THE GRAY CAPTAIN

*

THE
GRAY
CAPTAIN

✻ By Jere Wheelwright ✻

1954
CHARLES SCRIBNER'S SONS
New York

COPYRIGHT, 1954, BY
JERE H. WHEELWRIGHT, JR.

Printed in the United States of America

A

Library of Congress Catalog Card No. 54–8693

Two distinguished Baltimoreans,
S. STERETT McKIM *and* GRAEME TURNBULL,
discussed with me the germ of this book.

※

It is dedicated to them and to a third:
CLARENCE WATSON WHEELWRIGHT, JR.
*Airman, Second Class, United States Air Force
missing in air combat, Korea, 1952.*

⋙※⋘

"LIFE IS ACTION AND PASSION; THEREFORE IT
IS REQUIRED OF A MAN THAT HE SHOULD SHARE
THE PASSION AND ACTION OF HIS TIME AT PERIL
OF BEING JUDGED NOT TO HAVE LIVED."

❧ OLIVER WENDELL HOLMES, JR.,
Associate Justice, United States Supreme Court

*Captain and Brevet Colonel,
20th Massachusetts Infantry, 1861-1864,
three times wounded*

THE ROLL OF COMPANY "I,"
First Maryland Infantry Battalion,

called by courtesy the "Second Maryland Infantry," Confederate States Army, showing those present for duty the morning of June 4, 1864:

Captain	STOWELL
First Lieutenant	BRICE
First Sergeant	HAMMOND
Second Sergeant	McCOMAS
First Corporal	KIRK
Second Corporal	HODGES
Privates:	ABBOTT
	BEELER
	BUFFORD
	BURKE
	CABELL
	CARNEY
	DUVALL
	HEENAN
	HENDERSON
	HINES
	HOLBROOK
	HUBBARD
	LUCAS
	MATTHEWS
	NIEDLANDER
	RABY
	RADECKE
	REEDER
	SMITH—"GERMAN"
	SMITH—"HOME GROWN"
	WATTS
	ZOLLINGER

THE GRAY CAPTAIN

✵

I

A ROAD is Man's most characteristic monument to himself. By its existence it commemorates his necessity, his restlessness, his urge to escape. It need not be a finite path or trail or highway, but may pass imperceptibly through the oceans and the sky by means of sea lanes and airways, preserving to itself a permanent duality, half physical, half spiritual, the road and the reason for taking it. There are infinite varieties of both, but the catalyst is the manner in which the journey is faced and the judgment of a man in the end depends only upon that.

One particular road was blocked. A gravelly trace, rutted and trampled, it led through Hanover County in the state of Virginia—on this third day of June, 1864, still a part of the Southern Confederacy, at least as far as the low rise of ground which it first skirted and then crossed. Beyond that crossing, it was part of the Federal Union. The frontier was a gouge of ground ridged on either side by opposing breastworks projecting upward like the lips of a wound. Behind them, heaping and burrowing with bayonets and tin cups, tired, filthy, sick of the sound of Miniés, were those of the road's wayfarers who had not reached its end.

The afterglow of the sunset was a fading arc in the sky, and the dusk was a rising flood from the valley of the Chickahominy; the air growled and vibrated with heavy reports. It had rained earlier, but the clean tingle of the shower had given way to a nose-tickling, depressing odor of burned gunpowder. A sticky warmth was thrusting itself into prominence, a Virginia June snapped after heat like a trout after a fly.

A middle-aged farmer from out Lynchburg way with gray

1

hairs in his brown beard, a homespun, butternut-colored uniform and a bullet in the lower thigh, leaned upon his Enfield rifle with the same weary slouch as once he had leaned upon a plow handle.

"The Second Maryland Infantry? Couldn't rightly say where it is, but there's some of yo' boys up there. I heard some feller with a camp-meetin' bellow damning the Maryland Line for not keepin' formation, so if you looks . . . "

His drawling, pain-wracked voice rose to a shout. "Oh, Christ!" he cried in helplessness, and fell groaning to his knees while the shell whoop grew louder.

The officer who had made the inquiry flung himself flat, his sword jarring part way from its sheath and the small portmanteau he had been carrying flying from his hand and rolling over on its side. The shell, trailing a spark of fire, struck with a thud on a hard spot in the road's surface, bounced crackling through a stand of bushes and disappeared into the ditch with a fan of water and a deep-toned splash. There followed a boiling hiss that fizzed itself to blessed silence.

The two men, the one upon his face, the other kneeling against the upright Enfield, did not move until the sound had died away.

"Put out the fuse, I reckon," said the Virginia soldier shakily, and pulled himself to his feet hand over hand up the rifle barrel. The officer rubbed his fist across his lips, leaving a reddish earth smear. Then he too rose, rammed the sword back and spat to clear his mouth.

The Virginian was pointing gravely to the portmanteau.

"Your baggage is over there, Mister." If there was a touch of sarcasm in the tone, it was succeeded instantly by diffident pleading. "You wouldn't like to cut me a stick with that sword of yours, would you? This rifle makes a mighty heavy cane."

"There's a field hospital at that house," said the Marylander gruffly. "It's not more than a couple of hundred yards. Better not throw away your gun. No sense being demoralized."

He picked up the portmanteau as if it were a snake, already sorry that he had made the return thrust, but the ironic remark about his "baggage" had rankled. A portmanteau in an army as stripped as was this of Northern Virginia was on a

2

par with a trunk. The other had obviously thought him a "bomb-proof," uprooted from some safe administrative post by the Confederacy's urgent need. He could not refute the insinuation as had that Major in Richmond who had answered the jeers of passing combat troops by throwing back his cape and showing his missing arm. Yet within a few yards of where he now stood, on the old field of Gaines's Mill, he had been desperately hit in '62. The field hospital where he had directed the Virginian was in the same building to which he himself had been carried. The doctors had leaned over him and told him they could do nothing for so terrible a body wound. Somehow he had contrived to live, and since so many others had died, had managed at last to get new combat orders: "First Lieutenant Thomas Brice to the Second Maryland Infantry for duty." That bearded old bastard was patronizing him, was he? What the hell could he do, pull his shirt up and his pants down to show the seamed bullet scar? He slung the portmanteau into the bushes.

He went on, keeping to the road as it wound first south then east through rolling country where groves of ancient trees towered like castles above the lesser timber. He knew where he was. His way would take him to New Cold Harbor and to another battle that was laying over the first. All morning, tramping or begging lifts along the Mechanicsville Pike, so brief a journey from Richmond, he had listened to the warning that had knotted his stomach, the sound of artillery, sharper and higher than any thunder and, more terrible still to one who had the knowledge of its meaning, the crashes of musketry volley firing, a crackle and tear like sheets being ripped across. In the afternoon the noise had diminished, the smoke clouds which had ridden the sky had sunk to a rim above the trees, tinged, now that the light was fading, with reddish-yellow flashes.

The dusk was increasing, but the shadowed fields and woods, the swamps along the creek below him did not make their friendly night sounds. No whippoorwill called, the peepers were buried in the mud, only the mosquitoes hummed in swarms about his face. For a brief space the road would be crowded, a people walking in darkness, ambulances, ordnance wagons, stragglers, wounded and details. The smell of blood, of sweat, of horses, the grind of wheels, creaks and dull jars, groans and snatches of talk. One sentence, seldom more, a question, perhaps, and an answer.

"It's that kind of bacon. I can tell, my stomach's growlin' at it already. . . ."

"Is there a branch around? I got red clay a foot thick on my tongue."

"We piled 'em up good today. Burned my hand on my barrel I fired so much. . . ."

"Where's John Conroy? Tell me where he is. . . ."

"I keep sayin' I ain't seen him. Put your arm aroun' me, now, an' stop demandin' what I don't know."

Soft Southern voices made sharp by pain or urgency.

Then in another space, so unpredictable as to be startling, the road would be empty, like a forest path, for the trees and the bushes bulked larger and closer as vision narrowed.

Occasionally there would be a whipping rush as a spent bullet finished its trajectory across the fields. A Frenchman named Minié had invented this particular type, a conical projectile hollowed out at the base, and it had been received with enthusiasm by every war-waging agency in the world. In this part of it, the accent had been lost. The flying slugs were called "minnies," harridans who killed more men than did the random shells which burst in a dark rose.

Brice hunched his shoulders and walked on aching feet. He had spent the last of his pay on a pair of boots, the sort affected by the dandies of the Army, reaching almost to the knee. He had given two hundred dollars Confederate for them, and they were chafing him along their full length. A fine figure of a man was Brice, a fathom long with broad shoulders, but the two years passed in hospitals and in the easy duty of the Adjutant General's office in Richmond had blurred the lessons hard-learned by the lean sunburned infantryman of the Foot Cavalry. The boots were stirring memories, and the sweat that was gathering under the frock coat with the gold embroidery on the sleeves and the two thin stripes on the high collar was asking him a question. He was back at war again, had he forgotten?

4

The shape of houses showed ahead of him, and the glow of a lantern held near the ground. An angry voice called to know if he was the ration detail from the Fourth Alabama, and when he denied it, repeated the question querulously and unbelievingly. He snapped back, and there was a quick exchange of personalities, nerves speaking rather than minds. A line of infantry formed in a scrubby field gave a gusty breath of laughter.

"He tol' you an' tol' you he wasn't, Sergeant. Seems right earnest and excited about it too."

Brice drew level with the lantern's position and paused uncertainly. This sparse scattering of buildings must be New Cold Harbor, but how far ahead was the line? A battery on the spur of the rise was firing slowly but methodically. Number One gun would flare at its muzzle, a brilliant gust of light and smoke with cannoneers shadowy behind it and the piece running back on its recoil, the dusk would rush to fill the void like thunder after a lightning bolt, to be shattered in regular succession by the flame and report of Numbers Two, Three and Four. The minnies were hurrying by with their varying notes, most with a whistling hiss but some with a screech and others with a high yowl as they ricocheted end over end. A shell smashed through the roof of a shed with a splintering crash of shingles, and a sentry in the lee of a porch called a needless warning:

"No passing beyond here. The works is just a little piece ahead."

Another shell with too short a fuse exploded high in the air, a brief dirty flash, far less vivid than the muzzle blast of the racketing guns. Someone cursed the lantern, oblivious of the sheltering bulk of the house which concealed its glow from the Federal lines.

"Hold it steady," said the man under its light. He sat cross-legged on the ground, frowning intently as he wrote with a pen, dipping it occasionally into a tiny portable inkwell set upon an empty ammunition box. There was a huddle of gray and gold about him, a General and his staff.

Brice made his way over to them with unspoken relief. Staffs usually knew the troops in their own area far better

5

than the line whose knowledge was likely to be confined to their own brigade and very little further. Keeping respectfully in the background, he touched a junior on the shoulder. The aide turned, his spurs giving a tiny metallic jingle. His boots were dirty and his trousers splattered with dried mud; the rest of him was above the lantern's light and was only a pleasant voice and the smell of fatigue.

"The Second Maryland? Breckinridge's Division? Yes, I can help you, I've been over there three, four times today. This is Hoke and they're on our right. They're holding a swampy bottom in front of a ridge. The Yanks broke into it this morning and drove out Echols. The Marylanders took it back along with Finegan's Florida Brigade." The friendly tone hesitated an instant. "They were pretty badly mauled. I know they had to use their bayonets. . . ."

Brice said nothing but looked across the rapidly narrowing vista of where he must walk. The other gave a short humorless laugh.

"Not a pleasant prospect, is it? Wandering around a field of fight in the dark. But I'll loan you a courier to show you the way. It's not far, division fronts have got pretty narrow since Grant came into the Wilderness. Here, Keith. . . ."

He gave an order, and the courier mounted, Brice walking at the side of the horse. They went across a flat plateau to where the ridge thrust up again. The dusk had thickened until it was almost full night, a star or so was showing. Brice tripped over trailing vines and once over something soft and yielding, a dead man from the feel of the contact, some unlucky victim of a stray shell. He took hold of the stirrup leather to support himself and stepped warily. The horse was plodding, the animals were as tired as the men after the long day and the long days that had gone before; it had been a hard campaign for underfed beasts and soldiers. Without warning the occasional crack of a sharpshooter's rifle rose to a sputter of firing, there were faint yells, then the crash of a volley. The crest of the ridge erupted in flash and bellow.

"You're about there. I got to get back," called the courier in a quick, merging succession of words, spurring his mount

6

so that it wheeled and sent Brice sprawling. He rolled into a depression in the ground and lay dazed for a moment by the fall and by the noise, bitter at the panicky desertion. The air blasts pushed his eardrums inward. Artillery was firing as fast as it could load, and the battle roar soared up with a smash of rifles, a deep full-throated shouting that Brice had heard before, answered by the high, shrill, irregular squalling of the rebel yell.

Overs were bursting beyond the dead ground in which he crouched, sweating and near terror. The combat soldier who declares that he has never been frightened is either a fool or a liar, and here, alone in the flashing darkness, Brice had none of the drugs which dull the hammer blows of pressing danger. There was no responsibility for others to blur his sensations, no observing eyes to give him a stiffening of pride. At any moment there might be a sudden rush down this side of the slope, a mob of unknowns racing to the rear and then a futile, groping struggle against other unknowns, shadows whose substance might be enemy.

He jerked out his Colt and felt with his thumb for the hammer. To stay where he was might have been the best course, but the same instinct that makes men crowd together in time of peril sent him seeking others, his pistol held upright, ready to chop down. Twenty steps brought him past a screen of cedars growing along a demolished rail fence to a scrambling, cursing, stamping confusion of soldiers and horses. A fire was dying in a shroud of sparks as someone kicked it out, but there was enough light left to show the limbers of a battery in action on the ridge being hastily hooked in. If the line was broken, there would be a furious rush to carry off the guns, and to be in front of the galloping teams would mean a fatal trampling.

There could be no comfort in such company, and he ran behind the limbers, a nightmare rush in his heavy boots. Overhead and low, a shell exploded, and he heard the ragged tear of a splinter go past him, the rip of it drowned in a simultaneous shriek, a horse and a man screaming together.

"Cut that wheeler out and put that driver on the limber!"

7

bellowed a brazen voice. Brice ran on until his boots splashed in water, and he fell on his knees in a stream, his Colt flying out of his hand.

He groped for it in mud and sand, but when he felt metal and pulled it out, the charges were wet and the weapon useless. Cursing in a shaky monotone, he let the water run down the muzzle. Though the night was striped with flashes, how could he draw the soaked loads, pour in powder, ram home the bullets and cap the chambers when he would have to work by touch alone?

He squatted on his heels, head raised, nostrils flaring. There were forms near him, and he could hear the thudding of feet as the din died down. The infantry firing exhausted itself in nervous spurts, the beat of the artillery was slackening. Back where he had come, the fields were spotted with fresh fury, Hoke's Division writhing in the foam of full battle, but on this front of Breckinridge's it had subsided. Sounds once submerged in clangor reached the surface.

"We've been whipped! They're coming!" whimpered a lost voice, and he grabbed vainly at a scurrying figure. He knew now where he was, for it was a known experience. The stream's tiny ravine had channelled into it the debris of the fight, the wounded, the demoralized and the skulkers. Victory or defeat equally sloughed off this scurf of pain or terror. He had been hairline close to fear himself, but he had read the message of the diminishing and static roar: the line had neither been broken nor rolled back, the attack had been repulsed. His shakiness sought a relief and found it in anger.

Still gripping the pistol, he seized the next runner by the collar. Hands clutched at him frantically, and a boy's voice squealed, "Whar's the rear? Oh, whar's the rear?"

He shook the youngster in a hard grip.

"Goddam you, quit your bolting! Get back to your command!"

The boy trembled and sobbed, and Brice shook him again.

"Get ahold of yourself! What's your regiment?"

The youngster stopped crying, and his teeth clicked audibly together. He tried to answer, but his voice was not yet under control. The stars were clearer, and Brice could see better.

Another man, tall and gaunt, was trotting towards them, shoulders bent forward. A stray shell exploded too far away to be dangerous, but the fugitive made a frightened leap and began to run. Brice released the boy and grappled with him.

"Where are you taking off for?" he demanded in a snarl. The other struggled, then stiffened and became passive as the useless .44 jammed into his stomach.

"I'm wounded, hit bad. I'm huntin' the hospital."

"Show me where."

"In the leg. I got to get it dressed." The thick voice had taken on a whiney note. The boy had fled from death rushing at him in the dark, this other was a confirmed skulker, ready with excuses.

Brice pushed the pistol muzzle deeper into the shrinking belly. "You're a liar, sir! You jumped over the moon when that shell went off. Get in front of me, both of you, and we'll march back to where you came from."

He heard a fresh gasp like a hiccup from the boy, but the two fugitives started on their way. The branch had an easy fall and there was no difficulty in keeping to its course now that the dark extreme between the dusk and the night had been bridged. The human ebb they breasted that followed the water's flow was better defined and had better reason for its quest for safety. White bandages, black bloodstains, still figures on litters, were legitimate passports. No one spoke to them nor did they speak; the wounded, such as were not preoccupied with pain or shock, did not need to be told his errand. The cannon had almost entirely ceased, even the row on Hoke's front was dwindling.

He watched the boy who dragged his feet, his head on his chest. Brice was ambitious but he also was a combat officer. He liked rank, liked command, hoped for more of both before the war was over. He had gained one step before he had met that bullet. Others had gained many more, but they had been at Second Manassas, at Sharpsburg, at Fredericksburg, at Chancellorsville, at Gettysburg—more recently in the Wilderness or at Spotsylvania, slaughters that took officers in droves but opened the way for the juniors. "A bloody war or a sickly season" had been an old toast in the British Navy,

9

and it applied with equal force to the Army of Northern Virginia. Officers must expose themselves or the men of a critical service would not follow. It was a wasteful system but it had produced what was to be called "that incomparable body of infantry." Had it been less wasteful, had command reserved itself to the rear, the Army of the Potomac would have been in Richmond two years ago.

Brice had his own battle record, First Manassas, the Valley Campaign, Gaines's Mill. He had seen trouble through the smoke and knew the narrowness of the way that led across the mire of self-preservation gone wild. He had barely succeeded just now in treading it himself.

"You, youngster," he said in a neutral tone. "What is your command?"

The boy's head came up with a jerk. His voice was thick with humiliation.

"Grandy's Battery, sir. The Norfolk Light Artillery Blues."

The line was almost reached, the breastworks swelled across their way. The minnies still were whipping by, but the artillery was swabbing hot guns.

A hard voice spoke out of the darkness. It had informed itself by starlight though the powder smoke still drifted, rank and heavy.

"What you got there, skulkers?"

"One," answered Brice shortly. "The big fellow. Does he belong to you?"

"We know him," said the voice, and added, "to our sorrow. All right, we'll take him off your hands."

Armed men stepped to the straggler's elbows.

"How about the little one?"

"Just a lost sheep from Grandy's Battery. Who are you?"

"The Twenty-sixth Virginia, Echols' Brigade. We've had a right rough day, but I see you've brought our shame home to us. March, you! Grandy's guns are on our line, walk over there and you'll find them."

Brice slid the Colt back into its holster. "Come along," he said to the boy, and took his arm without force.

Side by side they followed the works where the axes rang and grunting men shoved toplogs into position as headcover against the rushing minnies. One thudded with a smack into the wood as they passed, but the boy gave no more than an involuntary start.

"Grandy's Battery?"

"Here, sir." A burly Sergeant stepped away from the bronze Napoleon twelve-pounder which brooded over the parapet.

"I have a man who says he's yours."

The Sergeant peered and nodded.

"He's ours, sir. Joined two weeks ago."

Brice propelled his companion forward. "He got lost in the dark. I've been guiding him back."

"Obliged to you, sir. Willy, get over to your mess." The boy said nothing but vanished behind the piece. "I'll so report it, sir." The Sergeant's tone was full of understanding. "He's only fifteen and it's his first night action."

Brice made no comment but instead asked his usual question. The Sergeant could not tell him but brought his Captain, who also seemed a man of understanding after a few muttered words from his subordinate. The Second Maryland? Surely; it was down in the hollow below the dip. This was the reserve line. Echols' Brigade had been surprised by a dawn attack and had been withdrawn to the top of the ridge. The Marylanders had relieved them. He'd be glad to show the gap in the works that led down to where they were. . . .

Brice grinned to himself now that he was the one from whom understanding was required. The Yankees had waded into Echols and trampled him, but the Lord in His Heaven forbid that the Norfolk Light Artillery Blues admit that Virginia troops had left a position in a hurry. He was grateful for the proffered help and said so.

"Have you eaten?" asked the Battery Commander.

"Not since this morning."

"We have a scrap of cold cornbread. . . ."

"Bless you for that."

This was hospitality indeed in an army that was existing fairly close to the borderline of starvation. Brice ate the cornbread gratefully beside a fire of red coals kindled in a dip and surrounded by weary men, some of whom went to sleep as they talked in dragging voices. He begged a drink of water

11

from a canteen to take the scratchy residue from his throat and reloaded his pistol. The Battery Commander himself took him back to the works and left him by a trodden path which dropped abruptly down a scrubby slope.

"Hol' on a minute, sir," said a sentry. "Litter party's comin' up."

Four men with grunts and slithering feet wrestled a stretcher to the level ground. The blanket-wrapped burden was silent but let out his breath in a sighing groan, as a bearer nearly fell to his knees. Question and answer were exchanged in whispers.

"Yes, sir. We're from B Company. This is Lieutenant Stone we got here. Follow the path through the swamp. There's a picket where it branches. Go straight ahead; if you turn left they talk Tarheel—North Carolina troops there. Don't let Charley scare you."

Brice did not waste time inquiring who Charley might be, but went over the edge where the crumbly earth slid noisily under his bootheels, bushes brushing at his coat. The swamp was about him, the smell of mud, of shattered trees, the foul residue of burned powder. There were shadows enough to rob him of the starlight, and he groped his way, placing each foot in front of him and feeling with it before he set it down. Occasional minnies bore him company. The deeper he penetrated the worse the smell became, for there was blood in it now. Twice he heard squelches and groans. The first time, he challenged fiercely in a whisper and was answered by a startled stir and a pungent, nervous warning.

"God blast you, don't yell so. The Yanks is just across. We're huntin' for wounded."

He stumbled almost on top of a man who crouched against a tree trunk, staring rigidly to the front. Brice identified himself hastily. There is need of haste when sentries' fingers are near the trigger. There was no reply, and after a moment he reached out to tap the shoulder, whispering again more urgently, then drew his hand back with a jerk, for the man was more than naturally rigid, a dead infantryman killed in the morning counterattack.

From farther along the path came a grim chuckle.

"Advance and be recognized," said a low, carrying voice. "I heard you telling Charley who you were. North Carolina to the left, Maryland straight ahead."

Brice obeyed but was halted before he reached the picket. "What did you say your name was?" The tone was suspicious and the lock of a rifle clicked. "Brice? There's no Lieutenant of that name with us."

Whisper of further explanation, a low call for the Corporal of the Guard, more squelches and a watchful command. A short walk with a rifle muzzle held against his back, then again the loom of works ahead of him.

"Captain Crane's in the glory hole there."

The "glory hole" was a deep pit almost chest high but shallow enough to permit firing over its edge, smelling of turned earth and foul water. It was inhabited by the Battalion Commander, his Adjutant and the Sergeant Major. A stub of candle burned in the ring of a bayonet thrust into the wall on a slant, and the lined, deep-socketed faces looked up at him.

"I know him," said Captain Crane. The Lieutenant Colonel and the Major had both been wounded and left at Gettysburg when Lee had retreated, and he was the senior officer who had survived the attack on Culp's Hill.

Brice stepped down into the pit, his boots sinking into six inches of liquid mud. There was no need to introduce himself, since he had visited the Battalion in the spring when it had been guarding the railroad at Hanover Junction. He shook hands and produced the War Department's order.

Crane read it and passed it to Laird, the Adjutant. The latter laughed when he too had held it near the candle.

"Reinforcements, by God! The first we've seen. Where are you going to assign him, Captain?"

The Battalion Commander pulled at the short imperial he affected.

"B has no officer left. I was thinking. . . ." He stared meditatively at the newcomer without intentional rudeness while he considered. "Let's see, you haven't been in the field since Gaines's Mill. The war's changed, Brice, both the men and

13

the methods. Reckon that's of a piece with all wars. What you learned in '62 won't serve you too well in '64. We'll season you a little."

He turned to Laird.

"Stowell's not been feeling too hearty of late. We'll send him to I."

Brice bit his lips. The uplift of spirit which had been given him by the sight of known faces was lost in disappointment and anger. So he wasn't to get a company though one offered itself officerless. Yet there was nothing he could say. Crane was well within his rights.

The Adjutant had been looking him over.

"Have you got a blanket?" he asked.

"No. I'll have to draw one from the Quartermaster."

"He hasn't got any."

Laird spoke to the Sergeant Major who was leaning against the side of the pit.

"See what you can scare up for the Lieutenant. He'll need an oilcloth too. There may be a dead Yankee left with a pair on him, though I doubt it. Our boys are pretty quick to swap spoons with them."

The Sergeant Major climbed out of the hole and departed. Crane and Laird chatted in a desultory fashion with Brice, asking the latest news from Richmond, but so tired that they gave the impression of only half listening. Occasionally a rifle cracked along the front, there was a sound of digging, but Brice heard an undernote like a groundswell of anguish, groaning and muffled crying, sometimes with half-grasped phrases repeated over and over again. He tilted his head back and listened while the two others sat with graven, inscrutable expressions.

"Yankee wounded," said Laird at last in a quiet voice. "I've never seen it so bad. They're piled out there three deep, scrambled in with the dead."

Brice found himself using the same restraint when he asked, "Are we getting any in?"

It was Crane who answered, his load of responsibility edging his words. "A few, but very few. We can't go out much beyond the picket line. They attacked at dusk, as I reckon

14

you know, and they may attack again. Sharpshooting is very bad."

"Grant will ask for a truce tomorrow," said Laird. He sounded as if he were trying to convince himself.

"Will he?" Crane was pessimistic. "If he does, he admits that we whipped him today, and he isn't the sort to admit a whipping."

The Sergeant Major tumbled over the edge of the hole. "Oilcloth and blanket, sir, all complete. Blanket ain't much, I'm afraid. Our boys has done what you said, but I got this one off'n a dead man and wrapped him in a worse one. 'Fraid it's got graybacks in it."

Brice nodded his thanks. He had forgotten another thing about war. Tonight he would sleep in a dead man's blanket and tomorrow he would be lousy.

"Good luck to you anyway," said the Adjutant. "Sergeant Major, you'd best take Lieutenant Brice along to Captain Stowell."

Crouch and stumble between the glory holes, behind the piled logs, step high over sleeping men, answer the low challenges. The ground in front of them was sedge and brush with dark windrows and heaps upon it that moved and struggled until the field itself seemed to crawl. It complained in its agony with babbling and moaning. Brice was sweating, his stomach heaved.

"Christ!" he muttered.

"Yes, sir," said the Sergeant Major.

Starlight and the smell of death, of unwashed men, the stink of unlimed sinks. Voices whispering in anger, disputing among themselves but not too loudly lest they draw a sharpshooter's bullet:

"We can't bury 'em with only tin cups to turn the dirt. I tell you we got to have the spade."

"You can't have it; the Old Gentleman says so. We got to use it to make a parapet."

Brice felt the Sergeant Major's restraining hand. There rose the ghost of a chuckle, startled out of the macabre night in spite of itself.

"This here's I Company, sir."

15

II

BRICE stirred in his sleep and returned to full consciousness in successive stages. He felt first the dull ache of his still weary body, gridded by the inequalities of the ground, then heard the intermittent whip reports of rifles, followed by a grunting and stir in the darkness. As he opened his sticky eyelids a hand fell on his shoulder and shook him.

"Heave out, sir. It's dawn and we're standing to arms."

He muttered an unintelligible acknowledgment and sat up, throwing off the blanket. The arm on which he had pillowed his head pricked him with returning circulation, but there was an uncomfortable addition, a nibbling and itching under his frock coat. Reaching inside his shirt, he scratched vigorously, and the form kneeling beside him chuckled.

"You got company, sir? Reckon we all have."

Brice was savage with discomfort and fatigue, and his mood was in his tone.

"Who are you?" he demanded shortly.

The grunting in the nearby darkness had been followed by a fit of coughing. A voice still wheezy from lack of breath took over the reply.

"That is First Sergeant Hammond, Mr. Brice. It is customary in this Army to man all positions at dawn and at dusk in case Grant should take it into his head to attack. You will keep that in mind in future."

"Yes, sir." Brice's mood was not helped by the irony which he sensed in Captain Stowell's order.

Another fit of coughing gave Brice time to button his coat and reach for the sword and pistol which leaned against a log of the breastwork. He had slept in his clothes, including

16

his boots, so there was nothing else for him to put on.

"Sergeant Hammond will take you along the line and show you the Company's position, Lieutenant. You will familiarize yourself with it."

"Yes, sir," Brice repeated, and stood up, his knee joints cracking.

"Stay down," the wheezy voice warned him. "The light's beginning to show and there may be enough of it for a Yankee sharpshooter to put a bullet through your head."

Brice stooped below the protection of the works. He almost expected Stowell to add, "You will keep that in mind in future," and bit his lip with chagrin.

"We'll cruise this way, sir," said the impassive Sergeant, and led off at a crouch.

The dawn was knifing the night with blades of light, but without the chatter of birds or the rustle and stir of life awakening. Rifles cracked irregularly, a few guns sent over their shells, only the field gave off its monotonous, heart-cracking crying. It had centered itself upon a single phrase, thin and gasping. "Water!" it repeated, "Oh God, water!" Whatever cool the darkness had held was being routed by heat, and the noonday would be hotter still. Already the corpses were bloating and the death smell was becoming stronger, permeating everything.

"This is Sergeant McComas, sir," said Hammond, indicating a busy shadow which was stirring laggards from sleep with its foot and sending them to join the other dim figures which were manning the parapet.

McComas did not come to attention, for to do so would have put his head above the safety line. Instead, he saluted with a jerk of the hand to his eyebrow.

"We have two men out in front, sir," he reported. "They have the Captain's permission."

The voice had a vague familiarity to Brice.

"Do I know you?" he asked, since he could not clearly make out the other's face.

"Yes. I'm Henry McComas. Used to live on Madison Avenue."

"Of course," said Brice, and shook hands.

17

A sharp challenge from the parapet was answered by a muffled response, and a voice called along the line, "Don't shoot, it's them."

A long, dark-clothed bundle was shoved across the head-log into the arms of the man who had challenged. He lowered it to the ground with unintentional roughness, and it screamed sharply.

"Goddam it, Beeler," said a neighbor, "you hurt him."

Two figures in lighter clothes vaulted the works to a yowl of minnies. The bulkier of them wrung his hand as if he had been stung, then set it to his lips and sucked noisily.

"Burned me!" he exclaimed, and stood panting. Empty canteens were hung in clusters from each shoulder.

"No more!" said Hammond with authority.

"Reckon not. They ain't stoppin' to ask us what we're doing. The pickets'll have to hug dirt today. Anybody got any water for the poor devil? We've used ours up."

McComas produced another canteen. "It's out of the swamp, but I guess it's as good as we've got."

These forms and voices among which Brice had moved became individuals in the brightening gray. Against the background of the logs, the bark still on them, which supported the earthen overlay, butternut men were watching the little group around the wounded Federal. Their faces were blackened by powder grains, some only in rings about the mouth, others smeared like minstrels. The bitten cartridges of yesterday's fight had left their residue, and there had been no time for amenities. Hammond, very tall and lean, the bones of his skull etched clearly under the shrunken skin, was pillowing the weaving head on his breast while a shaggy-browed Irishman, having thrown off his burden of canteens, was taking the cork from the fresh one. The second rescuer was feeling for the wound, disregarding the trickle of blood which stained his own wrist. He was short and very round as if some joker had poured him into a barrel and then hammered him down to take its shape. Brice, watching the bulging muscles under the checkered shirt, thought him fully capable of serving the joker the same way and then walking off with the barrel.

18

"Privates Burke and Lucas," said Sergeant McComas, a poised well-bred youngster of not more than nineteen with a little yellow beard of soft hair. "This is the third they've brought back, and they've given water to a lot of others. With your permission, sir, I'll pass the word again for the Surgeon."

"Better find a litter and carry this fellow to where he is," directed Brice, but McComas shook his head.

"Captain Stowell's orders are that no one is to leave the line of battle under any circumstances until we are dismissed from stand to arms."

"But . . ." began Brice, then cut off the words. Stowell was perfectly right. Four men at the handles of a litter were four less rifles should the Federals suddenly storm out of the woods from which their attacks had been issuing. Furthermore, his own countermand would be remembered and would afford a good excuse for a drift to the rear in a hot action. At First Manassas he had seen as many as six solicitous companions escorting a single lightly wounded comrade out of the fire.

McComas, after a moment's wait, cupped hands and shouted that Dr. Snowden was wanted on the right. The varying voices of men took it up like a chant, fading away as the words were passed from Company to Company.

Brice walked to the works and peered cautiously through the narrow gap left for the rifles between the main entrenchment and the headlog. A few yards away were the rifle pits in which squatted the Confederate picket line while beyond them the trampled pastureland ended in a red zigzag of turned soil, the Federal first line skirting a raddled wood of pine and broadleaf. Whitey-gray puffs of smoke jutted from it at irregular intervals, sharpshooters stinging any careless exposure.

The penalty was the same for both sides. As Brice watched, Beeler fired his Enfield, withdrew it from its rest on the lower log and began to reload. The same neighbor who had cursed him for his carelessness in handling the wounded Federal instantly shoved his own muzzle through the gap and searched for a target.

While Brice strove consciously to grasp the outlines of the

19

enemy's position, his subconscious dragged his eyes down to the littered space between the outposts. Here lay the dead, some on their faces, others staring blindly upwards with open mouths, bodies mangled beyond recognition of their humanity, corpses piled upon corpses, while between them and over them and under them still stirred the agonized living, choking with pain and thirst. Their cries came to him poignantly, and he beat his clenched hand upon the rough bark in helplessness.

The squat, powerful Lucas was beside him. He too looked out and turned his eyes away. He spoke aloud with the resonance of an exhorter.

"'Heaps upon heaps,'" he quoted, and then repeated it. "'Heaps upon heaps, with the jaw of an ass have I slain a thousand men.' Wonder who ordered those attacks?"

Beeler looked up from his busy rammer as he tamped the cartridge down.

"Yes, it's a pity. All those shoes out there and us not able to get them."

Brice turned away just as a shout came from around a traverse: "Dismiss from stand-to-arms!" Except for the sharpshooters and the sentries, the men laid their rifles against the logs and clustered around the rescued Northerner.

"What's your name, boy?" Burke was asking in a soft brogue, but the other only clutched feebly at the canteen and sucked noisily. Hammond, propping him, was staring downwards.

"What's he got here? Lieutenant, take a look, sir."

He worried the short blue jacket off the arms and held it up. Sewed across the back between the shoulder blades was a cloth label. "Malachi O'Brien," it read in sprawled writing. "Sixty-sixth New York."

They looked at each other.

"They've all got them," volunteered another soldier. "The ones we buried last night had them too."

Hammond's terribly thin face was twisted. "Poor devils, poor devils. Looks as if they knew what they were in for and prepared for it. Yet they kept a-comin'."

"Thought you had no use for bluebellies," remarked a shock-

20

headed youngster whose hair protruded in bunches through the holes in a wreck of a hat.

The First Sergeant gave him a bitter stare, "Who would, after Camp Chase? Don't be puny-minded, Matthews."

"You were a prisoner, Sergeant?" asked Brice.

"Yes, sir. Captured at Gettysburg and just exchanged."

That would explain his emaciation. Camp Chase had a grim reputation, as hard a one as Libby and Andersonville in Northern minds. Exchanged he might be, thought Brice, but there could be little gain for him, coming from a starving prison to a starving army.

The Battalion's Assistant Surgeon, Dr. Snowden, arrived out of breath from his haste.

"Well, who got it?" he demanded brusquely, pushing through the group. "So you brought another one of them in, did you? Let's see if we can keep you from having wasted your trouble."

Abrupt though his manner was, the men gave way for him, laughing. In itself, their attitude was a tribute. Snowden was no contract surgeon, a licensed butcher of the helpless, as was too often the case. He saved the medical whiskey for the wounded instead of drinking it himself and improvised surical instruments from forks together with remedies from plants and herbs to eke out the shortage of both caused by the blockade. His prematurely balding head bent over the wounded man and his hands were gentle.

"Two ribs fractured by a ball. Haven't pierced the lung yet, which is lucky considering the way he's been manhandled. Also there's a bullet in the left leg. All right. If stand-to has been dismissed, I'd thank you kindly for a litter."

Hammond gave a perfunctory look at Brice, then issued orders. "Matthews, go fetch the stretcher. It's leaning against the traverse. Then you and Duvall and German Smith and Home Grown Smith can carry him where the Doctor tells you."

The three whose names had been called as bearers stepped forward and stood waiting while Matthews went to the traverse. German Smith, whose real name was undoubtedly

Schmidt, was a ruddy, big-nosed, broad-shouldered, round-sterned twenty who bleached rather than tanned so that even his blue eyes were washed out. There had been a great German emigration to the United States, and Baltimore had received a large share of it. Home Grown Smith was dark and very thin with a hacking cough that made Dr. Snowden raise his head and look at him.

"Send that man to me at sick call," he said sharply.

"Yes, sir," said Hammond. "Hubbard, you take Home Grown's place."

He leaned over the Doctor and said something in his ear. Snowden listened, still busily bandaging, then nodded.

"I'll see the Old Gentleman right away. The usual prescription is hot toddy, warmth and rest—a pleasant memory. However, I'll send along the toddy if you'll tell me which one of these rapscallions I can trust. The evaporation of whiskey is appalling."

"They won't touch it," answered Hammond, but gave a precautionary glare at Hubbard who wiped his mouth and shuffled his feet.

The Sergeant came over to Brice, pulling a battered notebook from his pocket and making notations in it with the stub of a pencil.

"We've one more firing bay, sir. If you don't mind, I'll take muster as we go."

The works were built in zigzags, and Brice followed him around another bend. This section of the line was populated by a Corporal and four Privates, one of whom watched from a loophole while the others sat cross-legged and stripped to the waist while they searched the seams of their shirts for the ever-present and ever-multiplying lice.

"Corporal Kirk, sir," introduced Hammond, followed by a hasty, "Goddam it, keep your head down," as the man came to attention. Just in time the military-minded soldier relaxed into a crouch, for a minnie whined over while another spatted into the earth rampart.

The Corporal grinned nervously while the names were checked off in Hammond's book.

"Three more of the boys have gone for the rations," said

Hammond, closing it with a slap and shoving it into his hip pocket. He smiled at Brice. "That may seem an over-allowance, sir, for the amount we've been issued, but we live in hope." He pointed to the far traverse. "Other side of that is H Company. Beyond them it's Maryland again."

Brice understood his meaning, having listened to bitter complaints when he had visited Hanover Junction. This Battalion was the successor to a famous Regiment, the old First Maryland in which he had served. That command had fought with great distinction under Stonewall Jackson, but had been disbanded in '62 when its enlistments expired—those short-term enlistments for a short-term war, still blazing in its third year. Most of its veterans had naturally taken the easier course and transferred to the cavalry or the artillery, where the life was pleasanter and the expectancy of living enhanced. Those who were left, even including the others who came through the Federal lines to enlist, were not enough for more than one strong battalion. Reorganized, therefore, as the First Maryland Battalion, called by courtesy "the Second Maryland Infantry," it had been so shattered at Gettysburg that the Confederate War Department had drafted into it a detachment of military prisoners which had been formed into a separate Company. Most of them did badly, a number did well, and one stoutheart of few morals was to represent it at Appomattox, but its very presence was gall and wormwood to men who had crossed the Potomac when they could have sat safely at home merely by taking the oath of allegiance.

Brice and Hammond returned to the middle angle just as the wounded Federal was being placed upon the litter. Dr. Snowden stood back, and the bearers took their places at the handles. German Smith unlaced the casualty's shoes but, instead of placing them beside him on the stretcher, tossed them to McComas. Brice watched with surprise, then, as the stretcher was lifted, exploded in indignation.

"What the devil are you doing?" he shouted. "Robbing a wounded man? Put those shoes back!"

McComas, Hammond, even Dr. Snowden were staring at him. In hot wrath he took a step forward.

"Put them back, I say. That's an order!"

23

"Wait a minute," remonstrated Snowden, but a newly familiar, wheezy voice broke in.

"Lieutenant, I'll have a word with you, if you please."

Captain Stowell stood, hunched-shouldered, at the entrance to the bay. His bulky body sagged and shook with coughing, his nose was swollen and his eyes were sick, but the grizzled beard bristled forward over the outthrust jaw.

"Doctor," he asked, "can this Yankee walk?"

"No, and not for some time yet," said Snowden quietly.

"Then *my* orders stand. McComas, if the shoes fit Raby, give them to him."

Brice clenched his fists, but the beard was jutting now at him.

"You will come with me, sir," said the wheezy voice harshly.

Red-faced and furious, Brice hesitated; then the habit of discipline brought him forward, stiff-legged. Stowell stepped back to where the traverse hid them both from the watching men.

"Mr. Brice," he said, "you and I must reason together."

III

WEARY and ungraceful, the Captain sat down on a hummock of earth, supporting himself at the last minute by an outstretched hand. Sixty years old, far over the usual age of a combat infantry officer, the brown face with its tracery of red veins above the grizzled beard reflected the effort that had kept him in the field since the First Manassas. He had coped with declining strength and nervous energy and, more serious still, with the burden of continuous, grave responsibility until his expression had reached a governed stability. Too old to be promoted, too conscientious to seek release, he had no prospects. Either his body would fail, or peace would come —there was nothing between those extremes except death or a wound.

He coughed heavily, and Brice, still seething with anger, watched the jerking shoulders without sympathy. In the Old Regiment where Brice had known him casually, Stowell had been a faintly comic figure—an elderly man puffing into action at the head of those much younger must be either ridiculous or appealing—but in those times he had shown no sign of becoming the sour martinet which his Lieutenant considered him. Yet in spite of the effects of his illness, Stowell kept his dignity. The short jacket of faded gray was pulled well down, neither wrinkled nor bunched over the slightly protruding belly, the long trousers, patched at one knee, had been brushed, though the red mudstains still faintly streaked them; the clumsy brogans had been scraped. Even the neatly trimmed beard gave him an advantage over Brice's day-old stubble.

The Captain leaned back and wiped his lips with a soiled handkerchief. He spoke abruptly.

"You're a good soldier, Mr. Brice." The hardness was gone from his tone. "You spoke your piece fully and fairly. When we were in the Valley I might have done the same myself."

Though he was taken by surprise, Brice was not mollified.

"I'm glad to know that, sir. I think I was right," he snapped insubordinately.

"Were you?" The question levelled like a pistol. "The Valley is a long time ago, longer than you realize. Since then we've lost the Mississippi, Sherman has crossed into Georgia, and Grant is here and damned close to Richmond. Our Quartermasters have a sinecure since there's nothing left to issue. Most of what we do get comes from the enemy. We must rob Peter to pay Paul, even our own dead as well as theirs. I had two of my boys killed yesterday, and their shoes are on somebody else's feet right now. I'll show you why we do it, and if you can think of a way out, I'd be right happy to hear it. I'm not being sarcastic at your expense, Lieutenant. I mean it."

He raised a croaking shout.

"Corporal Hodges! Send me Private Raby!"

A stir and a scuffling beyond the bend, a gruff admonition, and a pinched and limping sixteen-year-old appeared with a nervous salute.

"Private Raby reporting, sir."

Stowell indicated the soldier's feet with a curt gesture. They were bare except for a rag tied around one sole. A cut, infected by the dirt, suppurated above an ankle.

"Have you a suggestion, Lieutenant? If we move again, this man cannot keep up on the march."

The latent urgency in the words cut deeply into Brice's anger. Stowell might be begging the real question, but except on moral grounds the need could not be denied. He shook his head reluctantly.

The Captain spoke to the boy. "Sergeant McComas has some shoes we just took off a wounded Yankee. I hope they'll fit reasonably well. I told him to save them for you."

When Raby was out of earshot, Stowell reached out and gently touched Brice's knee.

"Have you ever read the regulations of the Continental

26

Army? A Prussian wrote them, Von Steuben, but they make very good sense to me. They say in effect that the Captain must be the father of his Company. We've come rather far from them in later years, probably because they were made for a civilian army, and our present ones were written by professionals for professionals. Von Steuben may have got to the root of the matter. Ours have stopped fitting the times. No, I'm not arguing that discipline should be relaxed but that officers should pay more attention to their men than to their careers."

He rammed his fist into his palm impatiently.

"We've got to think of our own few first, Brice. How are we to go on if we don't? Grant has got the numbers. He can afford to be wasteful—God help those poor devils out in front of us. He doesn't have to look to George Washington and Valley Forge for a lesson. We do, if we want to learn how to keep in the field without supplies and without replacements."

He had been talking rapidly and with extreme intensity. Now he stopped with almost a visible jerk as he wrenched his mind back to the immediate situation.

"I beg your pardon," he resumed after a short pause. "I get to lecturing and I forgot that you've got to listen. We always have to return to my taking the shoes off a live man who's been hurt; you would have thought nothing of it if he'd been dead or at least hale. Yes, I know he'll need them later and I don't like to dwell on it, but in the meantime we've got to keep Raby from going sick, or, by God, Malachi O'Brien of the Sixty-sixth New York will be getting a new pair direct from a Yankee quartermaster in Richmond."

Brice's indignation had subsided to some extent. There was an uncomfortable memory in the back of his mind that he too had been re-equipped with a blanket and an oilcloth, accepting them for his own necessity without inquiring where they had originated. While he could not carry Stowell's logic to the same conclusion, he had to admit to himself that he could think of no easy argument in rebuttal even if he had been allowed to use it. He was glad when Dr. Snowden joined them.

27

"Sorry to interrupt, Captain, but I've got to be getting back and taking care of your Yankee. I promised Hammond I'd take a look at you. If you'll let me listen to your chest, I'll send you a toddy." His manner was the cajoling one he might have used with a refractory child.

Stowell's grim expression suddenly relaxed, his teeth gleamed in his beard. "Why don't you just lay on your hands? Any man who can keep a stock of liquor in this Army can work miracles."

"Hush, now, and let me hear your organ music. I picked me out a hospital orderly with gloomy and immediate ideas on the Second Coming. He feels he can't afford to backslide, and since he can't, he's damned both ways if anybody else will either. I'll send your drink along by one of your litter bearers."

"Not by Hubbard!"

The Doctor, ear to the chest, winked at Brice. " 'The Captain should be the father of his Company,' " he quoted. "I wasn't listening but I'll swear that came into the conversation. Hubbard's one of the wayward children."

He took his balding head away and rebuttoned the jacket. "You're better, though I reckon you think I'm a liar. If it does any good to tell you, which I doubt, spend the day in your blankets. You got a Lieutenant now to do the work."

The Doctor departed laughing, and Sergeant Hammond took his place.

"Roll call complete, sir. All present or accounted for. Dr. Snowden wants Home Grown Smith to report to him at sick call so I'll ship him along."

His lips suddenly curled upward.

"The spade is mustered and present, sir."

"Good," said Stowell, and again the teeth shone through the beard. "Lieutenant Brice will take charge today. I'll be laying in my blankets in the middle angle with the toddy inside me, I trust. You'll find me there if you need me. Brice, I would suggest that you send the spade and two men to dig a sink between them. See that it's covered from stray bullets, but open enough for you to scare out anybody who makes camp there."

He was interrupted by more coughing. "This damned cold. . . . I don't like the men drinking the swamp water. Have Sergeant Hammond send back for some purer from the nearest branch. Let most of them rest, though. We'll take 'em out in front to build abatis as soon as it's good and dark. There's nothing like a row of felled trees with their branches pointing forward to distress an earnest night attack. At least we're not on picket duty. It's B Company's turn tonight."

Hammond looked doubtful. "It ain't going to be easy to cut those trees after dark, sir."

"I know. That's why we'll do it late this afternoon and drag them up behind the works."

The Sergeant's eyebrows raised. "The Yanks have plenty of guns and plenty of ammunition and they'll use them both if they hear the axes."

His tone was respectful, but Stowell made a scythelike sweep of his open hand.

"Use your ears, boy, use your ears. There's axes being used in their woods yonder right now. Reckon they're as worried about us as we are about them. They're not going to open on us with their own working parties out."

He went on with the ever-present nagging problems that made up part of his daily routine. Firewood, food, facilities for washing, cartridges—Stowell apparently had catalogued every need in his mind, and methodically brought them forth to be dealt with in turn. When he had finished, they moved into the angle and made room for the ration party which had been waiting to pass around the bend.

Stowell settled himself in a corner, Brice beside him, a sharpshooter's legs a yard from where they sat. It was hotter even than the dawn had promised, and the inside of the works was being shaded with blankets draped across bayoneted rifles thrust upright into the ground, the edges caught under the triggers. Thin smoke from little fires laced the sky, clean wood smoke unalloyed by the metallic cloying of powder, as the bacon was cooked and the cornbread warmed. The bacon was rusty green, and the cornbread would grow sour after the second day so that diarrhea and heartburn were accepted as quite normal consequences, but at least rations had been

29

distributed. Not the least virtue of the Rebel infantry was its endurance of empty bellies, of gnawing, morale-shattering hunger.

The Captain's orderly, an Irishman named Heenan with a horsy look and the build of a groom, brought them the same food as the men were eating. Brice, still a trifle finicky after the feeble luxuries of wartime Richmond, looked at his portion distastefully but forced it down. As he licked the bacon grease from his fingers he caught another smile from Stowell. The Captain had preserved his sense of humor. Perhaps it was only a medicine against discouragement and discomfort, but it was an almost universal remedy in the Army of Northern Virginia. Sullenness, even fanaticism, for the most part had broken down already and had contributed their share to the deserters, the deadbeats and the professional stragglers.

"I sympathize with you, I do indeed," said Stowell. "I would give a year's pay for something that would *taste*, the stronger the better. At the beginning of the war I dreamed about canvasback duck, terrapin and saddle of venison served the way they do at the Maryland Club. The second year I settled for lamb with currant jelly. Now it has resolved itself into onions, raw and unadorned."

Laird, the Adjutant, was picking a way among the blankets towards them. Stowell waved him over.

"We still have some conveniences," he remarked. "Here comes the Baltimore paper, Cold Harbor edition."

Laird squatted, grinning. "The latest grapes from our own correspondent at the front." He was using the contracted form of "grapevine," the Army's current term for rumor. "I passed the toddy on the way. Bussey's giving it an armed escort through H Company. Grant's been stopped; they say it's the same everywhere along the line as it is out there." He jerked a thumb to indicate the field beyond the parapet. "Marse Robert's sent word that the artillery is to bombard the Yank positions every night at nine in case they try to slip around our right."

"Glad to know that," remarked Stowell. "Brice, here, is going out to build abatis after dark. We'll hold him up until the fuss is over."

"That's fine. Captain Crane wants abatis along the whole front." Laird's face darkened. "There's no truce flag come over yet. I can't make it out. Either Ulysses is too damned bull-headed to care for his wounded or else's he's planning to try it again. What troops made the attack, do you know?"

Presumably he thought Stowell had been in his blankets, so the question was addressed to Brice.

"The Sixty-sixth New York," the latter answered. He knew that much from the prisoner.

"Barlow's Division of Hancock's Second Corps," finished Stowell quietly. "The dead men had the red cloverleafs on their caps."

Laird was scribbling in a notebook that matched Sergeant Hammond's for dogears and dilapidation.

"And who's on our right?" he continued, knowing that I company was on the extreme end of the Battalion's front. Normally, A Company would have been in their position, but in yesterday's commotion the formation had been reversed.

"Florida troops," said Brice hesitantly.

"The Eighth Florida, Finegan's Brigade," again Stowell amplified.

Brice's good humor vanished in a fresh surge of irritation. Whatever he tried to do, Stowell seemed to make him look bad at it. His ill-temper made him forget that the Captain had only been ensuring that the report was full and correct. He bit his lips and paid bare attention to the joyous military scandal which Laird was whispering in a mirth-laden voice.

"You know General Breckinridge had his horse killed yesterday. Seems that Stoddard Johnston, his Assistant Adjutant General, wrote a dispatch saying that old Breckinridge had received a bruise that would prevent him from taking the saddle for several days. Some joker on Marse Robert's staff sent a note back sayin' that they hoped Breckinridge wouldn't suffer from sleepin' on his face. The General's fit to be tied. He's been arresting Johnston every hour on the hour ever since."

He took his departure with a jingle of spurs, the harmless swagger of a mounted officer over those whose heels were unarmed, and Brice rose, still remembering to keep his head down.

"I'll see to it that the morning orders are carried out, sir," he announced frigidly. Stowell looked up at the tone, seemed about to speak, then apparently thought better of it and settled back in his blankets. Brice went in search of First Sergeant Hammond.

The long day passed peacefully enough except for the incessant sharpshooting. The field wailed and the smell of the dead grew stronger. The bodies were swelling and turning black, but, at least on their front, no bugle sounded, no white flag was waved over the Federal parapet to request a truce to remove the wounded. The crying and the odor together soaked the senses.

"Grant's tryin' to stink us out," said Hammond grimly.

Brice had advanced another step in his acquaintance with the men. He talked to Hammond, more freely to McComas with whom he was renewing friendship. The First Sergeant, he learned, was a merchant mate who still flavored his remarks with sea terms.

"Only went coastwise," confided McComas cheerfully. "If you want to make him real mad, say that and sniff. The boys call him 'Offshore Gus.'"

Brice found that he had one other personal acquaintance in the ranks, Dick Reeder, once a choirboy at Mount Calvary Church, now an accomplished forager. There was a story about his having made off with a hive of bees and then falling over a stump while still carrying them.

"Dick rode a wagon to Gettysburg after the bees got through with him," chuckled McComas. "Said he was mighty lonely and depressed what with all those fat Pennsylvania hens cackling to join the Confederacy, but he had plenty of company going back. I reckon there were a lot of us who would have hunted out hives if we'd known what was going to happen to us."

The axes thudded off in the Yankee woods, the rifles cracked, occasionally a gun boomed. Towards nightfall Brice routed out his own axemen, and the swamp joined the woods in the crash of falling trees. Here Hammond and the spade came

32

into play, levelling a way up to the works where the ex-mate had contrived a runway of logs with levers to roll the materials for the abatis over the parapet.

"That spade," commented McComas, "ranks next to the Battalion flag. The Old Gentleman" (he used the term quite naturally) "thought it would come in mighty handy to have around, but whenever he'd collect one the boys would throw it away on the next march. It's an awkward thing to carry. After we'd served about three of them the same way, he had the next mustered and reported in at every rollcall. Says he'll cloud up and rain on anybody that loses it."

Just before the dusk stand-to-arms, Stowell sent for Brice. His cold, in spite of Dr. Snowden's encouraging prognosis, was still heavy, and he sat with a blanket hooded over his head while he talked.

"Ten men'll do it," he croaked hoarsely. "Take McComas with you and leave Hammond at the runway you've built, to count them out and in. Be mighty awkward if somebody got hit and left outside the works and we didn't know it. Be sure you notify the pickets and the Florida regiment so nobody gets to shooting. Lucas and Burke want to go for Yankees again, but I told them they couldn't. It'll be ticklish enough as it is without them wandering around all the way out in front. I'd come with you, but I haven't got enough voice to make myself heard. Sure you can handle it?"

"Of course," said Brice, still a trifle sullen.

"The password's 'Chantilly.' Tell your men."

The stars were out when the party mustered, crouching in the lee of the parapet. Brice struck a match and looked at his watch. The hands pointed to nine, and the Confederate batteries opened as if the tiny flare had been their signal. For half an hour the air was crisscrossed with the hurtling comets of the burning fuses, for the Union guns instantly took up the duel. Shells flared as they burst along the ridge while the front line hugged dirt and blessed the orders that were making both sides plaster the rear areas rather than the works. When the firing had died away, Brice touched Hammond's elbow.

"We'll go over now," he said. "Drag up the trees."

33

He cupped his hands and called softly, repeatedly, through the loophole, "Party coming out. Don't fire."

"We hear you," came the answer from the picket line at last. "Come ahead."

Brice stepped back and followed the bark of the backlogs with his hand. He would pass the word to the Florida sentries who manned the next angle.

The group around the incline blocked him, and he waited, hearing the scrape of wood, the soft grunts and curses as the men levered the cut trees up the slope. Suddenly there was a clear snapping sound and a heavy slide.

"What the devil happened?" asked Hammond in a fierce whisper. "Watts, I'll kick your ass if you don't get your back into it."

"Don't blame me, blame whoever cut this goddam lever. It busted." The low voice was breathless and equally angry.

"Get the spare, then."

Backs bent, figures groped, but without result.

"We'll have to cut another, Lieutenant," whispered Hammond apologetically. "I had the spare right handy against the parapet, but some fool's carried it off."

"And wake everybody up across the way? Use the handle of the spade."

Brice lifted himself over the parapet and dropped to the face of the work.

"Couple of you come here and help me ease the timber down," he called, and men joined him while Hammond whispered names, his lowered voice barely audible to Brice. A tree emerged over the edge, teetered, and slid across while they tugged at its branches. Others followed and more men, slithering over the toplog like lizards.

"McComas!"

"Here, sir."

"Start dragging that stuff into position, points towards the Yanks, remember. I'll stay here and help haul the rest." He remembered the first of the names which Hammond had called. "Niedlander and Duvall, stay with me. The rest of you go with Sergeant McComas."

He knelt down and stared across the scrubby meadow. The

34

advanced rifle pits, the dark heaps which squirmed no longer, but moaned still, the substance of the woods beyond, showed no sign of moving shadows. His own men had spread out; branches crackled as they set the trees in position, an axe whacked as someone hammered in a butt.

"Not so much noise," he called, but the last word was lost in a sharp challenge from farther on the right.

"Who goes there?" it demanded loudly.

Brice leaped up, frantic with rage. Didn't that bastard know there were men out in front?

But did he? His stomach tickled as if it were brushed with tiny wings. Too late he remembered that he had forgotten to warn the Florida troops.

"Friends!" he shouted with a bursting throat. "Chantilly! For God's sake, don't fire!"

IV

THAT instant of desperate realization made him leap forward, waving his arms in front of him as if to push back the threatened bullets. The Florida line made a projecting salient, and the raw conscript from St. Augustine, taking his turn as sentry in what his Company Commander undoubtedly thought was an innocuous post, was making pictures in his imagination. He saw the blurred figure as a threat, a Federal night surprise and an officer waving to his men to change direction. The answer and the password made no impression; inexperience is ruled by its interpretation of actions, instinctive reaction blurs the meaning of words. He pulled his trigger and screeched alarm.

His mates could not be blamed for their response. The sentry's nerves seemed justified; here were scurrying figures where no friends could be anticipated. They snatched their rifles and blazed through the loopholes. It was not long before the frantic shouting, not only from the working party but from the Floridians who manned the nearer angle and had correctly diagnosed the situation, made them cease firing, but in the meantime the impersonal minnies had struck home.

Across the field a picket from Michigan had shouted and fired at the yelling and the whipcracks. The Federal works spattered flashes that blended into a rising rattle while a cannon sent case shot into the what the gunners were equally certain was a Rebel rush. Tomorrow a General, sharing one of the frequent misconceptions of war, would report that the Rebels had attacked and been handsomely repulsed.

The demoralized working party ran for the shelter of their own line or flung themselves on their faces, some with their arms clasped over their heads. Brice, still upright and bellowing, felt a tug at his coat as a bullet passed through the skirt of it. He had returned to a sensation he had not felt since the First Manassas, the feeling that he was watching, raging and scornful, while this thing that was really himself strove desperately to cope with the disaster its forgetfulness had caused.

The flashes seemed to ring him about as the Union rifles commenced. Someone panted past him, groping for the parapet; there was a dull whack and the man plunged headlong into the earthen face. Brice reached for shoulder and crotch, heaved the weight up and slung it across the top. That madness of effort too was normal for the circumstances, his body had galvanized its strength to fight for its life. Someone else was screaming with pain, and he ran heavily towards the sound, a faint thread in the turmoil. A glancing bullet rapped his cheek, and the shock of it brought him to his knees. Another man fell over him and knocked him full length, a man who cursed loudly with lurid blasphemies, repeated senselessly as if he did not know what he was doing.

Brice snatched at the other's leg.

"Get back! Get back, I tell you!"

The cursing man struggled free. He had gripped the one who had screamed and was lugging him by the arms. Brice scrambled to them and helped just as the first charge of case burst and whirred by like pellets from a huge shotgun. The minnies were coming through the switchy brush with a sound like driven hail, but the rescuers lifted and panted, staggering together like a six-legged monster. Once again the turned earth was under their feet, once more Brice strained and pushed as the still screaming body went up and over.

His companion leaped for the top and vanished, but Brice was turning back again when he was grasped about the neck from behind.

"You've done enough. Get in!"

A beard was in his mouth as he writhed his head around in protest. Other hands clawed at his coat, then fastened. He was lifted, half strangled, and felt first the roughness of the headlog, then a swooping fall to hard ground. Breathless and choking, he lay inside the works, the artificial strength draining away and leaving him weak; sick with useless regret.

37

The flare of a match cupped in a hand struck his eyes.

"Lieutenant Brice," said Hammond's voice. "Looks like he's been hit in the face."

"How many more to come?" croaked Captain Stowell from immediately above Brice's head. He could feel the beard against his ear and knew now who had ordered him to safety.

"Three," came Hammond's answer. "Holbrook's dead, he was the one the Lieutenant slung in first. Corporal Hodges was the other that the Lieutenant and McComas brought in together. He got it in the belly and he's just died. Couple of others have been hit but not too bad. Goddam those Florida fools."

There was a sound between a grunt and a gasp from Stowell, quickly repressed. "The rest better not try coming in yet. Who are they?"

"Matthews, Hines and Zollinger."

The Captain's voice took on as much volume as his inflamed throat would permit. "No firing from this front, understand? Pass the word along. I'll tell those other sons of bitches myself."

An unfamiliar shadow pushed in among them.

"Who's in command here?" it asked.

"I am."

"Well, I'm the Major of the Eighth Florida. 'Fraid it won't do much good if we tell you we're sorry, but why the devil didn't you let us know that you had a party out in front of the works?"

Brice could speak now. His faint voice came out miserably.

"He's right, Captain. I forgot to tell them."

The words were audible even over the rattle of the Federal rifles. Brice sensed the stir and the shifting of bodies as the men understood.

"Holy Mother of God," said Heenan, who had stooped with a canteen.

"The blind, stupid bastard." It was a mutter from the background, unidentifiable but savage in its scorn.

Stowell spoke in a quivering monotone. "Thank you, Major. We still have three outside. Will you be sure not to fire?"

"I'll see to it myself." The Florida officer was already hur-

38

rying off. It was no further business of his; such things had happened.

The silence still hung until the Captain rasped a command.

"McComas, cover those bodies with their blankets. The rest of you get back to the loopholes. Hammond, I told you to pass an order, get about it! Niedlander, go along to Dr. Snowden and tell him he's wanted. You wounded men, wait here till the Surgeon comes."

Brice's face was numb from the bullet's blow, but he had reached his feet. He had no impulse to offer an excuse, knowing that there was none that would be acceptable against the testimony of the ragged bundles over which blankets were being draped. Stowell pushed him down again.

"I said that the wounded were to wait for the Surgeon, Brice."

He could not read the tone, but his self-disgust made him defiant.

"Let me go out again, sir. The firing's stopped. Goddam it, they were my men an' I ought to have the right to try . . ."

"Hush up!" Private Watts had not turned his head. He was listening intently and now brought his eyes to the level of the loophole under the toplog. "Somebody's callin' us."

The muffled insistent voice was answered and identified itself.

"It's Zollinger," reported Watts. "He's got Hines with him. Says Hines has got a broken leg. A fellow from the picket line is helping him carry him back."

Brice clawed his way up to the top of the works and sat astride them. Captain Stowell's head rose beside him.

"Lieutenant," he said quietly, "you seem spry enough. When these men are in, I want you to build fire steps in this bay. The parapet is too high. You can use the logs from your runway, they're right handy."

There was no emphasis upon the words, their inflection was unmarked by either blame or palliation. The perfect normality of tone and instructions shook Brice as nothing else could have done. If he were ready to return to duty, then duty was waiting for him.

"Yes, sir," he acknowledged, choking his shame into steadfastness. "Here they are."

Hines's teeth ground as they lowered him but he made no sound. The shock of his injury still mercifully held off the worst pain. Zollinger helped the picket over.

"This boy's got a ball in the shoulder," he announced. "Don't know how he contrived to help. . . ."

"Groundhog case," muttered the picket. "Nothin' else to do. God, what a mess. Goin' to break the stock of a musket over the next Florida head I sees. . . ." Very undramatically he collapsed in a faint.

"Wrong head he's goin' to bust," growled the background.

The Captain wheeled. "Sergeant McComas, take Carney and buck and gag him."

"Now, sir?"

"Right now."

McComas stirred to action. In the dark shadow of the trench, the minnies still seeking overhead, Private Carney sat in an awkward posture, his hands tied in front of him and a stick passed over the arms and under the knees. He could not move without rolling over, and a cloth tied over his mouth kept him from speaking.

"Release him in an hour," said the Captain. "If they attack, cut him loose. Watts, stand sentry over him."

Hammond burst into the firing bay.

"Matthews is back, sir. Says he squinched down between the trees they'd toted out for the abatis."

"Very good." Stowell had not raised his voice when he had ordered the punishment for Carney nor did he now as he continued. "Lieutenant, I'd see about those fire steps."

His bulky figure moved slowly into the next angle of the works, and Brice was left alone with the men.

They did not look at him, nor did they speak. He had shown indubitable courage after the disaster; had it not been his own fault and no one else's, he would already have won their good opinion. Hodges and Holbrook, stiffening under the blankets, would have been sacrifices to chance or to obedience to orders from the higher levels of the Army hierarchy; even the decimated blue regiments opposite blamed Grant and not their Colonels. In fact, the bond would have been tighter forged by the recognition that they suffered mutually. But here in this narrow trace of ditch and parapet he and his butternut infantrymen faced only the stark fact of his failure. Hodges and Holbrook would indecently soon become merely names mentioned by chance in recollection; only the living exist for troops in combat. But that moment of forgetfulness would stick and rankle, dragging at the feet of the patrols he led, making the heads of the pickets he posted turn uncertainly towards the flanks, ineffacable by time but solely by example. Nor would this last be easy; he could not afford another mistake, and his men would be watchful, distrustful, during the period in which he proved himself.

Stripped to the core of him by fatigue and reaction, Brice flogged himself into movement. He walked across to the timbered incline and took hold of the nearest log. It was heavy and his strength had passed with his ordeal, but he strained and lifted at it, drawing his breath hard between his clenched teeth. He gave no command, but worried the embedded top from the parapet and dropped it into the trench. The weight of the next might be beyond him, but he would try. He put his arms around it, braced his feet and lifted, his muscles cracking. Then the burden lightened, the two Sergeants had laid hold of it too.

Still wordless, they dragged it clear and carried it to where it would prolong the first. Brice's palm was bleeding where a stub had scratched it, but without complaint he plodded back to the partly denuded incline, the Sergeants behind him.

Two other shadows were struggling with the third log.

"Goddam it, Zollinger," muttered the taller disgustedly, "hoist your share, will you? Don't leave the whole job to me."

V

THE day was the time for rest, the night for work. The sun might beat down unmercifully, the friable gray soil with its streaking of red clay might dry into puffs of clinging dust, but tired men must learn to sleep in sweat and dirt. The death odor was becoming monstrous, drawing further strength from the decaying carcasses of horses and mules scattered about the rear areas. The artillerymen and wagoners were too busy to dig the pits required to dispose of this animal refuse; only the dead men who did not lie in the disputed ground could be shuffled under the surface. The lines could be located by the persistence of the smell; those few visitors who came out from Richmond, government officials for the most part, went away nauseated. The soldiers had no option, they stayed.

Yet still no flag came. If it were bad enough in the trenches, the suffering wounded were dying in hell.

Hodges and Holbrook had been buried during the final depth of darkness before the dawn when the troops would go to the parapets, the Rebel infantry, sallow from underfeeding, cuddling their rifles and searching with strained faces until the deceptive light grew honest enough to assure them that there would be no further attacks. Ten thousand men, most of them seasoned veterans from the Army of the Potomac, had been killed, wounded, or were missing on the rolls. After the war, when the Federal dead were buried in neat, precisely arranged cemeteries, the unknowns outnumbered the known and even those whose pathetic headstones still ask an unanswerable question. Headstones with fragments of names, with initials and nothing more; scraps of identification from rotting clothing or blurred letters. But the Confederates rest more quietly. Save for a few they have gone back into Virginia, sinking like Hodges and Holbrook into unity with the fields

42

and the swamps and perhaps with the song of the birds who come back when the guns stop.

It was Sunday the fifth of June, Brice's second day in the line. He went about his work silently, expecting sullenness but finding it only in a minority. The majority of the men treated him with reserve, very careful to continue the military formalities which would have begun to slough off as they grew used to him. A military organization takes its tone from its leaders. General Lee had set the standard for the Army of Northern Virginia, a leaven which worked down through the corps, the divisions, the brigades to the smallest squad, enhanced or lessened by the individual characters of the Lieutenant Generals, of the Corporals and every rank between. The final forging of I Company had been accomplished by Captain Stowell. Wise, humorous and disillusioned, he had shaped his men, an equally disillusioned assemblage of scholars and dockrats, young for the most part, veterans for the most part, whose early dreams of glamorous war had long since been dissipated. Among them Brice was still an anachronism, better understood by the others than by Brice himself. His development had been arrested by the wound at Gaines's Mill, so that he had not yet emerged from the illusion of glory, from the self-conscious veneer of hardness which characterizes the beginner who has not yet cut his military eyeteeth. The horror of battle with its accompaniment of fear and violent death and mangled bodies, its smells and its sounds, is merely a preliminary phase; the final one is the endurance of utter monotony, month in and month out, the same faces, the same food, the same duties unending. The disaster he had inadvertently caused was the first sobering douche.

As if it were an established custom the barrel-like Lucas gathered as many about him as were inclined and could be spared from duty, and after a reading from the Bible led them in prayer. He was not a minister nor even well educated, but sincerity rang deep as he prayed that those who had been taken from them might be granted eternal rest. At the end he paused, then added simply:

"Lord, let them Yankees get some sense and bring in their wounded. Amen."

Brice listened somberly. The bass of the tone and the mocking screech of the minnies matched his mood. All of us who are young, he reflected, or most of us anyway, are in this war. Into his mind flashed the sardonic endorsement of D. H. Hill on a request for furlough: "Approved for the reason that if our soldiers are not permitted to visit their homes, the next generation will be composed of the descendants of cowards and skulkers." General Hill was a sarcastic old buzzard who probably knew that he was being unjust to many folks, but the Army had laughed at the apt expression of its own feelings. There were too many groups who were outside this war altogether, the politicians struggling for power, the speculators, the contractors and the workingmen who were handling more money than they had ever seen before—all of them far away from the stinking ditches of Cold Harbor.

The men were rising from their knees, Captain Stowell among them. Brice replaced his hat and watched his commander lumber back to his blankets. There was another tough old buzzard, bucking and gagging Carney in the front line on his own responsibility and in defiance of Army regulations. Carney must have suffered plenty of mental anguish during that hour, even though the Captain had inconspicuously returned and leaned against the traverse, his drawn sword partly hidden under his cloak to make certain that the prisoner was cut loose if the pickets fired. Yet the men apparently did not object; he had heard them laughing unsympathetically when Carney had been released. They treated it as if it were a family matter, something private among themselves, something to which he did not belong. Well, he'd better go look at his fire steps by daylight. It was important that they lie solidly against the front of the works and be properly aligned.

He had not taken two strides, crouching automatically out of an already ingrained respect for the Yankee sharpshooters, when another memory struck him. How far was he really apart from the knit entity that was I Company? He had heard last night what he was not supposed to hear, disembodied voices talking in the darkness. Laird, the Battalion Adjutant, had come hotfoot. An F Company working party which had been just leaving the works when the firing had broken out had also had a man wounded. What was the situation here?

44

Stowell had reported it and had said flatly that the blame was entirely his. He had failed to make sure that the Florida regiment had been informed. Since he was in command, he had been derelict in his duty. Probably Laird had better assessed the blame, but in the face of that uncompromising reply had made no remark and gone back to headquarters.

Brice spun around as along the works came a series of yells, spreading from angle to angle. The Federal lines took notice of the sound and sputtered with picket firing, but the timbre of the squalls was joyous.

"What in hell's that?" asked McComas, hastily shoving a Testament into his pocket. "Grant's quit or something?"

Little Raby, flushed and open-mouthed, dashed around the traverse. "Boys, wait'll you see the rations! Fat bacon and onions run through from Nassau!"

The ration party followed him, grinning from ear to ear. "For once he's not lyin'. It's no grape," called Burke, arching his black brows humorously as he set down his load.

Captain Stowell kicked his blanket off.

"Count the onions," he ordered. "We'll issue them evenly." Involuntary saliva stained the corner of his beard, and he wiped it away, but not before there were covert chuckles. "They're not cooked?" he demanded.

"No, sir. Them food destroyers at the ration train have never laid a hand on them."

"That's your Irish optimism," growled Home Grown Smith, his hacking cough unabated, spots of high color on his cheekbones and his throat bound up by a pair of socks tied together. "They've had their hands on them all right, the goddam thieves. Do what the Captain says and find out how many they've left us."

"They look mighty small," said Private Duvall, peering hungrily into the sack.

These small grumbles were no more than a customary accompaniment to rising morale. I Company was happy. It laughed at last, regardless of the muffled wailing that still drifted across the parapet, regardless of its new dead, of the dirt, the smell and the lice that crawled and bit under the ragged clothes. Like Captain Stowell, the men too had craved something that would taste, something that was neither musty

45

nor sour, the unfamiliar sensation of a full belly. The satisfaction of a need that seemed so simple yet was actually so great put them in a mood of forgiveness. Even Brice recovered a measure of good will.

The little fires were kindled, "picket fires," the Army called them, twigs and sticks in no larger quantity than was necessary to cook the bacon and boil the coffee. Some messes had a community frying pan, others employed skewers hastily whittled from sticks. The Old Gentleman (Brice was beginning to use mentally the same term as the men) had put his onions in his hat and was peeling them carefully with a claspknife, discarding only the very minimum of unedible skin. The sharp, biting exhalation made his eyes water, but he cut rings from the remainder and ate them with relish from his dirty fingers. There were no forks in the First Maryland Infantry Battalion; even the few that had been in the officers' mess chest had been utilized by Dr. Snowden as surgical implements.

The Captain, chewing slowly to prolong the enjoyment, looked up and met Brice's amused glance. For the first time since that fatal sally outside the works, he smiled.

"You may bring us luck after all. It seems to me that yesterday I was making mention of onions and here they are. It seems right unfortunate that I didn't emphasize the lamb with currant jelly."

His eyes shifted to the groups about the fires. The coffee had been served out, and the men were staring at what they held in their palms. There was hearty swearing and a buzz of complaint, though a few merely poured the substance into the tin cups in which the water bubbled.

"I thought so," said Stowell, listening. "Rye substitute instead of real coffee. There's a grape that it causes impotence. Watch Cabell and we can tell if we'll hear about it. He was reading law when the war started and he does the talking when they take it upon themselves to point out my shortcomings or ask for information. He can outargue Hammond, so Hammond lets him come to me to be dealt with. That boy can beat a preacher at a horsetrade."

Private Cabell, like a judge in ragged robes, considered the problem his clients were putting before him. The officers in their corner of the firing bay could hear a little of what was said, but could not determine whether Cabell was being asked to approach the throne or merely advise. Apparently it was the latter, for his pronouncement had a mixed reception. The wrangling continued.

"Ask the Old Gentleman," demanded young Matthews lustily, nursing a fire with his battered hat, but Raby objected equally loudly.

"It wouldn't make no difference to him. Look how old he is."

Sixteen was appalled by the ancientness of sixty, and the nearer men were red-faced with suppressed laughter, but the Captain threw back his head with a guffaw. "I've done my duty already, three daughters and a son. Thank you, Heenan," he said to the horsy orderly who had just appeared. "If you don't slop over the rest of my coffee, I'll take the risk."

After breakfast Brice stretched himself at full length along the flank of the traverse, his folded blanket for a pillow. The spent bullet which had glanced from his cheek had left him with a recurrent nausea caused by shock. Utter fatigue strove to drag him into the depths of sleep, but discomfort fought every inch of the descent. Except where the contusion of the minnie had caused a wide black bruise, his light skin had contrasted with the dark red or brown of the faces of the others who had been weather-beaten while he had sat in an office. Now every exposed surface flamed with sunburn made worse by the irritation of the gritty dirt which smeared him. Flies and mosquitoes, the latter rising in clouds from the swamps and the standing water along the Chickahominy, joined with the lice to infest him with a barely endurable itching. He threw a portion of the blanket over his head, but its weight stifled him and he alternately slept and woke, occasionally drawing his limbs up like a wounded man.

Once when his lids parted he saw Stowell writing on a pad held against his knee. While Brice wondered vaguely, the Old Gentleman finished a page and began to address one of the yellow Confederate envelopes. After the first line he frowned, then beckoned First Sergeant Hammond and held a whispered conversation with him, low enough to respect the ears of the Lieutenant who they thought was sleeping, but loud

enough nevertheless for him to hear. Brice felt the sickness
and the heartache surge up again. There were still mail car-
riers, "blockade runners" they were called, who made the trip
to and from Maryland, secret figures stealing across the rivers
in rowboats and dodging Federal patrols. Stowell had asked
the address of Holbrook's family in Baltimore; he was writing
to the kin of those whom Brice's forgetfulness had destroyed.
But even his bitter brooding could not endure against exhaustion, and he drifted off again to his tossing slumber.

While he slept a pattern was being formed, unknown to
I Company. In the distant valley of the Shenandoah the Fed-
eral General Hunter was killing General "Grumble" Jones at
Piedmont and routing his small command.

In the afternoon the axes went to work again. The abatis
building must be resumed or the front would not be safe from
surprises. This time it was the Captain who led the party
over the works when the bombardment had died away, the
Floridians notified, Brice and Hammond side by side check-
ing the names at the restored incline. Brice had made no
foolish offer to lead. He knew as well as Stowell that nervous-
ness must be steadied by the officer they trusted.

There was no incident save one. Home Grown Smith asked
to be of the detail, and the Old Gentleman, graven-faced,
considered briefly and consented, giving the soldier his spare
handkerchief to stuff into his mouth should he begin to cough.
Brice could read the nuances in the request and its answer,
the thoughts that were not expressed. If Smith was dying of
consumption, he would sooner have the quick mercy of a
bullet. The doctors knew no remedy for tuberculosis, and
Smith had no future in the barnlike base hospitals save to
pass alone in the bright flood of a hemorrhage.

When the work was done Burke and Lucas were allowed
to returned to their furtive expedition, stealthy fingers groping
under blue coats to feel for a heartbeat, ears alert for a gasping breath. Twice they brought back bundles that smelled of
gangrene and urine to such aid as Dr. Snowden could afford
them.

The sixth was a Monday and hot. It was also the fourth full
day—full hell—for the Federals who had been hit in the dawn
attack on the third and who were still lying with swollen

tongues and feebly scrabbling fingers where the rescuers, their lives in their hands, had not been able to reach them. Federals and Confederates alike had sent out men of good will to save those nearest the works, but there was a belt of suffering that stretched along the middle ground. There the wailing was finished, few could make a sound. Others had died and were swelling with the gases of decay, their uniforms stretching under the rising pressure. Over them still whined the minnies, for no picket dared trust the motives of a moving shadow. That night the grape spread down the Confederate defenses that Grant had at last sent over a flag.

Brice had kept to himself, not thrusting his presence among the men except as was necessary to carry out his duties. In his blankets during the light, helping to lever the trees up the new runway during the darkness, he had done some hard thinking. He had passed through the first stage of self-justification, the insidious temptation to excuse everything by arguing that he was entitled to one mistake, no matter who had paid for it. He had met that head-on. Was he to learn from it or retreat into deliberate forgetfulness, trying by swagger and sternness to make the others forget too? He knew better. Was he to impress the quietly gallant Lucas and Burke, the savage Beeler, the skull-faced Hammond by a cheap pretense that he was a harder man than they were? There was nothing left but to endure until his own mark was on him for better or for worse.

Captain Stowell must have watched his lonely struggle with more sympathy than Brice realized. After the stand-to-arms at dawn, the routine of orders and the report of rollcall, he joined his Lieutenant in their chosen corner and sat filling a battered briar pipe. His cold was better, but one puff of smoke and he knocked the pipe out again with a wry grimace.

"Be a day or two yet before I can enjoy it," he remarked, and leaned his back against the traverse.

"I was a bookseller in Baltimore," he continued, scraping out the clogged bowl with his knifepoint. "Maybe you've been in my store on Lexington Street, though I'll admit I don't recall you before we met in the Old Regiment. When I saw this trouble coming, I began to read my own wares, being careful, of course, not to soil the pages. I read everything I could find on war and how to wage it. Old General Knox who did so much with Washington's artillery was a bookseller too, and did the same thing before the Revolution. Maybe before he got through with that affair after Yorktown he had the same experience that I did. Nothing I'd read seemed to help very much. What did was what I learned 'endurin' the war,' as some of the boys say. If I had to do it over, I wouldn't spend so much time on Napoleon's *Memoirs.* I'd study some plain infantryman's yarn, if he tells the truth, which most don't."

He put the pipe back in his pocket and straightened out his legs with a tired grunt.

"A company officer isn't a General," he went on slowly. "He doesn't need to have more than a smattering of education in what they call the science. Once he knows the drill and a few tricks of the trade, he's got all the knowledge he needs. Except that he's got to know soldiers, something all except the really big Generals forget. Soldiers are always pretty much the same. Whatever war they fight in, they're complaining about the same things and have to put up with the same things. It's easier for me than it is for you. Once I showed them I could take them out on a field of fight and was interested in them, they gave me that same interest back. This is a young Company for the most part. They've mostly assigned me the children."

His expression was hard to read, there was bitterness in it and sorrow and pride.

"The men forgive me a lot just because I'm old enough to be the father of most of them. I can tell a boy not to make a fool of himself when a youngster like you has got to be regulation. There's only a few I've had to be tough with, like I was with Carney. He's further along in years than most of the Company, and he's spent most of those years along the docks where they don't make allowances for others. Even then, that kind don't get far with their grudges, not if your boys like you."

He settled himself for a nap and pulled his hat over his eyes.

"I'll say this much for you, Brice. You've had a poor beginning but you're looking it in the face."

VI

TUESDAY the seventh was hot in the morning, hot at noon, hot in the furnace for the very few who still lived in the middle ground. The messages had to go back and forth between the headquarters, the truce arrangements completed and the front lines notified. Then at last the white flags fluttered from both parapets and Federal parties scrambled over with water and litters and doctors. Yet this late there was little they could do. The spades and not the scalpels were called for, and the burial squads, overwhelmed by the magnitude of their task, must send back for more help.

The Marylanders watched from their own works. Any aid they might have offered must necessarily have been refused; even those whom Burke and Lucas had rescued were prisoners at best. They sat in rows along the toplog or thrust their heads above its shelter. Crouching men took the cricks out of their backs without fear of minnies. Brice's working party could walk with impunity over the space where they had grovelled or run that bloody night.

They talked very little when they were overlooking the field. Their rifles had helped create that stinking ghastliness which was being covered with clean dirt like a dog's mess. Even the conviction that the Yankees had asked for what they had got, coming down South and trying to tromple everybody and everybody's rights, did not entirely compensate for the sight of the dead bodies thumping into the shallow pits, whole rows of them, elbow to elbow. The earth was the Lord's, and the fulness thereof, but Man always wanted a share and more than his share—so he killed for it.

Brice walked out through the narrow gap in the abatis, his

smudged handkerchief in his hand as a sign of peace. Lucas and Burke tramped behind him.

"Duty," he told the pickets, lounging but watchful in their pits. "We're on duty."

The three advanced into the field, picking their way among the dead. The burial parties had not reached this far as yet, and it was not easy to find a place to put one's feet. A Michigan Captain waved a handkerchief in return and strode towards them, followed by a Corporal and a squad with an empty litter.

"These men brought in five of your boys," said Brice, indicating Lucas and Burke. "We got a list of the names if you want them."

"Good of you," said the Federal Captain heartily. He took the list, then offered his hand to the three Confederates. "Any more still living out here?"

"'Fraid that one's gone," Lucas told the Corporal. "We felt of him last night an' he's cold."

"Deceivin', ain't he?" said the Corporal. "Up on his elbows like that."

The officers stood together while the men scattered to search.

"I brought you fellows some newspapers," remarked the Captain, holding out a package. "New York ones and not too old."

"Thank you," said Brice. He drew out a plug of tobacco and made a return gift. They talked together, not volubly but as quietly as two chance acquaintances, but now their handkerchiefs were held to their noses. The smell was such that one of the litter bearers suddenly stooped over and vomited. Save for the color of the uniforms and the thin raggedness of the rebel Privates, there was little to differentiate between the sides on which these Americans were fighting. All were dirty and all had the same stamp on their faces, combat men, unmistakably marked by their calling.

Lucas and Burke had shown the Corporal over that area which they had covered by night, but had been unable to discover any survivors. They drifted back with the litter, talking among themselves and even exchanging grim jokes.

"Looks like the only way we'll get to Richmond is by swapping Generals," said the Corporal.

"Faith, you've been tryin' hard enough to make that little jaunt," Burke was returning the compliment. "I remimber that at the beginning of this war we was saying that we could beat the Yankees with popguns. Maybe we still could, but you wouldn't use popguns."

Brice shook hands again. "Reckon we'd better be getting home. Come on, men."

The groups separated, the Rebels facing for the first time the irregular trace of mound and interlaced trees which was as familiar to the Federals as was the corresponding one along the skirt of the woods to them. They stared at it curiously, rather astonished to see that it appeared fully as strong as the other. Burke voiced their thought.

"Looks like we're better moles than they are or our officers crack a longer whip."

Brice felt a quick twinge of cheerfulness. Burke had made a joke indirectly at his expense, the first fissure in the men's reserved attitude, but he only grinned without replying.

The parapet sitters had noticed the bundle under Brice's arm and broke out into a babble as they vaulted over.

"Yankee papers! Can we see 'em, Lieutenant, an' find out what's goin' on in that benighted land?"

"Got to show 'em to the Captain first," warned Brice. There was neither censorship nor propaganda to keep the troops from reading enemy journals. Each side read the other's—and went on fighting.

"The illustrated papers that cheer the boys in blue with sketches of the glorious deeds they did not do," said Beeler with a snarling grin.

The would-be lawyer Cabell, scratching under his jacket, feigned astonishment.

"Hark to that now. Beeler's getting him an education and beginning to talk in rhyme. If he keeps it up he'll be the Shakespeare of the sinks."

"Hesh up, both of you," said Lucas sharply. "I've been out there an' I don't feel like laughing."

Brice found the Old Gentleman taking advantage of the

truce by trying to wash out his remaining handkerchief in the swamp. He had a small piece of soap, but the task was a hopeless one for without a bleach the cloth merely assumed a dark gray hue. He hung it on a bush to dry and began to mend a tear in the sleeve of his jacket, sewing backwards as men do. He pulled the needle slowly through the material, squinting at it and muttering under his breath.

However, he had a budget of news that was even fresher than that in the Yankee papers. Laird had been along from Battalion Headquarters and had told him that General Breckinridge, whether or not he was still able to endure the contact of his saddle, had marched for the Valley with two brigades, twenty-one hundred troops. Hunter was advancing up the Shenandoah's course, leaving bright flames and black smoke behind him as the Virginia Military Institute and the home of the state's Governor burned. More Yankees were coming—when they combined, Hunter would have close to seventeen thousand men, or so the staff estimated, with nothing to stop him except the few remnants of the dead "Grumble" Jones's command and the Home Guards.

Around Cold Harbor, Laird had admitted, things were a mite confused. The Maryland Battalion had been left on this front, detached from Breckinridge but without the slightest inkling as to what General below Marse Robert himself they were now responsible. He reckoned it might be Harry Heth but he wasn't sure.

When the white flags were lowered on the eighth, and the sharpshooters were busy again, the days slid by as the armies watched each other in a stalemate. Occasionally a local attack flared and crashed, sputtering out with its accompaniment of casualties. Lee was too far outnumbered to risk much, and Grant had had a surfeit of assaults. There were military refinements in the line now. Communication trenches were winding their way behind the busy tools of the working parties across the open spaces, once traversed only by night and dangerously. A gun had been emplaced directly behind I Company's position and treble-shotted with canister. The Virginia artillerymen were available for talk and argument and had brought with them a new and hotly debated grape. They were making balloons back in Richmond—yes, they were, I tell you it's so—and they were going to load them up with explosives and float them over the Yankees. No sir, the blue-bellies weren't goin' to like it when that stuff came a-tumblin' down on their heads. . . .

"What if the wind shifts?" asked Cabell sardonically, and nearly had a fight on his hands.

Fixed rifles had been aligned on low spots in the Federal parapet. They were a real help to a sharpshooter. All he had to do was to look along the sights of the Enfield until somebody carelessly stepped into them, and then pull the trigger. The only objection was that the Yankees did the same thing.

I Company had a fairly large proportion of men of German extraction, though only one, a tallish, heavy-jawed Private named Radecke, had been born abroad. Zollinger and Beeler, though lumped in with them under the general term of "Dutchmen," were second or third generation. Niedlander and German Smith still occasionally used the language of the old country, though by now its purity had been so debased by the unconscious adoption of English terms that Radecke groped to follow them. Except for Beeler, whom they found uncongenial, as did most of the Company, they messed together and had adopted little Raby into their group. Brice had been amused to hear them talking together, Radecke on the one extreme, Zollinger and Raby on the other, the remainder in the linguistic center, gradually evolving a still weirder mixture of German and English as a sort of lingua franca.

This day the lines had done little quarreling between themselves. It was towards sunset, and, except for an infrequent shot which they had come to accept as a familiar accompaniment to their lives, the men were resting quietly, awake but relaxed until the coming of darkness and the resumption of the alert. Radecke, cross-legged with his hat pulled down, began to sing in a sweet, true baritone a succession of German lieder. No one interrupted; faces turned or eyes closed, they listened while the terrible homesickness of men whose families were in enemy country tightened their lips. As abruptly as he had started Radecke stopped. He stood up, his head next

55

to a gap between the toplogs at the point of the angle where the builders had not been able to join them. The dull whack of the bullet brought him to his knees, his hands at his face and blood trickling between them. When they picked him up they saw that the minnie had gone through both eyes.

Somehow it seemed that it wasn't right that the evening should have been so terribly marred. Possibly it was the reversion from a momentary dream into a harsh reality that so affected them. I Company's sharpshooters glared down their rifle barrels and sought with gently twitching muzzles for a target. Next day they had it, as Brice heard from McComas.

A couple of crazy bluebellies got into a fight and rolled out into the open with the other Yanks whooping and yelling and running out too, like as if it was a ruckus down on Light Street by the docks. Beeler shot one. They saw him flop, and he was still lying there when it got dark. Maybe if it hadn't been for Radecke, the boys would have felt a little mean about it— it looked like a good fight and the Rebels were enjoying it too.

Their turn came around for night picket. Companies performed this duty in a body and in regular rotation, the others spreading out so as to cover the portion of the line they vacated. There was always an accordion-like effect of expansion and contraction going on, firing bays changing ownership to the accompaniment of grumbles both by those who were regularly assigned and by those who temporarily replaced them. Neither, according to the common belief, ever knew how to build a proper parapet or how to do a real job of policing up the area. H Company, the former military prisoners, would relieve I in this case, and the grumbling was intensified. H Company was regarded sweepingly as a den of thieves, which was partially untrue, and even the promise of the friendly Virginians that they would keep an eye on their few belongings failed to pacify the complaints until Captain Stowell detailed Beeler as a guard. Beeler might be an unpleasant soul but he had his uses.

They mustered before dusk, and Sergeant Hammond went along their line, dropping a ramrod into each rifle to be sure that it was loaded. The percussion caps were fitted to the nipples and hands felt in pockets for extra cartridges. These were carried loose, cartridge boxes being so much useless weight to lug along on a march and, if a man didn't forget and put a hot pipe among them instead of into his haversack, they were regarded as perfectly harmless. Captain Bussey brought his followers into the angles and exchanged a few not too cordial remarks with Captain Stowell. Bussey was sensitive about the reputation of his rapscallions, and the Virginians' helpful whistling of the Rogue's March did not add to his good humor. Then I Company filed along the trench towards the center of the Battalion front.

It was a new experience for Brice. Having held the end of the works, they had never had another company pass them on its way to picket. The Marylanders exchanged greetings as they traversed their own familiar world, no longer isolated by H Company on their left and the absolute necessity which required that each unit hold its own section of the line without visiting the others. Officers he knew called to him or shook his hand, old friends over whom he might have crawled the night he had joined but whom the thirty or forty yards which had intervened between his post and theirs had separated as far as when he had been in Richmond and they at Hanover Junction. There were other comments too, low-pitched but intentionally audible. His finery, soiled though it now was, came in for quiet jeers from the lounging Privates.

"Come out of that coat," said a voice. "I can see your legs stickin' out so I know you're in there."

"Who sent for the militia?" asked another with false earnestness.

Brice took it calmly. It was the routine dose which an officer had to swallow and most of them grew both to expect and rather to enjoy it. If they objected actively, the very objection would become a treasured memory, on a par with General Breckinridge's bruises and General Elzey's abrupt and involuntary descent from his horse during a formal review.

Then the order came to stand to arms, and the last of their brief journey was made behind the rigid backs of the manned parapet.

The Battalion Commander was waiting for them and talked

briefly to Captain Stowell. Hammond went down the line with the orders. Don't shoot unless you're certain you see something, don't leave the rifle pits unless there's an attack, then fire and run for the works through the gaps in the abatis, the password's "Buckshot," we'll be relieved at dawn. He added more when he reached Brice at his proper place in the rear of the Company. The Captain would locate himself in the middle of the picket line. Hammond would post the pickets on the left, the Lieutenant those on the right. If he was ready, they'd go over.

"All ready," said Brice. He did not look at his shadowy men, silent in the darkness. If they doubted him, he would know it when the test came, not before.

The single file began to move jerkily ahead. As each man mounted the parapet, he leaned over and offered a hand to the one behind him.

"Crawl till you're clear of the gap," came a warning from an officer nameless in the gloom, as Brice reached up to meet McComas's grip. "They've got a fixed rifle on it, but it carries high."

Brice's boot struck softly against a log, and his stomach slid across the top of the parapet.

"Hold onto my foot," whispered McComas, and they snaked their way along, the trampled grass brushing their faces. Low voices from a glory hole, and Hammond's detachment crouching off into the deeper night.

"Brice?"

"Here, sir."

"Get going. I'll be here with Heenan. Captain Thomas is sending a Sergeant with you to bring back the pickets you relieve."

Brice took the strange noncom's sleeve so as not to lose him.

"Don't let your canteens rattle. Pass it along," he told Mc-Comas.

He was in the too familiar field again with only the stars to see by. Yet the field, watched with sidelong intentness, had a difference. The bushes and the bullet-ripped cedars grew out of it, better defined now that their bases were not buried in the dead. As he slunk along, the turned earth on the edge of the pits would hunch up from the soil, there would be a low challenge, an answer, a momentary pause, and one of his men would slip in and an A Company man lift himself out. A stealthy, silent tiptoeing like children at a game, stooping so they would not be outlined against the sky above the works and the abatis; then at last the final post, the final relief. The A Company Sergeant reversed his line and departed, leaving Brice with McComas at his heels to advance until he had the challenge of the Florida outposts.

He was resolved that if his example were needed to restore confidence he would not fail. One by one he visited the glory holes, staying briefly with each picket and sharing his watch. Lucas, Cabell, Watts, Zollinger, all of them alert, all of them veterans to whom this was an old and familiar task, Burke, Niedlander—then a stooping figure throwing a whisper ahead of it:

"Lieutenant Brice! Lieutenant Brice!"

"Here with me," answered Niedlander.

Heenan, the Captain's orderly, flung himself flat beside them.

"Captain wants Sergeant McComas to report to him."

"Anything gone wrong?" asked Brice quickly.

"Nothin' that I know of, sir. The Captain's goin' to have a look at the left."

McComas trailed his rifle and held his canteen close to his side. The two left at a quick walk, and Brice resumed his rounds. Corporal Kirk and Home Grown Smith were the last pickets before Stowell's command post. He made the few extra steps and found McComas alone in it.

"Hammond's boys are a little jumpy but they're quieting down," reported his Sergeant and friend. "Reckon the Old Gentleman's bein' fatherly or bustin' somebody's head."

There had been an occasional shot from that direction, remembered Brice. He turned back to patrol his own section of the front which lay dark and unruffled. With McComas taken from him, he was alone and that much the more determined that he would not fail on this assignment. Monotonously as the night passed so passed he, lying and watching with the sentries, listening to the sounds—the pickaxes and the spades at work over the way, the far-off rumble of wagons, the soft "All's well" that floated along the opposing outposts as it did down their own. Nothing unusual, nothing alarming—only the recurrent rifles and the boom of a gun at long intervals. Not a shot did his sentries fire, a quiet night save for the early quick bombardment that Lee had ordered for nine o'clock. Then at last the whispers and the stir that announced the arrival of the day relief.

He tallied the names as the new guard stepped into the glory holes. Home Grown Smith, Kirk, Niedlander—all with him, all safe thus far. The first step in his rehabilitation in the eyes of his men had been successfully taken. They reached the junction with the Florida Brigade, and he felt his way back along the waiting row who leaned upon their rifles, counting them and making a retally of the names.

Then, suddenly, he grinned. The old bastard, the old fox, the old—gentleman! Now he understood why Stowell had sent for McComas. It was to give him, Brice, the whole responsibility without the support of an experienced Sergeant. Unostentatiously he was to have his confidence rebuilt and, to ensure that it was, the Captain had arranged that his detachment be the pick of the Company. Lucas, Burke, Zollinger and the rest would not be stampeded easily. No wonder Stowell had stayed on the left, rather than on his right. No wonder he had not even appeared from dusk until dawn.

He made no mention of it to Stowell when they were inside the works, nor did the Captain ever bring up the subject. Of course, he had yet to be tested on day picket which would come soon enough. Nevertheless, it would not be so searching. To make rounds when the sharpshooters could see was plain suicide, and the officers would stay in a glory hole, hugging dirt like the others.

However, that duty was postponed. On the night of the twelfth Laird came again, this time with orders. The three of them read the formal paper by matchflares behind the traverse where there was no danger of outlining a head against a loophole. I Company was to draw three days' cooked rations and report to Lieutenant General Jubal Early of the Second Corps as guides. Start before daylight.

They discussed it, bright-eyed, in whispers. Marse Robert had got sick and tired of Hunter and was sending Old Jube with what was left of Stonewall Jackson's infantry to abolish him. The risk of detaching them would be enormous with the Army of the Potomac so strong, but that wasn't their affair. The subject they debated, hot and eager, was why was I Company to go? The orders were authentic enough and signed by Walter H. Taylor who was General Lee's own Assistant Adjutant General. They had come direct from Army Headquarters straight to their Battalion without passing through any General; possibly even the staff had not been able to work out the chain of command. But again, why I Company if the Second Corps was going to the Valley? They were solidly Baltimoreans.

They stared at each other while the last match died. You don't suppose—it couldn't be that they were going into Maryland, going to Baltimore, going home?

VII

"Hurry!" said Captain Stowell, Brice and the Sergeants. The courier who had brought the order had had no easy task to locate a single unattached unit in an army of over forty thousand men, and he had been very late. If the dawn caught I Company before it could leave the line, there was risk of casualties. The ridge that curved above the swampy piece was too steep for communication trenches, and, though barricades of earth and logs had been erected to cover the most exposed stretches of path, all movement must stop with the light. Yet there must be delay, a racking wait while eyes nervously searched the sky for the first tinge of gray. The Florida Brigade must take over the vacated firing bays, for the Marylanders were too extended already.

Captain Crane arrived from headquarters and went on around the far traverse to complete the arrangements for the relief. Meanwhile, Sergeant Hammond collected the detail that was filling sandbags, chased the deadbeats who had sheltered themselves at the sink in the hope of avoiding work, and saw to it that the sentries were temporarily replaced by the first who stood up in marching order.

In the pitchy darkness, thicker by the added gloom of parapet and traverse, a groping, swearing ferment of kneeling figures made ready for the move. Each soldier wrapped his blankets and such few extra clothes as he might possess into the oilcloth, lashed it tight and then tied it together at the bottom so as to make an elongated doughnut. He put his canteen strap over one shoulder and then put the roll on top of it where it embraced him like a friendly python. On the opposite hip he slung the haversack, soiled and greasy from contact with past issues of bacon. The invaluable tin cup, holding about a quart, depended from the belt or from a strap sewed to the jacket. If a mess possessed a frying pan or skillet, one member rammed the filed-down handle into his rifle muzzle. This was full equipment, style of 1864. If a man must carry all he owns, he embraces poverty with a cheerful heart.

The knots were stubborn when they had to be tied by feel; blankets and oilcloths crept from one roll into another either accidentally or helped by the unscrupulous; quick quarrels flared. Brice heard the smack of a fist and tore two struggling Privates apart.

"Quit that! Quit that now! We'll straighten everything out come daylight. Ought to be ashamed of yourselves—grown men fightin'. . . ."

He stooped over his own roll, felt around with increasing vehemence, then, forgetting his good counsel of an instant before, made his own complaint.

"Some son of a bitch has stole my oilcloth."

There was a quick burst of laughter, followed by a fresh challenge in a different voice:

"Damn you, Watts, you've got my pipe!"

"I haven't, but I just stepped on it. What'd you go and leave it on the fire step for?"

"Why in hell don't you watch where you put your feet?"

"Burke!" boomed Hammond. "It's your turn to carry the spade."

"*Again*, Sergeant darlint?" answered the soft brogue.

"What do you mean 'again'? You've seen so little of it that I'm goin' to have to introduce the two of you."

Finally the slap of a hand against the earth of the parapet and a muttered comment. "I ain't grudged a single cupful of dirt I've done throwed on this here pile."

When at last they were ready, sitting in a row on the fire step and looking oddly bulky, the questioning began.

"Where we goin', Lieutenant?"

"Is it true that we're marchin' on Washington?"

Brice made no answer, and the men began to speculate among themselves, meanwhile listening for any unguarded comment he might make.

"Washington, that's where we're bound. Marchin' right around Ulysses Grant an' leavin' him sittin' here."

"One company? Pull your ears and you'll find they've grown to full jackass length. The rest of the Battalion ain't coming."

"Where'd you hear that?"

At last they reached the truth as they accepted it: "Boys, we're goin' to Baltimore with Jubal Early. No, it ain't no grape. A man from H Company just told me. Said he heard it from a fellow who got it from old Crane's orderly. He heard 'em talking to the courier. . . ."

The row of heads turned simultaneously in Brice's direction.

"Is that so, Lieutenant?"

"Tell us, sir."

"Boys, I'm not allowed to say."

Florida infantrymen filed into the bays, grumbling full-throated but silenced by the mutter from the sitting rank.

"We're goin' to Baltimore. Hear that, you crackers? Us and the whole Second Corps. Just heard it from the Lieutenant."

Brice, who had said nothing of the sort, was wondering what kind of a reception he would have from Captain Stowell were the latter to hear the rumor attributed to his subordinate when a deep-chested chuckle sounded beside him.

"In the next bay they're saying I told them."

The Captain turned to the Florida officer who accompanied him. "Well, you've seen our line. This is as far as it goes."

"Kind of puny parapets," said the thin shadow of the Floridian in a disparaging drawl.

"Maybe so, but better than yours, sir," retorted the Old Gentleman, unruffled. "Now if your sentries will take over from mine, we'll be getting along."

I Company collected about him in a dark cluster, and Hammond called the roll rapidly from memory. "Spade!" he ended sharply, and Burke's voice rumbled in answer:

"Present and cuttin' into me collarbone."

"All here, sir," reported the First Sergeant, as if the Captain had not heard the entire transaction, and they filed along the works.

The rumor of their supposed destination had spread, and

there were excited questions as they zigzagged through the trenches, but few answered. I Company was looking at the sky and judging time anxiously. The trifle of dawn breeze was ruffling the leaves of the few trees that were still left standing in the swamp. "Keep closed up and hurry," came the order down the file, and they followed each other at so short an interval that each stepped on the heels of the man ahead. Brice and the others at the tail were in a stumbling jogtrot.

They wheeled sharply where the path began, Laird the Adjutant marking the turn.

"Keep your bowels open, and you'll be all right," said Dr. Snowden who stood beside him. The glory hole in which Battalion Headquarters had been located when Brice had arrived was now a very fair bombproof, roofed over by logs with a thick layer of dirt piled on top. However, it was still damp; the Sergeant Major's shoes splashed as he crawled out of it.

"Tell the Monument Street girls to wait for the real soldiers," he growled, but there was envy in his tone.

They wound through the swamp, a very different place from the gloomy labyrinth of Brice's entering journey. The path was wider and muddier; their feet squelched in it or resounded on wood where corduroy had been laid over the deeper holes. The timber was thinned by the axes, and the writhing snake of men licked their lips with a feeling of nakedness. But the smell of the place was the same, a memory so implanted in their minds that they would never sniff a marsh again without its coming back to them, subtle and dreadful. Behind them came a faint cry of "Stand to arms!" and a minnie threshed through the bushes.

The ground steepened, and their worn shoes slid with the pitch of it.

"Goddam you, can't you travel?" McComas kept asking in a shaking whisper that was full of impotent rage, and the file rammed their rifle butts into the ground and thrust themselves along. Another random minnie slapped into a red gum's trunk, and Brice bunched his shoulders in a shrinking, useless effort to reduce the target. An absurd thought repeated itself over and over in his mind: "I don't want to get shot in

65

the back. How'll I explain it?" The individual trees were beginning to stand out, the shadowy bushes were revealing their shape. Soon the sharpshooters yonder would be able to line up their sights.

Then, startling but welcome, rapped the challenge, "Who goes there?"

A gasped-out answer—Stowell must have suffered for breath —confirmed by a gabble of other voices. The line lurched forward. The desperate impatience subsided into relief, hearts slowed their rapid beat, and I Company, sweating and blown, were behind the works of the support position.

"Better squat down, boys," advised a Virginian of Mahone's old Brigade which had relieved Echols, "them minnies you passed will be catchin' up to you right soon."

The halt was a brief one. As soon as his chest stopped heaving, Stowell was on his feet and leading down the reverse slope of the ridge. The minnies had ceased to hum close, though a few still passed well overhead. The Company was keeping no formation, and Brice found himself beside Reeder who nodded upwards as a bullet tore its way through the air.

"Funny, isn't it?" commented the former choirboy. "You can set that sound to music. "It's a swell from E flat to F, then it retrogrades to D."

Brice gave him a tired grin. "Does it? I like the retrogression best."

By chance and the lie of the ground, they were still following the original route which he had traced coming up to join. The little branch ran roiled, its banks trampled into mud, and pools of water standing in the maze of footprints. Its course was littered with discarded bandages, stale with old blood, with rifles, articles of clothing and worn-out shoes. Yet it was the only landmark he could identify except for the battered houses of New Cold Harbor off to his right. The rising sun dispelled his lingering impression of enormous distances traversed amid death and mystery. Instead there was a vista of fields and woods, smirched by the effects of the battle, stinking carcasses of horses, abandoned wagons, fences stripped of rails and trees split by shot.

The ration train was some two miles to the rear to make

it safe from long-range bombardment, and the Company trudged wearily towards it, accepting fatalistically the chance that some blind-fired shell might land among them. The men were silent, walking as if they were pressed down by a weight; the full reaction on them. It had been rough at Cold Harbor, mighty rough. In ten days they had lost four killed and three severely wounded, only one of whom, Hines, had much chance of returning. There were left of them two officers, two Sergeants, one Corporal and nineteen Privates, including their single representative at the Commissary whom they would pick up. When they had been reorganized from the Old Regiment in the autumn of '62, they had had three officers and eighty-five rank and file. Disease had taken more than combat, but the wastage from death, wounds, transfers, sickness, prisoners and missing had been irreplaceable. Brice and little Raby had been the only new faces in their ranks since then. And they were regarded as a lucky unit with a good commander.

Fortunately they had a stimulant against the too vivid impressions which their recent immersion in the sight, feel and smell of hardship and danger had added to previous ones as grimly vivid. They would be forever changed within themselves, never able to find complete understanding except among others of their own kind, never able to express by any medium the depth and breath of their ordeal, never able entirely to escape from the acid of it, bitten deeply into the shadows of their subconscious. Yet now, trudging towards the white wagon covers sheltering beside a patch of woods, the new tenuous hope swam to the surface and bore them up.

Not that they entirely believed their own story that they were bound for Baltimore. Too many recalled the march to Gettysburg when every strategist in the ranks was sure that a few days would see them marching down Charles Street. A few had continued stubbornly certain even when the decimated columns were falling back on the Potomac. Still, since the belief was so necessary, they rationalized it to serve its present purpose.

McComas, his rifle slanted almost horizontally over his

shoulder as Daniel Boone might have carried his, held a bundle out to Brice.

"You might as well have this. It's the Sergeant Major's oilcloth. I grabbed it while he was telling us to have the Monument Street girls wait. If he's going to be one of those real soldiers they're to expect, he'd better learn not to spread an oilcloth to dry on a bush before it's light enough for him to keep an eye on it. What a recruit's trick!"

Brice took the gift without hesitation. The Confederate service had much in common with Napoleon's Grand Army. The members of both were highly individualistic, and the discipline in each case had to be geared to that fact. There was far more give-and-take between officers and men than would ever exist among the Federals, blighted by the influence of the British theory of rigid separation even after the coming of Grant.

The Sergeant ran his hand across his yellow beard. "We've come a mighty long way since Jack Wambeizie fired our first shot back in June of '61—at a lightning bug, as I recall. Reckon my conscience is buried somewheres along the road—and a pretty fair distance back."

His drawn face equated itself between fatigue and dry humor, and he called out loudly enough to carry to the head of the little column:

"Isn't it time to look into the haversack, Captain?"

Other voices eagerly took up the question, and Stowell turned his head good-humoredly.

"You've been resting behind works for a week. Wait until we need it."

McComas managed a wink at Brice. "Let's see, it was me who told you about the spade, wasn't it? Well, here's something else you'd better know. The Old Gentleman carries a bottle of liquor in his haversack which he's saving for a real emergency, or so he tells us. He drinks all right, but not out of that. Only time he ever opened it was after Gettysburg when we'd lost pretty near half of the boys who went in. He gave us a pull all round and got another bottle, the one he's carrying now, in Pennsylvania during the retreat, though how our goddam cavalry happened to overlook it, I don't know.

68

We live in hope that he'll break down again and give us another swallow, but he can be right firm like you've just seen."

The wagon train was parked hub to hub, its wheels and underbodies still splashed with dried mud, and fully half of the stained canvas covers bearing the big "U.S." to show where they had originated. Beyond it were long rows of picketed horses and mules, gaunt beasts which had cleaned up every blade of grass within reach and gnawed the bark of the trees. The infantrymen watched hopefully while the Commissary officers prepared to issue the three days' rations, then slumped dejectedly. It was going to be bacon and cold cornbread again without the luxury of onions. Even the coffee continued to be rye substitute. The wagoners and Commissary troops left them strictly alone. Combat troops in that mood were mean folks to fool with.

Captain Stowell, after an angry but useless argument with the issuing officers, let the Company fall out to eat. They made fires of broken boxes at which they brewed their odd-tasting drink, and a few cooked their bacon. But the majority bolted the meat raw. It shrank too much in the frying pans. The three days' rations disappeared in one meal, and was hardly enough to satisfy them. Why carry food which might spoil in a haversack, when the stomach was a better, and a too ample, container?

The Old Gentleman sat on a stump, his tin plate cleaned of its unappetizing contents. The resiliency which the others drew from their still green strength was beyond his body's power to furnish. His reserves must be of mind and will. Brice, watching him without intrusive curiosity, was for the second time conscious of the other's age. This was far too late in the war for ideals to be buoyant; what later generations would call "combat fatigue" was an endemic disease. Just a few days before, a Lieutenant Colonel in a Massachusetts regiment had written home: "It is still kill, kill, all the time," and in those few words had summed up the outlook and the despair of the sacrificed youth of both sides. If Stowell continued, it must be on a simpler, earthier basis, and Brice thought he knew what it was—this Company that were his children.

Reluctantly, the Captain straightened his back. His eyes came alive again and centered on Brice's sword which the latter was using to toast his share of the bacon.

"Useful tools, swords," commented the Old Gentleman with gentle sarcasm. "Mighty handy for cutting brush too. They can be dangerous though. I carried mine in my teeth when we were scrambling up Culp's Hill, and it broke two of them. The only blood I shed at Gettysburg was what came when Dr. Snowden yanked out the roots. Then I tried putting my hat on the point of it—it looks so fine in the lithographs—but that wasn't a success either. The damned thing just slid down the blade until it was over my wrist. Furthermore, it ruined the hat."

He looked up, startled, as a chorus of bitter jeers broke out from the men. Then he gave a tight smile.

"I see Hammond's scared out Henderson. He's our Commissary detail back here with the wagons. The boys are sure giving it to him. He says he suffers from a 'wasting disease,' and there's none of them believes him, including me. Still, it's too much trouble for the Sergeants to have to keep watching him all the time, so I reckon I indulge him to save them." His voice took on a contemplative note. "You know, this war does peculiar things—and that wasn't in my books either. Henderson was a good soldier once, now he can't be trusted in a line of battle. I don't believe in calling a man a coward, there are some who'll fight like hell one day and run like a cottontail rabbit the next; and the more fights you're in the more the rabbit side gets prominent. Henderson came out with us in the Old Regiment. Reckon he's just been out too long."

"Captain!" Hammond was running towards them. "Henderson says there's a mail orderly around here with letters from home."

Mail! Even Stowell rose hastily to his feet, and Brice scorched his mouth on the last of his bacon. I Company ranged like bird dogs, and before long returned, hustling a cadaverous soldier who carried a leather sack.

"It's him, and he won't give it to us!" squalled Raby, tears of rage and disappointment making clean furrows down his dirty cheeks. "Says he can't open it until it's delivered to the Battalion!"

There was an ugly menacing sound from the press of men, but the mail orderly hugged the bag close, his stupid, obstinate face set.

"Them's my orders," he said.

The Captain strode forward. As Brice followed, the Lieutenant sensed a rapid movement beside him. Abbott, a quiet, brooding nonentity who had made no particular impression before this, had snatched up his loaded Enfield and was trying to bring the muzzle to bear.

"Kill the bastard!" he muttered thickly, and continued to mutter even after Brice had wrenched the rifle from him.

The Old Gentleman had sprung into the line of fire. Now he turned upon the frightened orderly.

"Maybe you're being overattentive to your duty," he began grimly, then his patience snapped. The kindly, tanned face set in a burst of furious anger.

"I'll hear no more foolishness. Give me that, sir! I'll take the responsibility."

He handed the bag to Hammond.

"Sort it, Sergeant!" he ordered, and stood back, as formidable in his thin-lipped quiescence as he had been in his outburst. He said nothing to Abbott nor did Brice expect him to. The explosive reaction of overstrain was better overlooked since it had not resulted in tragedy.

Hammond was calling out names and tossing letters into reaching hands.

"Abbott!" he shouted at last, and flipped an envelope. There was a snatch, a rip of paper, a quick look and a despairing gasp. Private Abbott stumbled away, the sheets fluttering to the ground. Lucas detached himself from the group and walked after him.

"Reckon he may need me," he said quietly, as he passed the officers. "Hammond'll save my letters."

Stowell caught a hurtling missive out of the air. "Abbott's wife was sick when we heard last, two months ago. Looks like he's been told how she made out."

71

Fifteen minutes he gave them and himself to read of the things that mattered most vitally in their other lives, those private existences which their uniform had thrust into the background. Then the order was given to fall in, and they marched off, this time in ranks.

The pace was the quick Zouave step in which the Old Regiment had been originally drilled and had left as a legacy to the successor Battalion. When the bits of news had been exchanged, the talking died away. Too many memories usually meticulously swathed in deliberate forgetfulness had burst through their protective wrappings. Abbott swung along blindly between Lucas and Burke.

The two officers led the column of fours at a good rate. Brice was rereading snatches of his letters. Baltimore had split wide open on the war, and partisan bitterness had grown as the casualty lists arrived both from the North and from the South. The espionage of the Unionists on the Confederate sympathizers may have had justification, but there was a malignant side to it. There were some who found it a convenience for satisfying personal grudges, what with the garrison on Federal Hill so near and so receptive to whispered denunciations. His lawyer father had argued a case which had brought him into collision with another attorney who favored the North. His mother was ill from worry lest there be a trumped-up charge of treason against him and a trip to Fort McHenry where the political prisoners were kept. Perhaps it was natural that she should have confided in her son, at least she may have excused herself in that fashion when she wrote the letter which could do no more than add to his anxieties while he was helpless to aid.

The Captain was equally silent. He too must have had something to disturb him, for his expression was careworn and gloomy. Then he shrugged off his moodiness and addressed himself to Brice in a low tone.

"Has it occurred to you that in spite of all this urgency, nobody's thought to tell us where to find General Early?"

VIII

BRICE found nothing odd in the fact that neither he nor his Captain knew the whereabouts of a Lieutenant General. Their outlook was that of the ordinary regimental officers who might know their Brigadier well, their Divisional General less so, and their Corps Chief by sight. Under normal circumstances they would have taken advantage of this chain and inquired their way up it, trusting that the more rarefied strata might have the information they needed. However, belonging to no organization higher than a Battalion, these sources were closed to them.

I Company's tiny command echelon was in a predicament familiar to most veterans who have made a daylong search for some place or unit, possibly to find it at last three hundred yards from their starting point. Whoever wanted them to hurry had thrown a most effective obstacle in the way of their compliance.

Stowell pulled his beard thoughtfully, too experienced to fret. "We'll start for the left," he decided. "The Commissaries at the train said that nothing as big as a Corps has gone by this morning. I make it a practice never to believe Commissaries or couriers either, but even they couldn't be wrong on that. 'Fraid we'll have to ask our way." He grinned wryly at Brice. "You'll have to exercise yourself. I don't want to take the men into cannon range."

Brice groaned mentally. "I'd better begin at New Cold Harbor," he said reluctantly, measuring the distance with a jaundiced eye. "General Hoke was there once."

"At least there's a house still standing, and staffs are partial

73

to houses. Let me know how the boots and you make out." The Captain's tone deepened. "Better make the best time you can."

The day continued the hot spell with a hearty and enthusiastic sun beating down. The country was badly watered, and the men were both thirsty and dusty, but they passed the morning enjoyably, watching their unfortunate Lieutenant trudge towards the line, halt for animated debate with passing couriers, and return with a fiery face and little more tidings than that the Second Corps was thought to be still further on the left. Then they would hoist their rifles to their shoulders and move off in that direction until another promising house sent Brice on his quest again.

"'A horse, a horse, my kingdom for a horse!'" chuckled Cabell, as he watched Brice approaching after his third journey. "Reckon that's what he's saying. Look, he's stopped another courier. What's he doing?"

The resting soldiers peered under their hands.

"He's sure giving it to him hot and heavy."

"No he ain't. Looks like he's pleadin' with him. You don't suppose he's tryin' to buy that beast, do you?"

The interested group broke into a roar of laughter as they saw Brice sit down beside the courier who had dismounted. Each was pulling at his footgear.

"By God," said McComas, "he's swapping his boots for the other fellow's brogans."

Brice had stopped couriers with a double purpose, both for information and possible exchange. The Rebel horsemen were so ill-equipped that many rode in ordinary shoes, and the Lieutenant had at last found a size that fitted. When he came back to where they sat, his face for the first time showed some cheerfulness.

"Got it!" he called to the Captain. "Early's already left for the Valley, moving by Gordonsville and the line of the Virginia Central."

He arrived closer and lowered his voice. "Got a lot more too. Grant's gone; he's crossing the Chickahominy bound for the James, they think. Our pickets have gone beyond their works, and the whole front's empty. Reckon those minnies we got this morning were no more than a parting blessing from the rearguard."

"So!" exclaimed Stowell. "I was wondering why I hadn't seen a shellburst. Well, we'll pursue Old Jubilee, faint but persevering. We must be at least six hours behind him already which isn't pleasant to dwell on. My map will take us as far as Gordonsville or thereabouts. Beyond that we'll have to ask our way since it doesn't show the Valley. Why won't they ever fight on the map we have and not keep running over the edge?" He clapped Brice on the shoulder. "Cheer up, boy! We won't have to send you ahead on a scout, we can ask as we go."

When they marched, angling away from the once quiescent lines, Hanover County was astir with galloping staff officers and the rumble of wagon trains. The life and movement were flowing off to the southeast, leaving behind it a barren countryside, furrowed with the trenches, its timber thinned to make revetments, its fence rails burned in campfires, its springs fouled, its crops ruined, its houses battered by shot and its people starving. There is nothing on earth that can approach in sheer, ugly, heartbreaking desolation the abandoned field of a great battle.

Stowell was studying his map, its outer surface stained by his sweat. The heat beat down in pulsating waves that matched their strides. Even so small a force raised a cloud of gritty dust. Brice looked over his shoulder at the marching Company, scarecrows lifted from their poles and set a-walking across what was left of the Confederacy. Campaigning in Virginia had given the Rebels a maxim. If one must choose between a covering for the feet and one for the head, go barefoot. Casualties from heat prostration or actual sunstroke invariably littered the path of any hard summer march: get you therefore a hat by whatever means you can. The men had faithfully obeyed, though the wreck Matthews wore might have been a mere token of his conformity. Most had low-crowned slouches of black or gray, a number wore captured Yankee caps, the tops collapsed towards the long visors and still bearing either the crossed rifles of the Federal infantry or the cloverleaf Corps badge of Hancock's stormers. Cabell was haloed with a very wide-brimmed straw which had originally been manufactured for a field hand, while German Smith had an oddity, a civilian's silk stovepipe which he had snatched from a passenger peering too curiously out of the window of a Virginia Central train at Hanover Junction.

Their clothes were as conglomerate a mixture. The regulation gray, ranging in shade from very dark to a charcoal-washed white, was in a definite minority to brown homespun, since that was what the Quartermaster had distributed the last time they had made an issue from their scanty stores. Corporal Kirk's chevrons were sewed to a threadbare black broadcloth, a memorial to a merchant in Pennsylvania who had reluctantly parted with it for Confederate bills. Jackets and trousers seldom matched, and both were usually patched in startling contrast to their original color. Zollinger, for example, would sit upon a faded rainbow cut from a quilt. The only strict uniformity was the powdering of dust, so thick and clinging that many times in this war the only distinction between opposing troops was the flag that waved over them. Virtually every man had pulled his socks above the bottoms of his pants to keep small stones from working inside and down to the sole of the foot.

Their shoes, Brice noted, were in pretty good condition, thanks to the Old Gentleman's policy. At least there were no clumsy sheaths of cowhide, shaped roughly to fit and permitted to dry that way, an expedient to which the crack Texas Brigade had been reduced. Such expedients might be a last resort, but if no footgear was issued, the men could not buy replacements. Not with the pay of a Rebel Private set at eighteen dollars a month, and the Richmond storekeepers asking eighty-five dollars a pair.

They were gaunt, dirty and odorous. The sweat from the stiff pace beaded their faces. Except for the youngest of them, they bristled with unshaven stubble. For lack of a change, they wore their underwear until it literally fell apart on bodies swarming with vermin and plagued by itch. Soap was scarce. They might bathe in the streams, but water unaided could not remove the grime which was so ground into them that such fortunate beings as came up with a cake found themselves shedding a layer of outer skin when they washed.

"Lord!" said Brice to the Captain. "If we ever do get to march down Charles Street, the Marshal and the police are going to throw the lot of us in jail."

"Not while we got these," came Hammond's voice from behind them, and he slapped the butt of his Enfield.

"Offshore Gus is gettin' persnickety," drawled Watts. "Don't know that I wouldn't settle for jail just to be home again."

The grim chuckles had a definite note of agreement.

In the early afternoon they fell out next to a house which had a well in its front yard. The bucket and rope were still left, though the windlass had collapsed from over-use. There might once have been a fragment of lawn, but that had been beaten out of existence by many feet, just as the fruit trees had been girdled by the hungry horses and the gate torn from its hinges. The house itself was intact to external appearance, a structure of the common type with a stone ground floor and a second story of wood. As they were filling their canteens, a woman came out on the porch and stared at them as if they had been a mile distant rather than twenty feet. She was tall and young, but her dress was stained with grass and earth, and her face matched those of the soldiers, sallow and soiled, with deeply sunken eyes.

The Old Gentleman took off his hat. "I'm afraid we're making free with your well, ma'am," he said politely. "I hope you don't mind."

It was an effort for her to collect herself. Brice saw her hands clasp until her lips quivered from the steadying pain.

"Nothin' much left to mind about," she said levelly.

The men were drinking in turn, the water dripping from their chins. Knowing their inability to give comfort, they paid only covert attention to her.

The woman spoke over her shoulder to another who watched from the doorway. "They're ours," she said, as if that were any consolation. Probably it had been Rebels who had been responsible for the desolation in the first place, particularly if the house had been unoccupied. An empty building of any sort was regarded as a windfall, and the troops had made free with it. Still there were no signs of pillage, which would have been the case had it fallen behind the invader's lines.

Two small boys in patched clothes had followed her onto the porch. A little girl with a smudgy face and matted yellow hair slipped past the second woman and clutched at her mother's skirt.

Big Niedlander squatted down and beckoned to her. "Hello, honey," he called softly with a reassuring grin, but she hid her face in the cloth.

Niedlander's voice was very gentle. "Look what I got for you. It's a button that I'm cuttin' off my coat right now. It's real brass an' if you shines it up with some sand, reckon it'll wink at you."

A tear-stained eye, a nubbin of a nose, peeked out from the skirt like a timid and sorrowful mouse, then whisked back into shelter. The elder of the boys left the porch and came nearer the friendly soldier, shifting his weight from foot to foot.

"You got anything to eat?" he burst out.

The mother's face flushed and she spoke sharply. "Hush, Johnny, you're not to beg."

The stung, bitter pride in her tone wilted as the little girl began to sob. "I'm awful hungry," she wailed, and the men understood at last.

Niedlander still squatted without looking up. "Now of course you are," he said heartily to the child. "When I was your age I was always lookin' for something to eat. The Government gives us cornbread which you sure has a right to since you're a Rebel too. Here's a piece, an' your maw won't mind your takin' it because, as I says, you're entitled to it. You can have the button too if your maw's agreeable. That's from me."

Brice followed his lead. "It's really quite simple, ma'am," he said urbanely. "The Army can issue rations as it sees fit. We will provision you and make a return to the Commissary."

The hesitant obstinacy shattered under his matter-of-factness. The mother flung her arms wide.

"The Lord will provide!" she cried in passionate faith. "Wasn't I telling you that, children?"

78

I Company emptied its haversacks of what little remained in them, piling the food into the hands of the youngsters. The mother could hardly take her eyes from it, but she clung desperately to her manners.

"Can't tell you gentlemen how much we're obliged to you. When the firing started we took to the woods. We've been hiding in an old cabin down by the branch, and all we've had to eat was the rabbits my Johhny here snared. We just came home to this."

Her re-won composure quivered beneath her measured tone. "I'd ask you into the house, but it seems they must have used it for a hospital. There's blood all over the floor, and there's . . ." Her voice went up. "I'm sorry, but there's a pile of arms and legs what they cut off stacked in the parlor."

"Of course, ma'am," Stowell was speaking very calmly, and his hand was on her elbow. "Now you and the children and your friend sit down and have something to eat, and we'll at least get rid of that for you. Sergeant Hammond, start someone to digging a pit with the spade, and the rest of us will carry those things out and bury them in it."

It was no pleasant task, for the hot weather made the interior smell like a slaughter pen, and the flies rose in dark veils, but in half an hour the job was done. I Company went on its way, and that night slept supperless, to rise also breakfastless and take the Gordonsville road. The small kindness they had done gave them a temporary lift of cheerfulness, but they had lost that half hour irrevocably. Early and the Second Corps had gained at least a mile.

For the next three days they tramped steadily and swiftly. Old Jube was forcing the pace, for Hunter was threatening the important depots at Lynchburg and Charlottesville. I Company must conform, cutting rest periods to a minimum, soaked with sweat, black with dirt, the heat so great that their lungs seemed to be robbed rather than helped by the breaths they drew. Occasionally a rolled blanket was slung to the roadside—even that much weight might break a man down.

Marching eventually took on its own repetitious time-beat, just as had the life in the Cold Harbor trenches. The days were almost exact duplicates of each other from dawn to dusk.

79

A little talk at first, perhaps a curious glance at a passing courier or at a group of Early's stragglers limping along, a side look at a dead man, stricken by the sun or exhaustion, lying with a dropped jaw under a stone wall; then, as the temperature mounted, only the shuffle of their feet and the clinking of their equipment. When it drew towards sunset they would break out in a rash of questions.

"Where are we?"

"Captain, when are we goin' to camp?"

"Much farther to go, sir?"

And that unanswerable one which Brice found particularly exasperating:

"Where's the spring?"

Officers were supposed to possess a peculiar omniscience. Perhaps for once they could point it out and save a weary man the trouble of looking for it.

The prime question was, as always, food. The Second Corps might have rations of a sort on its wagons, but the "guides" toiling far in the rear must live off the country and lose more time doing it.

When at last Stowell signalled the halt, they could not drop in their places as their weariness demanded. The foragers, one from each mess, had to drag themselves from a slough of exhaustion and go out for whatever Louisa County afforded, which was not much in that land that the locusts had eaten. The most generous inhabitant could part with little more or face starvation on his own account, yet the prowling soldiers had no choice either. They must wheedle or beg or frankly steal.

The third night was rough. They were in a patch of woods near Trevilian Station on the Virginia Central, a moribund railroad, cut at present by a raid. Wade Hampton had beaten Sheridan here a few days before, and the familiar stink from a dead battlefield fought against the smoke from the fires. Stowell had shaken his head when McComas had asked if the marching was to end soon. A courier had told them that Early had continued on to Charlottesville at the same killing pace, and those extra miles weighted them down. Hunger was becoming a stalking reality, creeping into their brief conversations, where they dwelt upon past meals down to the last loving detail or planned imaginary feasts. Even Reeder, for all his reputation, had been able to produce during the whole march no more than a single scrawny chicken and a haversack full of flour. Raby had almost collapsed, Niedlander had carried his rifle for him, and German Smith massaged his knotted leg muscles as he lay prone.

Reeder and Zollinger came into the firelight, and the men looked up eagerly only to slump again at the former's headshake.

"Nothing. We went over to the field and had a look for Yankee haversacks, but they've been cleaned. Thought we might at least bring home some horsemeat, but they've been dead too long, and in this hot weather . . ."

Suddenly the sentry yelled, a high note of exultation.

"Carney! Look what he's got!"

The forager was grinning. In his arms was the carcass of a pig with a bullet hole behind the shoulder.

"It's a wild one," he explained loudly, one eye on the Captain. "Found it wanderin' in the woods and shot it."

There were such pigs which had returned to a semi-wild state, escaping from looted farms, but Brice privately doubted that this was one of them, particularly when he saw the care with which the skin and bones were buried after the animal had been butchered. Not that Brice was so principled as to raise the question. His appetite made him perfectly willing to accept the familiar excuse that the pig had turned dangerous and that Carney had shot it in self-defense. He even shared in the apprehensive looks which the men cast at Stowell, until they saw that the Old Gentleman was smiling in his beard.

"Another groundhog case," he muttered to Brice. "I apologize for the pun as I'm apologizing for the hog."

Unobtrusively he had kept his foragers within bounds. "You've got to watch," he told his Lieutenant later, wiping his greasy fingers on the grass. "If you see anybody with money or silver or anything like that, he'll have to prove to us that it was given to him, or else we'll prefer charges and see that he gets a court. I'll not stand for pillaging."

"Carney and Beeler, I reckon?" asked Brice, but the Captain shook his head.

"Not Beeler. Carney and Watts and Matthews."

"That youngster!"

"Surely. He's quick to learn, and he's in the wrong mess, but that's one thing I can't change."

At least the fires were comforting to the chilling sweat in the slight coolness of the June evenings. The tired men, fed at last, lounged briefly before they stretched out to sleep by couples, the blanket and oilcloth of one partner underneath, the other's on top. Yet even in that short interval diffident figures appeared, waiting in the rim of the firelight until the Old Gentleman lighted his pipe. That mail had brought its problems, and there were some who took them to the Captain. Brice picked himself up and wandered off to sit on a log, his strained leg muscles aching, until the rumble of quiet voices had ceased. Wives could be unfaithful, mothers demanding, or girls forget the plans and promises that had once seemed so bright. In '64 the home front robbed the armies. Good men, hearing that crops had failed or that there was hunger, death and sickness, would steal away, sometimes ready to fire upon anyone who tried to bring them back. Except from the conglomerate H Company, the Maryland Battalion had not had a deserter thus far, and Brice was prepared to give some of the credit to the elderly officer rousing himself to counsel when he was dead for sleep.

He came back to the fire and drew off his shoes. The Captain was still sitting close to it, his short blackened pipe gripped between his teeth although it had gone out. Brice had begun to watch him as he watched little Raby and Home Grown Smith, now spitting blood, and Hammond, unsteady on his feet after the day's march. He was wondering which of them would collapse first.

Stowell saw his eyes on him and smiled grimly. "'Physician, heal thyself.' Reckon I don't feel up to it right now."

His lids came down in sheer weariness.

"My wife has written me that my son is coming out."

IX

THE flat, toneless remark caught Brice completely by surprise. The Captain had been so resolutely cheerful, so utterly self-reliant, that this unexpected confidence, this betrayal of deep feeling, left him at a loss what to say. In fact, he was wondering what he could say that would bring consolation to a man more experienced in war and command than was he.

To cover his uncertainty he filled his own pipe, making quite a business of it. Though he naturally approved of young Stowell's motive for enlisting, the hard disillusionment of experience made him fully understand the father's anxiety. The demand for replacements was so great that the Army of Northern Virginia maintained few recruit schools and those for only the most primary drill. Many newcomers would join a regiment at once, losing the priceless opportunity of becoming acclimated and learning how to take care of themselves. The wastage among them was much heavier than among veterans.

"How old is he?" he asked at last.

"He was sixteen in February."

The Old Gentleman's eyes were on the blanket-wrapped cocoon which marked where Raby slept beside Zollinger. The boy had thrown away his own roll, but his messmates were sharing with him. The same age or a little older than the Captain's son, and not thriving on hard marching and underfeeding.

There was no sense in expressing what he really felt, thought Brice, and did his best.

"Well at least he's got to get to Virginia before he can enlist, and that's stopped a lot who've tried it."

Stowell shook his head slowly. "Stopped them safely, Brice? There are some who've been killed on the way or captured and thrown into jail. Take a look at Hammond if you want to see what a Federal prison camp can do."

"Your boy's pretty young, sir. If they catch him, they'll put it down to pure damn foolishness and send him home."

The Old Gentleman was tamping down fresh tobacco with his thumb. He drew out a letter, glanced at it, then rolled it into a spill and used it to light his pipe.

"I'm grateful to you for the thought," he remarked, as the blue smoke curled from the bowl, but his tone was still lifeless. "Perhaps for once I've let myself look on the gloomy side and for me that's worse than a mistake. Matter of fact, what bothers me most is Murray's age. If he were eighteen, now, I wouldn't feel so bad. Eighteen can take care of itself pretty well."

For the first time he turned his head so that Brice was looking at him full-face instead of in profile. For an instant the Lieutenant was shocked. It seemed as if the Captain had changed overnight and for the worse, until he realized that the whitened beard and eyebrows and the deeper graving of the lines came from the powdering of dust. It had been a dry camp, and the available water had had to be used entirely for drinking.

"You ought to feel proud, sir," said Brice feebly.

"Should I? Well, perhaps I do. God knows we have so many children in this Army that we ought to be used to their coming so early. Look at George Booth from the Old Regiment. He was just under seventeen when he commanded F Company at the First Manassas. What's more, he's still alive which is a little unusual." His words became more accentuated, though still dragged to a low register by fatigue and emotion. "No, I'm not telling you the whole truth."

He paused perceptibly as if he would not go on, but he too needed the same comfort he had been ready to give his men, a sympathetic listener.

"I wish I didn't know as much as I do about boys. I wish I hadn't watched them until I learned who was most likely to make a good soldier and who wasn't. The people who don't

84

know keep talking about the 'only child' having the real bad time, but that's not so, not as I've seen it. The ones who suffer most are the youngsters who come from a family of girls with them the only boy in it. Their mothers make pets of them, and their sisters make a fuss over them until they come around to believing that they're entitled to a little more consideration than anybody else. It's harder for them to realize that they've got to stand on their own feet. Reckon you've noticed it yourself?"

"Yes," answered Brice reluctantly. "I have."

"That's the fact of it with my Murray. We had four daughters, but Nellie died. We had him rather late in life to replace her. His mother thinks the world and all of him, and I've been three years away. Could anybody have a worse start?"

Brice made an attempt at a reassuring laugh. "I don't think that follows. Maybe he's kicked over the traces at home. At least his mother's letting him come, which I'd take for a good sign. Seems to me if she was as fond of him as you say, she couldn't bear to part with him."

Stowell let the pipe smoke drift slowly between his lips. The fires were dying down, and there was no stir about them. Abbott, the first of the night sentries, was leaning on his rifle, fighting his private sorrow against the thin ringed moon and the whippoorwill's calling.

"Mrs. Stowell is a masterful woman and a busy one," came the quiet voice across the embers. "She's right active at church sociables and she likes to visit and talk with the other ladies. Not that it bothered me. I was busy enough with my store, and when I came home there were the children. I used to read to them. Ever seen a boy's eyes in the firelight when you've got Sir Walter Scott open and he's being Ivanhoe in his own imaginings? Perhaps Mrs. Stowell thought I was a dry old stick, but she was a good wife for all that. She talked a lot of duty when we thought Maryland was going to secede, but she said 'our' and not 'your.'"

The whitened eyebrows lifted and the set mouth relaxed into a wry smile.

"No, she didn't run me South. Matter of fact, she didn't want me to go at all, thought I was too old. I came because it was a matter of principle. Now she's sending the boy, and I reckon it's more of a sacrifice for her than you give her credit."

The artificial stimulus of his emotion left him; again he looked over to where Raby was sleeping.

"If you're as tired as I am, you haven't been thanking me for keeping you up. Better get what rest you can. We've got to make Charlottesville tomorrow. Old Jube won't be pleased with us for being late, but, damn it, I can't march the men four days on empty stomachs."

Brice rolled up in his oilcloth and his blanket, taking a last precautionary look at Abbott, hands crossed over the muzzle of his Enfield, the whippoorwill still plaintive and the moon riding high. When he awoke, the moon was down, the whippoorwill had stopped crying and the air was full of the smell of dawn, but the sentry still in the same pose. He had to look twice before he realized that it was Carney and not Abbott.

McComas was shouting and pulling men to their feet, not unkindly, for some of them needed help. Hammond, usually the first up, was on all fours, his head lowered. With an effort he scrambled to one knee, but there was sweat on his face. Brice came over to him and took him by the arm, lifting until the Sergeant was planted on his legs.

"Are you all right?" asked the Lieutenant of the white face.

"Of course, sir," the tone was fiercely resentful. Almost staggering as he walked, Hammond went among the men, cajoling and rebuking. Corporal Kirk shrugged his shoulders.

"He won't be needing these," he said, and kicked Hammond's blankets aside. "I'll carry his rifle if he's willin'."

"He won't last the day," commented McComas quietly. "Maybe there's some more that won't either. Forced march again?"

"'Fraid so," said Brice, and glanced at Captain Stowell who was belting on his sword and pistol, his fingers fumbling at the buckle.

The fires were rekindled, what was left of the pork was quickly cooked. Hammond ate his standing as if he were afraid to sit down. Zollinger was rubbing Raby's legs like a trainer with a racehorse. Home Grown Smith stepped to one side and spat out a long string of reddish mucus. The First Sergeant, steadying his voice, barked the familiar roll.

"All present, sir, and the spade."

How many will be tonight? wondered Brice, and unlatched the high collar of his coat.

"Column forward!" cried Stowell in the long rolling cadence of command, and I Company swung down the road, the ever-lasting, ever-renewing road that the infantry must travel.

"Goin' to shower," said the Captain, as he set the pace. "At least it ought to settle the dust."

Brice looked back along the swaying shoulders at the silent men, heard the shuffle and clink. Which of them will go down first? Niedlander was again carrying Raby's rifle, and Lucas had Home Grown Smith's. Nearly a third of them had thrown away their rolls. He dropped back along the short column, was about to offer to take Hammond's Enfield, but thought the better of it and took Matthews' instead. He trotted back to the head of the line and opened the top buttons of his coat. The sweat was already running into his dirty under-shirt. He became aware of Stowell's touch on his elbow.

"If I should not be able to keep up, Lieutenant, you will take the Company through to Charlottesville. We must re-port to General Early tonight."

Startled by the formality, Brice did not answer.

"Do you understand me, sir?" came the gruff question. "This Company must be in Charlottesville, whoever falls out. I rely on you."

"I understand, sir."

There was no need to say more; the order had been given and would be obeyed. Brice was fully aware of the stark necessity of the warning. He appreciated the pain that it must cost the Captain to have to admit even the possibility that he would be physically unable to do his full duty. There was no sense in offering vain consolation. Mere sympathy was use-less without the means to aid. Early's stragglers, thicker now, were pitiable enough, so many lame and hobbling with bleed-ing feet and gray faces, but I Company itself was not to be envied. What had it to give—its haversacks empty and its tramping men hardly different except that they were still in formation?

Stowell was speaking again.

"Take the rear, Mr. Brice, and see that the column is closed up."

The sky had turned dark, the sun was hidden, but the heat, confined under the clouds, grew worse. The Company split into two files, walking on the edges of the road to make less dust, but not even that remedy availed. The dirt highway, so cut and trampled, had sprayed its sandy surface into the grass, and the feet scuffed it up in clouds that made breathing difficult. To the dry coughing of Home Grown Smith was added that of others, hacking and spitting from parched mouths as the grit worked into their windpipes. Occasionally a soldier would run a few steps to one side to draw a few clean breaths.

"Column left!"

The sign at the fork said "To Charlottesville," but it was not needed. The wheelmarks were plain enough, the discarded equipment and the worn-out men showed where the Second Corps had also turned. Brice's lips were cracking, his throat burned; eyes and nose and ears were clogged. The pace never slackened, the sweat steamed off them, and Raby was sobbing. Niedlander, tallest and strongest of the German mess, crossed from the other file and said something, then put his arm under the boy's shoulder. Heenan was leg-weary like one of the horses he had once tended. He stumbled and nearly went down. If Beeler had not given him a jerk as he passed, he would have gone on his face.

The Captain croaked a question, clearly audible in the silence of effort.

"Want to get rid of the spade, Burke? You can if you want to."

"Jesus!" exclaimed McComas from his place at the rear of the opposite line. "We *are* bad off."

The indomitable Irishman managed a note of forlorn gaiety. "Not yet, sir. It balances me rifle."

88

Thunder began to rumble, and the sound of it brought heads up.

"What's that? Early's run into Hunter?"

"No, it's the right kind, the good Lord's artillery. . . ."

The last stifling, almost unendurable blast of heat before the rain brought a restless mutter from the tortured column. Watts's arm went up and another roll went into the ditch. Reeder's followed his.

"Can't stand this," gasped Heenan and stopped. Brice put the flat of his hand between the shoulder blades and shoved. "Close up!" he gasped, feeling as if each word drew a harrow of pain along his inflamed throat. "No halting!"

Raby was sobbing again, his knees buckled, but Niedlander was almost carrying him by now. Zollinger dropped back beside them and took some of the weight.

Brice's shoes were full of sand in spite of his protective socks; the dust had so mingled with the sweat that his skin erupted under the constant irritation. Heenan staggered back to be met by another push and a harsher command to close up. Hammond was weaving as he marched, but still clutched his rifle. Scabbarded bayonets, even dry canteens, were being discarded. Cabell too had begun to lag and was limping.

Outwardly a stern, implacable disciplinarian, Brice actually shrank from the mock brutality he might have to show, though he admitted its necessity. Cursing, abuse and even force must be used on those poor devils whom exhaustion had put beyond the feeling of shame or devotion to duty—any means which might bring out a final spurt and keep them with the Company.

Men in the leading files began to run forward.

"A branch, boys!" called Corporal Kirk, and Captain Stowell's dry rasp was almost cheerful.

"Ten minutes' halt when we get to it."

It wasn't particularly good water, but nobody questioned its purity as they lay and sucked it up, or threw it over their faces. The feel of it, warm and nearly stagnant, was still an impact on their hot skin. They paid no attention to the dead horse that lay half in and half out of it save to pay the carcass the single respect of drinking upstream. The wind stirred, a puff of chilling coolness, then the rain came down. They revived like fish thrown back after flopping on the bank. Even Raby seemed better, though Brice noticed that he was flushed with fever. The Old Gentleman put back his turnip of a watch.

"Time's up! Fall in the Company, Sergeant."

The renewed marching was easier at first, though even that trifling halt had stiffened them. They had not yet exchanged discomforts as they were bound to do, since the rain proved both soaking and persistent. The relief from the scorching heat gave them a false strength that made them step out even better than when they had broken camp, but Brice knew better than to relax his vigilance. There was no true resuscitation reflected in the tramp of feet. It was not yet noon, and there would be no nooning, for the haversacks were empty. Trouble had merely moved a few paces to the rear. Soon it would be catching up with them.

Yet he could let his mind rove for a little while, could let it deal with thoughts instead of confining it, not altogether of his own volition, to the constant concern over the weaker men. He himself was bearing up well—those months of extra feeding in Richmond had given him a reserve of endurance that was more than the others had, just as they in turn exceeded Early's soldiers who had been in the Wilderness and Spotsylvania, while the Maryland Line had garrisoned Hanover Junction. The Second Corps was shedding off pretty fast. There must have been close to a brigade, officers too, who had broken down and were scattered along the road. A forced march! What meaning could that convey to civilians who had never experienced one, to newspaper critics who got their reports by telegraph and thundered in the Richmond journals? They would draw their own conclusions without the practical knowledge, like a man telling a woman about childbirth.

The rain beat steadily, and the dust, thank God, was settled, but their clothes were becoming soaked, the haversacks dripped and the wooden stocks of the rifles felt slippery under their hands. Nobody stopped to drape an oilcloth over his shoulders. They had learned better than to confine the sweat under its stickiness. Their long, uncut hair, the straggly beards of the older men, were beaded with moisture.

Someone in the column grumbled aloud, "Wish'd I'd been wounded at Cold Harbor. Hope I'll be wounded in the next fight."

Brice understood. To be wounded meant at least temporary withdrawal from battle and marching and discomfort. It might even bring a discharge. Not that they could go home. . . .

McComas raised his head with an angry jerk that sent water flying from the brim of his hat.

"You thinkin' about Radecke? Reckon he'd trade."

Their feet slopped instead of slapping. Puddles splashed their legs. Raby, chilled after being roasted, was in trouble again; his messmates had returned to his side. Hammond looked badly. When he turned his head, Brice noticed how much more pronounced was the skull effect. The Old Gentleman, however, showed no signs of weakness, except that he had slumped in the same way that Brice had observed back at the ration train after they had left the trenches. So his son was coming out, was he? Well, if the boy felt he had to come, maybe he'd be luckier than most what with his father being a combat officer. He should get understanding which so many others wouldn't.

Still eager to take his mind off the merciless marching, at least until fatigue or responsibility called it imperatively back, he dwelt upon the idea. The times called for understanding. Without it there could be no common plane upon which a young soldier and his parents could meet. The family must make allowances for what they themselves had not borne, must help without dictation, must shape themselves to the changes that war had made and make the best of them. How many would do it?

Wet and tired, Matthews' rifle loading his shoulder, Brice was in no condition to speculate objectively. He was beyond evaluating the recurrent truth that the normal standard of one generation might become abnormal to the next. When events move rapidly, change keeps abreast of them. The comparatively youthful elders could hardly succeed to the age of dictation before they would already have become anomalies to the younger who had experience far broader and more terrible. A fellow participant might have a bond, an equal outlook.

"How far to Charlottesville?"

The slow-moving farmer, who was leading a bony mule which hobbled on three legs, pointed ahead.

"See that rise? Only a few miles beyond. . . ."

"You hear that?" McComas shouted. "Step out, boys. It'll soon be over."

He grinned sardonically at Brice. "Two big lies, one right after the other. Bet you it's nearer twelve or fifteen, but we might as well try and be cheerful. Reckon he's tryin' to salvage that mule. Did you see the harness galls on it? Cut out of a wagon, I suppose, when the trains were passing. I could have told him the poor beast couldn't live, but since he was doin' his best for us, I wasn't goin' to cast him down. What time is it?"

" 'Bout one, I reckon."

"Well, I give Raby another half hour and Hammond another three quarters."

The countryside was changing its dress. The thickly wooded, marshy lowlands around the Chickahominy had been displaced by rolling grass, and there was hickory in the groves, outguards of the nearing Appalachians, but the dreary day obscured its beauty. Discomforts added themselves in regular rotation: first the clammy feel of soaked trousers against the moving knees, then the gradual wetting of the whole body as the rain penetrated the outer clothing, finally the increase in weight as the fibers of the cloth absorbed water. Cabell's limp was worse; Heenan had drifted back until the short man was just in front of Brice who gave him a methodical shove as he periodically lurched. Twice, Home Grown Smith had choked and spat his red-tinged warning. Hammond was weaving between the third pair of files instead of at the head of them, but still repulsed all efforts to take his rifle from him.

Then Raby went limp, his feet dragging between Niedlander and Zollinger, who had to stop or else drop him.

"He's fainted, sir," said Zollinger.

Captain Stowell halted the company.

"Let him down," he said quietly. "Sergeant Hammond, fall out and bring him along if you can."

Someone shook Hammond's shoulder.

"You hear what the Captain's saying?"

The words had penetrated at last. Hammond's eyes, redrimmed with inflammation, came to life. "I won't fall out, sir," he said stubbornly, as if he were repeating a theme which had rung continually in his brain.

"I gave you an order, Sergeant. You are to bring up any stragglers."

The flush left the skull cheekbones. The nearly exhausted man, saved from collapse with his pride intact, managed a salute.

"Yes, sir."

"Column forward!"

Heenan turned his twisted face to Brice.

"I can't."

"March!" said the Lieutenant harshly, and spun him impersonally around.

One last look before they passed out of sight. Hammond had set his own and Raby's rifles against a tree and was leaning over the boy's mudstained form.

They swung by a gray-bearded man who was trying to chop a log into stove lengths outside a cabin.

"How far to Charlottesville?"

"'Bout four miles beyond that bend, sir."

Four miles! The bend was reached, and the distance accomplished, but there was still no sign of house or steeple. Did any countryman know the measure of a mile? Brice's pistol holster was chafing his thigh, the Enfield on his shoulder made his collarbone sore, and he shifted it to the other. In spite of the monotony of "close up, close up," the tight formation was lengthening itself. Cabell and Heenan were obviously on their last legs. Where, for God's sake, had Charlottesville got to?

If anyone had asked them, they could not have told how many hours they had been tramping. Time and weariness were so mutually entangled that they wound into one like a ball of yarn. Their perceptions dragged as did their stride. There was nothing to seize upon; the sun stayed behind the drizzling clouds, and that tree beside the road up ahead might be a hundred feet away or a hundred yards. The rise and fall of the ground was more pronounced, there was an impression of hills and, off to the left, the sound of a river. Cabell had given in at last and was left by the roadside. Heenan was breathing noisily, and Brice passed him by, seeing that no further prodding would avail. Others were weakening. Like cattle in a drive, they fell back into the "drag" and were herded along by the Lieutenant and the Sergeant. Abbott was there now with Hubbard and Home Grown Smith. Except for the grasshopper chir of "close up, close the column," no one spoke save once when Smith gasped out to no one in particular:

"It's a hell of a long way to Baltimore."

Duvall began to hobble and curse. His left shoe had separated between the upper and the sole. He fell out long enough to take the pair off and hang them by the laces from his rifle barrel.

"Might be able to cobble it," he muttered, as he caught up again, barefoot.

Burke stopped long enough to unsling his roll.

"The Captain said you could throw away the spade," reminded Brice, as they came abreast, but the other blazed darkly:

"Dommed if I do. I'm going to plant it in the middle of Charlottesville and knock down the first man who asks me why I'm carryin' it."

Imperceptibly the column was slowing down. Was there a lag in Stowell's step? Brice remembered his orders and peered ahead anxiously. The old fool was carrying a rifle, he fumed to himself. That's pushing duty too far. Even the strongest Samaritans were suffering under the double weight. Then the Captain stopped so suddenly that Brice thought he was admitting failure.

"Rivanna river crossing, boys," said the hoarse voice. "I remember it from when we were stationed here in '62. It's just a step now, and that's no countryman's guess."

The bridge when they reached it was broken. A wagon had gone through the center planking and lay on its side in the stream with most of the structure beside it. However, the water was low enough to ford, and they slipped and stumbled down the bank.

"Confederate pontoons," McComas announced with hollow cheerfulness. "March straight through in column of fours."

They waded across, rifles held high, and struggled back to the road again. Cracked voices took up encouragement.

"It's no distance now, the Old Gentleman says so. Can't help it if you can't go no farther. You try an' keep puttin' one foot ahead of the other an' you'll see that they still work."

With surprising resonance McComas began to sing:

"Maryland, ain't you happy?
We'll anchor by and by.
We'll stand the storm, it won't be long,
We'll anchor by and by."

Haven't heard that since the Old Regiment, thought Brice, and added his own off-key contribution though the words came more in gasps than in time. These boys fool you, he reflected. I remember him as a grubby kid when I was beginning to shave and wearing my first boiled shirt. Never thought he had it in him then. Reckon it's when we get away from home that we know what a man's really like.

"I see the town," came a yelp from Matthews, and the song died. The last of their breath went into the final spurt.

A locomotive bell rang faintly, wheels rumbled somewhere and fires sparked in the gathering night. I Company of the Maryland Line came into Charlottesville, past parked artillery. They were swaying from fatigue as they tramped down a street, but they were proud. By God, they'd made a march.

"Halt!"

Home Grown Smith could not stand without aid. Duvall's feet were bleeding. Captain Stowell had unhooked his sword from his belt and was propping himself on it.

Nobody looked at him, not even the small boys. They were no novelty for Charlottesville in '64.

X

THE drizzle had stopped, the sky was clearing; soon there would be stars, but the rearguard of the emptied clouds compressed their view of the town to a single street. It was as muddy as a country lane and had spewed a slippery film onto the sidewalks. The shops and buildings had peeling paint, loose boards and sagging shutters, a general air of ricketiness. Though as yet the invaders had not reached so far, war had already attacked Charlottesville, winning its first victory over neatness and repair and continuing to drive until all material things assumed the uniform shabbiness which characterized the whole of the exhausted Confederacy. There was a raw frontier air about its appearance, a suggestion of impermanence as if it were some mining settlement in the foothills of the Sierra Nevada or in the Superstitions of Arizona rather than Thomas Jefferson's hearthstone under the first rise of the Alleghenies.

The thinning crowd which still lingered at the stores confirmed the impression that Virginia had moved West. The women were in homespun or in renovated dresses, probably a combination of several remnants from more prosperous times. The male civilians showed the same signs of makeshift or diligent husbandry, while the ubiquitous soldiers with their raggedness, their tan and their hairiness might have been miners in from the creeks. A few were noisily drunk and falling afoul of the Provost Marshal's details. Into the overlooking rooms where the lamps were kindling, the voices came like readings from a play, snatches of happiness, comedy, tragedy or sorrow or of a great casualness, no scene ever quite completed.

I Company lowered their rifle butts into the mud and sagged against the support of the weapons. They had had more than their usual allowance of hunger, exhaustion and pain, and for a time their bodies were in charge. The sweat still trickled clammily into their wet clothes, their muscles twitched, and the fingers of the hands which had swung free as they marched were swollen with blood. For perhaps ten minutes, too tired to talk, too tired even to think, they yielded themselves entirely to their deliverance from that continuity of effort.

Two elderly Home Guards, the first gray-haired and thin, the second gray-haired and fat, splashed through the mud as they crossed the street. They had to turn out of their way to avoid the Marylanders and made casual comment as they passed.

"Pretty badly used up, aren't they?"

"Smell worse'n most too."

McComas took his chin from the muzzle of his Enfield. "I heard tell that they burned a company of Home Guards at Staunton to keep them from falling into Yankee hands," he drawled.

Zollinger chimed in, hot eyes on the fat soldier, "Oh, Captain, Captain Stowell, sir. We've found the man who swallowed our bass drum."

Burke pointed to the spade standing vertically in the mud in front of him. "Ye wouldn't be after askin' why I'm carryin' *this*, would you?" he demanded in a thick and hopeful brogue.

Though a few continued in their torpor, the exchange had aroused most of them. Their Army life had inculcated a habit of dependence on their officers, and their heads turned towards Stowell, still leaning heavily on his sword as if he neither heard nor noticed. Brice handed back Matthews' rifle and ploughed across to him, McComas at his heels.

"Are you all right, sir?" he asked.

There was no reply, and Brice repeated the question more urgently.

"Maybe we ought to look in the haversack," suggested McComas nervously. "He sure needs a drink."

"It hasn't come to that yet," muttered the Old Gentleman, his voice furry and the words blurred. His head came up.

"Find General Early and report to him that we are here." As habit had made the men look to him, so habit strengthened him to try to respond. Brice could see the fatigue-drunk mind trying to grapple with the familiar list of tasks.

"Rations—reckon the General will have to give us those. A place to camp with water and firewood handy—we'll burn a fence if we have to. Send Sergeant Hammond . . ." The voice trailed off.

"Hammond's bringing up stragglers, but here's Sergeant McComas," Brice reminded him huskily. What's got into me, he snarled silently at himself. I've known him two weeks, and here I am getting sentimental about him. "We'll take care of everything," he went on aloud.

"Obliged to you," said the tired voice politely, then rallied to admonish firmly, "Report to General Early first."

Brice prowled away in search of someone who could tell him where headquarters might be located. He pushed along the sidewalk through the crowd which was so preoccupied with its own concerns that it was profoundly indifferent to his. The first officer he stopped smelled strongly of whiskey and merely inquired, "Does your mother know you're out?" The second professed ignorance, but a brisk young cavalryman clanking a ponderous saber pointed a finger southward.

"Early? He's gone on to Lynchburg. Hunter's supposed to be gettin' near there."

The pit of Brice's stomach fell out. Gone to Lynchburg! Where Early had gone he knew that Stowell would insist on following.

"How far is that?" he managed to ask.

"'Bout sixty miles."

They were blocking the thoroughfare, and a whorl of impatience was forming about them. The cavalryman said, "Excuse me," and went on his way, leaving Brice facing a bulky, elderly person in muddy boots, a sodden gray cloak and a high hat like that of German Smith.

"Cheer up, boy," he rumbled. "The infantry took the cars. Reckon if you've got to go, the old Orange & Alexandria can creak you through. It still runs after a fashion."

His broadness was twice the obstruction to the sidewalk that the cavalryman had been, but he seemed disposed to gossip.

"Are those your men? What command are you?" he demanded.

"I Company of the Second Maryland Infantry," answered Brice, puzzled whether to classify him by his dress as a soldier or a civilian.

"Gordon's Division?"

Brice was impatient and suspicious at this inquisition. He was about to tell the other to go to the devil when he saw the three gold stars of a Colonel embroidered on the high collar which showed momentarily above the cloak. He came to attention and explained their predicament.

"I thought you might belong to Gordon," said the Colonel, apparently still disposed to gossip. "He's got most of what's left of Edward Johnson's troops, the regiments that were wiped out at the Bloody Angle, and three men and an officer are liable to tell you that they're the Thirty-third Virginia." He sensed Brice's mood and changed his tone. "Tell you what. I'll scare out somebody with authority to issue you rations and send him along. It's only a step out of my way. And if you're bound and determined to find General Early, see that big house down at the end of the block? The one with the hip roof and the four chimneys? There's a staff officer of his staying there. I don't know his name, but he may know something about you."

"Thank you, sir," said Brice, warming to this unusual Colonel who would concern himself so helpfully with the affairs of others.

The heavy face scanned his and measured the muddy street. "On second thought, I'll scare him out too. Thank God I usually ride a horse. It'll take a few minutes. Tell your Captain that Colonel Nelson says to wait."

"Nelson," wondered Brice, shoving his way back to the street, and then recognized the name. He was the one they called "the Old Colonel," well along in his sixties and commanding a battalion of the Second Corps artillery. That high silk hat was part of the tale. It was on a par with Captain Stowell's spade and haversack. The eccentricities of these ancient warriors were cherished by their men because of the homely illusion they created.

McComas met him next the curb. "He's better now," he reported, and led him to the Captain, who was walking slowly along the line, talking to each soldier. He had stopped in front of Home Grown Smith who still maintained his feet, though he held to German Smith's belt to keep from swaying—pale dark face next to blond paleness.

The Old Gentleman's voice had lost its fuzziness. "Better report to the hospital, boy," he said.

The bedraggled Private shook his head stubbornly. "I'm comin' along to Baltimore, sir."

"I could order you in," continued the Captain slowly, watching the red fever spots above the cheekbones.

The sick man lurched a step forward and clawed at him. "You promised me . . ." he began, but Stowell cut him off.

"Very well, have your way, but remember, it's up to you to keep up."

Brice made his report. "Now, that's right kindly of him," said Stowell with a faint echo of heartiness, and moved over to Matthews.

"You look pretty chipper," he remarked, then lowered his voice so that only Matthews and Brice could hear. "Next time don't be so quick to give up your rifle. You could have carried it a few miles further without burdening somebody else."

A Commissary officer appeared, gave them an order for rations and told them where to find the train. Colonel Nelson's energy was bearing fruit.

The Captain returned to his work.

"Sergeant McComas, Burke has carried the spade long enough. Assign it to Beeler."

The Old Gentleman was assessing strength and weakness, dealing with his men as individuals, not as impersonal units. He had shown that he could be a disciplinarian, could march them to the extremest edge of endurance, yet strive throughout to mitigate hardships, both mental and physical. More than that he could not do, and Brice already realized that the Company knew as much.

"The Maryland Line?" asked an amused voice behind them, and they turned to see a young staff officer in sword and sash and glittering boots, barely muddy, coming up with a broad smile.

"I Company?" he continued, still with that edge of laughter.

"That's right," said Stowell stiffly.

The staff officer paid lip service to an apology. "I'm sorry, but you see it's right funny. Old Jubilee has been raising hell about it. He thought he needed guides, and he forgot that he already had the Maryland cavalry with him, not to speak of a couple of batteries from your state. He told an aide to write to General Lee and ask for a company from your Battalion. 'One company,' he said, and whoever was making notes put down the numeral instead of spelling it out. When they made the fair copy to be sent to headquarters, I reckon they misread the '1' for a capital 'I', so here you are."

Stowell and Brice stared at him speechlessly. The youngster's grin broadened, his voice was barely under control.

"It got worse mixed up before they got through. General Early said later that he wanted men from around Frederick and Hagerstown, but that didn't get into the despatch when it was sent. Reckon they thought he knew just what he was after when he was so specific about I Company. Where are you from, as a matter of fact?"

"Baltimore," Brice answered in a cracked voice.

"Good Lord." The staff officer bit his lips hard, eyes crinkling with mirth. "Well, reckon it was a mistake."

He strode away with laughter trickling back from him.

The men had heard; he had not bothered to keep his voice down. There was a rising angry note from the haggard ranks, dying away under the blight of despair. Brice was too incoherent with fury to get out a word. The terrible marching, the achievement of endurance made futile and frustrated because of a ridiculous error. Cabell, Heenan, Hammond, Raby —broken down and abandoned like that dying mule, the dignity of their failure smirched by that scourging guffaw. He cursed savagely and clenched his fists. It was well for the staff officer that he had not lingered. Then Stowell's curt command hushed him.

"Stop that! Your men are listening, sir! If you give way, so will they."

The Captain's eyes were burning too brightly, but he found strength in this fresh emergency.

"We have a decision to make, Brice. What do you advise?"

"What is there to do except go back where we came from?"

"And forget our duty? Our orders are to report to General Early. Do you think that goddam baby *is* General Early?"

Brice spun to face his Commander. "And go sixty more miles, even if it is by train, to be laughed at again?"

Stowell clasped his hands behind him. His cold appraisal

took Brice back to the day he had protested against the appropriation of the wounded Federal shoes.

"Is it any concern of ours whether or not the General chooses to take it as a joke? As for going to Lynchburg, I had no such idea. If the railroad is running, the telegraph line must be open that far. Would it be too much of an inconvience for you to go to the station here and send a request for instructions?"

The sarcastic inflection made Brice flush. He felt that he had shown to poor advantage. The far more tired Stowell had kept his wits and his temper while he had stormed uselessly. He waited in shamed silence.

The Old Gentleman was writing the message on a corner of the stained map with a stub of pencil. His head was bent over his work, but his lips moved as he spoke in a low tone.

"I think Early is going to Maryland all right. Marse Robert isn't going to lose the chance of threatening Washington if Hunter can be routed. And, by God, Brice, I want to go along! The men need it. If we just take them back to Petersburg and the Battalion, I'm right afraid that the Maryland Line will have its first deserters. You can't pick them up and then throw them down like this. I've said as much in this despatch, and I'll be damned if I care what Early thinks about me for saying it."

"Do you think he'll keep us?" asked Brice, his eagerness overcoming his good sense.

The other tore off the corner with the scribbled message and stuffed the remainder of the mutilated map back into his pocket. With a faint shadow of his usual whimsicality he arched his brows at his Lieutenant.

"You really want to ask that? I thought not. Get this off as soon as you can and join us at the Commissary train."

He tugged at the bottom of his short jacket to straighten out the creases and pulled his belt straight.

"I wish I could answer you," he burst out. "I'd like a day's rest here myself so I could make a few inquiries. General Elzey had a camp of Maryland recruits at Staunton. Of course, when the Yankees came they had to skedaddle, but I'd like to know if my son, Murray, ever got there."

That fleeting loss of control seemed to make him ashamed.

He brushed his hand over his beard and with the gesture resumed command both of himself and of his subordinates.

"Well, they heard that fool. We'll have to post sentries tonight—reliable ones. I'd hoped to spare them that since we've caught up, but there's going to be some we can't trust for a while, not after what's happened."

He waved Brice on his way and did an about face. His steady eyes swept his men.

"Fall in, two ranks!"

Weary feet soughed in the mud. The bodies, brittle as dry branches, obeyed automatically, but the expressions were blank or sullen. Will and determination had sunk very low even among the sturdiest. When McComas dressed the line, his commands and the responses were equally mechanical. In spite of his duty, Brice lingered. A few passers-by were watching critically, and it touched him on the raw that they should be witnesses to the nadir of I Company's morale.

Stowell waited quietly, then spoke in a normal tone.

"We're asking for orders. Whatever they are we'll obey them like men. Reckon while we're waiting we'll open the haversack."

There was a stir, a raising of heads. He had caught their interest. The tradition of the haversack made its opening an event, gave a transitory victory over their depression. McComas smiled faintly, and Hubbard wiped his wet mouth with the back of his fist.

In that fleeting instant of revival, the Captain's voice assumed a baying resonance.

"They're looking at you!" he cried. "Remember who you are—the Maryland Line!"

He was appealing to the fierce unit pride which outlasts most ideals, to the brotherhood of adversity which is not petty but in its way ennobling. They had won the deference of their peers, expected to hear, "Them's the Marylanders," uttered with respect. They considered themselves the direct successors of the older Line which had been equally proud under Washington and Greene. The cunning reminder that they were being watched braced their front.

"Shoulder arms! Right wheel! Forward march!"

103

Bone-weary and overwrought, they still made an attempt to keep formation and squelched down the street with a ghost of jauntiness.

An artilleryman standing behind Brice spoke to another consideringly.

"I saw them fellers at Gettysburg, and what I saw I liked first rate. Don't see no cause to change my opinion."

The mood of sympathetic exaltation took the weary Brice to the railroad station and back along a heavy road until he found I Company's camp.

It was not hard to find, what with big fires burning to dry the sodden ground and silhouetting the whole Company which lined a rail fence waiting for him to come.

"There he is now!"

"Step out, sir, *please!*"

"Captain 'llows he ain't goin' to pull the cork until you get here!"

Brice made his report while the men clustered thirstily in the background, holding their tin cups.

"Very good," acknowledged the Captain. Smiling benignly but with a certain eagerness in his movements, he opened the haversack and held up the bottle.

"All here?" he inquired.

"All except Lucas," said Watts commiseratingly. "He don't drink liquor. Belongs to one of those sects what breaks for the woods and bellows when you pulls out the popskull."

The Old Gentleman ran his eye over them and pointed to Matthews. "Fall out. Seventeen's too young to tangle with whiskey."

"Aw, sir!"

There was a mutter of approval, though the motive was probably a desire to reduce the number of participants. Even as it was, there'd be only a swallow for each, but it would be a bright spot, the solitary one in what had been a right trying day.

"Get on over to Lucas, kid," admonished Niedlander. "He'll tell you it's a direct intervention of Providence to save you from sin."

The Captain pried loose the cork with his knife and measured equal allowance until the bottle was empty.

"Weather's broken twice today, this ends the second dry spell," said Hubbard with a grin, and tossed down his drink. The grin wiped away abruptly.

"Goddam it!" he shouted. "This ain't whiskey!"

Carney confirmed him in an amber spray, the others tasted and raged, even the Old Gentleman swore with a fluency that he had not learned from his books.

"That's nothin' but water colored with boiled oak bark!"

Their faces were flushed, their fists balled. There was no humor to them in a situation which had robbed them of a consolation so badly needed. In unmeasured, furious terms they blasted the crafty Pennsylvanian from whom the Captain had purchased the bottle. Then Watts threw the pack onto a new scent.

"I tell you it was Heenan! He was boilin' oak bark one day an' I asked him why. He said, the damn liar, that he was tryin' to make something that would taste like tea."

Others affirmed him angrily, recalling that the horsy orderly had had access to the haversack when he cooked the Captain's rations and that once or twice he had displayed a cheeriness foreign to his usual gloom. He had stolen from all of them, and they talked of him as they would of a thief.

"He'll come back, and we'll be waiting for him!"

"We ought to buck him ourselves!"

Stowell had decided that their vengeful hysteria had gone far enough.

"All right!" he commanded. "Quit this shouting. . . . What is it, Brice?"

The Lieutenant had reached into his own haversack and held up another bottle.

"I was thinking that there were right smart of us to be gaining any benefit from just one jug," he drawled. "So I got me another in Charlottesville."

He handed it to the Captain. "Here, sir. See how far this'll go."

"By God," said Carney, the man who had been bucked. "There's some use to the Long Boy after all."

XI

LIEUTENANT BRICE perched in a cane-bottomed chair set unevenly on the grass and watched a camp kettle that was bubbling furiously. He had retained his pants, but the remainder of his clothes were spread out in the early afternoon sun, a reasonable, pleasant sun, not the choking, blazing one of the past few days. He still wore his hat, and to the covert amusement of the lounging watchers was observing a ritual about it. Whenever he stood up to stir the contents of the pot, he would tilt it to the back of his head, but when he sat down he would straighten it again with the regularity of clockwork.

"Going into town, Lieutenant?" inquired McComas, his silky yellow beard recovering its vanity under his comb.

"Whenever the Captain gets back," Brice confirmed. "I know some people here, claim kin to them, as a matter of fact. I stayed with them when I was convalescing."

His freshly shaven face was nicked in a fashion that showed the stubborn resistance his stubble had made to the razor, but it showed also a relaxation which had not been present the previous night.

I Company had regained its normal pitch, though traces of the strain abode in the shadowed eye sockets and the subconscious twitchings of those who drowsed. The men had slept, had enjoyed both supper and breakfast, something of a pleasant novelty, and, most heartening of all, knew that they were to remain with the Second Corps. The curt return wire had come ordering them to stay with the reserve wagon train until they were needed. At least they could still nurse the possibly delusive hope that they were on their way to Baltimore.

106

The strategists among them had already analyzed Early's future movements to their own satisfaction and had come surprisingly close to reading that General's mind. With keen insight they had classified Hunter as a bluffer rather than a fighter and were sure he'd run from the action that they had heard was going on at Lynchburg. Those Germans he had with him weren't like the Army of the Potomac for whom they had a profound respect. With Hunter out of the way, Old Jube would come a-hellin' down the Valley; reckon the Yanks in Harpers Ferry were already buyin' trunks.

Brice rose for the tenth time to peer into the kettle and swear. He was engaged in boiling his shirt and underwear in an attempt to rid them of graybacks, the doughty and persistent lice which several of the spectators were assaulting in a different but now familiar fashion by picking them off the seams and cracking them between their fingernails. Though most of the clothes had been washed, the vermin ignored cold water and, to Brice's exasperation, were apparently just as impervious to hot.

"Botherin' 'em any, sir?" inquired Reeder solemnly.

"Dry up," said McComas with mock severity. "You're watching another Stonewall Jackson. He's flanking 'em."

"I've heard they don't like salt," ventured German Smith, and roused a chorus of jeers.

"Who told you that? A grayback? He was foolin' you. Salt's a treat to them."

"Anyway, where'd we get any?"

Their laughter came more easily under the cloudless sky with the Blue Ridge faint and brooding on the far horizon, with the cushiony feel of soft grass under them and the smell of its crushed spears soothing those who dozed. The stacked rifles were like rows of stunted wigwams waiting for the squaws to spread the covers. There was even a scattering of straw for the ones whose blankets had been left along the Cold Harbor road. They had camped in the home pasture of a brick house with porches almost reaching to its roof, and its owners had contributed buttermilk, a couple of chairs and several fascinated children to whom Niedlander was explaining the working of his Enfield. It took very little to reverse the surface mood of these infantrymen who had learned to be sparing in what they demanded as luxury.

Beeler pointed with his pipe. "Somebody comin' yonder."

The soldiers turned to look, even the sleepers who had stood sentry last night before the message came were aroused and sat up. Brice fished his garments from the kettle and spread them on a bush. If it was Heenan who was coming up the lane, he might have to interfere to keep him from bodily harm. The victims were nursing a dangerous grudge.

"Who is it? Is it him?"

"If it is, I'll break his damn neck."

Corporal Kirk strode officiously to the edge of the red clay track where the water still stood in pools. "This fellow isn't built like Heenan," he announced, and put his hands belligerently on his hips. He had a professional grievance of his own. The Captain had issued passes that morning to part of those who wanted to visit the town, but Hubbard was missing without one.

"Wonder if Heenan'd dare come back right now?"

"How should he know the Old Gentleman would open it? That wasn't Gettysburg yesterday, though it came mighty close to it."

"It's Cabell!" exclaimed the Corporal. "He's caught up."

The straggler's messmates went into immediate action. Lucas and Reeder trotted to meet him while Burke threw a small heap of sticks together and lighted them with a burning twig from Brice's fire. Abbott began slicing fat bacon into a skillet.

"We got cornmeal enough to make 'coosh'?" he asked, and Burke nodded. "Coosh" was a nauseous-looking and worse-tasting compound of meal cooked in bacon grease which three years ago would have staggered them internally and externally.

Cabell was still limping, but he was carrying the rifle he had retrieved before he fell out. Captain Stowell was strict about retaining arms. He reported to Brice, who was in charge while the Old Gentleman sought news of his son in Charlottesville.

"Next time, Lieutenant, I'll know enough either to wear a

whole sock or none at all instead of trying to march with one that's a latticework on the bottom. It blistered hell out of my foot. The others? I haven't seen any of them."

The camp relaxed into its lethargy only to be aroused again by the arrival of Hubbard, magnificently drunk and escorted by two heated members of the Provost Guard.

"Is this yours?" asked one, propelling him towards Sergeant McComas. "We got a note for you about him. Seems he ran into your Captain downtown."

He held out a pass with Stowell's name scrawled at the bottom. "Look at the back," he admonished.

Brice turned it over and saw a line of writing with the Captain's signature repeated. "This side is genuine," it said. "The pass isn't. Give him the water treatment."

Hubbard was removed under Kirk's supervision to the bank of the shallow creek that ran through the bottom of the pasture where Lucas and Beeler held him while the Corporal methodically dumped buckets of icy water over his head. They did not bother to remove his clothes.

"It must have worked on him quick," said Burke wistfully, and one of the Provost Guards whispered out of the corner of his mouth:

"Persimmon whiskey. First mouthful gags you but clears the way. We get it off'n the folks from Ragged Mountain. Keep a few jugs back of the guardhouse at a right reasonable price. Watch out for the Officer of the Day but don't pay no mind to the Sergeant. He's in on it."

"I'll work a pass tonight."

By late afternoon Brice's clothes had dried and he dressed with meticulous care, finishing by greasing his brogans with a piece of bacon rind. The Captain had not returned nor had the passes of the first detachment expired as yet, but the Lieutenant and the remainder who expected to go into town were beginning to suffer from the impatience of anticipation. They were watching the lane and moving about restlessly. Hubbard was being dried out in front of a fire by his messmates and was trying to beg coffee from them, having traded the last of his own ration for the persimmon brew. His urgent appeals were disregarded as a buggy drove up and a one-armed Sergeant alighted, leaving a second man to hold the reins over the horse.

The newcomer picked out McComas's chevrons and spoke to him as one having authority. Their voices buzzed together briefly, and McComas gave an exclamation.

"I'll be damned! Well, better tell the Lieutenant about it."

The one-armed Sergeant, a fine-looking fellow, was very military about his reporting. He saluted stiffly, waited for the acknowledgment, and spoke in curt phrases.

"Sergeant Rixcy, sir, the Baltimore Light Artillery. Right now I belong to General Elzey's camp of instruction that used to be at Staunton. I've fetched along a recruit, sir, that General Elzey himself ordered me to deliver to you. I've had some trouble finding where you were."

General Elzey himself! Why was he. . . ? Brice fell upon a conclusion, then tried to dismiss it, but the answer that came to his question was the one he feared.

"Private Stowell, sir, Murray Stowell. The General says for you to carry him on your rolls and he'll see that the Battalion is notified."

Hell and damnation, thought Brice, and he could see from McComas's expression that the other shared his feelings. General Elzey must have thought that he was doing Captain Stowell a kindness to send his son to serve under him, but Brice could see a hundred instant objections. However, there was nothing he could do about it. The assignment had been ordered by higher authority. Still, he had some trouble getting out the routine words of acknowledgment.

"Very good, Sergeant. Is that him in the buggy?"

"Yes, sir," answered Rixcy, wooden-faced.

"McComas, here, will take charge of him. Can you drive back alone?"

"Easily, sir." The Sergeant permitted himself a grim smile. He probably sensed the atmosphere. "The horse isn't too spirited even for a one-armed fellow to control. Matter of fact, I may have to carry him the last part of the way. The livery stable has had all its good ones impressed."

The news had spread with low-voiced rapidity, and the men

were gravitating towards the buggy. The two Sergeants went to it and spoke to the occupant who wrapped the reins about the whipsocket and climbed down. Brice had a quick look at him as he turned to take his Enfield and his equipment out of the vehicle.

Bigger than Raby, his coarse homespun uniform, dyed butternut brown, nevertheless hung on him like an unmade bed, and the bottoms of the trousers were turned up to prevent their dragging on the ground. Probably the Quartermaster who had issued it had had nothing near the right size. His hat was the only article that fitted, and it was a decrepit black slouch that might have been salvaged from the Second Corps' discards. Brice was thankful to observe that he carried the full outfit of blanket roll, haversack, tin cup and the less essential bayonet. If he had lacked anything, there was nothing with which to make up deficiencies, for I Company had descended even below the necessary minimum. One of the Captain's errands in Charlottesville had been to see if replacements could be obtained for lost equipment.

McComas was marching him across to where Brice stood, and the latter made a hasty effort to assume a pleasant expression for what heartening effect it might have. Joining any new unit begets a preliminary nervous excitement, and he knew from experience the strangeness the recruit must be battling.

Hubbard was still partly drunk in spite of the heroic treatment to which he had been subjected. His scornful, maudlin voice rang out.

"For God's sake! He won't fill his old man's shoes."

The phrase had a double meaning that was altogether too apparent. The unfairness of it irritated Brice, and his pretended cheeriness gave place to a scowl just as the boy came to attention before him. Murray Stowell's expression was a compound of bewilderment and hurt. Undoubtedly he had heard Hubbard and had taken the officer's frown as directed towards himself.

The misapprehension added to Brice's anger so that without intention he barked like a martinet:

"Do you know your drill?"

"Only a little of it, sir," was the stammered reply. A lock

111

of the thick brown hair escaped at that moment from under the hat and fell over the boy's eye. His hand came up to brush it back, then fell hastily to his side as he remembered that he was at attention. He was very pale, more noticeably than Brice considered the experience called for, and his skin was spotted with reddish pits.

"What's the matter with your face?" the Lieutenant blurted tactlessly, and grew angrier still as he saw McComas's lips quiver with suppressed laughter.

"I had measles, sir," Murray Stowell faltered. "They just let me out of hospital."

The Sergeant came to his help. "Rixcy said as much, sir. Said the lad got sick soon after he arrived in camp and he barely knows the drill with arms. We can take care of that," he finished cheerfully.

Brice held out his hand, and young Stowell took it in a startled fashion that nearly finished upsetting McComas's equanimity.

"I'm glad to see you," ground out Brice with a final unsuccessful attempt at heartiness. "Your father's in Charlottesville, hunting for you, I believe. The Sergeant will show you what to do until he comes." He transferred his glower to McComas who at once became demure. "Enter him on the roll and draw an extra ration. Who's on the Commissary detail?"

"Henderson, sir," was the answer, but McComas added unnecessarily, "again." That detail was eagerly sought, and though Brice agreed with the Captain's reasoning in keeping the shaken soldier back with the train, the Company as a whole did not. In fact, there was a latent resentment against the apparent favoritism.

"I didn't ask you to comment," said Brice coldly. His underlying vexation against General Elzey focussed temporarily on his humorous friend whom he could cheerfully have kicked.

Having dismissed them, he leaned morosely against the fence for the next hour. Sergeant Rixcy had found a few acquaintances in camp, and after a short visit with them drove off, the old horse's broad hoofs spraying the standing water, and the buggy's wheels sinking deeply into the red clay. The men were questioning young Stowell for the latest news of

Baltimore. Brice was just as curious, but he would get his later at second hand from McComas. Instinctively he had avoided the pitfall of displaying too much attentiveness to Murray at the beginning. If he had done so, he might have established an impression among the Company that the Captain's son was a privileged character and made the position twice as difficult. He dwelt with misgiving upon the Old Gentleman's probable reaction to Murray's arrival. He had good cause to respect the Captain's consistent adherence to his principle of command. Fair, impartial, yet never pampering, and demanding the strictest performance of duty—how was the father to square with the officer? Perhaps cleverer men might work out a compromise, but he did not believe that Stowell could do so.

He broke off the long stalk of a weed and tore it absently into small pieces. Brice had taken a liking to young Murray in spite of the mutually embarrassing quality of their encounter. He'd better rally around and efface that first erroneous estimate that the latter must have formed. It looked like he'd have to apply Stowell's policy towards the Company as a whole towards the boy individually, and watch him as closely as an officer legitimately could. The Captain would never favor him. In fact, as an adherence to principle, he would probably lean over backwards to avoid favoring him. Brice tossed the last scrap of the weed viciously away. One of the few men in I Company that the Old Gentleman could not be a father to was his own son.

Private Bufford passed him talking volubly to Private Duvall. They had been to town, and the latter exhaled an aroma of spiritous liquor. Brice came out from his meditation with a feeling of faint surprise. That Bufford should talk volubly was a real departure from the impression he had formed of him. To Brice he was hardly more than a name and an accustomed vision of a stocky, dark-complexioned figure, with the splash of an old scald on his forehead, who turned up silently in the right place at the right time. McComas had told him that Bufford had been a fireman on the Baltimore & Ohio Railroad, and he was popularly supposed to have spent the entire war thinking up something to say but never quite reaching his goal. However, something had happened to rouse his professional ire, and the floodgates of his tongue were opened at last.

"That Early!" he declaimed violently. "Never saw a lawyer yet that wasn't sure he could run anybody else's business better than the feller what's doin' it, an' now that he's General he's got a chance to try it out with nobody to stop him. I tell you he's got that Orange & Alexandria so snarled up that they're still carrying reinforcements down to him what should have been in Lynchburg yesterday. He made 'em run all their teakettles and their cars here and held them in the station till he had 'em all at one end of the line before he'd let any start back. Reckon he thinks a railroad runs like the tide, everything moving in one direction. Ain't he ever heard of passing sidings, or doesn't he believe they have any since he didn't invent them? The stationmaster told me that he said he'd shoot any railroader what didn't do what he told them to do. Reckon it'd be better if he shot himself an' let 'em run it, the dried-up atomy. . . ."

The indignant voice passed out of earshot, but left Brice chuckling. "A dried-up atomy" was an excellent description of Lieutenant General Jubal Early, the egocentric, irascible and sarcastic Corps Commander.

The mud soughed again, and Captain Stowell spoke to him. "Hello, Brice. Sorry to have kept you waiting, but it took a while to wheedle the Quartermasters."

Brice turned as slowly as he could to meet the bearded face, meanwhile trying to improvise hastily a neat and not too abrupt speech which would announce Murray's arrival. The Old Gentleman was too preoccupied to notice his confusion. A gentle alcoholic aroma surrounded him also, but he was in no manner, as the phrase was, "overtaken."

"Carney and Matthews are in the Guardhouse," said the Captain jovially. "Drunk, of course, and fighting. Understand they picked on a little Georgian who wouldn't be roostered. He beat the two of them up, and the Provost Guard took charge of the remains. Did you get Hubbard back?"

"Yes, sir," muttered Brice.

"Good. We'll let our warriors spend the night in the pen

and put them to work tomorrow policing up the camp. I know the men say I'm always hunting extra labor, but they usually manage to volunteer for it the way these have done. You got any more to contribute?"

"No, sir. No trouble in camp."

"We'll get a few additions to our involuntary toilers tonight if I'm not mistaken. Burke probably and Watts for a certainty. Still I'll give them the passes. It won't do them any harm to get a little elevated after what we've been through. Any of the stragglers come in?"

"Only Cabell, sir. He's all right."

The Captain had got a full look at Brice's face.

"What's the matter? Anything wrong?" he demanded sharply.

"Not a thing, sir, like I said."

Stowell's voice grew strong. "If there's nothing here then . . . Have you heard anything about Murray?"

The neat little speech had failed to arrange itself satisfactorily. Brice came out baldly with the facts.

The Old Gentleman stood stockstill. Brice could watch the play of expression from amazement to full comprehension as the import of the words sank in.

"Is the boy all right?" Stowell asked very slowly.

"He's just over the measles. Reckon that was why he didn't write and let you know that he'd gotten through the lines."

Deep in thought, the other put a clay-streaked shoe on the lower rail. Brice kept his eyes averted and went off on a mental tangent. Albemarle red clay made the worst walking in the world, his bacon rind shine wasn't going to last him to town.

"It would be all right if we weren't on detached duty," said Stowell after a long pause. "If we were with the Battalion, I'd ask Crane to transfer him to another company. I'd welcome him then. I could talk to him, I could advise him and let him find his own level with somebody else responsible for him." He began to speak in short explosive phrases. "Captain Torsch or Captain Thomas would have taken him—they're both fine men and would have given him a chance to make his way. Now because of this goddam 'favor' I can't help him. I dare not help him. It's bad enough that the men believe I'm favoring Henderson."

"I'll do my best for him," offered Brice awkwardly.

"I know you will. But even you mustn't favor him. We've got to think of the others, and if they once get the idea that we're doing that, they'll make life a worse hell for him than . . ." the voice hesitated, "than I'll have to."

He clicked his tongue, and with the tiny sound lowered the mask of authority over his feelings.

"Send him to me, Lieutenant. I'll see him. And have McComas prepare the rest of the passes for me to sign. Go on into town, you don't have to be back until morning. The wagon trains aren't to move for a few days yet, so we'll have a little while to ourselves."

The gray cluster broke up as the officers approached. The Captain stopped near the fire, and McComas touched Murray's arm. They started together, the Sergeant with the regulation stride, but the boy trotted past him with a glad smile, and McComas halted abruptly.

"Father! I'm sure glad to see you!"

Stowell's composure cracked. He took a step forward and hugged his son, patting him on the back and pushing him away to look at him. Brice, McComas and the others were ostentatiously busy about small unnecessary tasks that kept their backs to the reunion, but Hubbard stared and laughed jeeringly.

"You low-lived son of a bitch!" snarled Abbott passionately, but it was too late. The Captain had heard.

"You're a soldier now. You have your duty to do. Begin it properly." The words were stern, but the tone shook. The boy blinked in a startled fashion, then came to attention and saluted. The Captain returned the salute and looked into the fire. "That's all I have to say."

"That hurt 'em both," said McComas between his teeth, as he and Brice ended their pretended conference. "Look at the kid."

Murray Stowell was coming back towards them. His head drooped and his eyes were full of tears.

"He hasn't growed yet, he doesn't know what's happened to his old man," McComas went on helplessly. "How'n hell will we explain it to him?"

"Hey, young'un," called big Niedlander. "Spread your blankets over here with us."

"Fine," exclaimed Brice explosively but under his breath. "There's good men in the German mess. If they adopt him like they've done Raby, maybe he'll get along all right."

"Surely," McComas agreed, brightening. "The two of them will be playing together like hound pups. Do 'em both good. 'Fraid Matthews is turning into a deadbeat since he's started living with all the other deadbeats in the Company. This kid will do better."

There was a sharp hail from the lane.

"Lend me a hand here. I've got Offshore Gus."

Zollinger, returning from town, was helping Hammond through the sticky clay. The Sergeant was still as they had been yesterday—muddy, nearly exhausted and stinking with sweat. His Enfield was slung by a strap, and he leaned far forward as if he were afraid the weight of it might drag him over backwards.

"Give me that," cried McComas, running to his side, but the death's-head turned on him fiercely.

"In this Company we comes back with our arms," it growled.

Hammond pushed Zollinger aside and reported to the Captain.

"I carried out your orders, sir. Met Heenan on the way, but he had to go into hospital. The doctors say he's got malaria. They don't know when he'll rejoin because they've got no quinine, and they're using white oak bark instead, which don't seem to do much good. Raby won't be back either. I had to leave him at a house by the way. He's a mighty sick boy, an' he was out of his head."

He looked Stowell straight in the face, and there was a challenge in his tone.

"I done my best, sir, to bring up the stragglers. I tried to carry him, but I reckon I was too weak to tote him farther than the house."

XII

WHILE the second batch of passes were still being made out, Brice started for Charlottesville, but before he could cover the short distance to the outskirts, he heard the echo of cheerful voices behind him. They mingled with the hum of others from the camps of the train, the whinnying of horses, the grind of wagon wheels, the town sound of an army. The glowing sunset promised a continuance of the good weather, but the rainwater still filled the ruts without draining off and had permeated the clay only enough to make a thick gumbo. His footprints were wells that began to fill almost before he had stepped out of them. The bacon rind shine was erased as he had anticipated, and his pants were damp and red-streaked nearly to his knees. "I'm not walking," he muttered disgustedly. "I'm plowing a furrow."

At the first curbstone he scraped the thick-soled, flat-heeled brogans as clean as he could, noticing that the leather was cracking. Perhaps he had made a bad bargain when he parted with his boots, but the latter would have reduced him to the same condition as Cabell had he worn them on the march. However, he shrugged the misgiving away and with it the depression he had felt since Murray Stowell had reported. If it was too bad about that situation, it was worse about Heenan's being in hospital, much worse about young Raby. Yet how could he help even Raby who seemed most in need? He couldn't borrow a horse and ride a twenty-mile round trip to visit an ailing boy for whom the odds were that he could do absolutely nothing. Horses were too precious to be loaned and, for such a lengthy journey, impossible to be hired. The machinery of the Army would account for Raby eventually. He fell back upon the fatalism which had mostly faded during his long convalescence but was renewing itself in battle and marching. As quickly as possible he must forget about the sick men except insofar as the chance remained that they might rejoin. To dwell too closely upon death or suffering sharpened the perception of both to such an extent that a life of which they were so insistent a part might become unbearable.

His cousins were glad to see him. The elderly Mr. Bambridge opened the door himself, for they no longer kept a servant except a cook. Cousin Mary, his wife, embraced Brice and so did the married daughter, Cousin Nannie (her husband absent in Wilmington as a Lieutenant on the *Tallahassee*) since they were within that degree of relationship known throughout the South as "kissing kin." The fuss they made over him was welcome; already he needed a contrast to the constant association with men. The pitch of their voices, their soft coloring, the tiny fragrance of sachet about their clothes —had an element of novelty to his senses, comparatively brief though his separation from such things had been.

"We'll cut the ham for you, Tom," declared Cousin Mary. "If we can't kill the fatted calf, we've still got what's left of the fatted pig. With that and the salt pork and the black-eyed peas, reckon we can make out to feed you."

"Coffee, too," said Mr. Bambridge. "Admitting that two thirds of it is acorn, the rest is real. We can color it a trifle, though there's too many of us for one cow to keep in cream. We keep her in the cellar so the soldiers won't be milking her."

"Too many of us?" Brice asked inquiringly. A cow in a cellar was too usual for him to remark on it.

"The house is full of refugees," explained Cousin Nannie with a snap in her tone. "Most of them are mighty nice, but there's a couple I could get along without. They don't seem to appreciate that we're not making ends meet too easily, and they act like we're robbing them because we don't give them fried chicken and mush with every meal. I hate to hear them picking on Mother."

"Hush, child. At least we give them plenty of mush, though the chicken's only a beautiful memory."

"Come in and meet them," said Mr. Bambridge cheerfully. He could afford to be cheerful, since he spent most of the day at his warehouse, away from nagging complaints. "We've got a selection that covers Virginia from Saltville to the Northern Neck. Take your choice."

They looked at each other and laughed, then scrutinized Brice and laughed again.

"No use worrying about which one he'll choose," said Nannie. "I'll bring her out to meet him so he can sit beside her and not have to knock down three or four getting to her. Reckon now she'll stay for supper since he can take her home afterwards."

With a mischievous flirt of her brown ringlets, she crossed the deep hallway and opened the door to the sitting room. Voices came out of it like those from Pandora's box, a querulous one that demanded why the police didn't clear the drunken soldiers off the streets and another that affirmed that the Government should issue coffee to civilians the way it did to the Army. Brice, who knew that part of the tippling came from the desire for temporary forgetfulness and part from the craving for sugar, which the alcohol supplied, cursed that uncharitableness under his breath and viciously prayed that the second lady would get her wish and have to get along with the bitter, unadulterated rye brew. He gloomily contemplated a trying evening. Then, just as in the myth, Hope came out of the box too.

He called her that mentally, for she made the prospects brighten just by appearing. She was gray-eyed and humorous of mouth with hair as black as the gown she wore, the cloth over the broad hoops at the bottom narrowing to enclose a slender waist and then flowering again to cover magnificent shoulders and a deep bosom. Hope had a sweet voice, a little drawly, as she acknowledged the introduction. Only her name wasn't Hope. It was Charlotte. Miss Charlotte Talcott from Lynchburg way, refugeeing here while Early drove off Hunter, and staying with her uncle who was a professor at the University.

"She's in mourning for her two brothers," whispered Cousin Mary rapidly. "One was killed at Malvern Hill; the other died

120

of fever last winter in the Chimborazo Hospital in Richmond. Her father's with the Army of Tennessee."

Brice made his manners, very conscious that his right knee was coyly visible through a rent in the trousers. His sewing had not survived the sucking of the clay. For once he sank his dislike for staff officers and wished he could be like them with a red sash and a fine horse pawing at the door, instead of a road-battered line infantryman whose Richmond finery had already paid the penalty of smoke and mud and the toasting effect of campfires. She was the prettiest girl he'd ever seen, prettier even than Hetty Cary of Baltimore who had become almost a legend.

Of course, he would be delighted to escort her back to the University after supper, an avowal which he made with such fervency that they all giggled. Before he could muster his small talk, Cousin Mary invited them to the sitting room to meet the others.

Brice recalled it as a center of coziness and comfort, but it had been contracted into a stuffy den by the number of people who had crowded into it. There was an emphatic odor of warm humanity in spite of the open windows which admitted the breeze and a few burly June bugs droning towards the just-lighted lamps. Most of the huddled chairs were occupied by women, though one held a shrunken octogenarian who barely raised his head as Brice entered. Two little girls about six and eight respectively were wiggling on hassocks, but the shrill squeaks from the kitchen mingled with a bass mumble proclaimed that the rest of the young were pestering the cook. When the introductions were completed, the six-year-old climbed into Brice's lap and stared covetously at his buttons, while the elder, after demanding why he didn't wear his sword, took possession of Miss Charlotte until Cousin Nannie mercifully called her off.

He progressed through the usual preliminary stages of conversation according to the time and place, matching mutual acquaintances and discussing the latest news of the battles at Lynchburg and Petersburg. Already he could identify the harpies, but the other ladies, in sympathetic alliance, turned away their searching inquisition and left him to talk to Miss

Charlotte. When they were called to supper, he escorted her in and took a chair beside her.

The silver, the linen and the china were far too grand for black-eyed peas and pork, but the thin crimson slices of ham were at home among them. Under cover of the babble of conversation Miss Charlotte managed a few confidences and confirmed Cousin Nannie's estimate.

"There's just a couple of nuisances. Most of them are run-of-the-mine people like we are, pushed out or burned out of their homes and making the best of it. We'll have one advantage after this war's over. We'll know which families to marry into and which to avoid like the plague, since we've seen them at their worst as well as at their best. Look at poor Mrs. Contee there. She's had an experience that's really marked her for life."

She indicated a small woman in a rather handsome black silk dress; a delicate-faced, highbred lady with slender hands that were already too thin and veiny from work and privation. Not so long ago she must have been a real beauty.

"She's from the Northern Neck," said Miss Charlotte's drawly sweetness in his ear. "A Miss Hungerford who married a Contee. They were very happy, I've heard, and he was most attentive to her—which isn't invariably the case."

She laughed, and he whispered back:

"Must have been easy with her just as it would be with you."

"Now is this young man just being overly polite or is he being bold?" she soliloquized, and went on with her story.

"Anyway, Mr. Contee was a fine horseman, and he got her a pair of matched bay colts. He broke them for the carriage and gave them to her for her birthday. Right after that the war began and he went into the Army, the Ninth Virginia Cavalry, I think. He was killed on the Rapidan in a skirmish, and she took it mighty hard. The colts meant a lot to her, since they were the last present she'd ever have from him."

The woman on the far side of her made a remark, and she turned her head to answer. Just then they rose from the table, but Brice, still tactically impeccable, maintained his place when they were back in the living room.

"Go on about Mrs. Contee," he requested.

"Oh, yes. I was telling you about the colts. Well, you know the Northern Neck has been fairly hard hit by Yankee raids, that's why she's in Charlottesville, though I reckon she's jumped out of the frying pan into the fire. They mostly land from gunboats and take everything they can, including the silver. She didn't mind so much about losing that, but she was set on preserving the pair. She did it for a while. They had a good place down the bed of a branch with a patch of woods to hide them, and the neighbors functioned well enough to give warning, but finally what turned up was Yankee cavalry from an unexpected direction. They rode into the yard just as she came back from church in the carriage."

There was no humor in her voice now.

"She pleaded with the Yankee Captain, told him what store she set on the colts and why, but he just laughed at her. Said that the only thing she had proved by her talk was that they had been the property of a rebel and he was going to seize them. He looked them over while his men were taking them out of the carriage and had his saddle shifted to the one that caught his fancy. As he mounted, Mrs. Contee who had stopped begging, spoke to him.

"'Sir!' she said. 'Since you've been so uncharitable, I pray that that horse breaks your neck before you get out of the yard.'

"He laughed again and reined around. Just then one of his men fired his carbine at a pig. The colt shied at the shot, and the Captain was thrown. He hit the stone pillar at the end of the drive headfirst and it killed him dead."

Brice whistled soundlessly. "That's having Providence answer you real quick."

"I don't think I'd like it to happen to me," admitted Miss Charlotte. "I reckon she really didn't mean it."

The children were waiting in the living room and gathered around him with squeals and pushing. There were little boys among them, and Brice knew the inevitable first question before it was asked.

"How many Yankees have you shot?"

Why were the very youthful males invariably so bloodthirsty, he wondered, and brought out his pat answer.

"I don't know. I've been a lot too busy trying to keep them from shooting me."

Nannie pulled up a hassock. "There's an affinity between children and soldiers," she smiled. "They adore a gray uniform, but there's a penalty attached. You'll have to tell them stories."

"About the war," came the chorus.

"I've seen the battles," boasted a girl of eight. "It was all over smoke, and the windows rattled."

"The fighting during the Seven Days," explained Nannie. "She was in Richmond then. I would have thought she'd have seen enough. . . ."

"And the wounded soldiers came back in wagons and they dripped. . . ."

"You be quiet," said Miss Charlotte. "Listen to Lieutenant Brice."

"They know too much about it already," he muttered. It was a hard assignment that the girls had set him. To draw on the too vivid memories of Radecke, the red stream spurting through his fingers from his blinded eyes, of Corporal Hodges screaming with the agony of the belly wound, and then to thin the crimson and the pain down to a wash of quaintness and humor.

"Cavalrymen get out of it by talking about their horses. Was there a dog perhaps?" whispered Miss Charlotte.

"No dog." He pitched upon a yarn that he had heard from the Old Gentleman. "There was a big fight at Gettysburg up in Pennsylvania, and our Battalion was in it. They had charged up a hill and had got behind a stone fence. The Yankees were trying to drive them out, and they were still trying as it got dark."

He gulped, and the fascinated faces showed signs of impatience.

"Anyway, when it was real dark, this Yankee officer came into our lines, thinking they were his own, and yelled to cease fire. Captain Torsch was very mad. He grabbed him by the collar and dragged him over to Major Goldsborough. 'Give him the devil, Major,' he shouted. 'He came into our position and tried to interfere with me in the discharge of my duties.' Funny things happen in battle."

"*What* funny things?" asked the eight-year-old, puzzled.

"Charlie Henry told us about his horse what would shake hands with him," said a little boy scornfully.

Nannie and Charlotte were shaking with mirth. "A trifle over the heads of your audience," commented the latter, but she intervened firmly. "Mr. Brice is too tired to tell you any more. He's been marching all day. Now you all go on up to bed and let him rest himself."

There was a howl of protest, but a reinforcement of mothers overcame resistance. One of the latter, clutching two wriggling sons, smiled tremulously at Brice. "I overheard what you said about their knowing too much about it already. Do you know that a man told me yesterday that at Cold Harbor there were two small girls who came out every evening right to the batteries to watch the guns being fired? They wouldn't be chased away even when the enemy shells burst, but seemed to enjoy the excitement without being the least frightened. I wonder if these children here realize how much there is of death and sorrow about them."

Nannie looked up at her. "I think they sense more than they say. Seeing them makes me feel sometimes that it was better that my own baby died."

During the short interval when the girls were upstairs helping to bed down the young, Cousin Mary cross-questioned him in a low voice.

"Is there anything you need, Tom, that we can get for you? I always feel so badly when I think of your being from Maryland with no chance of getting a box from home. You know how fond of you we are."

"Not a thing," exclaimed Brice hastily, though he remembered with longing the contents of that discarded portmanteau. "You've been much too kind already. Matter of fact, all Virginia has."

Cousin Mary pursed her lips and listened to the interminable complaints of the vinegary ladies.

"Some of them haven't been, not to anybody. Too many think of this war just as it affects themselves, but it'll catch up to them, either now or in after years. Never saw that selfishness paid off. Why, I've even heard that there's some who have signs posted on their property, 'No soldiers welcomed here.'"

"I've seen them," confirmed Brice quietly. "Wonder how much attention a Yankee raiding party would pay to a notice like that?"

"None at all, and I'd be glad of it." She looked at him closely. "We're going to make up a little package for you, a few handkerchiefs, socks, fresh underwear and a clean shirt. Mr. Bambridge's going to get them tomorrow—no, it's Sunday. The day after, then. We have some homemade soap, too."

She coughed as if she were embarrassed. "If you need any money . . ."

"No, no."

"As you wish, then. Don't blush about poverty, Tom. I've heard that the Army hasn't been paid."

As a matter of fact, his pockets were empty, and the paymaster had not yet appeared. He doubted if the whole of I Company could have raised fifty dollars Confederate among them.

Nannie tapped him on the shoulder. "Charlotte's leaving," she announced. "I know better than to try and stop you, but you've got to promise to come see us before you march off. I know that's a sacrifice but I require it. My pride needs a little soothing."

Brice laughed. "From me? One of the worst broken down members of the Southron chivalry? Well, you'll have it, for what it's worth."

His farewells said, he went out to the hall where Charlotte was waiting in a black bonnet with a white band that was very fetching. As he opened the door for her, the piano in the parlor banged out a few notes of "Bonnie Dundee" under the fingers of Nannie.

Charlotte had a chuckle that was as attractive as her voice. "Nannie loves to pester people, but I've never known anybody to get mad at her. Straighten your brows, Mr. Brice. If you keep on frowning, I'll have to make an exception to what I just said."

The moon was thickening, the night was warm and friendly, but she would not flirt. She listened pleasantly and responded in the right places and with the right manner to the stereotyped courtesies and compliments which were her due. Yet her level sincerity robbed the interchange of most of its frivolity. Brice had first seen her from the attitude of a field soldier, the entire emphasis on her sex and her looks, but already he had a disconcerting awareness that he was dealing with mind and character as well.

The University of Virginia adjoined the town, and even the most leisurely pace at which Brice could dawdle brought them in sight of the Rotunda far too soon. The moonlight touched the dome like the helmet gleam from some tall champion towering above the lesser buildings. The beauty of it silenced them as they turned off towards the East Range, where her uncle occupied one of the professors' houses.

"It's like a tombstone," said Charlotte in a half-whisper. "It breaks my heart to see it cut down to a barracks for refugees. If the Yankees come, I wonder if they'll spare it? They burned VMI and just about wrecked Washington College."

"Don't think about their coming," said Brice with a trace of kindly roughness.

"I try not to." She was herself again in an instant. "Thank you for taking me home."

"May I come call on you tomorrow?"

"So soon?" She laughed and relented. "Tomorrow evening, then. I am helping in the hospital, which keeps me busy all day."

Brice grinned. "I feel a twinge coming on already. Will you nurse me if I malinger into it?"

"Don't you try."

"I wish we were related."

"The 'cousinly kiss'? Don't you try that either!"

"I warn you. I'll ask Cousin Mary to trace a relationship. I bet she could in an emergency like this."

The knob turned under her fingers. "Keep that philandering young Lieutenant back in camp tomorrow evening and come as yourself. Good night, Tom."

The panels of the door were highly uninteresting after they hid Miss Charlotte's back. He was still tired and he decided against returning to the Bambridges'. At least that was the reason he gave himself; unadmitted was the prospect of a session of teasing at the hands of Cousin Nannie. He swung down the streets and gazed benignly on the town. He sho' had found *the* Charlotte of Charlottesville and laughed so inanely at the silly pun that passing soldiers snickered. That big Lieutenant was coverin' up pretty well, but the popskull was workin' on him.

There was a loud commotion on one of the sidewalks that promptly drew a crowd.

"Fight!" yelled a train driver. "Good fight!" and pelted towards the scene.

It was a pretty fair ruckus, thought Brice, and craned to see. There were more than just a pair involved. It looked more like a small riot, and the ecstatic crowd howled with joy. A flushed soldier without a hat trotted backwards, the ring making way for him. He kept on backing with tottering steps, then sat down abruptly in the mud and held his jaw. Another followed him, tossed like a sack by collar and pants, but Brice had begun to run. He had recognized the squat, hammered-down Lucas as the man who had done the tossing.

"Break it up!" Brice yowled, but the Provost Guard had already arrived and was doing it for him.

Lucas, with the expression of an aroused Old Testament prophet and the muscles of a Samson, was being disentangled from a gangling artilleryman who appeared glad to escape. The towering Niedlander, his jacket torn open and his nose spilling blood, was holding another man close and hitting him with short-armed jabs until two of the Guard hauled him away. Burke had just surrendered a serviceable club which he had improvised from part of a porch rail, and German Smith was on his back, his head against the curb with the wind knocked out of him. Other casualties littered the area.

The reliables, the steady reliables, brawling in the street!

"Wow!" a sallow soldier rejoiced in the accent of the deep South. "As good a fist-and-foot celebration as I've ever see'd. What fools tackled them wildcats?"

Watts, arriving too late, bawled drunkenly:

"I've been a-coming, boys. Let's beat up on the rest of 'em!"

He took a wild swing at the sallow soldier, who sidestepped neatly. Watts promptly lost his balance and measured his length in the roadway.

"Drunk but willin'. Reckon his feet were so tangled he couldn't get here any sooner," commented the intended victim, and forgivingly assisted the overtaken Watts into the Provost Marshal's office which was only a couple of doors away.

The Provost Marshal himself was conducting the interrogation when Brice finally managed to elbow his way into the building.

"You say they called you 'Dutchmen'?"

Niedlander was doing the talking. " 'Damned Dutchmen,' sir. Me and Smith here was talking German together, and a bunch of 'em started picking on us. Said we were stragglers from Hunter's Hessians and asked how much our relatives were making on the silver. We took it at first, but when one of them took the spoon out'n his buttonhole an' asked if we'd dropped it, I hauled off and hit him."

The Major looked across the table at Burke. "Don't tell me you're Dutch, too."

"Faith, sir, I brevetted meself one on the spot."

Lucas flexed his terrible arms, eyes still blazing with anger. "It wasn't right, sir, the man speakin' to Niedlander thataway. As the Book says, 'Frowardness is in his heart, he deviseth mischief continually; he soweth discord.' "

The Major hid his mouth with his hand. Like most Southerners of the time, he was a student of the Bible, and he finished the quotation neatly:

" 'Therefore shall his calamity come suddenly.' From Proverbs, as I recall. Well the promise was certainly fulfilled."

The indignant Brice got to the front at last.

"This is a damnable thing, sir," he roared. "These men are in my Company, and they're all good soldiers. There's no call for them to be insulted. . . ."

The Provost Marshal nodded.

"All right, all right," he said, but Brice in the full tide of his partisanship was not listening.

"By God, sir, if you throw them into the Guardhouse, you'll have to put me under arrest too. It's a damn disgrace. . . ."

"All right!" The Major was shouting loud enough to make the lamps flicker. "Didn't I agree with you? Take 'em back to camp, and I'll throw in your sot along with the rest of you."

He indicated the recumbent Watts who was being noisily sick at his stomach.

They tramped back along the lane, the dishevelled Privates alternating in dragging Watts who was nearly out on his feet. When it came Burke's turn as bear leader, Brice noticed that the Irishman had disappeared. He knew better than to ask for him; they would not lie, but a direct question would be resented. Burke had probably decided to continue his interrupted spree. There had been a token of persimmon whiskey about his bearing.

When they came in sight of camp, Brice dropped into step with Niedlander.

"Was the youngster with you? The Captain's boy, I mean?"

The big man was staunching a cut over his eyebrow with a sleeve of his ruined jacket. He considered a moment, suspiciously, then answered without evasion:

"No, sir. We left him with Zollinger. He said he'd seen enough of Charlottesville already, and he didn't want to come."

Brice felt a twinge of disappointment. If the boy had been along, if he had been in the fight, even if he'd only skirmished around the edges, he would have made a stride towards establishing a position. The act of participating, the shared episode, would have begun a change in his messmates' attitude towards him. Their unconsciously patronizing sympathy would have had an admixture of acceptance and respect. Men who must be together in close association set their own standards. He would have passed a test as old as the fighting instinct itself, the preliminary weeding out of those who cannot be relied upon in an emergency. It would have been an easy preliminary, too, not so hard as the ordeal of battle.

XIII

MORNING rollcall disclosed one unauthorized absentee—Private Burke. Sergeant Hammond was watching the lane for him out of the corner of his eye even after Lucas had begun his informal Sunday service. The broad man read a chapter from the Bible, cleared his throat and commenced his prayer. Brice, kneeling comfortably on the soft turf next to McComas, let his glance rove to Captain Stowell just ahead of him, his gaze fixed on the bowed head of Murray who was in the front row. Only in such moments had the Captain betrayed a more than impersonal interest in his son who was also his subordinate. It must be like a hair shirt to him, reflected the Lieutenant. Plenty of saints have undergone less of a trial. His wandering attention was jerked back to what Lucas was saying.

McComas had mentioned to him that it was the exhorter's occasional custom to wrestle in his petitions with the sins of the Company, but he had not hitherto encountered such an occasion. Now, apparently, Lucas had meditated upon last evening's brawl and had set out to bring to his congregation a feeling of individual guilt. If anyone objected, he stood ready afterwards to justify his strictures with a clear conscience and a hard fist. The few who had tried conclusions had been so badly worsted that even the most excoriated sinners were resigned to listening meekly and to enjoying the blasts that he levelled at others of their ilk.

The prayer started quietly enough with Lucas asking that the recruit who had just joined them be kept from the pitfalls that beset young soldiers, then picked up in interest when he mentioned that Zollinger had turned to evil ways and cajoled

Murray out of his spare shirt. He'd better restore it and also see that German Smith gave back the socks he had allegedly "borrowed." Brice barely succeeded in choking down a snicker and he observed that McComas too was having trouble maintaining his decorum. The "fresh fish" who came to the Army were regarded as fair game for promiscuous despoilment by the veterans.

Warming to his theme, Lucas grappled with the devil over persimmon whiskey and applejack, using as exemplars Hubbard, Matthews, Carney, the subdued Watts and the errant Burke. In a breathless hush on the part of his congregation he asked that the noncommissioned officers be spared from the effects of the jug they had smuggled into camp and buried in the roots to the right of the hickory across the branch. Might the straw they sucked from plug up and bust that they be not engulfed in a lake of eternal brimstone.

Brice chewed upon his sleeve and did not dare look at the flustered McComas. He noticed that Hammond had forgotten all about his absentee and was instead glancing apprehensively at Captain Stowell who remained unmoved. Then his own cheeks burned. Lucas' discourse was now upon the subject of swearing, a prevalent and dangerous backsliding which was particularly noticeable in the speech of "that fine young man, Mr. Brice." Might he see the error of his ways and stop cursing and blinding to the damage of his soul. The now enthralled listeners, their shoulders shaking in unison, waited avidly for some enlightenment as to the Old Gentleman's besetting offense against morality as Lucas saw it, but the preacher steered clear of that slippery ground. Instead, he ended by confessing his own inability to keep his temper and turn the other cheek to a bunch of low-lived artillerymen in town and asked for strength both to resist that temptation in future and also that of taking one of those chickens which the wise owners of the land on which they camped had carefully penned in the barn. There was a padlock on the door, but they had forgotten the small window in back. He would justify himself by nailing on some slats.

One counted minute after the "Amen," too heartily echoed by the delighted troops, the Captain beckoned Lucas, now reverted to his unprivileged status as a private soldier. Brice was close enough to hear what passed between them.

"Lucas," the Old Gentleman said, courteously but firmly, "I have every respect for your right to pray for us. I hope it does some good, and I think it does too. But since you're in the Army, you will render unto Caesar the things which are Caesar's and you will not petition publicly and aloud for anybody above the rank of Private. If you have anything to say about your superiors, pass over it in silence, and your congregation can fill in the gaps any way they want. If not, I fear that I must draw forcibly to your attention the separation between Church and State."

The day was soft and dreamy, the sun still tempered enough so that they could doze in the open field without seeking the shade of the trees. Rumor had been confirmed that Hunter had taken off for the mountains without a serious fight and that the Second Corps was in hot pursuit, or a pursuit as hot as could be maintained by troops who had already been marched almost to the limit of their endurance. The composite relaxation of body and mind grew more intense as anxieties resolved themselves, and expressed itself in a torpor so gripping that only the most necessary tasks were carried out.

Yet I Company's peace was not undisturbed. The Sergeants fruitlessly kept up their vigil for the return of Burke who could not be located even in that most logical of places, the Provost Marshal's Guardhouse. Nor would Corporal Kirk's over-military conscience remain quiescent while Murray Stowell remained uninstructed. His crisp voice, raised in admonition, carried to Brice as the latter stretched himself out next to the Captain and put his hat over his eyes.

"Are you going to report Burke as overstaying his leave?" he asked lazily.

"No," came the Old Gentleman's rumble. "He'll be back and with some damned excuse that will get him off the worst of his punishment. I swear each time it happens that I won't laugh, but the scoundrel has a way about him. He and McComas and that trifling Watts do us a lot of good. Between them they can raise a laugh when there's nothing much to laugh at. However, the boys are feeling their oats a mite. Be-

133

ginning tomorrow we'll give them four hours of company drill each day."

Brice said nothing. It was just like the Army. Get comfortable and right away somebody thought up something to keep you busy. At least he was losing nothing; Miss Charlotte worked all day in the hospital.

He brushed off an inquisitive fly and let his body go loose. Corporal Kirk's instructions to Murray Stowell carried to him clearly and disturbed his rest.

"Load in nine times," the Corporal announced. "At the command, 'Load,' come to the first motion of present arms, lower the piece to the ground and carry the hand to the cartridge box . . ."

"How can he? He ain't got no cartridge box," came a drawling remonstrance in another voice.

"Dry up, Zollinger."

"What he's tryin' to say is 'stick your hand in your pocket and feel around,'" commented Duvall.

The badgered Corporal continued, "At the command, 'handle cartridge,' seize the cartridge between the thumb and the next two fingers . . ."

"If some Yank hasn't shot them off by now," chirped another watcher. The Company was arousing itself to the new game.

"And place it between the teeth . . ."

"Assumin' you've got any left after chewin' on issue beef, full of bone splinters." That was Watts.

"The next command is 'tear cartridge'. . . ."

Kirk was repeating the passages in Hardee's *Tactics* almost verbatim. Brice visualized the book through half shut lids, even to the queer illustrations of elegant soldiers in frock coats and high, hard hats.

"Tear the paper to the powder and hold the cartridge upright near the muzzle."

"Don't look at it though," added one of the tormentors. "By this time your hand's shakin' so bad that you've spilled the powder."

"Goddam it, I told you all to dry up!"

"Of course, Corporal, wouldn't interfere with your pleasure, not for nothin'.'" Niedlander's tones were charged with deadly and meaningful sarcasm. "That's real Regular Army style. We ain't used nothin' but 'load at will' since '61. Maybe that's why we usually run 'em."

Brice chuckled under the shading hatbrim. The portentous term "Regular" had lost all meaning since they had served their own apprenticeship. He could not have said offhand which division of the Army of the Potomac was the professional one, or whether it was the best or the worst in that formidable organization.

"Good morning, Captain, good morning to ye." The full, hearty resonance of the greeting startled Brice so that he sat up abruptly, his hat falling off. At the same instant the Old Gentleman suffered an identical reaction, and they faced each other like householders aroused by an alarm of fire. Smiling and unabashed, Burke sat beside the branch in the position of the "buck," a stick passed through arms and legs in the prescribed manner and his wrists brought together in front of him though they were not tied.

"I thought I'd save ye the trouble of orderin' it, sir," beamed the Irishman. He must have avoided the lookouts, sneaked behind the barn and crept along under the bank until he had arrived opposite the officers. One look at his face and at those of the furious Sergeants and Brice exploded with laughter. He could not check it, and the sound and example of his mirth was too much for Captain Stowell's sworn effort to maintain his gravity. The beard quivered, then the mouth forced itself open in a guffaw.

"You damned scoundrel, you've beaten me again. Sergeant Hammond, put Burke to work policing up the camp."

Burke shot a betraying glance over the already immaculate camping ground. Hammond had had plenty of labor that morning. However, the Sergeant smiled grimly.

"Very good, sir. I was thinking that there are ladies in the house and maybe they don't relish the sight of a lot of men cruisin' around half-naked when they're washing their clothes. Seems to me a good solid screen would serve. If we felled a couple of trees and made one out of the branches . . ."

He dwelt upon the words, and Stowell hid a smile with difficulty.

"Of course, Sergeant. Burke's a good axeman. He can start after dinner."

Hammond relaxed his forbidding attitude and became human. "It's a grand dinner, sir, that the detail has just toted in from the Commissaries. Beef, dried peas, crackers, molasses and real coffee with a little sugar."

"I thought it might be," acknowledged the Old Gentleman. "I talked to the Commissaries yesterday. It makes a mighty big difference whether they think they're feeding just an ordinary infantry company or General Early's Personal Escort. Our orders might imply that that's what we are if you read them with an open mind. I was right convincing, I think, and I hope they'll keep on believing it."

The dinner was indeed good, even though the beef was blue and stringy. Nobody was so finicky as to object to its being boiled in the same kettle that Brice had used to discomfit the graybacks. This Sunday had a welcome resemblance to a real Sunday from before the war—worship and then a feast. Even Kirk relented enough to let Murray Stowell digest in peace. Only Burke did penance with an axe.

The Captain, however, grunted reluctantly to his feet, and announced that he was going to visit Heenan in hospital, upon which Brice roused himself to glossing solicitude.

"Let me go, sir. I need the walk."

The Old Gentleman stared, then twinkled. "A walk, Brice? You haven't had enough walking? You'd better be careful, son. Maybe you'll get an uncontrollable taste for it and start sneaking off each evening for a brisk ten or twenty miles."

"Heenan. . . ."

"There's been considerable change there too. You were agreeing with Hubbard who was advocating tearing up a sapling by the roots and beating his brains out with it." He reseated himself, the white teeth a gash in his beard. "I won't inquire further into this metamorphosis, though I reckon I can give it a name. However, I lay it on you to see Heenan before you see her."

Brice took the shreds of his dignity down the lane at a pace that increased from sedateness to a lively amble as soon as he was out of sight. Yet he could not have explained why Charlotte Talcott should have had so unique an effect upon him, so much stronger than the other Virginia belles he had met and flirted with. The fact remained that she did.

Miss Charlotte was not at the main hospital, by now fairly well equipped, but at a hasty makeshift established in a warehouse to take the overflow of cases, mostly fever and malnutrition, which the presence of the Second Corps had brought. He found her on hands and knees, her hair damp with perspiration, scrubbing at the accumulated layers of grime which the doctors had philosophically accepted. Soldiers were supposed to be hardy, and it was less than a generation since Semmelweiss had been hounded from Vienna for proving that childbearing mothers could be saved by a little cleanliness. Last year the Federals had shipped wounded away from Gettysburg in cattle cars with the dung still strewn on the floors. Yet keener medical minds were at last noting that where women were doing more than merely bathing the faces of "our poor boys," the death rate was tumbling.

When he stood over her, she looked up in surprise and, with a reaction entirely feminine, snapped at him:

"Well, Mr. Brice? Do you approve of me now?"

"Of course," he prevaricated. In his heart of hearts he did not. The period still demanded that its women flutter upon pedestals. He had envisioned her as a "ministering angel" doing something with hot broth and a spoon, not as a heated scrubwoman.

"I doubt it," she announced, reading his expression; then, sitting on her heels in what he privately considered an unladylike posture, she pointed the dripping brush at him. "Aroint thee, aroint thee to Acheron, foul spirit who interrupts my dream." Her smile took the sting from her words. "Can you wonder if I'm not just a mite annoyed at you? Last night you were quietly worshipping—or so you said, don't you dare deny it! Today you see your jewel turned to dross —all because of a scrubbing brush."

Once again she executed a bewildering change of mood. "Well, Thomas, you've seen me and, now that you have, may I ask what brings you here?"

"One of my men," he stammered. "Heenan."

"I know him, a little fellow." The brush pointed again. "Four pallets along. Thank God, we've at least got straw for them. Go see him and I'll be waiting for you if you still want to take me home. Oh, I'll be quite presentable, I assure you. I'm almost through."

Brice brooded down at Heenan, flushed and shrunken under a torn quilt. The spurious sympathy of his visit changed to a true regret. Heenan was very ill indeed. He wouldn't be back, probably would never see Baltimore again. What had brought him South away from his job as a Bishop's coachman? Why had he volunteered—for they were all volunteers from Maryland? The motivation of each man was his private secret, devotion to a cause, escape, the attraction of adventure, belief in the burning words of men too chary of themselves to risk what this devoured body had risked, a promise given in drink and a pride too great to recall it once given, all were accounted for and all forgotten now. The war had reached the dogfall of sheer endurance. He knew, for he had attained the same frame of mind.

Miss Charlotte came softly to his side.

"We have a doctor here who was a ship's surgeon," she whispered. "He said that he'd 'go out with the tide.' He's picked up camp fever as well as malaria."

"We'll strike him off the roll." Brice's voice rang with bitterness. "Is there any use waiting?"

"None. The Doctor says he won't come to. There's a Sister of Charity who has just come on duty. She'll stay with him. Reckon he'd rather have her than us, now."

He waited on the steps while she threw on a cloak, and they walked together to the University. Miss Charlotte's flash of pique had passed and so had his faint patronization. That a man should die was too common an event to let it cast a pall over a rare moment of pleasure.

"Black-eyed peas again for supper. I sure hope you like them."

"Nice of you to ask," he grinned. "What would you say if I told you I didn't?"

"Then I'd hope you'd enjoy the company because that and the peas are all you're going to get."

He reached into the pocket of his coat and brought out a shapeless lump wrapped in oilcloth. "I'm not so sure. I brought along my meat ration. It won't go far, but . . ."

She halted in mid-stride. "You brought along . . ." He caught her expression, and they burst out laughing.

"I thought it would go better than a bouquet."

"You were right."

Her gurgling chuckle was purling pleasantly around his heart, and his happiness expressed itself in a quotation.

> "A primrose by a river's brim,
> A yellow primrose was to him,
> And it was nothing more,

"Reckon the poet thought we'd join him in sneering at the poor devil who saw nothing to a primrose, but he was dead wrong. A primrose is no good in a stew, even for flavoring."

"Must we always let our stomachs edge into our conversation?"

"They don't pay much attention to whether we'd rather or rather not."

He replaced the package in his pocket and smiled down at her. The courage with which she could laugh at the spectre of constant hunger endeared her still more. It was easy to say that a cheerful soul overcame many an obstacle, but it was less easy to live up to the saying. Had the Army not found solace in its ironic grumbling, it would long since have dissolved, but at least it had the consolation of a burden shared. Miss Charlotte had to bear with the nagging problems of daily life, with the snarling complaints of those like the two old bitches who were making his cousins' hospitality a cross to them.

She was looking away at the darkening hills. "Charades tonight, I think. There'll be others visiting. Some of the cavalry guarding Rockfish Gap manage to sneak back, though they say they're on duty. You must give me ten minutes to myself when we arrive. Then I'll cast the scrubwoman for the princess, and woe betide you, sir, if you look at my hands."

She held them out ruefully, the smooth skin wrinkled and

roughened by the strong soap, but when he tried to mutter a sympathetic phrase, she put them behind her back.

"I'm not ashamed of them, Thomas. I've observed that there are three types of women. The first shout angrily that 'something ought to be done about it,' when anything bothers them, but don't do a thing about it themselves. The second go one step further and tell somebody else to take care of it. They can be right nasty and officious at times, but they keep themselves to the directing side, I notice. It's easy to point out that a floor needs to be scrubbed or dirty straw changed under a sick man or foul clothing cut off around a wound. There's got to be a third kind or the other two would simply rant themselves to death."

She tried to laugh lightly, but her hands were still held out of sight.

"Reckon I belong to the third kind."

"'Whence cometh our help,'" he answered humbly.

XIV

I Company rested five more days at Charlottesville with the trains and reserve artillery, while the Second Corps chased Hunter into the mountains and then turned north. Five days in which "General Early's Personal Escort" lived as well as Commissaries, and the weaker men recovered a portion of their strength. Even Hammond picked up and became his old self, a vigilant, efficient First Sergeant under whose caustic tongue the wild became tame and the lazy energetic.

"Offshore Gus is a lot better'n I am," admitted McComas, ruefully admiring. "He's got that Cape Horn bucko look about him. You half expects to see a belaying pin stickin' out of the front of his belt and the bulge of a revolver in his hip pocket. He's so rough the boys are proud of him."

"Who ever heard of a soft First Sergeant?"

"I've heard of poor ones, reckon that's the same thing. *Somebody's* got to be the Company son of a bitch. If it isn't the Top, then it's got to be the Captain. You notice how gentle the Old Gentleman's got now that Hammond's back? He was toughening up when I was his official Cossack. He even spoke to his son yesterday."

"What did he say?"

"Asked him how he was feelin' and asked three more of the men as well so's nobody could accuse him of paying too much attention to the boy." McComas spat on the ground. "Don't know why people can be so goddam small, but they are. You know and I know why he's handin' us that four hours of company drill each day, but there's mutterings that we're getting it so's to let Murray learn it. Not just from the dead-beats either, there's others taking it up just to have a grievance to pass the time. Soldiers are worse than women."

141

Brice felt guilty. He had promised himself that he would do his best to ease Murray Stowell's path and had done absolutely nothing about it except to speak to him pleasantly when they had met off duty. He had let that good intention go the way of most others, what with Charlotte occupying every minute he could get with her. However, I Company would have forgiven him. They too had met her.

Their acquaintance began at Heenan's funeral. She and the Sister of Charity had laid the body out decently and had found a carpenter to knock together a coffin. The two women followed the scant procession to the cemetery and waited while the Catholic priest read the office, and the three blank volleys (the balls removed from the oiled paper cartridges) were fired. Afterwards they crowded around to thank her, though a few did not venture to approach, feeling that they were too ragged to appear before a lady. She met them with friendliness and grace and severely affected Cabell, who turned up that evening at the University, to be well received by everyone except Brice. Even his reaction was solely that of jealousy. The mere fact that a man happened to be serving as a Private carried little weight socially in the Confederacy, unaffected by what were scornfully considered "West Point notions."

Captain Stowell, too, called in gratitude. Cabell and Brice were full of suspicion when he carried her off to a corner and talked long and intimately. They meditated upon old rams and elderly satyrs, upon the tendency of even the long-married to conceal their state under circumstances such as these, but they did the Old Gentleman an injustice .He left soon with a stately bow in the old-fashioned way, and Charlotte treated them imperiously.

"You might have done better than to glower in the background, the both of you. Tom Brice, that's your Cousin Nannie smiling at you, and you've hardly spoken to her tonight. Mr. Cabell, I've introduced you to four young ladies already, get over there now and make conversation."

When Cabell had fled, she touched Brice's sleeve. "The poor man, the poor old man. Why didn't you tell me about this awful thing they've done to him? I wish I had that wife of his in this house to hear a piece of my mind. She sits back in

Baltimore with a comfortable feeling of martyrdom and revels in sympathy. I've never met her, but that's just what she's doing, mark my words. She makes all the decisions and makes them her own way. Why, she never even wrote him for advice as to whether or not she should send the boy, but lets him go on her own account. His father's a Captain of infantry, but she doesn't consult him. If she was here, I think I'd—I'd hit her with that vase."

Brice, who felt very much the same way, grinned. "She's being patriotic."

"So she thinks perhaps, but I think otherwise. It's hard to be patriotic on ashcake and water, and maybe mine has got diluted enough so's I can't see the use of eating up our seed corn. The South's got to go on whether we win or lose this war, and already Congress is conscripting everybody from seventeen to fifty. But I'm going to help him," she finished with an air of resolution.

"How?" asked Brice reasonably.

"I'm going to take one weight off him. I'm going to persuade the Quartermasters to send a wagon for that other boy, Raby, if I have to drive it myself."

She was as good as her word, for three days later a grizzled convalescent rode into camp bareback on a mule with a message from her that Raby was in the Charlottesville hospital. The Captain and Brice went in, and she met them at the door with the Doctor.

"He'll get well," said the latter in answer to their questions. "He'll be ailing a long time enough. The war's stunted him. Worn out at sixteen! He ought to get port wine, eggs and broth, but the best we can do for him is give him a medical discharge and send him home."

"How?" asked Charlotte waspishly. "Home for him is across the Potomac."

Captain Stowell was comforting. "If he can't go back to Baltimore, at least he can go to his family. They came South last year at Federal request. I've heard they're visiting down in Amelia. It's a mercy afforded to mighty few."

"What happens to the others who get discharged?"

Stowell shrugged his shoulders. "That depends on the man

himself or who he knows. Some work their way through the lines and eventually take the oath of allegiance. Some have relatives or friends in the Confederacy and try to fit in with them. The few that can work generally can find it on a farm or in a factory and manage to scrape along, but there's a residue that collects in Richmond and goes to the bad."

"The Plug-Uglies?" commented the Doctor scornfully.

"By mixing with the Plug-Uglies," corrected the Old Gentleman. "There's a considerable difference between the genuine article and the discharged soldier."

To Brice this was an old story. He had heard too many caustic remarks while he was in Richmond about the Maryland riffraff which vexed the capital. He took the burden of replying onto himself with so much passion that they all looked at him.

"They're the dockrats, the toughs, the sneaking, murderous gangs that used to beat up people for voting against them and the Germans just for being Germans. The Whigs or the Know Nothings, they used to call themselves, with a pistol or a club that they'd use only if your back was turned. When the war broke out and Baltimore was occupied, they found they couldn't browbeat the troops like they had the police and the mayor. A lot of them came South to keep out of the penitentiary. They gave out that they were going to enlist, but you couldn't get them into the Army, not with dogwhips."

The Old Gentleman obviously agreed with the description, but he was also determined that young ladies should not be shocked. He figuratively shouldered Brice out of the conversation and addressed himself to Charlotte.

"You see, my dear, Marylanders have made good soldiers because most of them have been under fire already at the polls," he announced with playful gravity. "Yet the state's toning down. It is indeed. I recollect a little excursion that some of us made to Annapolis in the year '47 when I wasn't quite so long in the tooth as I am now. We took a boat down the Bay and tied up at the dock there. First thing we knew a fight broke out between some of our boys and the loungers —reckon both sides were a little elevated. Anyway, reinforcements arrived, and the rest of us who were encouraging the combatants and making a few bets on the side found ourselves being showered with rocks and bottles. The women and children got hit too. Now I'm a peaceful bookseller, but I didn't care for that sort of thing and furthermore I fear I'd been enjoying soft-shell crabs and Monongahela ever since we left Baltimore harbor, so I helped them get the rifles from the cabin."

"The rifles!"

"Just as I say. We loaded with ball and gave them a volley; hurt five of them, I heard afterwards. Pretty bad shooting, but I reckon the Monongahela was joggling our elbows. However, when I saw them bring down two cannon from the armory . . ."

"Good Lord!" said the Doctor.

"I went and soused my head in a bucket," continued the Old Gentleman serenely. Charlotte had begun to laugh. "A few of us got between the parties and stopped the fight. I got a lot of credit for it too, which I didn't deserve. People were so busy complimenting me that they forgot that I was the one who'd found the key to the arms chest. After that, the First Manassas was a familiar experience. What are you laughing at, honey?"

"At Tom Brice's expression," Charlotte choked helplessly. "His old war horse has turned into a hippogryph."

"Don't be too hard on him. Like most of you young folks, he doesn't believe that the older generation is entitled to a past." He turned to the Doctor. "Is it all right for me to see Raby?"

"Of course, but you won't see much except for a pair of eyes and a right short lump under a blanket."

"Sooner see that much rather than a blanket covering the whole of him. Brice, I suggest that you act as deputy for the Company and take Miss Charlotte for a walk. I want her to always remember that there are fields and flowers and birds and young men to flirt with. She's in danger of forgetting."

Brice looked after the retreating back. "He's sure broad on hints."

"If you don't care to take them, I'll release you."

"I didn't mean that and you know it."

She was giving him only nominal attention. "I don't wonder you're fond of him."

"Fond of him? I'd hardly think of it that way. Of course, he's a fine officer, but . . ."

"Don't qualify a compliment, particularly if it's a credit to you for paying it. He's certainly changed you."

"How do you mean?" he demanded, his vanity ruffled. "You've known me less than a week."

"What you're forgetting is that I've known Nannie for some years."

"Has she been gossiping?"

"I wouldn't call it that. She said you were right trying when you first visited them after the war had begun. You were bound to be a General and ride by your troops, doffing your hat with a smirk when they cheered you."

"I never said anything of the sort!"

"Oh, not in those words. I'll withdraw the smirk and express it as 'acknowledging graciously the plaudits of your men.' I read that in a Richmond paper once."

He was flushing with anger, but she went on ruthlessly. "Nannie said you were awful biggety even for a Second Lieutenant. You were, Tom, and don't deny it. You were trying to get onto the staff, and you were mighty critical. You don't think people noticed? They do, you know, particularly if you're an officer. Any Private can say what he wants, but he's got to watch himself if they make him a Corporal. He'll be criticizing full blast when some still small voice without stripes on the sleeve remarks that he's not worth shucks in charge of a squad. The higher you get, the more vulnerable you are. I may say that around that time I hear you were mighty vulnerable."

He stalked haughtily beside her without finding any quick defense.

"Just making you a First Lieutenant didn't change you, an Act of Congress doesn't go so far. You joined your Company feeling that it was just a steppingstone to higher rank. You weren't exactly popular, Tom."

"Are you quoting Cabell?" he sneered.

"Partly him, partly Heenan before he died, partly Raby and some others as well. Your boys have been nice to me. Do you know that they've sent me a share of their rations?"

146

"Have they?"

She shook his arm. "Come down, Thomas. Get off your high horse. They speak well of you now. They say you're a good officer, and they don't put any 'buts' to it. I haven't just sat and simpered these evenings when you've been telling me about what you do. No, I'm not devilling you, every man does it if he likes a girl. It's like moving out the first pawn in a game of chess. You've talked about the 'Old Gentleman,' as you call him, and about your men. I feel I could make a thumbnail sketch of every one of them. Best of all you haven't talked about yourself except incidentally."

"I'm glad I please you that far."

"Don't pretend you don't like the way I've finished, even if the way I started didn't sit well."

They were walking on the edge of a lane, dried now to red dust. A cardinal, redder still, lit on the fence and examined them through his black mask.

"His Eminence is considering us," said Charlotte with an effort at gaiety that did not quite succeed. "He's probably about to ask me why I'm so anxious about the mote in my neighbor's eye and forget the beam in my own. Tom, I'm a dreadful woman."

There was something in her tone that healed the injury to his ego.

"Why do you say that? Maybe it hurt, but it made me feel better to hear what you think."

"That's just it, Tom. I go around helping here and helping there—or so I fool myself into believing. Sometimes I do it with my hands, other times with my tongue. Then I stop and ask myself is it worth while? Am I just being efficient or am I officious? I don't seem to have any time left to be Charlotte Talcott, minding her own business, which is what I used to be. Captain Stowell was right when he told me to remember that there are fields and flowers. They're just like a starry night to make you feel less of your own importance when you've got all of God's creation to compare yourself with."

He had followed her train of thought without too much difficulty. Her frank self-criticism put them on an equal plane, and he took her hand in his.

"There's no cause for you to blame yourself. I'm too fond

of you ever to be offended by what you say about me."

Her mouth took on a humorous quirk. "Don't say something you might regret later. I took a liberty, and you've been right forgiving about it. Matter of fact, I'm fond of you too. I suppose that's why I talked as I did. It's in a girl's nature to criticize those she likes as well as those she doesn't."

Dark hair, gray eyes, proud, beautiful head combined to cause a flash of intense emotional feeling within Brice. He had flirted with many, had been, as he thought, in love with a few, but this was a wholly new experience. He heard his voice say hoarsely, "Charlotte, I think I'm in love with you."

Again her mouth was gay at him. "You only think, Tom? That's being conservative at least. Harry Cabell was a lot more definite yesterday."

Surprise and chagrin made him drop her hand.

"You mean . . .?"

She laughed, but the gaiety became forced. "No more than I said."

Reading his look, she moved away, spread out her dress and sat down on the bank that bordered the road.

"You're too quick to jump at conclusions, but there's no need to tower over me, Tom. You can sit down too—only not beside me."

Obediently he kept a space between them, but he had caught a glimpse of her expression though her face was partly averted. What he saw gave him a puzzled hope. His voice probed tenderly.

"Are you so sure you don't feel the same way I do—even a little?"

To his surprise she dropped her face into her hands.

"If I do, it just can't be so," she said, her words muffled and broken. "I think I'm going to cry. I've had nothing of late but solid doses of other people's pain and misery, so I think I'm entitled to weep a little over my own. And don't you come near me!"

There was a quality in her tone that warned him that she meant what she said. She cried as if her heart was breaking while the cardinal bobbed on the fence rail and Brice sat helpless and miserable.

At last she choked down a sob. "Have you a handkerchief?"

He pulled one that the Bambridges had given him from his pocket. Fortunately it was clean.

"Red eyes!" she exclaimed, using it. "I just can't abide them."

She raised her head and watched the cardinal flying away while Brice watched her.

"Two in two days!" she exclaimed while her hands clenched as though she was suffering physical pain. "Two more boys telling me they love me! And the worst of it is, I love you both. Not the way you think either! That's the trouble with men. It must always be how it affects them, not how it affects the girl they're after."

She knotted the handkerchief in her palm, and her expression was more than beautiful. Her inner spirit talked for her with passion and honor and charity.

"It's been like this for three years, and it hurts me so. You come in, the whole of you come in, and you want loving. You've been on the Shenandoah or the Chickahominy, the Rapidan or the Rappahannock, great mouth-filling names that all mean precisely the same thing—battle and murder and sudden death—and you know that eventually you'll go back to them. Like children you want loving, so you ask us to give it to you, and we want to do it—except we can't without cheapening ourselves. God knows I don't blame you—any of you. I can't even be scornful towards a harlot if she's satisfied that part of your nature, not with the sort of tomorrow that's waiting for you. But the hardest of all to deny are the boys who talk and mean true love and marriage. They're honest, and so am I. I can't snatch and then forget. I want loving as much as the boys do. I need it. I want somebody to help me when every day I've got to meet hunger and anxiety and selfishness and what I see in the hospitals, but I'll never prostitute my heart."

The sunset outlined her, erect and gallant, against its background, over-suggestive of bloody war and fading hopes.

"I gave it once," she said, her tone sinking to a deep wrenched-out whisper. "There was a boy in '62. He was a lot like you, Tom, tall and with the same swinging walk and eager vanity that didn't hurt anybody. Maybe you remind me of him, but I don't think it's that. He's dead at Cedar Mountain, and I reckon I'm through for the war."

She was on her feet, brushing off her dress with hasty hands.

"Let's go back. The trouble with us is that we're both lonely."

Brice walked silently beside her. He had understood, and the very understanding made his emotion deeper. The colors were fading in the gathering darkness.

"'Through for the war,'" he said slowly. "I think you're wise to say that. Heartbreak can't go on forever, not when you're young."

She gave him a quick glance and spoke to the evening wind.

"You may be right, Tom, you've been the hardest to deny and because you have I'll tell you my secret. I've studied things out for myself and I've arrived at a qualification. Maybe what I've endured has made me older than my age. I can look at the future without brooding on disaster. So if peace ever comes, perhaps I can trust my heart again. But if you want to come back to me, it will have to be a new beginning."

"I'll want to," said Brice soberly.

At three in the morning came the despatch, "Trains, reserve artillery and escorts to move at once to Staunton." Bugles blared in the dark, the infantry drums sounded the quick staccato of the long roll.

"I Company present or accounted for, sir. Sir, the spade is present."

XV

A DISMOUNTED staff officer stood at a street crossing, his mare's reins looped over his arm.

"Right there's the Staunton road. It leaves the University on its left. Fit yourselves anywhere you want in the middle of the column. That sunrise says it's going to be a nice dry day with plenty of dust. If you think that's bad, remember what red clay's like when it rains. I'd sooner smother than drown in it. Good luck, Captain. We halt tonight at the foot of Rockfish Gap."

He was a short man, even the pointing finger was stubby, and a honeyed voice commented from the shadowy ranks of I Company, "Looks just like a sawed-off signpost with a horse hitched to it, don't he?"

The ponderous wagons of the train passed successively with a thud of hoofs, a grind of wheels and the occasional sharp crack of a whip. The four- and six-mule teams were undergoing the auroral change from amorphous oblongs to crawling caterpillars with sixteen or twenty-four legs.

"Listen to them drivers cuss. Wonderful, ain't it, how they finds them words? Lucas is drawing aside the hem of his garments lest he be contaminated."

"You can't drive mules without talkin' their language. Remember Major Harmon, Old Jack's Quartermaster? He could start a mile-long string of wagons from the rear end just by the force and fervor of his remarks. Stonewall had to let him swear. Harmon said if he wanted his wagons, he'd better let the mules be told about it."

I Company embedded itself in the order of march between the Commissary and the Ordnance sections, took leisurely pace from them and chattered cheerfully. Its members had grown accustomed to starting off at dawn or thereabouts and were philosophic about times of arrival. No urgency was being demanded, and they faced the day with equanimity, particularly since they had eaten and their haversacks were full. Their strategists were already holding a council of war.

"Goin' west," said Zollinger approvingly. "Baltimore's getting closer. We always begin by heading in the opposite direction to where we'll fetch up."

"West doesn't mean anything," Reeder at once contradicted. "Second Corps is bound for Staunton, and we're just going there to meet them."

"Don't it? If Old Jube's going to take us right back to Marse Robert, he'd leave us in Charlottesville and pick us up as he passes through."

"Well, that's logical, but since when has the Army been logical? I reckon things will be about as usual. A General gets up late and finds his troops have started. He has a leisurely breakfast, picks his teeth, calls for more coffee—real coffee—then announces that he'd had a revelation in a dream that tells him to do the reverse of what he's been doing. So it ends up with us making a hell-bent rush back to where we started from."

Burke slapped the haggard Home Grown Smith on the shoulder. "Faith, boy, and don't you be listening to the scut. The Second Corps is going down the Valley just like we've been sayin'."

The wrangling voices, the dull rumble of the wagons, slammed back at them from the University buildings. People were beginning to appear at windows, and a woman ran out with a pail of milk which she dispensed with a dipper as long as it lasted.

"Baltimore! We're going to Baltimore!" yelled Matthews exuberantly to the watching faces, milling his arms in a circle.

"Hark to that now! If it's taken a full week to get through that thick skull, it's taken about the same time to get through Jubilee's. That settles it. You can always be tellin' what an old jackass is going to do if you watch a young one."

The deep-toned laughter ran along the Company, but there were a few who did not join in it. Abbott had taken the death of his wife very hard, his heart was in a farther City than Baltimore. Murray Stowell, shaken and disillusioned, was in the throes of a devouring homesickness, while Cabell and Brice were watching a certain shut door in the East Range. Every impulse urged them to double across the ragged lawn towards it, but that hundred yards was moated and walled invisibly. The People, the Democracy itself, not the Army, had established a harsh rule over them, had suspended their rights as citizens, had made them subject to punishment by military courts for offenses strange to the civil law, had set their pay arbitrarily at a far lower rate than it disbursed to a street cleaner, and was prepared to shoot them in case they objected to not being paid at all. The People in their united wisdom had decided that a Lieutenant and a Private had no right to personal concerns, no right to say goodbye to Charlotte Talcott, perhaps for the last time.

"'Come where my love lies dreaming,'" hummed McComas, and gave a quick, regretful snap of his fingers. "That was a damn fool thing to do. Bite my head off if you want to. I wouldn't blame you."

Only the noise of the column replied; Brice had not even heard. The East Range out of sight, he brought his eyes to the front.

"Close up! No straggling!" Hammond was in good voice.

"Stragglin' at this speed? Did you see that terrapin dash past in a cloud of dust?"

"He ain't meanin' it for any of us except Cabell and Mr. Brice."

"Watch what you say. The Lieutenant's lookin' at you slaunchways."

Brice knew he would go back to her, his choice was made for a certainty. Yet he was grimly conscious that his own volition counted for nothing. The true arbiter was disease or a bullet. He resolutely closed his mind to regret. Brooding and introspection, he knew from observation, were perils to be avoided by whatever means were possible. Some put faith of escaping in the poor reliance of liquor; his remedy would be to bury himself in detail. Perhaps that was why the Captain was being continuously meticulous.

153

The road unwound slowly. The even gait, the thrust of
shoulders, the slung or slanted rifles, the smell of heated bodies,
the clinging, acrid dust, the fences with the honeysuckle or
the Virginia creeper, green upon gray, were a sedative since
they were so utterly familiar. Charlotte was left behind in
Charlottesville, and he was on the Staunton Pike with the
marching squads in front of him.

"Close up! Step out, will you?"

And there's a wagon stuck, and we know goddam well who's
goin' to be called on to lift it out of the rut.

I Company, pessimistically certain, waited for the command
which duly came. Clustering about the wheels, they put their
weight to the spokes. The wagon lurched ahead, and they retrieved their discarded rifles.

"That lead mule would do better in the saddle and that
bastardly driver in the harness. So that's what we're goin' to
have to do as far as Staunton, is it? Dig 'em out an' carry 'em?"

McComas, marching silently since his ill-timed humming,
addressed Brice officially.

"If you don't mind, Lieutenant, I'll take a pull on some of
the willing horses and touch up the others. Did you notice
who was heaving at that rear wheel? Home Grown Smith,
and the wagon ought to be carrying him! Hubbard was holding his rifle for him, the damn deadbeat. Too bad the Old
Gentleman was on the opposite side and didn't see. He might
have spoken his mind."

Under the tactful and deserved rebuke, Brice surrendered
to the kindly anesthesia of attending to his duty.

"Since Hubbard's got the rifle, he might as well keep it.
Double forward and tell him I say so. If Smith gets prideful
and uppity, tell him that Hubbard's paying the penalty for
hanging back."

"Yes, sir. I'll improve here and there on your bare remarks,
though I think they'll still bounce off Hubbard like water off
a duck."

McComas, his errand discharged, dropped back into place,
and Brice moved over so they walked side by side.

"How's young Stowell doing?" he asked.

The Sergeant fiddled with the strap of his haversack.

"Bad, damn bad."

Brice was startled. "Why do you say that? He hasn't had much time to show anything, has he?"

"Time enough," said McComas darkly. He swung along without continuing until Brice prodded him with an elbow.

"You might tell me."

"I was going to, only it takes a little while to arrange ideas. It's like this. He joined us after he'd been in hospital not enjoying himself, and thought his troubles were over. Reckon he believed his father would fall on his neck like they do in the Bible, and the rest of us would stand around and sob with emotion. Be a Corporal in a week, maybe, and so on up with everybody saying out loud that it was only what he deserved. Instead, the Old Gentleman hasn't spoken ten words to him, and nobody pays him much mind except to curse him for being responsible for that extra drill."

"Still talking that damn foolishness!"

"Haven't I said the same thing? And yet there it is."

"How about Niedlander and his other messmates?"

"Fair to middling. They were right fond of Raby, and they can't help making comparisons. Raby was doing his best to lend a hand; Murray doesn't set himself forward to help unless somebody tells him to."

And damn Mrs. Stowell and the three doting sisters, thought Brice. The boy's used to being waited on.

"After a while I reckon they got sick of asking him to do things and began telling him to do them. That didn't set well either. He thinks they're picking on him. I heard Niedlander try to explain why they did it, but Murray just pushed his underlip out like a balky colt and didn't listen. Finally Niedlander lost his temper and quit. I don't blame him. If the Old Gentleman could just sneak him off into the bushes and tan his hide for him, it might help some."

"But he won't."

"I'm afraid not."

Another stuck wagon interrupted them, but when the column was again unblocked, they resumed their conversation.

"You've got good shoulders," remarked McComas. "I felt her lift when you rammed into that wheel. Getting back to Murray, are you going to speak to the Old Gentleman about him?"

"What good would that do? He's been away from the boy

so long I reckon he's afraid to talk to him like he would to any other youngster in the Company. He knows that Murray's liable to take it all as meant personally, and that carries a lot of weight with a father."

McComas laughed harshly. "Murray might even write his mother about it."

"What difference would that make?"

"Did you ever meet Mrs. Stowell? I thought not. I knew the family before the war. She's one of those women who acts like the leader of a wolfpack. If the Old Gentleman ever said anything she disagreed with, she'd bay out scornfully, 'Do you really think that?' and they'd all sink their fangs into him. I thought he was a pretty intelligent man myself, and now I know it, but she did her best to make him out a fool. There's been nobody around Murray the last few years to remind him that it's just possible his mother might be wrong."

"But the boy's fond of his father, you could see that when they met."

McComas pursed his lips. "Maybe he was, right at that moment, but not now. He thinks the Old Gentleman's attitude comes from just plain dislike. We're all supposed to be taking our tone from him. He told Niedlander as much. I heard him."

Lieutenant and Sergeant looked at each other in sour despair.

"He's homesick on top of everything else. You can see it plain enough," remarked Brice, more anxious to put forward a reason than an excuse for Murray's behavior. "Feeling that way, he's disappointed in us and wishing for his mother to come and take him back."

"Homesick!" McComas' mouth was a tight line. "He don't know what the word means even. I went through it. I came out when I was sixteen too, and my family throwing fits behind me. I was the baby of C Company in the Old Regiment, and nobody minded when I'd bawl as I did fairly frequently. Only I didn't think anybody was being mean to me—and neither did Raby, and I've heard him snivel in his blankets when he thought nobody was listening. I'm nineteen, rising twenty, if you're a horseman I can prove it by my teeth, and I've

156

served three years last month. I tell you that kid doesn't know what homesickness is, nor did I until lately. I'm so goddam homesick now that I'm almost scared to wander off into the woods for fear I'd make a beeline for Baltimore. I'm like that fellow on the line of battle what saw a cottontail rabbit make a bolt out of a fence corner and tear for the rear. 'Run, Molly, run,' he says, 'and if it wasn't for my character, I'd run with you.' "

He had sloughed off his buoyant courage, his eyes were so full of loneliness that an Italian master might have used them in a painting of Gethsemene, but his voice did not quiver or rise.

"You don't get real homesick until you've been out a good long time. You never get used to war, you never enjoy it, like some of our damn civilians seem to think. The glamor of the uniform wears off mighty quick after you've stood your first night picket or filled in your first sink, but they seem to think you spend your time admiring yourself in a mirror. There's never been an army that wasn't willing to quit fighting long before the people at home stopped being bloodthirsty."

He stopped himself in the full rush of confidence, looked at the ground, looked at the sky, and relapsed into the impenetrable reserve that was the bulwark of his individuality.

Brice's thought had run on exactly parallel lines, though he was twenty-four and had escaped the first devastating effects of that terrible disease. Disease it was, for there were those who died in the hospitals of pure nostalgia. His wound and the friends he had made during his convalescence had saved him from the dominion of despair, but he had skirted its borders.

"Homesick, is he?" The Sergeant came back to the Army of Northern Virginia again. "I see you've done some noticing after all," he continued approvingly. "I kind of thought that you were too busy to look. Do you suppose the Old Gentleman has done the same?"

"He's done it with everybody else. We'll have to assume that he has with Murray too."

"And isn't that a real comfort to him?"

The reddish dust was fogging the view until the wagon

ahead of them stood out as dimly as a far-off mountain peak, but they could see the gray Captain, solid and reassuring, in his place in the lead.

"He'll work it out," exclaimed McComas in a burst of admiring confidence. "He always has."

Brice let the statement go unanswered. His own feeling was bleaker. Only the Good Lord could work some things out or straighten out some people. Captain Stowell had his failures as well as his successes. Take Hubbard, for example: was it liquor, homesickness, or general cussedness that was making him so trifling and ornery?

The march was not a hard one, but it was an uncomfortable initiation for Murray Stowell. He learned the minor irritations of campaigning, the dry throat, the difficulty in breathing, the weight of his equipment, the trickling sweat, the feeling of nearly unendurable dirtiness, yet he was spared the worst, the unsparing urgency of the dash to Charlottesville. If he made any complaint, Brice was too far away to hear, but the Lieutenant noticed that the shoes under the baggy trousers were scuffing the ground instead of lifting clear with each step long before they reached the foot of the Blue Ridge. Maybe if he's that tired, it won't do any good to talk to him, thought Brice, maybe it won't do any good anyway, but I think I ought to try. I've postponed doing it too long already.

He was not given to self-analysis, or he might have realized that Charlotte Talcott had been right when she said that he had changed. He had not lost his ambition, nor was he content with a subordinate post. The chagrin still remained that Captain Crane had not given him the command of the officerless B Company the night he had joined the Battalion, but that feeling roused itself only rarely of late. He was not objective enough to consider that had he made the same mistakes as a Company Commander that he had made as Stowell's Lieutenant, his men might have distrusted his competence and hated him. In those hypothetical circumstances Crane might already have had to relieve him. Actually, however, his horizon had narrowed because he was interested in what he was doing. Though he might choose to regard his present service as only a passing phase in his military career, Stowell's example, the quiet hints that had helped him understand the character

158

of the corporate body of I Company, had been an absorbing study. His rescue from himself, his improvement in leadership, came from his being still young enough, pliant enough, and eager enough to learn from an instructor who could assess blame and award praise with impartial justice.

When they camped at the foot of the Gap, he roused himself and went from fire to fire, pausing for a few words at each. The Old Gentleman had already done so, a customary excursion of his so that he might assess the condition of the men, and Brice had usually accompanied him. This was the first time he had repeated the process alone, and there were some quiet grins from the wiser observers. I can't fool them, thought Brice, but let the blood be on my own head. Let them think I'm favoring young Stowell if they want to. I'm not the Captain. And if any deadbeat insinuates that he put me up to it, I'll take real pleasure in setting him right.

Niedlander was squatting on his heels, feeding wood into the little blaze. German Smith was arranging notched sticks on a slant over the flame so as to support the tin cups, and Zollinger was slicing bacon into the skillet. As Brice approached, he signalled them not to rise and addressed the mess generally.

"Anything left over for breakfast?"

"Just about enough for that, sir," answered Niedlander, and swivelled his eyes to watch Murray Stowell who was carrying a bucket towards them. The boy set it down with a violence that slopped water over the edge in a cascade, but Niedlander spoke mildly.

"No sense throwin' it away after you've toted it all the way from the spring. Here's the Lieutenant."

The last words were meant as a friendly warning, but Murray, looking like a clown in his ill-fitting clothes and with that lock of hair creeping down over his face, remained in a slack slouch.

Brice chose to ignore it. "How are you making out, son?" he asked.

"All right. Reckon I can keep up."

"Glad to hear you say that. It was right dusty today, and you did well. I was watching you."

Murray's reaction surprised Brice. Instead of gratification, his expression showed anger and resentment. Hell, thought the officer, he can get offended over nothing quicker than anybody I've ever met. Doesn't he realize that I'd be watching him anyway? Is he trying to read into what I said that I'm expecting him to fail?

"Sit down," he said aloud. "I wanted to ask about your getting through the lines. There's mighty few that do nowadays."

The other squatted on his heels, thawing a trifle at the friendly request. Obviously he treasured the memory of his single achievement.

"Well," he began, "my mother knew of a man who'd served in the Army of Northern Virginia and been discharged for sickness. So she sent me to him, a Mr. McGee who lives on . . ."

"Don't mention any names," said Brice quickly. He had nothing more in mind than a caution. I Company might lose a prisoner, and the prisoner might talk, in which case Mr. McGee would be lucky to escape with a term in jail, or Fort McHenry might have another hanging. Before the words were out of his mouth, however, he realized that Murray had misunderstood, had taken the urgency of the warning as a rebuke, a stinging blow to hurt pride.

"Then there's not much more to say," said the boy between his teeth. "That man sent me to another who had me meet a mail runner. The runner took me with him, and we crossed the Patuxent and the Potomac in skiffs, landed in Virginia and came across country. It's not too hard if you keep fairly far behind the Yankee Army."

Brice met Niedlander's look of resignation, and in spite of his annoyance he laughed.

"That's mighty succinct. It sounds like one of General Jackson's despatches. At least you're here, and that's to your credit. Well, I won't keep you and your messmates from your supper."

He had taken several steps away from the fire when Murray followed and gripped his arm.

"Did my father send you to me?"

Brice shook him off and flushed dull red. His good intentions added another paving block to hell.

"Stand to attention when you address me!" The pure venom in his tone made Murray's eyes go wide. "Didn't they teach you that, soldier? How insolent can you get? No, your father didn't send me to you. I was visiting your mess as part of my duty. Can you get that fixed in your kid's mind? I'll do it again, and the next time you remember to answer properly when you're spoken to. My concern with you ends with seeing that you're fit for duty with this Company, and it doesn't go one goddam inch further. Now get back to your mess!"

He spun on his heel and went over to where the officers' fire glowed. Private Watts, who had replaced Heenan as the Captain's orderly, passed him his plate and cup, then made himself scarce. There was thunder in the air. Brice was fully prepared to lock horns with the Old Gentleman himself if Stowell had shown any signs of protesting his fully audible outburst.

However, the Captain merely laid aside his pipe and began to eat, using his knife and his fingers in place of the long-vanished fork. He chewed quietly and spat out a bit of bacon rind. Holding another piece near his mouth, he looked at Brice for the first time.

"I think it did some good," he remarked in his usual tone. "He needed reminding that he was in the Army."

XVI

THERE was no hurry in the morning to tackle the steep grades of Rockfish Gap. The Train Commander had stared at them dubiously and decided to give his gaunt mules two hours' grazing before he put them to the trial. Then, with the escort to help at the wheels, they could get over the Blue Ridge to the higher floor of the great Valley.

I Company, dozing beside their stacked arms or foraging for roasting ears, sensed what was in the wind. They were fully prepared to malinger in a body, but First Sergeant Hammond stood like a sceptical lion in the path of the excuse makers. Already he had repulsed with abuse three hacking coughs, carefully imitated from Home Grown Smith's genuine one, and a parcel of strained backs, sore feet and assorted aches and pains. McComas and Kirk beat the edges of the camp and the nearby cornfields to bring back skulkers.

Captain Stowell comforted himself with his pipe and passed his pouch across to Brice.

"I'd suspect even Home Grown Smith at a time like this. Still I don't like it any more than they do. Manhandling wagons is exhausting work. Wonder how many have 'just stepped away for a minute and looked up to find the Company gone.' Here comes Hammond, and from the look of him, I'd say several."

"I never thought of them damned wagons until it was too late, sir," reported the Sergeant. "Hubbard, Carney and Watts had broke for the woods, but I caught Matthews. He said first that he was looking for wild flowers and then that he had dysentery. I cured him quick."

The Captain appraised the grades and the mules with equal

pessimism. "It'll be an all-hands job, as I've heard you say, Sergeant. Lucas will have to instruct us again on the evils of profanity. 'Here will be an old abusing of God's patience and the King's English.' That's from Shakespeare. I wonder if he ever trailed a pike in his day; sounds so."

Hammond drifted off, and the Old Gentleman reached for his haversack.

"Do you read much, Brice?"

"I used to, sir. Not since I rejoined, though. I'd like to carry a book or so, but it's too difficult. They're bulky, and they come apart when it rains."

Stowell produced an oblong package wrapped in oilcloth. "Ever thought of treating one like this? I can't get along without William. He always has something to say that fits in with what's happening. 'A snapper-up of unconsidered trifles,' that's Carney. If you leave your pipe or your rations loose in his vicinity, you'll learn how that phrase describes him to the letter. Look at that artilleryman there, 'another lean, unwashed artificer.' "

The sticky oilcloth gave a gruesome rip as he opened it.

"Remember Falstaff's soldiers? 'No eye hath seen such scarecrows . . . there's but a shirt and a half in all my company.' Reckon mine can't do much better."

He displayed a mass of loose pages stuffed into a broken binding. "Here he is."

"He hasn't kept very well," commented Brice in amusement.

"You have a point there. As a matter of fact, the book would have suffered a lot less if occasionally I hadn't had need of paper to light my pipe or for other purposes. I take the plays I don't like first. I've used up *Troilus and Cressida*, *Pericles* and *Timon of Athens*, and I'm coming to the fifth act of *Titus Andronicus*. As soon as I finish it I'll have to pick out another, and it's getting more difficult each time. Shall it be *Coriolanus* or *King Henry the Sixth* that will suffer my critical disapproval?"

He opened the binding, keeping his thumbs pressed firmly on the pages, but he was looking beyond the printing at a crowd of dismounted cavalrymen who were trudging past, officerless and in no order.

163

"What has Will to say about those fellows?" asked Brice, recovering from a fit of chuckles.

"Well, I can't think of an apposite quotation offhand, but I'll supply one from myself. Those Kitchen Rangers, those Buttermilk Scouts! All they do is forage the farms and steal everything they can lay their hands on. Brice, right before you is the finest collection of skulkers that ever stopped to fix a saddle blanket as they went into action and took six weeks to do it!"

Though the Captain's furious indictment was partially slanderous, Brice heartily agreed with him as would every infantryman within earshot. The rebel cavalry, particularly those from western Virginia who had never been under the strict discipline of the dead Jeb Stuart, possessed far more than their share of shirkers. The excuse was readily at hand, since the Confederate service clung to the bad system of making each trooper provide his own mount. Those who lost their horses or whose animals were ailing found an easy escape by marching with the train until another was found, and some would be mighty leisurely in looking. It was an abuse which was hard to curb, for the best soldiers also were prone to lose horses, only in their case it was usually to Federal bullets. However, the jealous and contemptuous infantry lumped all together and asked the sarcastic question: "Whoever saw a dead man with spurs on?"

Stowell abruptly slammed his book shut, retrieved a couple of fluttering pages and began reapplying the oilcloth. His voice ascended to a roar.

"Sergeant Hammond, fall in the Company!"

Hammond's instant answering bellow reminded the irreverent Brice of mastodons calling to each other across a primeval swamp. I Company fell hastily into line, Bufford vaulting a fence and exploding a shower of roasting ears from his haversack.

"Have the men take arms and then draw the charges."

Brice watched the tense faces become puzzled. To empty the barrels of the old loads and insert fresh ones was a frequent precaution preparatory to action, but there had been no sound of war in the camp.

"They're not to reload," ordered the Captain, "but have them fix bayonets."

Such bayonets as remained were hastily locked home. The Old Gentleman spoke in a dry tone, but his words carried. "I've heard it mentioned, though not to my face, that I'm always hunting labor. Well, this time you're going to help me recruit it."

"Don't we always?" came a low mutter out of the corner of the mouth of a rear-rank man.

"I think you boys deserve a rest from shoving at wagons while these cavalry stragglers stand around and watch. We're going to round up some and put them to work. Look real tough, threaten them if you must, but you're not to use any weapon."

"Not even our fists, sir?" came Burke's delighted question.

"I'll exempt fists. Mr. Brice will take half the Company and approach from one side while the rest of us take the other. I think I know where the game is thickest."

The Commissary wagons attracted the most flies. If one broke down, it might be deftly rifled. I Company approached from either flank, and the astonished cavalrymen fell back before the menacing bayonets.

"What'n hell you fellers think you're doin'?"

The Captain addressed the huddled assemblage. "You men are going to help the mules over Rockfish Gap. The teams are being harnessed now, and I'm detailing you to the wheels. Never mind arguing! My boys will release anybody who can show a wound. Sergeant Hammond here will listen to any others who have excuses; it'll serve to pass the time, but it won't do any good. Now fall in."

Some cavalrymen were ducking under the wagons and taking to their heels, but a squad of infantry pushed between at the double to check that route of escape. Brice, shepherding the forming ranks, saw a bulge in the mass of prisoners and hurried over. By some mistake the party which had rushed to block the fugitives had all come from this area, and no one was left to fill the gap but Murray Stowell.

The boy stood with his bayoneted rifle slanted across his

chest. His face was white, and the cavalrymen were edging closer.

"Grab his gun!" yelled a big fellow to another who wore a brace of pistols. "Kid, you're goin' to get hurt if you tries to stop us."

Fully a dozen were pressing near, a couple had already dodged past. The man with the pistols was only a step away when Murray abruptly brought the butt of his rifle down on his toes.

"Get back!" he shouted shrilly. "Somebody's going to get shot for sure." In spite of his shaky voice, there was a genuineness to the warning that halted the incipient rush.

Brice reached his side. His hard face turned the tide. McComas was running towards them with Zollinger at his heels.

"Good work, son," the Lieutenant whispered. "You bluffed them nicely."

Murray was shaking in reaction. It had been an ordeal for a sixteen-year-old, and the presence of the officer was a reassurance that brushed away dislike at least temporarily. He lowered his rifle butt gingerly to the ground. "I didn't bluff 'em, sir. It *is* loaded, and I was scared it would go off. Nobody has shown me how to draw the charge."

The train struggled up and over the Gap while I Company zestfully prodded its involuntary helpers into prodigies of zeal. Near the top of the grade McComas waved to Brice and pointed back where they had come.

"Take a look," he invited. "One of the best views in Virginia. It's my fourth time across old Rockfish and the first time I've had a chance to enjoy it." As Brice turned to sweep the great panorama, the Sergeant chuckled. "You know, there might be something to that youngster after all. He may be a worm, but he's shown he can turn."

On the downslope the cavalrymen were dismissed, and the Company re-formed into its usual march column. Their own stragglers began to turn up, their varied excuses drowned in jeers and laughter. The remaining exasperations of the day's travel were passed over good-humoredly even though the night blinded the road with them still on it. There were grunts and rattles as the ruts and ridges brought men to their knees. At last they saw the lights of Staunton, a feeble, steady glow that

was ringed about with tiny flame fountains, sparking sometimes in firefly towers, bright against the smoke.

"The Second Corps," came the mutter. "That's them."

Doubt and hope might be almost equally balanced in their
minds, but before them lay the visible indication of decision.
If when these fires died the troops who lay about them moved
north, their emotions would merge into an ecstacy, sharpened
almost beyond bearing, centering about a change of mental
phrase: "are we?" would alter itself to "can we?".

The trains rumbled on through the town towards their camping place. Staunton was smaller than Charlottesville and much
more shabby. It had been occupied recently by the enemy and
had stagnated commercially, but its turgid pool was full of
larvae—soldiers by the dozen. I Company was spruce beside
them, for they had been to Lynchburg and beyond in pursuit
and had then swung up the Valley to nearly complete a wide
circle. Fully half, officers included, were barefoot. I Company,
a tiny swarm of like beings, was too small to make even a
momentary swirl in the mass. For such a congeries of organ-
isms to live, there must be an established order and system,
and the Marylanders must find their place in it.

Captain Stowell summoned Hammond and Brice. "Take
charge of the Company, Sergeant, and go into camp. Mr. Brice,
you'd better come along with me. I have a feeling that we're
going to find General Early at last."

Application to only four officers produced one who could
give them directions to Corps Headquarters. "Two blocks and
then turn left. It's four or five houses down. Surely, you're
welcome."

Stowell walked with his chin on his chest, his beard hiding
the upper buttons on his jacket. He had been more given to
silence since Murray had reported, but Brice sensed a difference in this and guessed the reason. At this point he knew
more than the Captain and grinned secretly when the other
brought his head up.

"I reckon you're wondering why I'm taking you along with
me, Brice. I thought it would save time and trouble if I did."

They turned the corner, their feet ringing on the wooden
sidewalk.

"You may find yourself in command of the Company. If

that's the case, at least you won't have to be sent for. I have a feeling, a real definite one, that the General isn't going to be pleased with me. Now that I think of it, I've said that before, haven't I? Well, I'm repeating it. On top of our being late, he may regard my telegram from Charlottesville as being damned insubordinate."

"Still, sending it was the right thing to do, sir."

"I think it was myself, but I wish I hadn't been so damned tired, and I wish that young fool of an aide hadn't been so brash. Between the two, I got worked up. I acted my age, or felt it, and said what I thought. That first sentence won't sit so well with him."

Brice chuckled discreetly.

"It was very hard to read, sir. You recollect that you scribbled it on the edge of your map. I couldn't quite make it out, so I may have altered it some."

The two exchanged glances of complete understanding, and Brice continued:

"It *was* a little unusual in its tone, sir, though you certainly had good excuse. Even I knew that a Lieutenant General might not take it right when he's told that 'some goddam idiot on your staff has marched us here by mistake.' I sent it in more soothing terms, 'Owing to some misconception of orders, we have marched here, *et cetera.'*"

"Thomas, you ought to be a lawyer!"

"I am a lawyer, though a mighty fresh-caught one. I had been just admitted to the bar when the war broke out, but I've never tried a case."

Of the two adjoining houses, each with a sentry before it, the nearer displayed the Corps Headquarters flag, so they turned in there. Sabers hung from the hatrack in the hall, and they nearly collided with a stocky, handsome officer, a star on his collar, a sick-pale face and dark hair brushed back over his ears.

"Kyd Douglas!" exclaimed Brice. "When were you exchanged? I heard you were badly hit at Gettysburg and had to be left behind."

"Just in time for the Wilderness," answered the Major, shaking hands. Brice introduced Stowell, and Douglas whistled ruefully.

168

"General Early's been expecting you, Captain, I'm afraid with real eagerness. He's with General Gordon next door. I'm on his staff now, so I might as well take you over."

Douglas was from western Maryland, and Brice took advantage of that bond and his acquaintanceship to probe further.

"You seem to have heard of us."

The Major broke out in a fit of unrestrained mirth. "Yes, we've heard of you, Sandie Pendleton in particular. He's the senior on the staff, and somehow the despatch got through him though he didn't write it. Every time the General gets mad, which is right frequent, he always ends by calling in Sandie as a sort of postscript and going over the whole business at a hand gallop."

The Old Gentleman's expression was frigid, and Douglas became all courtesy in an instant.

"I hope you'll pardon me, sir. I reckon my amusement is very much misplaced. I assure you that you have my sympathy. I used to command a Company myself, and I entirely understand the problem you faced. However, I can't conceal from you that General Early is very much exercised. Your statement that you expected half your men to desert if they were sent back when the Army was to advance, he regards as blackmail. I'm only repeating his words so you'll know what to expect."

He stepped through a convenient gap in the decayed picket fence and led them into the second house. The deep hall from which opened living room and parlor reminded Brice of the Bambridges', but his attention had no chance for exploratory wanderings. A high-pitched, drawling voice with a sarcastic inflection was issuing from the half-opened door on the right.

"I know you're having difficulties, General Gordon, I know indeed, sir. But General Lee has the utmost confidence in you, and he probably considers that you can work them out."

The words were scrupulously correct, though the tone implied a doubt both in Lee's choice and Gordon's ability. That's Early, thought Brice, he's talking for the record. On paper it would read like a compliment which it sure isn't intended to be. Will he ever forget that he was a Commonwealth's Attorney and stop handling the people he doesn't like or of whom he's jealous the same way he would a burglar on the stand?

There was a family portrait on the wall, a mere daub. The hack artist had involuntarily supplied it with a basilisk expression. Some shift of Gordon's position carried him under it until the picture stared over his shoulder as if it were reflecting his inmost opinion. However, the tall, thin Division Commander with the fine eyes and the high forehead had also been a lawyer before he became a Major General, and his courtroom training aided him in keeping his temper.

"It is still a problem, sir," he said quietly. He spoke with so much resonance that the pitch of the voices sounded as if St. George were being interrogated by the Dragon. "My Louisiana Brigade, you will recall, is made up of the discordant fragments of two old ones, and, of course, Terry's is a conglomerate assemblage of the fragments of Edward Johnson's Division. The men don't like to lose the identity of their commands and to be with strangers, under strange officers. I don't know how much we can rely on them until the resentment wears off, which it will with time."

Early snapped up the admission. "They were excellent troops. They should be so still."

There was no answer for Gordon to make. He moved to where the door hid him, and his place under the portrait was taken by Early, an unhandsome, fiercely energetic figure whose six feet seemed less because of his habitual stoop.

The physical contrast between the two Generals was no stronger than their contrast in character. Early had graduated from West Point twenty years before but had gone immediately into legal practice. He was arrogant and utterly self-confident and had fallen into the habit of believing that he could assimilate any job and discharge it better than its incumbent, precisely as he had considered himself fully qualified to operate the Orange & Alexandria Railroad. Serene in that belief, he carped and criticized until the respect the Army felt for his ability was marred by what came very close to an active hatred for him personally. He had strategical concepts as great as those of Stonewall Jackson, but his execution fell short primarily because his men had little enthusiasm for him. He could use with facility the weapon of his predecessor, but he never could have forged it himself nor could he re-inspire it with a faith in him. In the end he was to wreck it and his own reputation in a bitter failure.

Gordon, on the other hand, represented the attorney class at its best. Accustomed to study, employing reflection to reinforce his desperate gallantry, he had served unflinchingly, and uncomplainingly, rising from Captain to Major General on his merits, and was to lead a corps before the war was over. Lee trusted him, and for that very reason had given him as his first divisional command the morale-stricken troops of which they had been talking. He had neither the advantages nor the disadvantages of a military education which may cut both ways depending upon the temper of a man, but the veterans of his old Brigade believed in him. Later his Division and his Corps would do the same.

In his new position under the picture, Early could see for the first time the group in the hall. He jerked his head imperatively.

"Damn it, Douglas, if you want to see me, why don't you knock and come in?"

Brice halted beside the doorway while the Major made the stiff introduction. "Captain Stowell of the Maryland Line, sir."

Early flushed and narrowed his eyes, the Commonwealth Attorney uppermost, while a big-jawed, pleasant-looking officer of Brice's own age but wearing the two stars of a Lieutenant Colonel arched his brows to make a background of comical dismay.

"Here's your man, Colonel Pendleton, here's the man, sir. By God, sir, the very one who blackmails me in the middle of a battle into keeping him with my Corps. Here's the Captain who cannot control his Company. Hell's blue brimstone, sir," he darted at Stowell, "how dared you send such a blasted insolent despatch to me?"

"It was not intended to be insolent, sir, but purely a statement of fact to aid you in basing a decision." The words were so close to being a paraphrase of what Gordon had meant when he had spoken of his Division that the erect Major General's lips quivered.

Early was too shrewd not to read the implied rebuke. His tone rose fiercely.

"It served its purpose then. It decided me that you were

171

thoroughly incompetent, Captain! How many deserters have you had already? You talk as if you're goddam used to them leaving you."

The Old Gentleman was fifteen years older than Early at a time when age enjoyed a certain veneration, and had been in the war long enough to lose any awe of a General that he might once have possessed. His own temper began to take fire, and his beard thrust forward to meet Early's.

"Not a goddam one, sir. And let me tell you this, that if they had left me, they wouldn't have run off, they'd have straggled to the front."

No American army has ever quite succeeded in turning itself into a machine, and the Confederate service was prone to speak its mind, but Brice held his breath. He expected Old Jube to explode into a court-martial at once, but Brice's own legal training showed him a way of escape, and he could not forebear taking it.

"We shall ask for a Court of Inquiry, sir."

Brice noticed Captain Stowell make a quick gesture for silence, but it was too late. Gordon, Pendleton and Douglas had all been looking uncomfortable, but the three of them and General Early were all staring at him now.

"And just who the devil are you?"

The high, sarcastic, furious voice struck at Brice's composure, but he was too intent and too angry to care. The slight had been on all of them.

"Lieutenant Brice of the Maryland Line, sir. I'm a lawyer and I tell you that I'll advise my . . ." he almost said "client," but changed it at the final instant . . . "Commanding Officer to ask for one. Our Battalion doesn't belong to your command. We heard at Charlottesville that it's Third Corps now. We'll have to report to them what happened."

A Lieutenant General of the old Army would at once have ordered him under arrest, but Jubal Early was a lawyer himself, with a quick perception sharpened by courtroom battles. Gordon and Douglas, both attorneys, grasped the implied threat as quickly. The request for a Court of Inquiry would go up through channels to General Lee. The story of that order would be read and commented upon by Captain Crane, a Brigadier, a Divisional Commander and a Corps Chief before it arrived at headquarters. Lieutenant General Ambrose Powell Hill was no particular friend of Early's and could be counted upon to look for an out if one could be found. The comic quality of the mistake would be enlarged upon and enjoyed until it sifted down to the lower ranks. Early was a proud, vain man, and to find himself a laughing-stock would be a deep wound.

He retreated agilely. "I have made no charges, young man. I need your Company as . . . as . . ." He hesitated while he tried to remember why I Company had been sent for in the first place. Gordon and the staff officers stared woodenly ahead, but their laughter was choking them. "Guides, curse it! Very well, I'll attach you to my Corps."

Catching Gordon's expression, he recovered his aplomb and with it his bitter sarcasm.

"General, since you have the ragtag and bobtail of the Army, I'll send them to your Division. You will devote yourself particularly to restoring their discipline. Judging by the insubordinate behavior of the Lieutenant here, they are no more than a rabble. Endorse their orders, Colonel Pendleton, and, Colonel, I'll see you later."

He jerked his head towards the door.

"Now, Captain, get out of my sight."

XVII

"TAKE arms!"

Hands tanned brown or brick-red reached to break up the neat stacks of rifles, and I Company fell in with its weapons.

"Bufford!" called Hammond inexorably. "You carry the spade."

The men relaxed from the position of attention. All of yesterday there had been hot debate, hope boiling in the kettle of their emotions. Could we win this war in spite of everything? Just supposin' we made a dash at Washington or Baltimore and took it, would they make peace?

Home Grown Smith had forgotten the others. He muttered to himself without regarding who heard:

"Lord, let me come to Thee at home."

Cabell, beside him in the ranks, looked out of the corner of his eye and raised the shield of his own voice.

"We could do it, I tell you so! They've lost a hell of a lot of men in the Wilderness and at Spotsylvania, and maybe Cold Harbor gave them their bellyful. There's an election coming up this fall. They must be getting tired of it. . . ."

"They sure ain't as tired as we are." Carney was taking the opposite side from force of habit. "There's so many of them they muster out whole regiments while we got to be told what a furlough is. . . ."

"What'd you do with a furlough even if you got one?" asked Niedlander caustically. "You ain't got nowhere to go."

There was a momentary silence, then Zollinger put their thoughts into words.

"Supposing we do win? Will Maryland be part of the Confederacy, or are we goin' to have to settle for the sacred soil of Virginia?"

"Oh, quit it," said Cabell wearily. "They don't all talk like that. Fellow in the Twenty-first Virginia was telling me yesterday how much they thought of us. Said they'd take care of us somehow."

"Offer you a job?" asked Watts, laughing.

"Matter of fact, he did. Said he'd see I was clerk of his county."

"Bet you he was a Private. Ain't nobody can talk as big as that 'cepting a Private."

"Don't you joke at Privates. They fetch up in surprising places."

Carney broke in again. "Better hold him to his promise. There ain't much more than ten thousand of us, and the Stowell young'un was sayin' they got mighty near that many just a-watchin' Baltimore from Federal Hill."

The veteran infantrymen could estimate numbers and odds as well as he could, and the reminder squeezed the humor and excitement out of them. They made no sound now, except when a restless shift of their feet brought a squeak of leather from the straps which held their equipment. They stared across the rolling fields, their hungry eyes watching the movement of the camps, the forming regiments. Staunton, too, had its hills. Betsy Bell and Mary Gray, lapdogs beside the Blue Ridge and the Alleghenies, drowsed near the town, and beneath them were the chalk marks of the radiating roads. The dust lay thick, for there had been no rain since that downpour which had caught I Company on the march. Jubal Early had reached a decision, the long roll and the bugles had heralded it to the dawn, the three days' rations in their haversacks, the forty rounds stuffed in their pockets had confirmed it, but the roads would declare it. Back to Charlottesville or north, down the Valley?

The fields were emptying, the troops, formation having been achieved, moved towards the gaps in the fences, the gates through the stone walls. Brice was hardly breathing; he strained to hear commands that the distance made inaudible. The fours came slowly to the road and then wheeled. . . .

High and shrill came a rebel yell from Matthews. "North! By God, they *are* headin' north!"

175

Burke, the veins of his forehead bulging, leaped across to Bufford and snatched the spade from his hands. He held it high above his head with a wild Irish cry.

"Here's your colors, boys. We planted 'em in Charlottesville, and we'll plant 'em in Washington and, begod, it'll be me that'll do the plantin' for you!"

The Twenty-first Virginia, a friendly regiment, shouldered its rifles at command and swung by, laughing at the flourished spade. Burke, all belligerence, shook it at them.

"Ye think it's funny, do you? We've made your backs sore too many times crawlin' over you to get at the bluebellies. I'm just tellin' you—get out of our way whenever you see this spade coming!"

The laughter stopped abruptly, flushed gentlemen of the Old Dominion began to fall out of ranks only to be shouted back into them by the Sergeants. "Sorebacks" had been coined by the North Carolina troops in retaliation for "Tarheels," and was a fighting word.

"Dry up, Burke!" drawled McComas. "Remember they're on our side."

"Attention—Company!"

Burke shouldered the spade, slung his rifle across his back and ran to his place in the ranks. Captain Stowell answered the appeal that the gesture made.

"Very well, Burke. We'll do it the way you want since our own colors are with the Battalion. And, Burke, live up to your boast, or I'll have a word with you."

General Gordon rode up to them on a handsome bay horse. With him was the Brigadier after whom the Brigade was named, General Terry. They pulled up beside Stowell, and Terry indicated I Company with a gesture.

"Here they are, General Gordon. The most independent pack of wolves in the goddamdest independent command in the Corps. I've got fourteen regiments with me, and not one of them will consolidate. They're damned if they'll consolidate, sir. They say they started off the war as Jackson's own Division of the Army of the Valley, and the most I've been able to do is persuade them to group themselves by their old Brigade units. They're the Stonewall and the Second and Third, although they're down to regimental strength and the regiments are companies. If that isn't problem enough, along come these Marylanders and are likewise damned in heaps if they'll merge themselves with anybody. They say their Battalion's at Petersburg, and they belong to that—troops of a different Corps, by God."

Gordon grinned down at Stowell's obstinate expression.

"Assuage yourself, Captain. There's no necessity for you to call your lawyer, I'll compromise. Sandie Pendleton told me your Battalion used to serve with what was the Third Brigade. If I leave you your separate identity, will you do it again?"

"Gladly, sir."

"You hear the offer, Terry. It relieves me that it's a peaceful one. You'd be wise to accept it, otherwise these Maryland Guerrillas may operate on their own."

"It's all right with me," said Terry, smiling. "I wasn't in the old Army, or I'd go stark mad. I've got a Brigade that's three Brigades in one, eight hundred men with fourteen flags and —what in hell is that thing?"

He pointed to the uplifted spade and to the twinkling Burke who was treating it with the grave reverence due the colors.

Stowell explained, and the Generals laughed so explosively that the horses curvetted.

"If I get through this war," said Terry, "I'll have no problem to find a profession. I shall open a lunatic asylum for the more violent cases only. Very well, Captain. That's your 'Brigade' passing now. Fall in behind it and tell Colonel Saunders that you'll cooperate with him. If he's puzzled, tell him I am equally so."

The Second Corps took the Valley Pike, the old road of Stonewall Jackson and of their own fame. Its organization was strong on paper—three Divisions, Gordon, Ramseur, Rodes, plus the demi-Division of Breckinridge—but they covered little space. The Confederacy was a descending curve, and the graph it drew was measured by manpower. There were no more resources to be tapped. Anything that was to be attempted must be done at once and with the means at hand.

The Foot Cavalry marched with a swinging stride and boasted that it could eventually break down any horse cav-

alry that tried to keep pace with it. The halts were ten minutes in each hour, the men lying flat on the dust-laden grass.

"Captain," said Brice, gazing ruefully at his shoes which
were showing definite signs of imminent dissolution, "suppose
this is only a raid to break up the railroad at Harpers Ferry.
The men are so full of hopes, I dread . . ."

"Calm yourself, Thomas." The Old Gentleman pillowed his
head on his elbow. "They won't be disappointed."

"How do you know, sir? Did General Gordon . . .?"

"No. You've heard every word he said to me. You ought to
read, my son, read a lot. I think I told you once that much
reading of strategy didn't help a Company officer. That's true
as far as it goes, but it sure helps him to gratify his curiosity."

He rubbed his brows free of the hard globules which had
been formed by a mixture of sweat and dust. His beard was
beyond such aid, but his smile thrust the laden hairs apart.

"I know because Jubal Early commands the Corps."

Brice was surprised, but he had learned that the Captain
usually had good reason when he expressed an opinion.

"That's right charitable, sir, but do you think we can do it?"

The Old Gentleman swung his haversack into place. The
halt was nearly over.

"If we're praying for a miracle, why begin by doubting it?
'The sword of the Lord and of Gideon.' A real professional
soldier would add up the odds and say it couldn't possibly be
done. That's why I think Marse Robert has picked on Old
Jubilee and not sent Anderson or A. P. Hill who think Army
style because they stayed in it. We've got an advantage—the
other professionals we face will double or triple our numbers
because they won't believe we'd try it with less. They'll scream
for reinforcements before they fight. Eventually it all boils
down to the Army of the Potomac."

"Hasn't it always?" Brice was looking sour. "Grant can ship
a couple of corps back by way of the James and the Potomac."

"That's why everything depends on speed. If we run into
them in force, we're finished."

The regiment ahead was forming ranks. Stowell clasped
holster and scabbard close to him and pushed himself to his
feet. "Fall in! Halt's over!"

The pillar of dust rose again over the heavy column, worse by far than when I Company had marched alone. The fields rolled backwards as the column tramped past, green-laden with grass and wheat, the little houses and the big barns like driftwood floating on the sea. Some farmers were doing well, their stock might be run off and their property looted, but the crops paid. Most of the Valley people, the small merchants, their families and the wives and children of the soldiers, did very badly, reduced to scavenging horsefeed from Federal camps to make cornbread or oatmeal. Such a woman stood wearily by a broken gate near Harrisonburg.

"Drive the Yankees out soon, boys," she called to the tramping regiments. "We can't stand it much longer."

XVIII

THE last days of the hot June burned themselves out in marching. July began with a monotonous evenness of pace and weather. There was no relief from the blazing dry spell, from the potholed, powdered progression of the Valley Pike. The Second Corps was averaging twenty miles a day, and the creatures of its dust suffered accordingly. The particles hung like a sea fog, but warm and gritty with the land, erasing the marks and settling in their lungs—even a man on the windward side of the column could see only the top of Massanutton's ridge like a green-cliffed island upon their right.

Home Grown Smith breathed the poison through his lolling mouth. The dark stain of it mingled with the bright blood in his sputum. His messmates shared his rifle between them, taking it without resistance on his part. His pride was gone, buried under the destroying dust like the fever flush on his cheeks. His mind too was failing as the disease took hold. His doubts and fears had been swallowed up by an illogical belief —if he got home, his present torture would be over forever. Sometimes he muttered at night, shivering beside a fire, talking of a bed with clean white sheets in a sun-bright room, the hands of his mother on his forehead. The Company, its disputation and expansiveness brought within bounds by the astringent of pity, saw to it spontaneously that the doubters did not express themselves within earshot. The Surgeon of the Thirty-seventh Virginia, summoned by Stowell for a look, had made an expressive gesture.

Although they were near the head of the Corps, they were far enough back to get their share of the jerky advance which made a nightmare of the rearguard. There could be no smoothness in the march of so large a body. After any halt, the column got under way with a shuddering jerk like a heavy train starting. Let a company delay for a moment in taking its place, let a battery stop to readjust harness, and the effect became cumulative on the following formations. They doubled or they crawled alternately. Nor was it easy to maintain discipline. In the dust and the mass of troops, individuals could not be watched. Men fell out to drink at every stream or well, to gather berries or roasting ears. Rations were being issued, but their bodies were impatient at salt pork and cornbread. Most of them would run to catch up, the juices making channels from the corners of their lips, but some fell behind and stayed behind. Hubbard was one. He was missing at night rollcall and still missing in the morning, a deadbeat, a beggar, a professional straggler and a menace to lonely women on lonely farms.

Murray Stowell kept in ranks. The dust had reddened his eyes and puffed his lids. It lay in shelves on the creases of his baggy trousers, but each night he answered to his name when they fell out to camp. Yet he received none of the affectionate attentions which his messmates had showered upon Raby. In his own way he was equally forlorn, but he was so preoccupied with his personal discomfort and unhappiness that he was sullenly oblivious to the others. He had resented the half-friendly jeers at the story of his involuntarily loaded rifle and had blighted even that beginning of interest. Had he seen the humor of the affair and accepted the teasing, or had he offered just once to perform a camp chore beyond the minimum which his mess demanded of him, he might have begun to breach the dislike which surrounded him. He did not whine, but neither did he thaw, and even the goodhearted Niedlander had begun to return his coldness. It was a young Company. Sergeant Hammond at twenty-seven was its graybeard after the Captain, and therefore it was intolerant. He was dismissed contemptuously. The men were too absorbed with the northward march and its implications to pay him much attention. Who cared about a crazy kid; weren't they going to Baltimore?

Brice managed to spare time enough to worry about him.

Yet he felt helpless, felt that their verbal skirmish had closed the door to confidence. Being honest in his interpretation, he did not realize that paradoxically he had gained the boy's respect. Murray was divided between hate and self-pity. In the first was included his father and the Company as a whole; like most of those who carry the dislike of military service from the impersonal to the personal, he did not understand the necessity of a partial surrender of self to fit the wryed pattern of war. But in his eyes Brice was different from the others. Firm and decided in manner, so assured where the youngster was not, he had set himself apart when he had complimented Murray on his stand against the stragglers. Sixteen finds a need for an example to set before it, though the choice may be good or bad. Brice's influence on him might be slight, it was too early in their acquaintance for any quickly given trust, but at least in his presence Murray Stowell bore himself like a soldier, not like a spoiled child.

Somewhere north of Mount Jackson, Brice limped out of the column. The leather of the brogans was so dry and cracked that pebbles worked into them as if he were wearing sandals. The noon halt was due very soon, but the discomfort was so acute that it demanded immediate relief. He made for the bordering wall and sat on it, feeling the reflected heat of the sun-beaten stone through the cloth of his trousers. Holding his shoes upside down, he shook them with care, afraid that even the motion might separate them further, and then put them on as if the operation were as delicate as adjusting a watch. Even the decrepit laces must be handled gingerly, for they were almost worn through. While the hazy files tramped past, he spat and blew his nose, a necessary preliminary after five hours in the cloud, then breathed deeply. His mouth was dry and furry, and he decided he could allow himself a few swallows of the hoarded water in his canteen. He tilted it to his lips and let the warm flat liquid trickle down his throat, then, as his eyes roved, came to a quick alert. A lane joined the Pike at an obtuse angle and on it was a long, trailing swirl of dust, hanging low and impenetrable, but the blur at its head was high and ghostly like men on horseback.

"What do you make of it, Lieutenant?"

A black gelding rattled its curbchain beside him. On it was an officer in a tall hat, the face under it framed in short, grizzled whiskers and as gray-masked as his own.

The hat gave him the clue immediately. "Cavalry, I think, Colonel Nelson," he reported, recognizing the elderly artillery commander of Charlottesville. "They might be Federals."

"I'm of the same mind as you. No sense in taking any chances. I'll arrange a little reception for them before they get too close. Double forward if you please and ask for some infantry support. I'm going to unlimber my leading battery. Doesn't look like more than a brigade of them."

Every unit masked itself in dust on these Virginia roads. In the windless day the dispersion was slow, and they must guess at what it concealed and judge the numbers by the length.

Brice ran; the Colonel shouted orders.

"Captain Kirkpatrick, left into battery in that field."

Gunners jumped from the limbers and set to work at the wall with pick and crowbar. I Company halted, wheeled and took shelter behind it, its rifles resting along the top. The Thirty-seventh Virginia formed on the right. As they completed their line of battle, the first twelve-pounder bounced through the opening, the iron tires throwing up sparks from the scattered stones. The dust cloud, however, continued its undaunted approach.

"They're goddam ambitious for Yanks," said Captain Stowell suspiciously. "I wonder . . ."

Brice judged the distance and thought it too short to use up in speculation.

"Shall we load, sir?" he asked fretfully, cursing the custom of large formations to march with their rifles empty. The dust cloud was in an almighty hurry. Two volleys would be a help, but three would certainly knock those bluebellies out of their saddles. If there was a longer delay, there wouldn't be time to get them in.

Kirkpatrick's leading piece was nearly ready for action. The gunners had opened the lid of the limber chest and were handing out shell and powder bag, the rammerman was poised. Colonel Nelson was standing in his stirrups and using a field glass, Now he let his hand drop.

"All right, Captain. Limber up again. It's just Mrs. Gordon."

The rear of the cloud was dispersing at last to reveal emptiness. The blur at the head of it was becoming distinct. The cause of the commotion was at last plainly visible—a small carriage drawn by a galloping pair with a small black boy on the box. Kirkpatrick's drivers reined hard on the horses, and the gunners laughed and lifted the trail of the second gun which they had just dropped to the ground.

A grinning artilleryman called to I Company, "It's the General's wife. Lord, she sure flushed plenty of birds this time."

I Company was both amused and interested. Mrs. Gordon was popular with the whole Army; everybody had heard of her. A sweet and gentle lady, she had the courage of a lioness and had defeated even General Lee in his efforts to send her to the rear. She followed her husband faithfully, watched the smoke of his battles, and had received him gallantly at the dressing station when he had been carried badly wounded from the field of Sharpsburg. As an additional recommendation she was a stranger to Army politics.

The Thirty-seventh Virginia fell in, guns and caissons wheeled with a flourish and went back through the gap. The carriage followed them with Colonel Nelson riding beside it, bareheaded. A lovely though begrimed face was thrust through the window.

"I'm so sorry, Colonel. I'm afraid I've disturbed you all. Put on your hat please. It's too hot to be polite. I was smothering back with the wagons and turned off to get some fresh air."

She began to plead as they ranged beside I Company, resuming its march formation.

"Please don't mention this if you can help it to my husband or General Early. I'm having trouble enough with both of them as it is."

Nelson beamed, but his voice held a mild rebuke. "So I understand. In fact Old Jube was saying in my hearing that if his men kept up as well as you did, he'd never have to issue another order against straggling."

"But that's a compliment! At least I'll choose to call it so whatever way he really meant it. May I come along with your

184

Battalion? I promise faithfully that I'll go back to the train tonight. It's just that I can't stand the dust."

The Colonel accepted at once.

"I don't know that you'll escape much even this far forward, but you're surely welcome. At least having you with us will make us less nervous. Now there I am using as much double meaning as General Early! But I'm ashamed of you, lathering your horses in weather like this."

Mrs. Gordon laughed. "I saw some Yankee cavalry over yonder. Just a scouting party, but I didn't want their company."

The Marylanders were following the Virginians, but her words came after them.

"I reckon General Gordon ought to be told. Still I'd feel much better if you'd do it instead of me. And, Colonel, could you maybe just say that you'd had a report about them and not say who from? He gets so nervous sometimes about me, and I dread being chased back to those wagons by an angry husband. I'm only going as far as Winchester. . . ."

I Company moved off, but Brice knew that that chance remark would cause another upsurge in speculation. Nor was he wrong: it was mouthed over and debated the rest of the day, and when they fell out by the roadside that night. Winchester was the key to the lower Valley, the hub from which stretched the Potomac routes. "Only as far as . . ." That argued that they were going further, and across the river was Maryland. Professional doubters like Carney were howled down, and the excitement grew when the Captain deliberately accepted the proffered baits and announced his opinion. Washington, crowed the optimists, you all heard what the Old Gentleman said, that's only two marches from Baltimore, and, by God, if they leave it to us, we'll do it in one. The faint-hearts renewed their courage; even Henderson, silent in anticipatory dread, grew haggardly gay. There'd be a battle, of course, there had to be one. The Yanks weren't going to let them walk right in and tour the Capitol, but it was better not to dwell on the thought, not to wonder who wouldn't make Baltimore after these bitter years. They formed their hope into a ball and packed their misgivings inside it, rolling it along the Valley Pike.

There were other Marylanders in the Second Corps, the cavalry and artillery of the Maryland Line and individuals or companies in Virginia regiments. The chance encounters between them were noisily happy, men from the same town or county swapping familiar memories. Even the Old Gentleman was moved to remind Brice of Guy's Hotel on Baltimore Street.

"Do you recall the bar and the oyster saloon in the basement next to the kitchen? I used to eat there noontimes and scuff my feet in the sawdust on the floor. Sometimes it had a pretty awful mixture of smells, particularly if they had cabbage on the bill of fare, but I'm right willing to forget that and remember only the oysters and whiskey. . . ."

"Whiskey with oysters?" Brice remonstrated. "I love them with beer, but I always thought the rye cooked the oysters in your stomach."

"Next time pour in the whiskey first, then throw in the oysters on top of it. Makes the nicest oyster fry inside you that you ever felt. We'll try it together."

The column poured yelling through Winchester, the band of the Stonewall Brigade tooting "Dixie" with breathless enthusiasm and the people shouting or running into the ranks for a moment's greeting. They were as much veterans as were the soldiers. They had known the color of the uniforms in the streets to change between morning and evening, knew the full roar of battle from the outskirts, knew bullets rapping into houses, knew the shells bursting upstairs while they crouched in the cellars, knew the bloody wounded and the wail of the dead march. It was hard to be from harried Winchester in this war, hardest if you were a soldier or belonged to a soldier's family. When they met as now, the rare sight of each other glinted with high emotion like sunshine through a crack in the wall of separation. The men must sum up at a single glance the hungry, wan expressions, the makeshift clothes, the feeble efforts to maintain a home—the women must assimilate as quickly the same wastedness as the regiments passed without halting or hear the news of death or wounds, sickness or captivity from a dusty, sweating Rebel, too hurried to soften the impact. The infantry listened with respect to the calls from the sidewalk.

"The Yanks pulled out yesterday, boys. There's some at Martinsburg and a whole slew at Harpers Ferry."

They halted for the night at Middletown Mills, well blown and dog-weary, but the grape came around that there'd be a fight tomorrow. Martinsburg, twenty-five miles away, was on the Baltimore & Ohio main line west from Harpers Ferry. The passenger trains would have stopped running by now. People of importance or self-importance would be inconvenienced. Senator This or The Honorable That would need more than influence to carry them through with the Foot Cavalry in the lower Valley. Freight trains would be blocked at either end of the division, produce of mines, produce of agriculture, of forests and factories held up, even the agitated telegrams throttled off the wire by military messages. The mail would be rerouted, only the troop trains would be moving. The disruption of commerce would come home to as many people as would the news of a battle. Merchants and bankers would rattle their newspapers and ask what Lincoln was doing about it, what the Army was going to do.

The Second Corps slept in the fields beside the Pike, cooked its breakfast and advanced. The uninviting prospect of twenty-five miles with a fight at the end of it hushed the column, brought the reassumption of what had been shed when they had left the Cold Harbor trenches. I Company had described a long right angle out of one hell and knew that it would sooner or later be pitchforked into another one.

In the afternoon there came a far-off wham that was taken up irregularly as if a drummer were trying out a soft drumhead. As the sounds travelled through the breathless heat, Brice felt a vicarious reaction born from the memory of closer firing, the same feeling as if the air rippled with each report. His stomach contracted as it always did. There might be some who escaped the nervous spasms, but he didn't believe that there were.

"Tollgate keeper banging the bar down," said McComas, wetting his lips. "Thank the Lord we ain't got to pay yet."

The speed of the march increased, the firing became more distinct. Under the flat grumbling of the artillery came the patter of small arms, interspersed with a rapid crackle that made even the most experienced look puzzled.

"What the hell's *that?*" asked Niedlander aloud, and a wounded cavalryman, walking his horse to the rear and nursing a dripping forearm, answered him.

"Spencers, seven-shot carbines. Little stingy guns, new. Yanks load them on Sunday, and they shoot the rest of the week."

Magazine carbines, thought Brice, so they've come at last. We'll never get them; we can't make them nor the cartridges for them. Heard that in Richmond. No machinery and no brass. Wonder why they didn't have them before? The Prussians had breechloaders as early as '48. God bless the Ordnance Department of the United States Army. If it had functioned right, we'd have been licked by now. But if they've got Spencers, we've damn well got to get into Washington before their infantry gets magazines too.

"Halt!"

The column stopped quickly.

"Watch what you're doing, will you? You've skun my heel with your goddam feet."

The colors were being uncased, the red battle flags drooped from the staffs. Burke stepped forward sturdily and raised the spade, resting the butt against his belt. Men reached into their pockets for cartridges and caps. The next order would be to load.

But it did not come. Instead, there were joyous howls from the leading files.

"They've skedaddled! Saw our infantry and decided that Martinsburg was played out. You ain't got no fight. Now ain't that just *too* bad?"

The silent strain broke.

"Suits me right down to the ground," said Watts. "I ain't mad at nobody."

Relaxed and easy, I Company resumed the march, catching up with the wreckage from the fight, dead men and horses in the road and in the fields, the clinging smell of powder, four men lugging a fifth on a blanket stretched between fence rails. Brice looked at Murray Stowell. The others might be hardened by harsh familiarity, but he was not. The most he had probably seen of violent death was perhaps a casualty from a runaway back in Baltimore. Here he had a selection of horror spread about him. Then came a shout from Zollinger.

"Hey, I know that feller! By God, he's in the Baltimore Light Artillery."

A dead cannoneer was spread-eagled beside the road as if he had been pitchforked into the air to land on his back.

"Sure it's us!" said a weak voice. A blackened, pain-drawn face looked at them from under a blanket. "Anybody happen to have any water?"

Half a dozen canteens were unslung and offered him. He emptied the first with greedy haste and apologized.

"Reckon I was too thirsty for manners. Can I keep another? I'm mighty dry. They left me here, but they're sending the battery wagon for me. No, I ain't hit bad, but it's queer, I feel cold all over. Right smart of a fight. They got them goddam Spencers, and some of our boys, Marylanders at that, pelted back along the Pike. Lieutenant McNulty got into battery here and just before I got hit, he was yelling, 'Get your runaway cavalry out of my way, and I'll let into them.' Reckon he did, 'cause after our boys picked me up they went on down the road. Remind 'em I'm here, will you?"

The Old Gentleman handed him his canteen. "We won't forget," he promised. "Step out now, we're blocking the column."

A hundred yards farther and they came upon the effect of McNulty's canister blasts, a tangle of mangled men and horses in a stiffening pool of blood and a humming cloud of bluebottles. A detail of Rebels was clearing the Pike. They had carried the wounded into the feeble shade of the stone wall, a row of men in faded blue. The worst hurt lay on their sides or their stomachs, cheeks pressed against the dried and trampled grass; the others talked jerkily among themselves or watched the dead being tumbled casually together in the ditch opposite.

"Break ranks or cut into the fields, sir," advised a sweating Sergeant, heaving at the stiffening leg of a horse. "Be a while yet before we can get these carcasses out of the way. They're almighty heavy."

I Company swung right where a panel of rails had been

thrown down by the preceding Regiment. On impulse, Brice strode over to a horse which still made feeble efforts to raise its head. Drawing his Colt, he stooped over, pointed the .44 between the ears and fired.

"Bet he never seen that either," said McComas, gesturing towards Murray Stowell. He took the boy's arm. "Put your finger down your throat and lose it," he advised. "You'll feel better afterwards."

It was still light in the camp beyond Martinsburg when a fuming mail rider arrived.

"Got a letter for Lieutenant Thomas Brice," he announced. "Had a hell of a time finding you. Next time tell your people to put the division on the address—or tell the lady. It looks like a woman writ it."

The men were grinning, only Cabell looked downcast. They were certain of the sender, for only Charlotte Talcott knew where they were. All other mail still went to the Battalion at Petersburg.

"She got a message for us?" called Matthews, but Niedlander squelched him.

"Be careful, youngster," he drawled. "Young love can put a blight on you—particularly if it's an officer."

Brice skimmed the brief note. Raby was improved with a discharge in prospect, a hope better than any medicine. She was sorry she had not seen them march out, but there had been a bad case in the hospital, and they had sent for her during the night. These were only preliminaries. The paragraph he sought came at the end.

"Maybe I'm just being afraid," she wrote, "but if that's my reason, I'm not brave yet. I can only say this—if you come back to me, you won't have to start from the beginning."

He put the letter in his inside pocket and told them about Raby.

XIX

THE Federal War Department's daily communiqué usually included a reassuring phrase in such familiar terms that it had begun to be quoted outside its context. It was read and accepted as part of the normal breakfast routine, a certification of safety that poured balm over the cities like maple syrup over hotcakes. Newspaper editors watched for it and held open a column on page one if it were absent, banks and brokers let it affect their quotations on gold or government securities. This day the filaments of alarm were quivering, all was not quiet along the Potomac. Harpers Ferry, said the despatches, had been evacuated. The Rebels were moving east in force.

The garrison of the town had scurried up Maryland Heights. There were fixed defenses there, thick earthworks revetted with gabions and fascines, covered in front with ditch, abatis and chevaux-de-frise. Tall lookout towers with platforms atop held observers with telescopes who studied the groves, the ravines and the hillocks where there were glimpses of men in butternut, then swept on to view the roads across the valleys. "Heavy skirmish lines here, but the main body of the rebels not yet in sight," was the report a tired courier brought to the B & O railhead where it was at once telegraphed to Washington. The observers expected to see more, needed to see more and, as Stowell had predicted, did not believe the truth. The whole of the Second Corps was before them, preparing to sidestep under the cover of darkness and cross the next natural obstacle, South Mountain.

The two-deep line of battle which was Gordon's Division had no intention of assaulting. Instead, the infantry lay on their stomachs, sat or squatted, and watched the gray-brown works, ribbed with the earth-filled wicker baskets, which decked themselves with pompons of dirty white smoke. Their own batteries were sending over a few shells which burst flashingly or threw up sprays of dirt as they ploughed into the face. Skirmishers popped halfheartedly at each other between the lines, but there was no feel of impending action. There had been a minor fuss over on the left a while ago, a tentative and hesitant sortie, but that had subsided. The clusters of men who were gathered behind every rise or fallen tree, the squads who sheltered in the depressions, were unconcerned. The tactical texts still demanded that a containing force such as this should be formed in mass and dignity, shoulder to shoulder, but then formal military thought always lagged well behind the front line. The universal belief of those more practical thinkers was that to survive "it was necessary to take judicious advantage of the shrubbery," and the Division twisted its front like a ram's horn to avoid making a target.

I Company was living up to the maxim in a new growth of hickory, interspersed with large and comforting stumps. Brice had selected a thick one and was resting behind it as well as he could under the persistent attacks of a force of red ants which were exploring his trouser legs. He would galvanize himself into action with a slap and a curse, then relax into a partially dreamy state enjoying the shade and harkening to the roaring echoes which the mountains provided for each shot. Since they were not being molested by the Federal artillery, many of the men were actually dozing. Either a sense of duty, the ants, or the discomfort from his bare feet (for the brogans had at last met their fate) kept his eyes partially open while his mind sketchily reviewed the last few days.

Memory is at once a sedative and an irritant, a crown and a cross. What was done or failed to be done at the time of happening must eventually be faced with a certain element of volition; may call for either repentence or justification, that easy road to hell which is travelled with arrogant assurance or logical explanation. Yet, particularly in time of war, there are some recurrent pictures which completely lack even a second-hand assessment, the visitation of hideousness such as young Murray Stowell had seen for the first time in that iconoclasm of God's image on the Valley Pike. These dark pits could only be skirted, not faced directly. Turn away the eyes, forget deliberately, or hope that time would wash them out. The ripped bodies, the congealing blood, the avid flies, were as vivid to

Brice as they undoubtedly were to the boy, but he made a thick mental brush-stroke over them, obliterating the sight as well as he could with the fresher experience of the Potomac crossing.

They had stripped to wade Boteler's Ford, clothes and shoes made into a bundle and carried on their shoulders. Naked as frogs, they looked at each other and laughed, making the inevitable ribald comments. The officers might have been fair game for "slaunchways" remarks, but the Old Gentleman retained both his dignity and a pair of ragged drawers, and the plaguingly critical glances at Brice had checked at the wheal of the bullet scar.

"Through the bowels! Lord Jesus, how'd he live?" a voice had whispered in carrying astonishment.

"So that's where they hit him at Gaines's Mill! Wasn't it Carney said he'd been hangin' around with the bombproofs?"

"Knew a Virginian from Chesterfield who got struck there. Only one I ever heard of before that came through it."

Murray Stowell's mouth was open, his gaze was fascinated. That was the sign when Death had nicked with his scythe but missed the full stroke. Brice could see the question frame itself in the boy's mind: Had it hurt? The absurd but natural expression of his dread.

They splashed across with laughter that changed to howls of pain as they encountered an underwater ridge of rock that was coated with marine shells, sharp and painful even to the most hardened soles. Glistening and streaming, they had mounted the farther bank only to fall as silent as if they had been universally gagged. This was Maryland, the warm dirt under their feet. Their status was changed. No longer were they strangers but welcoming their own allies on their own soil. On the way to Gettysburg they had shouted and even rolled on the ground, but the year between had concentrated their emotion, pressed it too deeply into them for demonstration. The Army of Northern Virginia on the march for Pennsylvania had not had the foreboding of the Second Corps on its way to Washington. They had gone up against the Philistines, and too many of their best had been slain on the high places—Culp's Hill, for one.

They had begun to dress, an uncomfortable process involving sweat-soaked clothes and river-wet bodies while the ford resounded with more splashes and yells, Nelson's Battalion of artillery crossing, the old Colonel in full panoply since he was mounted, leading across his naked cannoneers. Brice pulled on his coat and was sent almost sprawling by a heavy collision.

"Sorry," exclaimed McComas in hasty apology, then shouted, "Get ahold of them. Quit it, you kids!"

Murray Stowell and Matthews were flailing into each other with flying fists, their youthful bodies intertwining, their faces red with blubbering rage. The surprised men stared at them, then Niedlander swung Murray from his feet, and McComas yanked Matthews back by the collar of his shirt.

"Quit it, I said."

Matthews was too angry to subside even under that strong grip. "You goddam little puke!" he blurted to Murray. "Quit your bellerin'. If you're too good for us, why in hell don't you go home?"

McComas was bending his arm back in a hammerlock, and Sergeant Hammond was using his quarterdeck tone.

"Shut up, Matthews!"

Brice took a quick look over his shoulder. Captain Stowell had gone down to the bank to speak to Colonel Nelson. He hadn't heard.

"Just a couple of young'uns gettin' their exercise, sir," reported the First Sergeant. "No call to bring them before the Old Gentleman."

"Of course not," said Brice, his tongue in his cheek. The occasional fights which were bound to break out from too close association were usually concealed from the officers, and Sergeant Hammond's mendacious excuse had given him the chance not to interfere. Experience can modify the Articles of War more effectively than a General Order. It was better for Murray to have the Company's opinions beaten into him by the fists of a boy near his own age than to suffer the punishment ordained for fighting and inflicted by his father as the judge.

But what a black eye, what a beautiful black eye young Stowell had developed, thought Brice behind the stump on Maryland Heights and still slapping at ants. He could see it blooming, swollen and discolored, no further away than a fallen tree behind which Murray was sitting, his legs straight out in front of him. It was as conspicuous as those Yankee earthworks, but it was being carefully ignored.

A whistling hiss sent him grovelling behind the stump in an instinctive, war-developed reaction. A shell passed overhead and burst deeper in the grove, branches and leaves showering down to the whir and thud of iron particles rapping the trunks and the ground. The reverberation of the explosion slapped I Company's collective consciousness into a brief palpitation of activity. They crouched close in cover, the sleepers' eyes snapping open, betraying, naked and unconcealed, the terror of the first awakening, then changing to anger and surprise as their wits took over from their instinct. They drew their legs up under them, shaped their bodies to their shelter. Abbott, who had rolled into a patch of cooler shade, scrambled on all fours behind a boulder. As the shells continued to come, they endured stoically, motionless, with clenched teeth. They had no chance of retaliation, no chance of anticipating the regular screech and crash by making a comforting noise of their own, since their rifles would not reach the gunners. There was only a single piece firing, though a persistent one, and since it was being worked from a deep embrasure with poor traverse, most of the shells fell in their sector. By good luck, however, the Federals had either overestimated the range or thought there was a Rebel formation deeper in the timber, and their only danger was from shots which fell short.

The experienced veterans knew the military facts, which gave them some reassurance, but it did not give them any rash confidence. Some fool gunner over there might cut his fuse too short and land a shell among them to do as much damage as half a dozen deliberately aimed ones. Each individual missile was listened for, the noise of its arrival was analyzed with nerve-racking uncertainty, the stomach convulsed itself, the body poured off ill-smelling moisture if the sound seemed shriller or lower, differing in any degree from the last miss. The crashing explosion was a relief, but it was succeeded by a quivering pause as the piece was reloaded. The Old Gentleman had sent Cabell to the Brigade Commander with a request for artillery retaliation (what in hell were those goddam gunners doin', sittin' on their rumps and watching the bluebellies have target practice?), and Cabell's dodging departure was followed with envy. The black powder smoke reeked, driving away the normal smells and leaving only itself and those of their shrinking bodies.

Brice had begun to watch the men. He was no braver, if as brave, as a dozen of those under his command, but he had a compulsion that most of them did not, the responsibility for their well-being. The private soldier is free of many of the anxieties which afflict even a good Corporal, but in a situation like this he is at a disadvantage. Unless he creates a responsibility of his own, he has nothing to do but think of himself, to let the dread grow and fester without a counter-irritant. There may be nothing that the officer can accomplish, but he can at least vicariously spread his anxiety beyond his personal entity.

Henderson was flat on his face, his mouth drooling, his body quivering with each crash. Murray Stowell's eyes rolled in his head as if he could see each shell when it came, when it passed and when it disintegrated. Brice began to crawl towards him when the Old Gentleman's voice came through the grove, steady and calm.

"Matthews, Henderson, Stowell, German Smith, come over here, boys."

He was sitting in a little hollow, Watts crouching near him, and the briar pipe was sending up a curl of smoke. As he repeated the names, Matthews and German Smith slid over the lip, and Brice shook Murray's shoulder.

"Captain wants you," he said too loudly to suit himself, and repeated in a more normal tone, "Better go and see what he's after."

The boy started up, took his rifle in a shaking hand and doubled across, Brice following him more slowly. Henderson, his legs barely under control, passed, his face red from the slap which Hammond had given him.

"Hated to do it," growled the Sergeant, stepping behind a tree, "but I told him three times an' he didn't even hear me."

The Captain motioned them to sit down. "You can smoke if you want," he said. "You too, Matthews. I've seen you puffing on that thing you call a pipe, but you might try a better tobacco. If it *was* tobacco you were burning." He tossed over his pouch.

The hiss and bang of another shell made Matthews fumble the catch, but the Old Gentleman merely waited until the sound had died and began to talk.

"Bufford's mighty bitter, has been ever since we tore up the Baltimore & Ohio tracks. Said he'd ridden this division of the road as a railroad man and couldn't help wondering what would happen if a train went into the ditch. Might be one of his old friends running the engine. I told him that he was getting his professions mixed and to keep them apart while he was with us."

He had caught their attention with his inconsequential remark. Even Henderson was looking at him and not thinking of shells. Watts caught his purpose quicker than did Brice. His loose, sensual, cheerful face lost a little of its strain.

"Going to be hard on the railroads after this war," he said, first with the same loudness which had afflicted Brice and then with a self-conscious drop. "Too many of us and too many Yanks have learned how to knock loose a tie bar. If the train won't stop for you between stations, you just takes a rail out and builds you a fire. That stops 'em for sure. Then, if they don't let you ride free, you heats the rail and bends it. We might set up for a gang of train robbers."

Brice now had caught his cue. "We got more grievances, sir. Burke claims that Sergeant Hammond made him desecrate the flag."

"I hadn't heard of that," said the Old Gentleman gravely. "It's a weighty charge."

"Hammond was looking for the spade to dig out a culvert and found Burke leaning virtuously on it. Said he was now the color-bearer and he sure didn't intend to use the temporary colors of the Maryland Line to throw dirt with."

"Offshore Gus was stumped for a minute," said Watts. "He was breathin' through his gills like a fish."

German Smith laughed shakily even though another shell was passing. "He busted the two of them on the spot. It was Private Burke and the spade when he was through with 'em."

"What's the matter, Matthews?" asked the Captain. "Don't you like my tobacco?"

Matthews was scrutinizing the dying fire in his pipe, he had not sucked at the stem for the past minute.

197

"I'm enjoyin' the flavor, sir. It's mighty full and fine."

Cabell arrived panting, stumbled at the edge of the dip and slid down on the seat of his pants.

"Right informal way of reporting," remarked Brice, and realized with the words how much the distraction of the Old Gentleman's calmness had quieted his own nerves.

Cabell grinned. "Colonel Nelson's managed to get a section of the Albemarle Artillery into position. Ought to hear from 'em any minute."

"That's a relief," said the Captain, and knocked out his pipe with a deep chuckle. "Better knock yours out too, Matthews. Funny how foul a pipe tastes when you'd sooner be hunting a nice deep hole."

It was an admission in the form of a confidence and yet one which encouraged them all. It made Captain Stowell a sharer in their own experience, removed him from an Olympian detachment. From a man without nerves he became an example of how to control them.

The mountains rumbled back the echoes of two quick reports, and Brice, parting the bushes on the front of the rise, saw the flash and geyser of the shells striking the embrasure.

"Albemarle boys have started remonstrating with those sleep-disturbers. Just like throwing a shoe at a squalling cat on the back fence. The Yanks will shut up before long. They can't slew the gun around enough to answer."

The Captain looked for himself.

"They're hunting cover already. Well, you all better get back and try to snatch a nap. We're moving out after dark and heading for South Mountain. Watts, tell Sergeant Hammond so. Stowell, wait here a minute."

The group broke up. As Brice scrambled out of the depression he heard the Old Gentleman ask, "Well, son, how are things going?" and felt a twinge of emotion at the inflection of the word. "Son" was a common enough term when an older man talked to a youngster, but it seldom carried with it the depth of feeling he had caught.

The talk did not last long. Brice was picking a briar out of the sole of his bare foot when Murray subsided again behind the fallen tree. Covertly he watched the boy's face and was disappointed in what he saw. On impulse he walked over to him and squatted down.

"When are you going to grow up?" he demanded abruptly. "When are you going to try to realize that we're trying to help you, and you won't be helped?"

Possibly the father had touched upon the same chord. Murray reacted with what was now a familiar outburst of sullen anger.

"Don't you preach at me either! I'm doing my best, and nobody sees so."

Brice put his head down close to the boy's ear.

"You're doing your best? Well, it's a mighty puny one. You won't help your messmates, you won't be friendly, you try and answer me back with excuses when all I'm asking you to do is begin to think for yourself. Trouble with you is, you've been woman-raised and you see your own importance through a woman's eyes. If there were older men at home, they couldn't talk to you because they've no more knowledge of this we're going through than what they can get out of the newspapers. Even if there was somebody, you wouldn't listen. I don't blame you for that because every kid has to have his own ideas, I reckon, and to hell with advice. But their opinions and the women's opinions don't carry over into the Army. That's the last place left where men set their own standards. The only thing a mother can do for a youngster is to train him to be decent and unselfish, and most of them do it fine. The rest of it is what you make yourself, a soldier or a deadbeat. Whatever we are we've made of ourselves, every one of us."

He got up abruptly and went back to his stump, raging at his own futility. He considered himself a mighty poor substitute for the Old Gentleman. Brice felt that had the latter not been handcuffed by circumstance, he might have handled it differently and a whole lot better. Apparently a man who could not be a father to his son couldn't train another to act in his stead.

A little later he stole a look at the boy. Murray had his face buried on his arm laid across the top of a log.

Crying, I bet you, thought Brice. Now has he begun to see the light or is he just a mite sorrier for himself, which is perfectly possible?

XX

NIGHT march to Norristown, day march up and over Fox Gap and an entry into familiarity. They had wakened from bivouac in recognizable surroundings, and a few were finding landmarks. The Army was learning the country with the slow thoroughness of those who must travel on foot. It was beginning to sense the subtle dissimilarity in the blending civilizations that defy the easy labels of North and South, East and West, but constitute a patchwork beneath them. There were variations that ignored political boundaries, the Chickahominy differed from the Valley almost as definitely as did the Dutch colonies in southern Pennsylvania. On the western slope of South Mountain, the Shenandoah way of life reproduced itself with only a northing of language, the pronunciation of words more distinct, the tone harder. On this side there was a separate individuality, a contrast even to Virginia, though only the Potomac flowed between. These Maryland farmhouses were more substantial, built mostly of stone instead of wood, with bigger barns and wider fields, the timber less prominent. There were fewer gems of architecture, since the state's great houses tended to concentrate nearer to the Chesapeake, but the roads were better surfaced for heavier traffic. This was the broad plateau that rolled in beauty to the breaks above the Bay and the slow rivers which flowed into it.

Some of these folks are glad to see us, thought Brice, some of them are sorry, but the farther east we get the more there are who are glad. Western Maryland's pretty strongly Union, but we're coming into border country now. That pretty girl in the pink dress was waving a Rebel flag at us. She and the dress both looked fresh and rustley—she bought it new somewhere, hadn't had to make it or convert it. A good many people had brought out provisions and distributed them freely, those that didn't had to provide some anyway; soldiers were always hungry. There was a woman back a ways who had complained to him that she'd lost a whole week's baking of bread and was loudly indignant about it. Wonder how she'd have felt if they'd cleaned her out like he'd seen in Hanover County? Might have made her speechless, which would have been an advantage. Their only real losses, outside of their pantries, lay in horses. The Quartermasters were pressing those for Confederate money. He knew that it was necessary, but he felt more than a twinge of sympathy to see the big farm teams taken and hear the youngsters crying when some pet was drafted into the Army.

The column was hurrying again, but there wasn't much dust. It did not lie as thickly because of the crushed stone. The ruts were not as deep, didn't spout a cloud as the wheels rolled through them. Lucky they'd had that issue of shoes at Norristown, that's what General Early had been waiting for. He looked down at his newly shod feet with a mixture of relief and apprehension. The leather was stiff and chafing, but the heavy soles repulsed the diamond points of rock which had made a torture of the route from Boteler's Ford to where the Quartermasters had at last showered down. Of course, there hadn't been enough to go round, there never was any more, though he and Duvall had both been fitted. It had made them complete again, but Brice had not been able to escape the brooding thought that the delay had helped Grant also. While they had demonstrated before Maryland Heights, paddle wheels and propellers had frothed the rivers carrying troops north from the James, smoke and hiss of steam duplicated by the trains bringing the garrisons and reserves concentrating on Washington from the whole seaboard.

They had a beautiful morning about them, long view and bright sky fluffed with a few clouds. It was going to be hot, as usual, but at least there was a breeze. The fields were deep green, stippled with flowers, except where the growing corn rustled in lighter shades. Wings blurred little bodies as birds rose, a buzzard floated in slow circles high up, scolded by the crows. Above the steady shuffle and tramp the men were talking. They hadn't had time to get tired, no admonitory voice must raise itself in the monotonous croaking to close up.

"Hear that? Bob White a-callin'. Wish I had a gun."

"What's that thing in your hand, then?"

"No better than a stick for birds. You ever tried to hit one with an Enfield?"

The laughter took its tone from the day, clean and untroubled.

"Clear, ain't it? You can see the flies crawling on the walls of the houses over there even at two country miles."

"Pretty place. What town is it?"

"Frederick. Didn't you know?"

"Faith and would I be askin' if I did? I know you're a travelled man, Cabell, but you needn't be showing it off to a poor, ignorant Mick."

"I've been there too," said Duvall. "Have an uncle who used to keep store in Frederick. Best thing about it is the road out of it—the Baltimore Pike."

"By God, even the roads are talkin' about home. Somebody drop back and tell Home Grown Smith. Kirkpatrick's Battery are giving him a ride on a limber. It may cheer him up."

"Wonder if he'll know what you're saying? I think he's past understanding much."

"Hey, Burke, what are you now? Color-bearer or engineer detachment?"

Over the march sound and the wheel rumble a rifle spat from the eastward, then more, a sputtering sharpness. A gun answered the alarm with heavy confirmation. There was no diminution, instead the firing spread and rose.

"Color-bearer," said Burke grimly.

The too familiar girding began. When Duvall tossed away a pack of cards, the laughter rose again with a changed note of brittleness.

"Throwin' his sins into a fence corner. Tryin' to fool the Recording Angel. If Duvall gets killed, he'll be clean. No tools of the Devil on him when he gets to the Pearly Gates."

There was no laughter, however, when the breeze carried off a snow flurry of torn paper, the treasured letters that must not be read by an enemy who might retrieve them from a dead man's haversack.

Brice drew out Charlotte's letter and followed suit. The marching, the skirmish at Maryland Heights, the prospect of battle, had been insistent distractions, but the thought of her remained with him, deepening in emotional intensity. He could no longer doubt the genuineness of this new-found love which centered upon her. She had given him a badly needed stimulus. He wanted her and wanted no harm to come to her. The Federals were the symbol of dread, and his fighting against them an act of protection. A cause is impersonal, however hotly believed in. Charlotte made it personal.

A staff officer galloped along the edge of the road, gazing intently ahead of him, standing in his stirrups with his hat-brim blown back.

"Lost something, sonny?" came the ironic inquiry.

"Now that's unkind. Can't you see his horse is running away?"

It appeared that the order he carried was for Nelson's Battalion. Warning shouts crowded the infantry into the ditch as the Colonel's high stovepipe led his guns by, four batteries, sixteen bronze Napoleons, the cannoneers clinging to caisson and limber and cursing with each bounce. The smell of the horses was strong, the sweat already marring their coats, the freshly impressed teams high-headed with fright. A mounted Sergeant stopped and let Home Grown Smith down from behind him.

"Some of you boys take him, will you? I don't know as he can stand up."

"Jesus!" exclaimed Niedlander. "He's took bad. Look at his face. This is a hell of a time for it to happen."

He and Lucas had Smith by the arms, but the sick man miraculously revived.

"Just give me a lift," he gasped in blurred words. "I can still travel."

"What's keeping him going?" inquired McComas irritably. "All he needs is a shroud."

Halt and advance alternated with dust and shouting; fragments of information came down the line. Plenty of Yanks up ahead. Going to be a fight this time and no mistake. The leading troops were deploying.

A byroad shook Gordon's Division free of the highway. They hurried between rail fences, heads bobbing, slung rifles now slanting over shoulders. The dust decreased, they could see more and breathe cleaner air. The march pace took them down a dip and then up a low hill. They were passing York's Louisiana Brigade, halted along the roadside.

"Look at the toy soldier there! Hey, youngster, you been measured for your coffin yet?"

"There's another one, not much bigger. Quartermaster can put 'em both in the same one, cherrywood with silver handles."

Matthews had heard the ugly teasing before. "I blew a hole through a Yank at Cold Harbor twice as big an' nigh as ugly as you," he retorted icily, but Murray Stowell had no answer to make.

When they had cleared York's front they were themselves halted, standing in column of fours and looking over their shoulders to the left.

"What's that stream down there? Kind of braggy to call it a river."

"The Monocacy," said Bufford shortly, and was confirmed by Cabell.

"I fished it once but didn't have any luck."

A cluster of mounted men rode up to them, the Brigade Commander and his staff. General Terry gravely saluted the uplifted spade before he spoke.

"Stack arms, Captain. We've been told we're in reserve today."

He gave a very human grin at the Company, turned his horse and trotted back towards the center of the front. McComas strode over to Cabell.

"Don't let me ever catch you again complaining about the bad luck you've had on the Monocacy. You're having the best you ever had right now. By God, we're going to sit out a battle."

There was a relieved stir, somebody laughed like the detonator to a bursting charge of talk. They stared at the higher bank which faced them across the stream, looked northwards to where Nelson's Battalion was in action, long smoke jets from the bronze muzzles and the black and red crackle of dry grass fired by the flaming gunwads.

"Well, Mr. Rodes's gang and Mr. Ramseur's gang can go into the lottery business all by theirselves," drawled Watts. "I don't want to draw no capital prize."

They began unslinging their rolls. Though the breeze still held, the sun was hot enough to be uncomfortable. Fence rails and muskets propped the precious new blankets issued at Charlottesville or Norristown stretched over them to make a patch of shade.

"If anybody's got any cards," said Duvall, forgetting the Hereafter, "we could have a game."

Captain Stowell had walked a little in advance to where the rise gave him a sweeping view. Brice completed his own shelter, substituting his sword for a rifle as a support, and strolled out to him.

"There's room enough for both of us," he invited. "Wish we had a julep."

"It's a wholesome thought," said the Old Gentleman without turning his head. "I've swallowed so many wiggletails and tadpoles in the water we've been drinking that I'd enjoy preserving them in alcohol. But I'm enjoying myself as it is. First time I've ever had the chance to look at a battle."

He waved his arm in an admonitory gesture.

"Look, Thomas. It's mighty interesting, and instructive as well. My portion before this has been more smoke than strategy."

Brice joined him in watching the blue lines of the enemy, the brown hummocks of earthworks, the flash of cannon behind them. There were Federals on this side too, a thin chain of men who crouched and fired at another such in butternut. The river ran like a natural frontier between flat fields on their side, rolling ones on the other.

"It's not much of a stream," he remarked.

"Fine," agreed the Captain. "It ought to be fordable."

"I can see three bridges," answered Brice sceptically.

"Bridges are purely for convenience. We don't like to get our feet wet. Watch the current instead. It's slow, and the water's muddy in spots. Snags are showing too."

Brice grinned. "You ought to have been a schoolmaster, sir."

"I took the easier path and sold books. Go on."

"Can't see the farther bridge very well, but the two nearer ones are plain enough. An iron railroad one and a covered road bridge. Why do they cover bridges, sir?"

"I don't know. This is no time for philosophic speculation."

"The earthworks are there, a couple of blockhouses and a lot of firing."

Below their own hill the river took a bend around a ridge, the outpost of others covered with growing corn and stacked wheat. There was a big house with a barn and outbuildings like a city block around it. It had an elevated porch and shutters on its windows. Some distance beyond it was another of brick.

"At least the water looks deep enough here, sir, to keep us out of the fight."

"That's why I'm indulging myself the way I am, Thomas. What would you do if you were Jubal Early?"

"Turn their right, I reckon."

"So would I, but I'm a Captain of infantry, not a General. I hope Old Jubilee thinks the way we do and turns that right, the further away from us the better. Thomas, I hate to break into your rest, but will you go find a wagon? I can't keep my promise to Home Grown Smith, he's broken down completely, even though he's kept up, but I'll carry him as far as I can. Maybe we can find some charitable soul who'll tote him along."

Hell, thought Brice, there's no rest for the wicked. He turned to go, but the Captain caught his sleeve.

"What's that going on below us? Damnation, some eager young man has found him a ford and our cavalry's crossing. Yanks have seen it too, they're starting to deploy this way. Find that wagon quick. Old Jube may get a new idea."

Brice went along the brow of the hill at a run, asking questions.

"No wagons here. The train's back near Frederick."

More than a mile away the white covers grouped together like tent caterpillars. Too far, we'll have to wait till after the battle. The guns were working steadily, but ragged volleys had begun much nearer. He panted back to I Company to find them centered about an agitated huddle.

"Home Grown Smith, sir. He's having a hemorrhage."

Smith, limp and unconscious, was being propped on a blanket roll. Blood was pouring in a stream from his mouth.

"For God's sake, somebody get a surgeon," Niedlander was pleading. They had grown to take a sort of professional detachment at the sight of wounds, but this bright torrent had shaken them. The triumph of disease rather than violence had carried them back to their civilian days. They were as helpless as a street crowd before the victim of an accident.

The Captain, arriving with long strides, looked up startled and dodged aside as a staff officer threw clods over him, low on the neck of his racing horse.

"Why in hell don't you look where you're going?" shouted Stowell furiously, then, as one thought jostled another, stared after him.

The blood stopped its flow, Smith's cheek was stained from the soaked roll.

"Who's going for the Doctor?" Niedlander was shouting angrily. "What's the matter with you all, why don't you fetch him?"

"Lucas went," answered Hammond. "Is he still alive?"

"I think so. I'm tryin' to see if his heart's still beatin'."

Another staff officer was spurring and shouting, "Take arms and fall in on the double, on the double, the lot of you. We're going in. No time to grab your blankets. Fall in quick!"

Harsh voices began yelling commands, other regiments snatched their weapons. The road was filling up, the shelters collapsing as the men cursed and complained.

"I tell you I know they're new ones, but we can't stop."

A drummer was rattling his sticks in the humming beat of the alarm signal, the long roll. Captain Stowell stood over his men. His voice was flat and hard.

"There's nothing we can do for him. Leave him. Every man in ranks. Quick now!"

Reluctantly, looking back, the men sought their rifles. Niedlander took his own, and the blanket it had supported flapped down over Smith. The Surgeon of the Thirty-seventh Virginia pulled it aside and knelt.

"Fall in, goddam it!" McComas was yelling unsteadily. Hammond marked the line, Burke had raised the spade over his head.

Captain Stowell paid no attention to the fuming staff officer.

"How is he, Doctor?"

"He might live, but I don't know," said the Surgeon, then added the helpless phrase that marks the limitations of medicine. "There's nothing I can do."

"You're blocking the next Brigade, sir. You've got to move off!" The staff officer was shaking the Old Gentleman by the shoulder.

Stowell threw him aside with a sweep of his arm. "Keep your hands to yourself, goddam you! Company right face!"

Lucas turned with the others, but his deep voice boomed out:

"The Lord bless you and keep you . . ."

"Forward march!"

"And give you peace."

Beyond the bend of the river the firing crashed, louder and deadlier. The Division was streaming down the hill, battle flags unfurled, each four feet square, the honors of the old fights embroidered on them, the bullet rips from the new ones making them ragged.

Burke swung the spade in a circle, the broad edge swishing in the wind.

"Guide on the colors! Mind now, guide on the colors!"

XXI

As THEY left the rise of ground, their vision narrowed. The sweeping panorama of the battle pattern contracted to hurrying backs, sunburned necks, long, sweat-matted hair protruding below ragged hats. The creak of leather, the rattle of loose gear in the haversacks, the feet upon the road were magnified in spite of the firing, no longer having to compete with voices. The self-withdrawal had been completed, no specious reassurance could avail against the fact of nearing combat.

Familiarity had brought no surcease to Brice's sensations, dry mouth and twitchy stomach. He wished he could stop and empty his bladder. If anything, his discomfort increased with each ordeal. Sooner or later one got hit or hit again. The more the exposure to bullets, shell or solid shot, the greater were the odds against escaping unhurt, and he had the liveliest recollections of impact, shock and searing pain following in their rigorous succession. It was hard to endure, the swaggering toughs had deserted or been tamed down by continuous warfare to the common level of apprehensive normality. Individuals like Beeler were an anomaly, swayed either by an intensity of hatred or reverting to a natural savagery, but even he made no pretense of superficial hardness. Brice had heard that he had been a butcher by trade. Perhaps the poleaxing of steers had been more than an unpleasant business with him, an expression of darker urges or a reversion to them.

The column halted suddenly. Terry's Brigade was the last of the three as the formation had evolved and suffered the worst of the telescoping jar. Rear ranks bumped front ones, sparking off nerve-sharpened tempers. The leading troops made a moving mound of bodies as they climbed a fence, step up and leg over and jump down.

"Turning off into the fields," commented McComas, keeping his tone to professional dryness. "Leading companies climb, hittin' each other with rifle barrels or butts, depending on whether the man who's carryin' it tips it high or low. Next lot is gettin' their hands full of splinters tearing away the rails."

The firing had increased, added to itself the wicked rip of volleys. Shells flashed their rackety explosions on the ridge across the stream.

The next gap was too narrow, a pioneer was chopping at a post with an axe, the white chips flying, but while he worked the companies continued to funnel through, jammed together and cursing. In the pause while they waited for their turn, a spent minnie thudded into the turf.

"Boys," said Watts, "I ain't goin' to be the first to run, but the way I feel now, if anybody does, I'll be right behind him."

"Ain't nobody going to run. Don't try it, I warn you," Hammond admonished in a growl, and McComas poked his extended fingers into Henderson's back.

"You hear that? I'll have my eye on you too. Needn't be thinking of dusting for the Commissary lines, you're going through with this."

His tone passed the bounds of duty; there was a flaring, contemptuous dislike in it, but Brice said nothing. They needed everybody in line. If harshness could keep Henderson there, then McComas was right to use it, the necessity left no room for weakness or sympathy. He pulled open the flap of his holster and checked the loads in his .44, then realized ironically that he had unconsciously reinforced McComas' menace. The poor bastard'll believe I'm going to shoot him if he bolts. Well, it won't do any harm for him to think so. The old days of enthusiasm were long dead, the sloughing off of stragglers and skulkers had to be stopped. The mathematics of numbers could only be corrected by permitting no subtraction.

They squeezed themselves through the gap, and it was again double-quick and stop, run and halt, spaced by the resistant fences. The cavalry was in trouble by the sound, their horseholders were leading the horses downstream to make room for the leading brigades as they came out of the river.

Lightly wounded were drifting by, relieved at escaping the fight and buoyed by the prospect of a furlough. They reported that there were heavy Federal lines of infantry behind fences, too hard to crack for dismounted horsemen. The hurrying files listened mutely to them but received with jeers the panicky tales of slaughter gasped out by the skulkers. Still, the blood-stains on the bandages made some men look sideways, and the shepherding voices grew sharper.

"Close up, close up! Don't straggle!"

The Monocacy had trampled muddy banks like greasy chutes. Two opposite paths with nothing between them but the river had marked the ford for the Rebel scouts. The infantry slithered into the blue water and turned it brown below their point of passing. Like finicky dandies, they held the skirts of their jackets high to keep the cartridges in the pockets dry, splashing in a spectrum of droplets. An officer curbed a fidgety mare and kept shouting over and over, "Hurry up! Hurry up!"

Hurry hell, thought Brice. The time to have hurried was before this, then maybe there wouldn't have been Yankees here to stop us. The comforting support of his heavy shoes rebuked him as he drove for a foothold on the yielding eastern bank. If we had, I wouldn't be wearing these.

A cavalryman with a boot off and rags bound around his leg was sitting calmly smoking while he waited for the ford to clear. He held up a blue cap with a Greek cross of lighter blue on the slanted crown.

"See that, boys? Army of the Potomac, that's what they are. Third Division, Sixth Corps. Wish you the joy of them."

The narrow space between the river and the sheltering ridge was packed with forming troops, York's Louisianians highest on the slope, Evans' moving downstream as their own column turned up. The Twenty-first Virginia was wedged in between and had a lively recollection of Burke.

"There's that spade again! Right appropriate flag for the Gravediggers' Corps."

"Gravediggers, hell! Graverobbers!"

"You've been thinkin' that up, brooding and meditating . . ."

began Watts, in so aggrieved a tone that there was a jerky laugh from both units.

"Close up! What the hell do you think this is, a militia outing?"

"Man, do I wish it was!"

The Monocacy came towards the ridge in a bend; the smell of the crushed grass gave way to that of marsh; rank growth swished about their legs. The Cold Harbor odor made Brice gag, and he was still swallowing uncomfortably when they came to solid ground and stopped. Orders came in hoarse shouts: face to the right and form the line of battle.

Four ranks dwindled to two, Burke in front of them with the spade, the Captain on the right with Hammond behind him. Brice and McComas were on the left in the line of file closers. On the bank from which they had come Nelson's guns were busy, the breeze carried the smoke towards them in small dying swirls. They were still in cover, the flank of the ridge gullied between patches of brush. The men watched the shells, listened to the minnies, their eyes hooded, their mouths partly opened as if they anticipated a wonder that they dreaded. York's Brigade started over the brow, red flags, blue St. Andrew's crosses, butternut men and sun on the rifles.

"Load!"

Haversacks and pockets disgorged cartridges. Brice moved from his place and began inspecting his platoon.

Murray Stowell, his black eye still prominent, stood between Abbott and Zollinger. The boy was fumbling with the greased paper as if his fingers refused to grip it, and the watchful Kirk called over to him:

"Do it the way I told you. I'll count for you. One—come to the first position of the present arms and lower the piece to the ground. . . ."

"Surely you recollects it," said Zollinger, looking up. He was already ramming home the charge. "If you does, you'll do well to be able to load at all. Don't you listen to him, but bite the top off'n the thing and empty the powder into the barrel. That's it! Now stick the bullet in, pointed end uppermost. . . ."

"That ain't military, goddam it."

Brice came over. "Never mind, Corporal. Go on, Zollinger."

The process completed itself. "Now put the cap on the nipple. Keep your hammer at the half-cock. . . ."

"Fix bayonets!" Captain Stowell commanded in his deep bay, and those who had them slipped the rings over the barrels and locked them home with a twist of the wrist.

"Watch what you're doin' when you come to reload, or you'll stick that thing into your hand," warned Zollinger, and reached over to be sure that the ring was properly in place.

"Still a-babyin' him," grumbled Carney, Murray's rear-rank man.

Zollinger wheeled angrily. "I'll hammer you right into the ground if you opens your mouth again. We've all had to go through our first fight. . . ."

Abbott turned his head. "And we're still just as scared as the young'un."

Brice added his own quota to what he was beginning to think was overmuch advice.

"Listen for orders and aim low."

Captain Stowell had come up but presumably agreed with Brice, for he merely put out his hand and touched Murray gently on the shoulder. Then he stationed himself before Henderson who had already spoiled one cartridge in the attempt to pour the powder.

The noise blasted into crescendo, cannon and solid volleys mingled with screams and savage high shouting. The rebel yell was no organized sound like the Federal cheering. Born of excitement, anger and fear, individually expressed, it drew its elements from the country and the frontier rather than the cities. The warwhoop, the fox hunter's cry, the roostering backwoodsman all participated. It went up in the smoke, the crashing, and the yowling minnies of the boiling cauldron on the far side of the hill, heard and sensed by Terry's Brigade waiting their turn behind their bulwark.

This is a tiger cub of a fight, thought Brice, returning to his post. By God, there may not be as many in it as at Cold Harbor, but everybody's right earnest about it. Seems to be growing into a full-grown tiger. Now damn that Surgeon setting up his hospital right here where the men can see the wounded, the bad cases all ripped up and maybe screaming and we waiting to attack. And damn that Yank gunner, why doesn't he cut his fuse shorter like he ought and not land that shell right in the middle of the Thirty-seventh Virginia?

It was luck again, this time bad. A tree frog grown gigantic might have made that shrill screech that was followed by a flash and a puff of smoke. There was death scattered on the ground and a heard agony. The Old Gentleman was still standing beside Henderson. He was talking quietly.

A boy on horseback with the gold galons of a Lieutenant on his sleeve passed from left to right at a gallop shouting for General Terry.

"And here we go," said McComas tensely. "The days of our youth! The old folks envy us this."

"Attention Company!"

Brice slapped his pistol holster to be sure the weapon had not jarred out, and drew his sword. The steel was gray, the point bore a black stain from toasting meat at the campfire. His reliance was the Colt, the sword was used mostly in signalling directions. He had never had to resort to it, hoped he never would. Captain Stowell was looking down the front of the Brigade, caught the commands and the gestures.

"Forward!" A long drawling shout.

"Right shoulder shift!"

They were climbing the rise through the crackling brush.

"Guide center!"

The bulge of the ridge was like the lip of the cauldron. They dropped into it on the other side, and the battle burst on them. The smoke wrapped their vision close, but there was a fence, a field of wheat shocks, then another fence with men in dark clothes behind it. Brice could see the sunlight flash on swordblades as the Federal officers directed the fire. They were the target, and the minnies came seeking them.

Reaching the first obstacle, post and rails set strongly, they went over it like seamen over a ship's side. Some climbed; others leaped for the top and rolled across on their hips. The Old Gentleman rose in state, set his rump on the rail and slid.

"Guide center!" he was bellowing. "Slow down and dress the line."

Brice snatched his hand away from the log and flinched. A minnie had rapped into the wood an inch away. He tried again, feeling utterly naked as he reached the top, and for that instant was silhouetted against the sky. They can't miss me now, he thought, but they did. He landed in the middle of the rear rank, hot, stinking bodies surrounding him, haggard faces glaring back, teeth showing between their lips.

"All right, all right, let's go!"

Reeder fell sprawling, his rifle flying from his hand, but the line went on, Bufford jumping over him. The wheat shocks were like scattered towers which must be avoided. There were yelled commands, and Brice repeated them. The formation would break, stream past, then reassume itself on the far side. He swung the flat of his sword as a barrier in front of German Smith's chest, holding him back.

"Guide center, goddam it. Don't run at 'em by yourself."

It was hard for the blond boy to obey. There was an impulse to dash forward and close with the smoky fence, beaded with flashes. If we get at them we can stop them from shooting, the dirty bastards who're trying to kill us. Brice pulled out his Colt with his left hand, just as the tree frog screeched again, and a shell went over so close that he thought his head had been carried away. Three-inch Rodman, rifled gun, said a part of his mind coldly, the other was busy with the drill book, the proper succession of commands so that the line might be kept, the attack have weight behind it.

The devilish howl of another shell ended in a squelching thud before it dissolved itself into a crash. He looked towards the sound, knowing the answer, and saw a thing that tottered, spouting blood, and another blown back into a heap of rags, a shoe coming off and whirling lazily in an arc. He did not know who it was that had been blasted into carrion, but he could see Murray Stowell, covered with a crimson muck, fall to his knees. He saw too the Captain's face as the old man stopped in his stride and dropped his sword point.

"O Absalom, my son, O my son Absalom!" Brice shouted, and did not know that he had until he saw McComas staring at him with open mouth and a sort of furious puzzlement.

"What did you say? I can't hear you," bellowed the Sergeant through a cupped hand.

I Company was stopping, bunching together in confusion, paralyzed by the Captain's halt. The men did not understand what had happened, thought they might have missed an order. The door was wide open for panic.

"If anybody runs, knock him down with your rifle butt!" Brice bawled to McComas and shouldered to the front. The flank Company of the Thirty-seventh Virginia had drawn ahead of them, an officer was waving angrily to him and mouthing something inaudible. The smoky field was naked to the flaming line of fence.

"Guide center!" Brice shouted at the top of his lungs. His sword indicated the enemy. Oh God, will they come out of it and forget that mess back at Cold Harbor? Will they follow me? If they don't, they'll break.

"Dress that line!"

Burke roared inarticulately and waved the spade, the Sergeants took up the cry. Captain Stowell turned like a machine, blind and unthinking, and took his place on the right.

Brice, still sick with anxiety, raised his sword above his head, then brought it down in front of him at arm's length.

"Forward!"

He dared not look behind. All he could see was Burke marching beside him, sturdy strides matching his own, but the Irishman was staring back over his shoulder.

"They're coming, sir!"

The Virginians had broken into a trot, raising the yell. To its high exaltation Brice added his own hoarse command:

"Charge!"

The stubble belt of cut grain between him and the fence narrowed as he ran. The Marylanders screeched behind him, the faster men were almost alongside. German Smith flung his rifle to his shoulder and fired. The damn fool has wasted that shot, but we don't need it. They're not waiting for us.

The Federal line was falling back on its supports, its speed increasing as the charge approached, the hunting cry harrying it. The blue fence turned butternut as the rebels arrived, knelt or flung themselves flat and aimed across the rails. A screen of smoke came down as their volley crashed out, ramrods rattled as the rifles were reloaded.

"Do we go on, sir?" asked Hammond out of a blackened face.

Brice looked to the left. The rest of the Brigade was lining the fence, firing methodically.

"Not yet, at least."

The First Sergeant spoke in his normal voice, equivalent to a whisper in the frantic noise.

"He's coming to himself, but I didn't want to tell him. We lost Abbott, Duvall and Reeder, besides his son. I don't think Reeder's killed though. He rolled over after he got hit. I saw him."

"Hush up. Here he is."

The Old Gentleman was walking with unnatural stiffness along the shaken-out fringe of riflemen. His face was gray and his eyes sunken, but he had dosed himself with duty and doled out his words with quivering governance.

"I want this indiscriminate firing checked at once, Sergeant. We may need the ammunition."

The Federal supports were meditating a counterattack and clearing the way for it with a shower of minnies, but he did not crouch as did Brice and Hammond. His head moved as he scanned the front and the exposed flank with compressed lips, but Brice noticed that he never once looked back across the field over which they had charged, the field that bore their dead.

XXII

THE soldier's maxim that it is less desirable to die for one's own country than to assist the enemy to die for his, explains much fierce fighting. The desperate struggles for the sunken road at Fredericksburg, the railroad cut at Second Manassas or the peach orchard at Gettysburg were disputes over the possession of cover and with it the opportunity of hurting the other fellow without corresponding injury to oneself. I Company's captured fence, having changed sides, dropped its shield before the Marylanders, who blessed it in improper language when its wood smacked some hound of a bullet on its questing nose.

The ripping sound of volley firing had been replaced by a rapid crackle, very like a forest fire, the shells mimicking exploding trees. Brice, peering cautiously between rails, was getting a typical infantry survey of the Battle of the Monocacy. He could see no more than drifting smoke, thicker along the opposing fence, a patch of stubble, scattered corpses and, lying intimately beyond the posts, the litter of a stormed position, abandoned rifles, blanket rolls, boxes of ammunition with the tops ripped off, sprawled bodies and a living man in blue. As dirty, though not as ragged as the Rebels, he crouched like a freezing rabbit, fingers interlaced over an ugly leg wound, lips tight across the make-up which the powder had applied to his face. It was impossible to drag him through to their side, but Lucas handed him a canteen which he snatched with a bloody hand and drained in gulps.

Brice, anxious over their exposed right, took the risk of standing erect and peering towards the brick house, its upper part floating detached above the ground fog of smoke. Three paces away the spade, its handle wedged through the upper logs, gave a resonant clang as a bullet struck its blade; two minnies cried past him and he dropped behind a post with a catch of his breath.

Henderson was using the same shelter. He pulled trigger, his rifle muzzle pointing towards the sky.

"Lower, man, lower! Aim before you shoot."

Paying no attention, Henderson thumbed back the hammer and pulled a second time. There was no answering report, nor, now that Brice thought of it, had there been one before. He snatched the Enfield away and examined the nipple.

"You've forgotten to cap it," he snarled, and jerked out the rammer, sounding the barrel. The rod checked almost at once instead of sliding deep.

"There must be five charges in there already," grunted Beeler from his ringed mouth. "He just clicks his hammer and then puts in another one, too scared to know what he's doin'."

He reached roughly into Henderson's haversack and brought out a fistful of cartridges. "Gimme these. If you can't do nothin' else, you can be my ammunition mule."

Brice stared down at Henderson who lay beside the useless rifle, his fingers clawing convulsively at the sod. We've got him here, but what good is he doing?

Matthews leaped to his feet. "Here they come!" he yelled, as the far fence gridded waving arms and moving legs. Figures like hunchbacks were scrambling over, one toppling forward in a dive.

"Give it to 'em!"

Beneath the roar of firing, the reeking smoke, the defenders emptied their Enfields and reloaded in a clogged frenzy of haste. Snatching quick looks to the front, they performed the successive motions with fingers that turned to thumbs: tear cartridge, pour the powder, ram home the slug, prime, cap and jerk the piece to the shoulder. Armed once more, helpless no longer, they glared into the cloud, looked over the sights, took their shot and returned instantly to that intense concentration always with the dread that they might be interrupted by bayonets. Lips dry, throats split with shouting, in a sandstorm of thirst, they pushed each other aside, scrambling towards vantage points, trying to stop the rush with bullets, Virginians and Marylanders intermingled.

"Get over to the right! Don't let them turn it!" came a bellow, and a rush of infantrymen nearly knocked Brice down. He changed hands on swordhilt and pistol butt, levelling the Colt at a big officer, red-bearded around a gash of a mouth, slouch hat with a gold cord, a blue coat open at the throat to show a gray flannel shirt. A bang, the kick of the recoil knocking up the smoking muzzle, and the shirt turned redder than the beard. The officer leaped into the air and slammed flat on the ground, his sword curving in an arc to land quivering on its point. A few other Federals came out of a cloud, breasting low, bayoneted rifles held out before them. Their expressions froze as they realized that they were alone. Digging in their heels, one or two fired at random, then they bolted back, blurred in smoke. The shooting continued at speed, then slowed to the forest fire's crackling.

The burned powder cleared with maddening deliberation, eddies making little pathways of sight. The officer whom Brice had killed lay prone; nearer still, a Sergeant rolled over and over tearing at his jacket. There was a fresh addition, quiet or moving, to the dusty blue in the stubble. The sword fell over on its side, and Brice looked away quickly, only to meet the sightless stare of a dead Virginian, propped up by springy brush as though he lay on a couch.

"They hit me," announced a voice with a tinge of amazement. Corporal Kirk was fumbling at a sleeve from which streaky red ran down the fingers. Cabell slit the cloth with a knife, then cut the tail from his own shirt and tied it above the bullet hole.

"Go to the rear," advised Brice, glad to dwell on someone else's handiwork beside his own. "You don't really need that tourniquet, but you better have a surgeon look at it."

A hatless Lieutenant, hair as wet as if he had been swimming, shouted to him, separating each word with a pant:

"Are you in command here?"

God, thought Brice, am I? He stared apprehensively along the fence and saw Stowell's bulky figure, apparently unharmed.

"No, there's the Captain. What's happened?"

"Fall back to the river, General Terry's orders. We're feeling for their flank, and we're not far enough to the left, too close to their center."

"Dust along, youngster," drawled Zollinger sardonically. "Old Stonewall always knew a flank when he saw one, he didn't have to feel for it. Times have sure changed."

Cabell gave Kirk a little push. "You get going now. Looks like the rest of us will be coming along right soon."

The ranks formed hastily and faced about. The officers dropped to the rear, nearest the enemy. Burke lifted out the spade and stood between them.

"Forward," commanded the Captain, his resonant bay replaced by a cracking shout. "Never mind the Yanks. They won't be following us."

The Brigade retrod the dry stubble over which they had advanced, broke formation and took the guide again beyond the wheatstacks. Brice followed with a final look at the fence, left to its dead, and the wounded Federal still hunched in a heap. He licked his lips, drew comfort from the Captain striding, numb with grief, ten yards away; from Burke carrying the spade with an arm crooked stiffly across the handle. The ordeal of retreating, their backs exposed to a checked but unbroken enemy, was a formidable one, but it was endured calmly and without haste. Jackson's old regiments maintained the stature of their reputation. There was no flustered increase in pace, no individuals darting from the ranks, harbingers of panic. Even Henderson was in his place. Beeler had his hand under his elbow but not with gentleness.

Instead of McComas, a Sergeant of the Thirty-seventh Virginia dressed the line of Brice's platoon and swore dispassionately in a soft voice. Combat evoked such changes. People appeared and disappeared, hardly noticed, the mind so preoccupied with its own emotional stresses that it forgot to observe and catalogue. In a confused fire fight such as they had just experienced, a change in position of only a few feet might put a man among strangers. Brice's reaction was vexation rather than anxiety. What in the devil was McComas doing, drifting off when he was needed?

221

"Dress that line. Not so fast there in the front rank."

One Sergeant was gone, another was performing his duty for him. McComas was probably doing the same for some company of the Thirty-seventh.

The Federals on their front, robbed of a target, had ceased firing. The Brigade was in a vortex of quiet, though only as a contrast to the thunder of noise where the others were hotly engaged. The brick house was completely hidden by smoke, but had been replaced in view by the larger one with the shutters and the porch, a yellow hospital flag fluttering from its roof. Brice saw Watts trot diagonally away from the far flank, his rifle at the trail. Where's he going? Hold on, no use yelling at him, the Captain's there. Maybe he sent him.

There was purpose in Watts' movements, and he recognized what it was when he saw the orderly stoop over a butternut heap. Looking at our dead, looking for Murray. That's the ground we passed over when we charged, we're retreating farther to the north.

Watts came loping back, hand cupped to mouth. His shout was faint but distinct in spite of the din.

"He ain't there. Found the other two but no sign of him, nor of Reeder either."

Dead men don't get up and walk away, not in 1864. Then Murray wasn't killed, only wounded. It must be so, it's got to be. The stretcher bearers wouldn't cart off a corpse, and there'd be no burial parties collecting dead this early. Brice rejoiced as the father must be rejoicing, but added a mental proviso of his own. I hope he's hit bad enough to send him to hospital for a while. If he's out of the way, the Old Gentleman will be himself again.

They halted at the original post and rail, the one they had climbed, and tore out panels. Brice waited, sweating and shrinking, for the screech of a projectile, meanwhile damning the farmer's careful husbandry. Most fences I ever saw on one place. Wish he'd have let his cattle run.

The Rodman ranged on them as they crossed the rise, but the shell burst harmlessly. Then the ranks broke into a running mob in spite of angry shouts. The river flowed below, and like a thirsty herd they rushed to the bank, drinking, filling canteens, washing wounds. Brice yelled without result:

"Fall in, I Company! Fall in, goddam it! Thanks, Niedlander, I *will* take a swallow."

Captain Stowell was shifting his weight restlessly from foot to foot, very unlike his usual rocklike stance. His eyes were fixed on the dressing station, so near and yet so impossible of attainment as long as he was in command. Watts wiped his mouth, spoke to him and started for it. Going to see if Murray's there, see if he's hurt bad, thought the observant Brice. The men were trooping into ranks, sitting down wearily, not talking much. A low voice muttered, "We got to go in again, I heard them sayin' so. Once is bad enough, but twice is pure hell."

McComas turned up, herding Carney.

"Those Virginia officers swear a lot better'n you do," he informed Brice nonchalantly. "Better go over and take a lesson. I fetched Carney along. Found him resting by the river and willing for us to get belligerent without his help. Who's that yelling?"

It was Watts again, indicating a smaller figure that trudged beside him.

"He's all over blood, but there ain't a scratch on him. Surgeon said so. Captain, let's find another bottle and open it right now."

He grinned slyly, less concerned with Murray's return than with a faint hope that the Captain might indeed have a flask available.

In two strides the Old Gentleman had the boy by the shoulders.

"This time I hope he does fall on his neck," said McComas gruffly to disguise his feelings, but a courier with a led horse was clamoring for attention.

"Maryland Line? Captain Stowell?"

Disregarding both courtesy and military etiquette, he did not dismount but brought the animals so close to the Stowells that they broke apart.

"General Terry wants you to send him somebody who knows this country. I'm supposed to fetch him back with me. General

223

says to bring your Company to the head of the column right away. We're goin' up the river an' hit 'em again."

The moment of strong emotion had passed, but Brice believed that the son had felt it as much as the father.

"Cabell!" he shouted. "You said you'd fished along here. Go along with that courier. Make a good bluff anyway; General Early's guides always aim to please."

The pleasure at Murray's return made his voice ring, and Cabell laughed.

"For a wonder I know it well. That big house with the porch is the Worthingtons'. I've stayed there."

He slung his Enfield and put foot to stirrup. Mounted, he reined the horse back, swept off his battered straw hat and addressed the Company.

"Stand to attention like you ought when I'm speaking to you. Before I bid you farewell I want to tell you that I'm sorry for you all, trudging along in the dirt. I was poor once myself."

He waved grandly, thrust in his heels and let the horse have its head. Spattered by the flying clods, I Company shouldered arms and set out to follow.

"Some day he's goin' to have to get off'n that horse, then I'll fix him," grumbled Zollinger. "The patronizing son of a bitch; didn't he talk like a General though?"

There was a disturbance on the riverbank. Sergeant Hammond was pulling at Henderson who fell back on his haunches after each heave.

"Don't skulk, you bastard. Disgracin' us all . . ."

But Henderson had collapsed. Even when Hammond deliberately drew back the hammer of his rifle, he remained squatting, though he threw up an arm to hide his face. The Sergeant put the piece on half-cock and doubled after the column.

"Don't do no good," he remarked to Brice in passing, shaking his head. "I'd have had to shoot him before he'd go in again. Reckon he's used up. And I recall when he carried the flag in that fight with the Bucktails."

I Company made a mighty short column, Brice noticed. Five gone since Charlottesville, not counting Hubbard who isn't much of a loss or Henderson whom I'm sincerely sorry for.

That leaves us two officers and fourteen rank and file. I can remember when the Old Regiment would detail that many for a single picket post. And we're not through yet. Wonder what's waiting for us up river? By God, I wish that kid had had one little wound, just enough to justify leaving him behind. The Old Gentleman is going to have to go through it all over again.

They were alternating double time with quick time, but they were still passing regiments when the latter faced to the left, the color-bearers raising the flags. We're not going to get to the head of the Brigade. Captain'll have to fit us in somewhere.

I Company came to the end of its endurance, or rather that of its commanding officer, almost but not quite far enough along, and fell in behind the Twenty-first Virginia who greeted them with catcalls.

"Followin' us up, Gravediggers? See we get a first-class funeral, two horses to the hearse, black plumes and all."

Burke turned the flat of the spade towards his tormentors. "See that hole? A bullet did that. It's the truth, I'm tellin' ye. Ye'll find that's one of the things a bullet does if ye ever get close enough to one to hear it."

The shot-pierced colors of the Twenty-first gave him a valiant lie, but the Virginians laughed. A good sound to Brice. It took everybody's minds off the ending of the ridge and what was beyond it.

He gulped air, fighting utter fatigue in spite of the gnawing fear that made his skin clammy. The ridge dropped away to a flat hollow bisected by a tiny run; beyond the trickle the ground rose in a gentle incline. The Worthington house looked upon them from shattered windows. The family was probably hiding in the cellar, the firing and the shouting dripping down to them through the shut door. A Rebel field gun was making for the yard, its team straining into the collars. Corn grew knee-high near the river, surrounded by another careful job of fencing.

Quite alone, a man sat a scrubby horse and watched them approach. He wore a red shirt, sleeves rolled to the elbows, gray trousers and long boots. Except that he belted a pistol, he might have been an overseer out to survey the damage to the property. But that impression was lost instantly as he wheeled his horse. Straight back, short beard, proudly carried head, a combat General among combat troops, he pointed up the rise and rode with them.

"Gordon, by God!" exclaimed Brice.

"Hurry up, boys!" called the Division Commander, and checked an incipient cheer with a gesture. The approving infantry discussed him in jerky phrases.

"Gets up along with the skirmishers an' tells 'em to let the line of battle catch a nap, they can drive the Yanks by themselves."

"Prettiest thing you ever see'd on a field of fight . . ."

Then, with a return of immediacy:

"There's still another goddam fence on the top there. He's heading for it. Maybe we can see what's happenin'. . . ."

But Brice had already observed a disturbing sight, heavy gray lines resting on their arms and still on the wrong side of the Monocacy. That's Ramseur, why hasn't Early sent him across? We're fighting this battle with one division.

There was a shout as the Twenty-first Virginia reached the fence. "Bluebellies a-comin'! Yonder are the bastards!"

There was no order to halt, the Twenty-first piled up against the obstacle, the Marylanders slicing into them and losing formation. Two hundred yards away the inevitable post and rails terminated the field; beyond was a regiment advancing in line at the right shoulder shift, very beautiful in conscious power with sunbeams sparking the bayonets.

A wild yell went up, "Come on, let's go at 'em!" but Gordon's calm tone carried.

"Keep quiet, we'll have our time presently. Some of you pull down the fence so we can get through."

Brice, big and active, had pushed to the front, was one of those who set hands upon the rails and unsocketed them. The rush of men propelled him past the posts, threw him into a swelling mob who disregarded his pleas to form. Excitedly they fingered their rifles watching the Federals advance.

"If they get to that fence first, they'll murder us!"

Most of the Twenty-first, a few of the Marylanders, were

through the opening, the contagion of mad impatience spread among them. A voice yowled, "Charge them!" and the madness exploded into frantic action. Screeching and howling, they ran across the field, their feet beating down the corn, their glaring eyes fixed on the blue regiment.

They won the race easily, rested their rifles on top of the fence and poured in a volley. Without cover, advancing elbow to elbow, the Federals could not be missed. The line literally staggered, its step broken, men plunging to the ground, spinning around, flinging their arms wide before they collapsed. By a common impulse they broke for the rear.

"They done read their drill books." With a grin that was more a snarl, Zollinger bit open a cartridge. "Reckon we amended them."

All of Terry's men were screeching exultantly. Their officers shoved them into some sort of formation, and the Brigade stormed forward at a lope. They had turned the Federal flank and they knew it. The Rodmans by the bridge were limbering up and hurrying off down the Baltimore Pike; there was a stream of troops following them, here fluid in a mob, there sticking together in partial cohesion.

Brice was yelping as loud as the others, running through an orchard where blue soldiers flung their arms aloft and shouted that they surrendered. The fight that some of Ricketts' regiments were still maintaining along the clay cut of the Washington road ended as the Virginians burst into it below them. Gordon's other brigades had finally broken the stubborn resistance of their peers from the Army of the Potomac, came yelling by the brick house. It was all high, Brice could feel it. High as the rebel yell, high as the red battle flags slanting forward, high as their hearts.

XXIII

It was far more logical that the mood of exaltation should pass than for it to have existed at all. At the sight of flight, the battle mixture, fear and anger, had bubbled over into excitement and relief. Yet this new compound was only a palliative, not a remedy. Its speedy evaporation left only the verities of hunger, thirst and fatigue.

Ramseur's Division crossed by the railroad bridge, hopping or tiptoeing ludicrously on the ties, and took up the pursuit, striking the Federal rearguard, taking prisoners. Gordon's intermingled formations looked about them, altered faces taking recognizable shape out of the red haze of extreme exertion.

"Don't know you boys. What regiment you from?"

Calls began:

"Tenth Louisiana, this way."

"Twenty-first Virginia, over here."

"Anybody seen the Maryland Line?"

Brice envied the men who at least had rifles to lean on. Spitting cottony saliva into the dust of the Washington road, he was certain that one good push would send him flat on his back with no desire to get up. He sheathed his sword and holstered the Colt, feeling the weight of them dragging at his belt until it nearly cut him in two. His first sensation was one of thankfulness. I'm still in one piece, I haven't been hit anywhere. Then his body began to ache, became an expanse of overused muscles stretching between centers of pain in his forehead and in his feet. Oh Lord, am I tired. . . .

"What do we do now, sir?"

German Smith's plaintive question penetrated to the middle of the upper throbbing. Brice ran his hand over his eyes, the palm of it picking up greasy, gritty sweat from his brows. Do they ever think for themselves if they haven't got an officer handy to do it for them?

Clenching his teeth against a sharp answer, he reluctantly

228

turned to face the little group who watched him with equal weariness. Five of them, McComas, Burke, Lucas and Niedlander, besides Smith. He hadn't the faintest idea where the others were and, at the moment, didn't particularly care. More of them would only have provided an addition of expectancy, waiting for him to conjure up on the spot a Commissary wagon and a spring of cold water. Then he remembered with sour satisfaction that his first duty was to find his commanding officer. The responsibility would shift automatically to Stowell, and his concern would be only with his own needs.

"We'll look for the rest," he announced, his thirst-swollen tongue shaping the words painfully. "Reckon we're in front, so we'll head back towards the river. Even if we miss the Old Gentleman, we can at least get a drink."

They shuffled after him, ragged, smoke-smeared, their faces scorched from the flash of the priming, a party of tramps returning from forced labor on a road, the spade no longer a standard but a prosaic tool. The Federal dead lay thick, their pockets already turned out, shoes and haversacks missing; the wounded watched apathetically or begged for water. The men began to glean. German Smith tossed away his civilian hat and fitted himself with a blue-crossed cap. Niedlander ran up the side of the cut and came down in a slide carrying an overlooked haversack.

"Coffee!" he exclaimed, examining it, and lethargy aroused to interest.

"They treat them damn well," said McComas, grabbing a discarded blanket roll. "Better fit yourself out, boys, we'll never see ours again."

Burke stooped over and picked up a daguerreotype. Shaking off the dust, he looked at it.

"Pretty little thing," he remarked, and passed it to Niedlander. It went from hand to hand, reaching Brice. The picture showed a girl with dark, tightly combed hair, a young mouth, a rounded chin, a pretty thing indeed. He gave it to German Smith, who put it in his pocket, pulling it out at intervals to peek at it. Nobody speculated morbidly on what had happened to the owner.

A Federal with a grizzled beard and a complexion that matched the clay of the banks lay at full length, his head pillowed on a corpse. He had been shot in the chest, and his breathing whistled through the bullet hole. Beside him Carney squatted like a buzzard, reaching for the watch and chain under the coat, but drawing back his hand as the dying man opened his eyes.

"What in hell are you doing?" asked Niedlander savagely.

Carney was unabashed. "Goin' through him, of course."

Brice saw the turned-out pockets.

"Stand up!" he rapped harshly. "Sergeant McComas, search him. We'll see what he's taken."

Lucas snatched Carney's Enfield while McComas drew four watches out of the haversack. There was a growl from the others, a dangerous anger, for half an hour before they had been in the murder mood of battle. Carney felt it, turned defensive.

"He was tryin' to kill us, wasn't he?"

Brice's headache was relieved by a surge of fury.

"Stop your whining! You know how far you can go, and you've gone further. Anything you need you can take, shoes or clothes or blankets or food. Even money or a watch, if you're low enough to do it, won't make you entirely a scoundrel in this Army. If you don't take them, the Provost Guard will. But four watches are too much. That's robbery, not necessity. I'm putting you under arrest and bringing you before the Captain."

Carney, disarmed and guarded, went with them, nobody speaking to him. The dying Federal was left where he lay. Some other rat will probably finish what Carney began, thought Brice, but I can't help it. All I can do is draw a line.

The orchard through which they had charged had become the bivouac point for the Division. The chorus of rallying shouts was dominated by Hammond with his seaman's bull roar.

"Maryland Line here! I Company over here!"

The Old Gentleman had shaped his back to the trunk of a cherry tree, its boughs already stripped of fruit. He had crooked his elbows across two branches until they crutched him erect. Though he was not in the extremity of exhaustion he had showed in Charlottesville, Brice sensed a shallowing of his reserves. He would not recover as quickly from this day's work. No will, however strong, could resist Time's arresting tap on the shoulder.

Only Hammond and Murray were with him, the boy naked except for his underwear and watching his wet clothes drying in the last of the sunshine. The bloodstains had mostly washed away, but some still darkened the cloth.

Stowell pointed a finger with a counting gesture.

"All complete," he said in a parody of cheerfulness. "I've let the others go foraging. Looks like there'll be something to eat. It's a land of plenty as well as pain. You'll find a branch in the hollow. . . ."

He noticed Carney without his rifle.

"You hurt, son?"

Brice made his report. Even as he strung his sentences Brice felt a rising shame. More than thirty years older than I am, and I'm running to him to pile on another burden. Couldn't face responsibility myself, and he's already found the spring and rustled up the beginning of a Commissary. When I come I just tote along more trouble. I've been cursing Murray for not growing up, maybe I'm kind of stunted and puny myself.

Stowell heard Brice through and asked a few questions. Carney, returned to sullen defiance, brought out his excuses. The Captain levered himself away from the tree trunk with a grunt of effort. His quiet, level voice changed to flat whip-cracks.

"Carney, you're a scoundrel, a thieving, slinking disgrace to your Battalion and your state. We've got to associate with you not because we want to but because we've got to have even you if we're going to take Washington. That's the reason why I put a sick man, Henderson, into the line of battle, and it's the same reason why I'm not holding you for a court-martial. We've got to have you as long as you can pull a trigger, but I'll have no mercy on you if you skulk or straggle. I'll hear no more excuses in future from you. Fall out of ranks in battle or on the march just once during this campaign, and your name goes to the Provost Marshal for cowardice or desertion, and I'll make the charge stick. But if you do your full duty, there'll be no black mark against you. Meanwhile, you'll stay here and Sergeant Hammond will have his eye on you."

Brice and his party went off to the branch, having to content themselves with roiled and possibly polluted water, but it slaked thirst and washed off the stinging particles of powder. Hundreds were using it and then dispersing over the field, taking advantage of the windfall of food and equipment. He soaked his throbbing feet, changed his socks and wandered through the orchard where the grass smelled fresh and the odor of blood was diminishing as the dead were carried out of the bivouac area. The Federal wounded were being tended with casual kindness. A canteen of whiskey was being circulated among captors and captives alike.

"Now you're the right sort of a fellow," remarked an approving Rebel, taking a swig, his Adam's apple bobbing as he swallowed. "Carryin' this here consolation with you. Sorry we had to stop you with a minnie to get to it, but you'll allow it was necessary."

The thin Vermonter in a checked shirt closed his fingers around the canteen and looked about him before he drank.

"Ayah," he drawled. "You bring us tobacco, so I guess it's even."

Somebody handed him a plug, and he bit off a chew.

"I don't hold with grudges. It ain't profitable. There's a man in our regiment lost his son down in Virginia. He came down here judging that he'd get his satisfaction by killing Rebels. Guess when the Rebels came he changed his mind. I saw him run back over the bridge when the rest of us were still shooting, selectman and all too. Ayah, grudges don't pay."

Nobody offered Brice a drink, so he plodded on, coming next upon a mixed group of Virginians and I Company soldiers laughing at a rabidly indignant prisoner.

"Yeah," he was spluttering, "I'm here and all because of a Thirty Mile Colonel."

"Maryland Yank," whispered Zollinger out of the corner of his mouth. "Says he's a Hundred Days' man, kind of like militia, but he used to be in the Army of the Potomac."

"Thirty Mile Colonel I calls him, an' that's what he is. One of them fellows what belongs to a staff an' is promoted up without ever gettin' more than thirty miles from home. Mighty popular with the ladies. You know, the kind that won't hear a word against him because he's so nice and talk their husbands into gettin' him a command. We were the poor bastards he commanded, upstream with Tyler's Division when you people busted through. We heard the yellin', an' he tried to give orders, but I reckon he was too excited to remember the drill. Everything went whichaways, and first thing we knew the head of the regiment was treadin' on the ass end of it an' facing both directions. I caught me a glimpse of a red flag an' a bunch of you Rebels comin' a-running, and I ran too, only the other way. I ain't ashamed of it. There wasn't a man who'd been in the Army of the Potomac that didn't know right off what was goin' to happen. Jesus, you couldn't have missed that huddle. You hit me here in the leg an' God knows how many others, but he got clear. I saw him ride off with his Adjutant. Reckon he's heading for Washington right now to explain how he got overwhelmed by numbers, and his men got panicky. They'll listen to him too. Nobody ever harkens to a Private."

The laughter held more sympathy than mockery, but Brice did not join in. He had caught sight of Corporal Kirk coming through the trees. Kirk's arm was in a sling, the black and dingy civilian coat from Pennsylvania had been ripped off at the shoulder, and he too was preoccupied with trouble.

"They took my chevron, sir, when they cut away my sleeve. Do you suppose I can get a new one?"

Brice stared but checked a grin when he saw the intensity of the Corporal's feelings. The reaction from strain and shock had swelled the minor loss into a disaster.

"Don't fret about it," he advised, as they reached their bivouac. "We can find you another."

"But where'll I sew it?" Kirk almost wailed. "I haven't got a sleeve to put it on."

The clustering men of I Company stopped laughing. Kirk's absurd grief had a pathetic quality, and they recognized its source.

"Here's a shirt," said McComas. "Found it in this blanket roll. It's gray too. Sew it to that."

"Did you see any of the others?" asked the Old Gentleman quietly.

"I saw Reeder, sir. A bullet had smashed his hand. They were hoping to save it, but the Surgeon said it would be too stiff for him to come back to the Army."

"There goes the best chicken thief we had," muttered Watts.

"What'll he do when the war's over?" said McComas reflectively. "He wanted to be a musician."

"Don't worry, this war ain't never goin' to be over."

Kirk was folding his newly acquired shirt over his good arm with McComas' assistance.

"Didn't see Home Grown Smith, of course. I didn't go back across the river. But they did bring in Henderson, right bad hurt."

"Henderson!"

"Yes, sir. Looked like he felt he couldn't go on an' tried to blow off a toe so's he'd get a discharge. He must have held too low and blew off most of his foot instead."

"Goddam it," exclaimed McComas irritably. "He couldn't even do that right."

So Henderson had solved his problem his own way. Brice shrugged it off, though it left a residue of bitterness. Do whatever you could and there was still some wastage. Yet his reaction showed the change in his own outlook. He was loading some of the failure on himself, not standing to one side and letting it fall entirely on the Old Gentleman.

The dead known, the wounded accounted for, I Company shared its captured rations among itself and built its fires from the wood of ammunition and hardtack boxes. Cabell arrived on foot to be greeted by hoots.

"So they found that horse you stole, did they? Sheriff after you?"

Brice had an instant of wishful thinking. If Cabell had managed to make off with the horse which, of course, was impossible, he would have confiscated it for the Captain. The command he had been so anxious to get was approaching him with the old man's declining strength, and he doubted if he wanted it. He did not shrink from the responsibility. In fact, he had resolved to shoulder more if it would relieve Stowell. Yet he well knew that the Company, on a par with the Second Corps as a whole, was losing its resilience. Too many casualties, too prolonged campaigning, affect soldiers as human beings. Crack troops thrust too often into fire find their breaking point descending to within easy reach. Fresh and ardent youngsters, if such were to be had, North or South, could shatter the best veterans who had pyramided their experiences. Stowell had managed to keep I Company still eager, but the edge was leaving it. The Monocacy had been the turning point, the culmination of effort. Baltimore was no longer discussed so eagerly, there was doubt among the campfire strategists. The Army of the Potomac had been here, or part of it. There would be more of it in Washington. The Captain might still be able to cope with that dejection, Brice could not. He admitted freely to himself that he too had leaned upon the Old Gentleman.

The sunset was hardly over, but the men were rolling themselves in single blankets and going to sleep. McComas sat cross-legged at a fire sewing on Kirk's chevron while the Corporal watched the needle, spasms of pain twitching his face. Once again Brice felt respect for his Sergeant. The tired young noncom had searched for a discarded coat until he had found one with the proper markings. Soldiers came as one found them, brutes, cowards, skulkers, malingerers, but the great majority solid and true with a few who owned their souls.

The little trickle of smoke from fading fires went from the embers to the sky. The list of the dead posed a question: why were Abbott and Duvall taken and Carney left, or Hubbard, skulking in the rear? Brice, dirty and worn-out, may have been in better condition to understand than had he been dressed in his best and relaxed in church. Life was a short journey, perhaps there was a good halt at the end of it. If there was, Abbott had been more than willing to find it. Duvall —who knew about any man, the true being that defies even the most friendly analysis? Reluctance to die might be an unknowing lie.

He looked down at the Captain, sleeping on his back. The self-governance was gone from the old face, leaving only the fatigue and the vain regret. He's dozed off before his rounds, Brice thought, I'll make them for him.

A question and a weary smile in answer from the noncommissioned officers and he came to Murray Stowell. The boy was still awake among the blanketed forms of his messmates, his empty tin cup dangling from a finger hooked through the handle, his eyes fixed on the last sparks. He gave a startled jerk as he became aware of Brice's presence.

"Don't stand up," said the Lieutenant in a low voice. "How are you feeling?"

"Oh, all right, sir."

It did not sound as if he meant it, but Brice appreciated his probable emotions to the fullest extent. Murray had not only fought his first battle but had undergone an extra trial at the same time, the sort of experience that stuck in a man's memory as long as he lived, thrusting up like a snake from under a rock to disturb his sleep in later years.

What was there to say? Understanding might either help or strip off the layer of forgetfulness which the mind was already defensively applying. Brice stood wearily considering the young, ravaged face. Murray too had reached a turning point. He might not realize it, Brice doubted if he did, but the older men would have begun to accept him, however intolerant the youngsters might remain. There was no one among them who would willingly have undergone that blood bath. They would credit him with not malingering but going in the second time, the hardest of ordeals. His participation might have been involuntary, but this time he had been there.

Brice's question sounded casual, but it was not.

"Did you have any coffee?"

The boy flipped the cup by its curved handle.

"Yes, sir. Niedlander gave me some."

And that was a gain. Murray had almost succeeded in setting himself outside his mess. That the luxury should have been shared with him was a granted privilege, not a right which he could demand.

"Try and get some sleep."

I'd better get some myself. How far was it to Washington? Was it forty or was it fifty miles? This drought won't break, there'll be heat and dust.

He took off his shoes and stretched himself on the blanket which Lucas had given him out of the spoils. The battle and the victory belonged to today, it would be as it might be tomorrow. Fatigue that rolled him under killed his emotions. There was nothing beneath his closing lids but the continued refrain of his earlier impression: "Oh Lord, am I tired. . . ."

236

XXIV

SHERMAN's definition of war was no more than a staff appreciation. The Major General might approximate the truth by observation, but any of his infantry Privates could have analyzed hell in detail. One particular chamber of it was marching.

There had once been a military theory that troops must be rested after great exertions, but it seemed to have been replaced by an experimental probing to determine the maximum limit of human endurance. Gordon's battered Division heard bugles sounding in the dark. In sweat-stiffened clothes they had slept upon the ground, with holes scooped out of the earth to ease the contact of hip and shoulder. Waking gave them release only from lurid dreams colored by violence, not from the discomfort of grimy, aching bodies or jangled nerves. This day would be set side by side with the others that stretched back to '61, as monotonous as the ranked crosses in a military cemetery, each one memorializing privations and tribulations, camps and columns, the thinning circle of intimates, the increasing clash of personalities mutually abrading by constant contact.

Blazing hot and a forced march, a ditto under the recent entries in the Corps Diary. Had there been any truth in the superstition that battles brought rain, it should have been pouring. Instead, the high clouds floated indifferently over without yielding a drop; even the breeze had died. They made thirty miles to another sodden, primitive camp.

"Washington tomorrow, boys."

"How many miles left?"

"Some few."

237

"Oh God."

Only the captured coffee, drunk black and loaded with sugar, gave them consolation.

Too short a night, too quick a dawn.

"Roll out and fall in. Special tour to see the Capitol. On your feet, all of you."

At a quickstep the Second Corps began the last stage in a deliberate mirage of hope, units at proper interval, rifles slung, exhortations blazing like a prairie fire under the smoke of dust.

"Close up, close up there! Maybe the Yankee Government'll offer us jobs provided we vote the right ticket."

"They'll make us postmen, that's what they'll do. We sure know how to walk."

They swung to their own music, no bands playing but the shuffle, rattle and creak that had been their accompaniment for so long. At first there was a hollow cheerfulness in the urging—maybe we can get in, maybe we can beat Grant there, meet only the fortress troops and the armed civilians from the departments who'll never stand a charge. But it was a long march—too long a march. The probe exposed the limit of endurance. The sun pressed its hand on their heads and bowed them, sucked the moisture from their pores, dragged them down like a wolf. As it reached its zenith, Brice could sense the failure begin and swell, read it in the short breathing, the red flush that showed in the sweat runnels that channelled the gray film. Fatigue and heat thinned the butternut rows, tossed aside the stragglers.

Kirk yielded early. Weakened by his wound, he weaved in his stride but managed to last to the third halt where they left him under a hasty shelter of fence rails. The halts were five minutes in an hour, but they came too slowly, and Hammond went down at noon. Brice, kneeling beside him, diagnosed the hot skin, the strong, rapid pulse and did not need the Surgeon's confirmation—sunstroke. He waited until he saw the Sergeant hoisted into an ambulance which would take him and other such cases back to Frederick where the hospital had been established. All this took time, and when he started after the Company he could not catch it. Not with the heat and dust that choked him down to a walk.

By afternoon the thick, solid ranks were spread like skirmishers. The regiments lost cohesion, it was a migration not a column that pressed along the Seventh Street Pike. The rasping chir to close up came from strangers, ghost gray, unrecognizable.

"Goddam it," croaked one in futile anger, "I started out with the Thirty-third Virginia, but in this hell's delight I don't know where I've got to. Who are you?"

"Second Maryland," replied Brice, sparing of words, since every time he opened his mouth he swallowed grit. A nearby voice gave the same answer. It was Niedlander. The big soldier was limping badly, but he had a rifle on each shoulder.

"Give me one of those," said Brice. "Whose is it?"

"Matthews'. I think he fagged out back a ways, but you can't see in this dust. It's as bad as the Valley along here and a lot hotter."

"Where's the Captain?"

"I don't know." Inflamed eyes made Niedlander squint as if he were trying to be quizzical. "Up ahead somewheres. I twisted my ankle yesterday, so I lost him and the others. Don't worry 'bout me. Tell the boys I'll be in round supper time. Tell them to keep something hot," he finished sardonically.

General Early had realized what was happening and slowed the step, his lawyer's mind appraising the weakness of his argument once he appeared before the bar of the Washington forts, but it was too late. The Foot Cavalry was foundered.

Brice threw the last of his strength into maintaining the faster pace. He plodded resolutely past field batteries, the horses with drooping heads, the cannoneers on foot, exhausted stragglers riding the limber chests. The air was hot in his lungs, his nose stung from particles of dust. How long ago was it that he had been kneeling beside Hammond, talking to the Surgeon, begging him a lift while I Company lengthened distance between him and them? The Charlottesville march had been almost as bad as this, but not quite. Nothing seemed to have been quite as bad as this. If he tried to keep hurrying, the sun would have him too.

The artillery left behind, he mingled with more infantry. A drooping figure with a dust-colored beard spoke to him.

"Glad you got back. Better go see to the Old Gentleman.

I think he's been waiting for you so's he can drop down like Hammond. That's him at the front, and I'm at the back, and there ain't many between us. I'm not even sure who's left."

Sergeant McComas raised his tired voice. "Get along, Carney! I ain't being rough with you. I'm saving you from a post and a firing squad."

Presumably someone had given the van an order to halt, but the burning throats had shirked the repetition of it. Instead, the following troops came upon a leaf drift of men who lay in the road, hoarding even the steps necessary to take them to the grass borders, and in their turn dropped to the ground. Brice picked his way to where Stowell leaned against the wall of a tollhouse.

"Hammond's in an ambulance."

The Captain raised his head, and Brice felt the same shock that he might have experienced had he been absent for years and seen for the first time since his return the effects of age upon some elderly friend—the rapid sculpture of time unsoftened by gradual approach. Stowell had failed at last, there was no need for the final admission: "Take over, Thomas, I'm done."

"Column forward!"

"What we goin' to do with him?" asked Lucas, but Brice had heard the grind of gunwheels, seen a welcome face.

The old Colonel readily proffered a lift. He leaned down from his horse and addressed Stowell directly.

"I'll hear of no refusal, Captain. It *is* a trying day."

Brice and Lucas hoisted their commander to a limber chest. As they settled him in place he whispered bitterly, "I'm ashamed to quit. It's not much farther."

Brice followed his eyes and saw the sign above the tollgate, "Four miles to Washington." Only four miles, but his mind alternated between elation and depression. The count of distance was as one looked at it; fresh, it was no more than an hour, but in their present condition there was a mental multiplication, miles evolved into paces and paces into effort, so much more to expend from depleted reserves. It would bankrupt some.

And if it did, it must not be because of him. The command was his now, even if it were temporary. He peered at the little cluster, separating features from the dust masks. "Mc-Comas," he mustered aloud, "Beeler, Cabell, Carney, Lucas —where's Burke?"

"Gave out a while back," said Lucas. "So did Bufford; Beeler's got the spade."

Brice continued the roll from memory. McComas was dozing on his feet, his chin on his hands clasped over the rifle muzzle. It would slide off, and the Sergeant would partially awaken.

"German Smith, Murray Stowell . . ."

How the devil had he lasted this far?

"Who's got your rifle, son?"

It was not a demand, merely an inquiry. The boy had managed to keep up, but it had been a near thing. His uniform was black with sweat, and his eyes, like all the others', had retreated into caverns.

"Lucas, sir. I can carry it now."

"Perhaps you'd better." He pointed to the sign. "That's all we've got left, and we'll be marching past the Capitol. . . ."

Lucas laughed and spat grit.

"Unless they send the po-lice out and run us all in for vagrants. 'Member when you said that? We'll last, though. Let's get out of this artillery dust. We got to show them that they can't keep up with infantry less'n they got a horse."

"All right," said Brice. "We'll pass in review before Abe Lincoln."

Pride mustered enough speed to get them past the cannoneers until they mingled again with their equals; then they relapsed into the weary shuffle which was all that was left of the long stride of the Foot Cavalry. There was no passing in review before Lincoln, no march past the Capitol—they had not expected that even in the final tenuous filament of hope —but at least there were no four miles to cover. Before they were halfway the order came to fall out and stack arms, though the skirmishers were rattling fire and cannon were tolling like a deep tocsin. The platoon of them that was supposed to be a Company gathered on the hillside and gazed upon the Promised Land.

Except possibly for Murray Stowell, they knew after the first survey that they shared with Moses a Pisgah sight. Their

view of Washington was the roof of the Soldiers' Home thrusting above the timber along Rock Creek with a signal flag wig-
wagging the news of their approach. The dike that shut out
their feeble flood was all too clear. It began with abatis and
infantry parapets backed by field batteries and duplicated
itself with permanent forts. There were naval and fortress guns
on platforms, large-caliber pieces that outranged the Napoleons, their cones of fire previously calculated and interlocked.

The Maryland Rebels analyzed and counted.

"Speaking as a soldier," said Cabell coldly, "which the regu-
lars reckon I'm not, having had only three years' combat, I've
got to admire. Somebody did a mighty good job of laying
them out."

There were long columns of troops filing into the works.
McComas pointed at them, lips drawn back in a half-snarl.

"See those linen dusters? They're not Army of the Potomac."
His tone carried with it the defiant contempt which has broken
many a supposedly impregnable position. "We can bust those
forts if Old Jube will only turn us loose. Militia'll never stand,
never has and never will."

The drawn faces tautened in agreement until Cabell spoke
again as a sane man might expose the passions of fools.

"What we goin' to attack with? There's not more than two,
three thousand of us here, the rest are scattered back along
the Pike. Don't know that I could even walk as far as those
goddam forts, let alone fight my way to 'em. Oh God, if we'd
been one day earlier."

For the first time they felt despair. They had marched themselves out and fought themselves out to clutch at a victory
which might be illogical but was still possible. They had made
themselves believe in miracles, but none had been wrought.
Everything before this had been endurable; checked forty
miles from home, the paper dragons of suppressed doubt took
on flesh and bone. There was no violent display of emotion,
only a darkening of spirit like a curtain being drawn. The fear
of final failure ceased to skulk, became openly admitted.

Being an officer might bestow some privileges on Brice, but
they did not include irrational optimism. Yet instinctively he
struck out at depression.

"Stop your complaining, Cabell. You think we could have made this march barefoot? Goddam it, ask Duvall or ask me, we started that way."

Too late he remembered that any question put to Duvall, killed at the Monocacy, must remain unanswered. The blunder did not trip him, but, instead, stirred him to belligerence.

"Think for yourself if you're fool enough to try, but don't try and do it for the rest of us. We've still got tomorrow."

He flung up a clenched fist in fierce exhortation.

"Perhaps Grant's troops won't get here tonight. Even if they do, we can still run 'em. Sergeant McComas, get back to the road and collect stragglers. The rest of you get the coffee boiling."

He was perfectly sincere, struck no false note. His own doubts were forgotten in trying to browbeat theirs, and he gave them comfort. Beeler rammed the butt of the spade into the ground with a single powerful swing.

"They'll recognize this, and them that don't the smell of the coffee will bring. Right now it'll bring the whole Corps."

"Don't go handing it out, now; we're going to need it all. Lucas, if you get charitable, I'll have words with you. Anybody got an axe?"

The afternoon returned to them their stragglers. They would come in, be revived with the black brew and one by one get out to the hillside and look across Rock Creek. The others would watch the effect out of the corners of their eyes, saying nothing. The Old Gentleman was unloaded from the limber chest and lay upon a blanket, but not before he too had made a brief examination. He made only a single comment:

"Dawn attack, if we're to try it. Count your cartridges."

The orders came—and three hours later were cancelled. Colonel Saunders' Adjutant brought the countermand, a thickness of dark speaking in sibilants.

"We didn't quite make it. A corps is filing into the works, maybe another. The scouts say they're still arriving. We might get in but we'd never get out. General Early's planning to demonstrate during the day and retreat to the Potomac after nightfall. Carry us back to Old Virginny. . . ."

"Dry up, will you?"

"Sorry, sorry as hell. I didn't think. . . ."

This tomorrow was hard to bear.

They spent it in line of battle, watching the bickering of the skirmishers, a house burning with a bright flame as the fortress guns cleared their field of fire, and a Federal sortie which got nowhere. The short double rank of them, lying on their stomachs with their Enfields ready, knowing they were to retreat, sought consolation neither in anger nor in grief. Their distraction was in a family of rabbits, abandoned by their mother, which Zollinger had discovered nesting in the grass.

"Look here! Poor little things!"

"Don't touch 'em! Don't even breathe on them! If the old lady comes back, they've got to smell the same way she left them or she'll quit them for sure."

"Then they're gone goslings right now. Anybody within a mile of us sure knows where we are unless they got a head-cold."

"It's mighty hot. I was thinking we could build them a shelter out of grass and brush."

"They're doing all right. No, goddam it, Zollinger, you can't take 'em with you. You ain't equipped to suckle no rabbit children."

Dusk at last, a stir and a consultation of officers. The Captain, somewhat recovered, twitched at Brice's sleeve.

"See that ravine, the one that runs towards the Yank lines? The Colonel wants us to picket it until the Division retires. Take four men and push along it. If they come, fire and fall back. We'll be in the woods here. When it's time for you to get out, we'll show a lantern three times; the Adjutant borrowed one off the artillery. I can't give you a noncom. McComas is acting First Sergeant, and Kirk is riding a wagon, so take the pick of the others."

The coming of night lowered the timbre of voices. Brice called for Lucas, Cabell, Bufford and Niedlander, then, remembering the bad ankle, changed the last name to Zollinger. They loaded mostly by feel, for the light was almost gone, and followed him in a slinking line into the ravine.

They were no Kentucky frontiersmen, but they knew how

to move with a minimum disturbance of bushes and earth. Brice had left his sword with Watts so there would be no telltale jingle. His Colt was ready as they followed the twisting depression with no more noise than a faint creak of leather and the occasional soft slide of a stone.

He pushed his hand behind him, and Cabell stopped as he felt it touch his chest. The ravine was a black pit; a Federal could have walked into them before they saw him. Brice noticed a patch of brush overlooking the gulley.

"We can do better from there. Lucas, stay here, the rest of you get up over the bank and into it."

They settled themselves in a semicircle, rifles at the halfcock; not talking. It was lighter aboveground, and they could see the fort-crowned hills beyond the Creek even without the gleam of watchfires and the glimmering of the battle lanterns in the gun positions. The peepers were making a tiny din, mosquitoes hummed and bit, night bugs swished or struck softly against the leaves. The wheel rumble had begun from behind both lines, Federal batteries and trains coming into position, rebel ones departing. Occasionally a gun flashed or a sentry fired at a sound or a shadow. Brice shielded a match with his hat and looked at his watch. One hour gone. It would be another at least, he thought, before they could expect the recall.

The whole night had a vibration to it, a sense of noise and movement, furtive and stealthy. The insects and the small animals went about their normal business, startling the men who tried to imitate their soft progress. One army was expecting a night attack, another was retreating, all done in whispers with the heart in the throat.

Lucas hissed, then clambered from the ravine so quietly that Brice was startled to feel him beside him.

"Somebody coming, saw him against the sky."

The hammers clicked back.

"Behind us," Lucas muttered, barely audibly, and thrust the muzzle of his Enfield through the branches of a dogwood. There was a brief rustle as the picket faced the danger, then it died away in breathing silence.

Brice considered rapidly. Could they have missed the lantern blink and this be an orderly from the Captain with the message to retire? Possibly, but equally possible was a returning Federal patrol. As his reasoning completed itself, he thrust his pistol forward. If it was an orderly, the Old Gentleman would have sent him up the ravine so as not to miss them. Whoever Lucas had seen was outside it.

"Yanks, I think."

The ambush was ready at his low warning. He could hear Bufford let his breath out as he squeezed his trigger. The grass stirred and he challenged, a demanding whisper like the swish of an arrow.

"Who goes there?"

The arrow struck home, drew a startled gasp and a tense answer.

"Don't shoot. I surrender."

"How many of you?"

"Only one."

"Come forward with your hands up. If there's more than one, we fire."

The toneless, unrecognizable voices were a debate between ghosts. The white thread tied to the front sight of Lucas' rifle shifted aside. He was leaving the first target to the others, would take another, if there was another, so the picket would not waste its fire.

The dark grew solid, a single figure with its hands over its head.

"I'm giving up," it said, and repeated urgently, "Don't shoot."

"Rebel!" said Lucas, and Zollinger muttered savagely, "Deserter! He thinks we're bluebellies."

He stepped from the bushes and rammed his Enfield into the man's ribs.

"Come into the bushes, you bastard."

He was close enough for recognition. They could hear him grunt with surprise.

"Good Christ! It's the kid. It's Murray Stowell."

XXV

In the first flaming heat of shame and anger they were close to shooting young Stowell dead. The Maryland Infantry had been kept free of desertion by the men themselves. They had established an unspoken accord which sprang from a unity of origin and purpose. It was by their own will that they had come to this time and place, whatever their gamut of character or personal differences. The successive bounds which had been set upon their hopes, the early recognition that Maryland could not be part of the Confederacy, followed by the fissure even in that foundation, had only intensified their group feeling. They huddled sternly together against every assault, material or spiritual. One man and one only in the Battalion, unable to endure the starving trenches of Petersburg, was to go over to the enemy.

Hubbard was a skulker and a drunken blackguard, but they knew him. He would come back eventually, full-charged with specious excuses. They had watched Carney closer than even the officers knew, but Murray Stowell's attempt had come as a complete surprise.

They dragged him into the clump of brush, rough hands gripping at his arms, cursing and menacing until the crack of a rifle and the whine of a minnie fired at random showed that they had been heard by a Federal outpost across the Creek.

"Quit it! Quit it!" Brice hushed them. "You're telling the Yanks where we are. No sense getting killed over him."

His harsh-voiced warning restored their caution. An advanced picket was no place for a scuffle, and the veterans knew it.

"Reckon you all can watch him," said Lucas, and dropped

back into the ravine. Bufford picked up his Enfield and flung himself down on the enemy side of the clump. Cabell and Zollinger kept their holds, but their faces turned towards Brice for orders.

The Lieutenant's temper was quick to cool under a jarring reminder from his conscience. He had begun to feel an indulgent pride in his ability to read the boy's character, to help him over an unnecessarily rough road. The judgment which that pride had brought upon himself stood between two angry, contemptuous soldiers. Humble and ashamed, he realized that he had underestimated the crisis which Murray had faced. Young Stowell had been unready to adjust, had been unhappy and unpopular but was beginning to slough off his baby skin. Then he had run head-on into gruelling tests which might have disturbed the balance of an older, more emotionally developed man. That ghastly anointment with the blood and brains of comrades, the shock of disillusionment at the sight of the forts, had burst open a door that was closing. He had listened with complete credulity to the optimistic strategists around him and had not understood that not even they entirely believed in what they were saying. Victory was at hand and with it home, an ending to what must have been close to a nightmare. When victory had been denied, when the retreat was ordered, that last thought was left to tempt him like the Devil in an older Wilderness. Baltimore lay forty miles to the north, and the Yankees surely would be kind if he said he was going to his mother.

Zollinger, tired of waiting for instructions, asked the prisoner a rough question.

"Where's your rifle?"

Captain Stowell's discipline still held. To abandon a rifle except for sheer inability to carry it further was a heinous crime—a new one added to the greater offense.

A remnant of self-respect made the boy raise his head. "I dropped it when you challenged," he muttered.

"Must have been that I heard fallin'," said Zollinger. "I think I know just about where it is."

He knelt and peered intently, seeking any silhouette against the lighter sky, black indeed but a contrast to the inky gloom of the bushes. Then he crouched off into the field, and they could hear him scrabbling around as he searched.

"Hunker down," commanded Cabell, and Murray squatted at his feet, voice and movement hardly louder than a beetle's clumsy blundering. A heavy shell from Fort Stevens trailed its streak of fuse far over their heads and burst above the Confederate woods; another followed it, but no more.

Wonder if the bluebellies are waking up? thought Brice. Guiltily he remembered the signal. Did they show it and we miss it, what with all the excitement? Well, they'll repeat it after a while. His eyes roved the woods for the lantern's blink. His responsibility laughed coldly at him. You've been thinking of a boy, you've been sweating and wondering what you're to do about him, and meanwhile you've failed worse than with him. You've got four others to think of who can't think for themselves, not while they're under your command. Lucas is a better woodsman than you are; he crawled between the lines at Cold Harbor and brought in the Federal wounded while the sharpshooters were firing at a breaking twig, but you can't consult him. From where he is in the ravine he could not possibly have seen the flash. He's waiting for you to give him an order, and what's more he's got to wait, otherwise we're not an Army but a militia—and militia never stands.

"Did you see anything, Cabell?" he whispered.

"Nothing, sir, even if I knew what it was that you were looking for."

"The lantern. Ask Zollinger when he comes in."

Brice strained his eyes, but the woods were a silent question. What was in them? The Brigade still or only the Old Gentleman watching grimly, weighing the problem of losing all to save a few? He found that he was still gripping the butt of the Colt and holstered it, his fingers paining him as he straightened them. I haven't seen the recall, but it may have been sent. If it was, that leaves four men and a damned poor officer to be the rearguard of the Second Corps.

Zollinger came back and passed the Enfield to Cabell. He too had nothing to report.

"But I wasn't looking for anything 'cepting that damned piece."

249

Another thirty minutes, and I'll send a man back. Tell him to light a fire if the troops are gone and then run like hell before they land a shell in it. If we don't see even that, by God, I'll retire an hour before dawn. Then it'll be my goose that a court martial will cook instead of the Yanks cooking my picket.

He squatted near the outer edge of the bushes, sweeping not only the friendly woods but the neutral field which might turn hostile at any moment, listening for splashes in the Creek. He had despatched Zollinger to join Bufford at the fringe opposite the Federal works and was annoyed to hear them talking in whispers, too low for the words to be distinguished. In spite of his vigilance his mind kept roving in rhythm with his eyes.

No sign yet. The lantern may have gone out, and maybe they can't get it going again. If it's failed them, they'll have trouble making a torch, there's no pine that I noticed. He chuckled soundlessly. The Old Gentleman would make one even if he rubbed his pants in powder and set them alight. It's a comfort to know he's there. He'll get the word to us somehow unless some General has come along and suppressed him. Don't know that I can honestly blame Generals. I'm sweating here because of four men, and they've got a lot more to worry about. Still my four belong to me. Only the very big Generals would think the way I do. Marse Robert would, but Jubal Early may not.

He lit another match and looked at his watch under his hat. Two hours and a half. That's longer than I had expected, thirty minutes longer. Well, only the staff tries to run an army on schedule. Some fool hasn't got the word, and it may be me.

Those shells that the Fort had sent over, had the artillerymen seen more than he did, or was it one of those alarms that seem genuine to the ones who fire, abysmally stupid to those who are fired on? Both bursts were high, shouldn't have hurt I Company if they were lying up there in the woods. Wonder if they know that the kid is gone? Wonder if they guess why? If the Old Gentleman doesn't know, I'm the one that's got to tell him, dragging his son back to face a court martial. If they shoot the boy, they may as well shoot the father along with him. He'd take it as a kindness.

Court martial—the words were on his mind since either Murray or he or both might have to encounter one. If you had a reasonable excuse, the Board was sometimes understanding, if not, it was unsentimental. All at once, on his stomach among the dogwood, smelling the heat-crisped grass and the warm earth, he mentally reverted to a lawyer again. Murray Stowell can ask for an officer to defend him. Suppose it was me—it can't be since I would have to make the charge—but I'll go on supposing it to pass the time while I lie here, chilled in the hot night with my responsibility and my sense of failure. What points could I make?

After all the boy had not admitted that he was deserting. He had not responded to the challenge by a direct avowal. His words had been something like, "I'm giving up," not, "I'm coming over to you." He had called that he surrendered, but so might anyone, surprised by the enemy in the dark. He would probably have acted the same had he been sent with the recall and run into a Federal patrol in the darkness with no chance of escape.

Brice smiled sardonically at his own reasoning. Better not ask him if anybody had sent him. That would be pure ruin to his case, and the Good Lord knew he hadn't much of a one whatever way you looked at it. Still it would be better if nobody put the question to him before it was brought out in court, better that there be no damning testimony from one of the picket. They mustn't be allowed to talk to him if they hadn't done so already.

He withdrew himself on hands and knees. "Cabell," he whispered sharply to the guard.

"I'm Zollinger, sir."

Brice was startled. He had left Cabell as sentry over the prisoner, and there had been a substitution.

"Where in hell is Cabell?"

"With Lucas, sir. Lucas and Bufford changed places, and Bufford's in the ravine."

Brice choked with fury.

"Who gave them permission to do that?"

"They did it for themselves, sir. You were out on the edge of the brush, and we didn't think you'd welcome our botherin' you."

251

Militia! Militia! Goddam undisciplined militia! He'd bring them all before the Captain, doing a country dance instead of manning a picket post, gossiping in whispers. . . .

"Who goes there?"

The challenge snapped from the ravine. Bufford might be a silent individual but he knew his business. No rattlesnake ever blurred his tail with sincerer warning of ready fangs. The whispering stopped instantly, once again the hammers clicked.

"Friend. I Company, Maryland Battalion."

"Advance friend and be recognized. Hold your gun muzzle straight up, and if you've got a pistol, keep it in your holster or I'll blow a tunnel through your guts."

"Niedlander," said the voice, and the bushes rustled faintly. "Don't be so goddam warlike."

Brice was on the edge of the gulley, Lucas beside him like a shadow. Their weapons reinforced Bufford's Enfield. But even as they aimed they recognized the newcomer.

"Captain says to withdraw. Wants to know if you're all blind. We've been blinking that damned lantern at you until McComas took it out and waved it. Hell, everybody's seen it but you. Even the Yanks sent a couple of shells to inquire why we was celebrating the Fourth of July so late. The Brigade's retiring. If you can't use your eyes, for the Lord's sake use your legs."

"Picket muster here," snapped Brice. "All right, Niedlander, we're coming. Zollinger and Cabell, bring along the prisoner. No nonsense now. I hold you two personally responsible."

"You picked up a Yank?" asked Niedlander, but the inflection of his inquiry warned Brice that he knew or suspected the real state of affairs.

"Soldier, you talk too much."

"Sorry, Lieutenant."

Murray and his escort went first. The others filed after them with Brice as rearguard. They moved in the same cautious manner as they had advanced, but they muttered among themselves. After a time whispers arose which Brice realized were meant for his ears.

"McComas and I missed him. Didn't tell anybody else but started huntin' him."

252

"Does the Old Gentleman know he's gone?"

"Can't say. Don't think so though. He was frettin' so much about this picket gettin' overlooked that he was too fussed to notice what was goin' on under his nose."

"The fool kid! I was right angry at first, but I ain't so now. A court will shoot him for sure."

"They ain't goin' to shoot a sixteen-year-old!"

"They might. Deserters are goin' to be right plentiful when we get back to Virginia. There's too much gloomy talk already. Old Jube might decide he's got to make an example of him."

Niedlander's deep rumble was pitched carefully for Brice's attention. "You know he might not have been desertin' after all. He took his rifle with him."

"That's the truth. He had it when he came to us."

A catch of breath, a calculated pause. "McComas and I decided he might have just got over-eager an' snuck out to join you all. Kids are crazy sometimes, like to go huntin' adventure when any sensible man would leave it for somebody else."

"I think you're right. Maybe Zollinger just jumped at a conclusion," Lucas approved.

"I ain't talked to him yet, but I got good reason to think that Zollinger won't be so damn positive with his wild ideas when he's answerin' the Judge Advocate's questions." Niedlander's tone was edged. "He and I and the kid belong to the same mess. Maybe he was cherishin' a grudge."

"Reckon *you* might say so at least. You'd have noticed it."

"I sure did," purred the big soldier.

Brice could have silenced them or ignored the pointed hints, but he did neither. He was listening to the corporate opinion of the elders of I Company and he was willing to do so. He too was seeking a way out for the boy, the father and himself. He could not avoid a haunting doubt of the court's mercy, a losing war was apt to be a harsh one. There was rising within him an appreciative amusement at this kindly conspiracy. The whispering and apparent insubordination among the picket was explained, together with the low colloquy between Niedlander and the others before they had begun their vocal persuasion. Brice was convinced that the quick-witted

253

Niedlander had originated the scheme, the others would have been too inarticulate without his lead. But they must have approved the big man's motive, must have undergone a change of heart. That almost shocked phrase, "They wouldn't shoot a sixteen-year-old," would be the reason.

"The kid just came out an' then everybody jumped on him. I didn't know why," said Bufford, loquacious for once.

"Don't think that any of us saw anything wrong except Zollinger, an' of course the Lieutenant had to take what he said as gospel," Lucas confirmed, and Brice shook with mirth. It could not have been easy for the soldier preacher to tell even that very white lie.

"You'd say that on oath?" asked Niedlander sharply.

"I would, God forgive me."

"Don't mar it." Niedlander must have sensed Brice's feelings, for his dry warning held a whimsical note.

There was a pause as they negotiated a turn of the ravine. The woods were getting closer, and the banks shallower. The talkers hurled their sentences quicker.

"It'll be black shame on him an' his father. Don't know which I'm pityin' most."

"Reckon the young'un's learned his lesson. Too bad. He wouldn't do it again."

"We'll damn well see that he don't." Niedlander's words carried a pledge.

"We sure will," Lucas added. "'Member when Matthews was almost as crazy? The Old Gentleman caught him asleep on picket, an' in Pennsylvania too with Yanks all around. Captain had words with him, then tanned his hide for him till he squalled like a panther, but he didn't court martial him. Matthews still ain't got much sense and probably never will have, but he makes out with his job right well."

"Cabell says he thinks he can get this kid off, an' Cabell's a lawyer."

"Like hell he is, he only keeps pretendin' so's he can get somebody to listen to him," Bufford answered.

This was the climax. Niedlander was the speaker and made the last plea for the defense. It was an invitation by innuendo.

"Mr. Brice is a real one. Maybe we better ask him."

There was no need to put the question. Brice had been relieved from his dilemma. How could a court ever convict with
every enlisted witness lying like—like gentlemen, and the only
officer accuser coming as close to perjury as he dared? He had
been proffered more than discipline could ask, a general assurance of responsibility by men whom he could trust and
who would keep their promise.

"Pass the word to halt," he whispered.

He squeezed past his men until he reached Murray and
twisted the boy around to face him.

"You swear you're goin' to behave yourself after this? No
more damn-fool antics? You know what you just missed?"

Murray must have heard snatches of that talk. His tone was
cracked but he got the acknowledgment out.

"I do. I'm awfully grateful. . . ."

"Gratitude isn't enough of a reminder. *This* may stick with
you a while longer."

More on impulse than on deliberate decision, Brice bent the
youngster over and gave him five or six vigorous whacks on
the seat of the butternut pants. He had laid violent hands on
an enlisted man, and his commission was gone if it were reported, but the chance of betrayal was nil. I Company had
witnessed and approved when the Old Gentleman had risked
the same penalty with Matthews; the picket chuckled now.
The homely punishment had brought the affair out of the
threatening shadow of military law back to a less legitimate
but truer perspective. A deserter had diminished to a fool kid.

"What's that?" cried someone not far away, and another
followed with a challenge.

"Friends!" called Cabell, laughter blurring the response.
"Just an I Company picket rolling home rejoicing."

"Quit roarin' like a bull an' come in then. Where in hell do
you think you are? You men captured a bottle?"

Since he was now a conspirator, Brice took the lead from
Niedlander. The complete change in mood, the sensation of
enormous relief, set him bubbling with humor. He snatched
young Stowell's rifle from Cabell and thrust it into his hands.
Armed, Murray was indistinguishable from the others. There
was no outward sign of his former arrest. Yet they must carry

255

the deception further. McComas it was who had challenged, and Brice must answer for them all.

They emerged from the ravine, and shadows came out from the brush to meet them. McComas might be in sympathy with their motive, but the sentry might not, and Brice could not recognize him in the gloom. Best not take a risk, he thought, and spoke quickly to the Sergeant.

"Private Stowell is with us. He came along without orders."

McComas had been concerned over Murray; Niedlander had said as much. Yet it would not do to trust too far to his wits in a moment of surprise.

"You needn't do anything about it," he continued. "I've taken measures. . . ."

"Sir, the Captain wishes to see the Lieutenant immediately."

The words were correct in form but noncommittal. Brice hesitated, but did not dare put a question with the unknown factor of the sentry present. As swiftly as it had come the humor left him. If the Captain had been informed that Murray was missing, Brice knew that he must lie. He dared not slight the iron devotion to duty that underlay Stowell's kindliness. As he went up to the trees he dreaded the fact which he had recognized from the beginning, that Murray was the one person that the Company Commander could not spare and be honest with himself.

"Well, sir," growled the deep familiar tones, an octave higher than was usual, "and where were your eyes? Did you expect us to set the timber on fire before you would condescend to notice the recall? I did not expect this of you, Mr. Brice."

Brice said nothing. He knew the Captain was angry and the reason for it, but he was praying that his dereliction was the only factor.

"Sergeant McComas, muster the Company."

The Old Gentleman stepped back a pace into the thicker shade of a beech. There was a whisper of names and answers, a growing thankfulness in Brice's heart.

"All present, sir."

"And the spade? Why don't you report that?"

"The spade is present, sir. Private Burke is carrying it again."

"Very well, then. We'll follow the Brigade."

XXVI

The Second Corps, having recrossed the Potomac virtually unpursued, moved back into the Valley and cleared it of the Federals who had sifted behind their advance. Though their own raid had failed and the newspapers brought word that Sherman battered at Atlanta just as did Grant at Petersburg, they pertinaciously refused to accept the logic of events. The participants in history seldom believe in it. For all we know, the defenders of Jericho may have been muttering, "Just let those bastards assault and we'll show 'em," at the instant their walls crumbled.

They even recovered a part of their cheerfulness, for the weather had broken with more rain and less heat. Rations were fairly plentiful, and they were maneuvering in an idyll of reasonable marches, not overlong or overswift. Yet their generation had passed its military apogee. The war needed another to replace it, less wise, less weary, less disillusioned. So much poured-out blood was clogging the gears. Federal and Confederate attacks lacked their former fury, defenders were more ready to listen for and heed the panic-burdened cry, "We're flanked!" Before July was over two of Ramseur's Rebel regiments broke in a minor action, apparently without cause, and four days later Early routed Crook because of a similar stampede, this time wearing blue.

"You can go just so far," remarked Captain Stowell from a chair on a farmhouse porch, watching the August sun broil the roofs of Winchester. "Then you can't trust anybody, including yourself. They say that harshness is the remedy, but I don't believe it, except in a few cases."

"Like Carney?" asked Brice with a lazy arch of his brows.

257

He was sitting on the porch rail and sipping buttermilk out of a china cup. Since there wasn't much of it, he was making it last as long as he could.

"Carney's the case in point. He came to me last week and asked if our agreement still held. Said he thought he'd kept his share of the bargain and was I going to keep mine."

"What did you tell him?"

"Oh, I announced that I was. It's a nice technical point for you lawyers to chew over, but I felt as he did—that the campaign ended when we got back to Virginia. This is a new one. Carney and I understand each other. I can't ask too much virtue of him, but I am asking for some, and he realizes what'll happen if he oversteps the line seriously. You can't keep a man on the strait and narrow by threatening to shoot him. He's bound to kick over the traces some time. He'll either get drunk or sass McComas or get into some other minor foolishness, and there I'd be. I was hoping he'd come to me about it. If he hadn't, I'd have sent for him."

Brice took another sip of buttermilk. "Things *have* pretty much gone to hell though. I was over to one of the Stonewall regiments yesterday and saw a sentry cleaning his rifle."

"On post?" asked the Captain, frowning.

"Just that, sir. He was outside the Colonel's tent and an officer came along. The officer asked him what he was doing, and he was mighty casual about it. 'Just wait till I get this here gun together,' he said, 'an' I'll give you a salute.'"

"Good God!" exclaimed Stowell, honestly shocked.

Brice watched him with quiet affection. The supposed negligence over the recall signal had long since been forgiven. The Captain had finally remarked that he supposed he was getting old since he had begun to hope that the young would have room for more than one idea at a time. As he had warned Brice to watch his front, he reckoned he should have sent somebody else along with orders to watch the rear.

Brice had appreciated the joke, but there was too much truth in it. Stowell was getting old. The collapse at Charlottesville had been confirmed by the further failure at the tollhouse, and in each case the rally had been less. There had been a spiritual weakening as well, a willingness to drift, to shift the lesser problems to Brice, that warned of complete exhaustion. Yet his decline had not cost him respect. I Company knew to a man that his interest in them was as strong as ever, though the weary body could no longer be flogged into obedience. They would spare him what problems they could, but urgency could not always be avoided. Brice was already having quiet consultations with McComas.

"We need a victory," said the Captain almost pontifically. "I tell you, Thomas, discipline can't replace a good, solid hope of licking the other fellow. It's got its uses, though. A smart guard mount makes the boys feel proud of themselves if there's others looking on. McComas is doing well. He's not as exacting as Hammond, but I reckon there's some sense to that. You can't demand too much form if you can keep the spirit."

Brice agreed demurely. He and the Sergeant had made the decision independently, the first fruit of their anxious counselling.

"I miss Hammond, though. I know it's a petty thought, but he saved me a lot of trouble. To be even pettier, he always remembered to muster the spade which this youngster forgets too often."

Brice looked away with a shadowed face. I hope they feed Hammond. Lord, let them feed him, he thought. Early had been forced to abandon the bad cases in the Frederick hospital when he had retreated, and Hammond was again a prisoner. Home Grown Smith might be with him or might be dead. They had not been able to trace him, and he was carried as missing on their brief roll. Kirk had been sent to hospital that morning. The bullet had carried a piece of cloth into the wound, and it had been suppurating. The Surgeon's talk had not been optimistic. The grim word "amputation" had been mentioned.

The Old Gentleman ran his fingers through his beard.

"I'm glad Hines reported back. How have you and he been getting along?"

"All right, sir." Brice had been pleasantly surprised. Hines had been wounded during the disaster to the working party that he had caused at Cold Harbor. He had expected resentment but had received a sort of wary tolerance instead. Apparently Hines agreed with the captured Vermonter that grudges didn't pay.

The bright day and the cool breeze refused to permit the depressing thought of their casualties to linger too long. There had been a big mail that morning, forwarded by the Battalion from Petersburg, and the time had not yet come to reap the harvest of it. No one as yet had appeared before the porch with their problems on paper to be discussed with the Captain. They would wait for night and the firelit bivouac to bare their troubles. How many secrets did he know, wondered Brice, this unsworn yet trusted confessor? Certainly he knew all about Charlotte Talcott, for Brice himself had talked, releasing the pressure of his inner emotion.

Charlotte's letters were in Brice's pocket. He had their assurance and he had answered them, writing on the paper he had bought in Maryland, pencil scrawls but perfectly sincere. The Captain's words matched Brice's own feelings. Why be afraid if you had found a treasure? Why fear if religious faith drew out the sting of death whatever happened?

Courage, not mere physical bravery, was what the Old Gentleman was preaching, Brice thought when he had left the fire and was alone. It kept you from scrambling around through events, made you the master of yourself, if not of them. The confessor had proved that, sitting there with a thick sheaf of letters in his hand. He had allied himself, and the alliance had failed, though not to his defeat. Brice knew their contents as well as did the recipient. The boy would be the subject, not a word about the father. Yet the man had had the victory whether or not the son realized his true worth.

"Thirteen men and a Sergeant!"

The Old Gentleman had spoken. Brice looked up, startled. He had never heard quite that tone. There was a lament in it like the coronach of a Scots piper.

"Sir!" he exclaimed.

"I'm getting senile," said Stowell abruptly.

The bees worked among the honeysuckle that shaded the porch. A robin snatched at a worm, then decided that a passing soldier might be an enemy, dropped it and took to his wings. Brice wondered what the worm did. Crawl back underground and hide? He wished he could himself, life for an infantryman held too many robins.

"Do we need another Corporal?" asked the Captain, so prosaically that Brice knew his mood had passed.

"For thirteen men?"

"I can still l'arn ye, Thomas. The grapevine has it that there are three Federal corps at Harpers Ferry, and Sheridan has just taken over the command. That means fighting. Suppose McComas gets hit? He's got to have a successor just as I must have."

There was more than a mere explanation in the words. The inflection on the last phrase showed a somber certainty.

"Are you going to ask for a furlough, sir?" Brice was feeling his way carefully, but there was no need. Stowell was frank.

"I should and I will. That is, if I hear what I want from headquarters. I think that's the orderly now. You needn't tell me I need one, Thomas. I know for myself. If I was a horse, they'd shoot me. . . ."

The lined face was lit with the humorous tolerance that fatigue had almost overborne.

"I reckon they've tried hard enough to do it, but so far they've missed."

A smart-looking soldier, though he wore a boot on one leg, a shoe on the other, saluted and handed over two envelopes. The Captain excused himself and read the enclosures without expression. Brice waited patiently. He hoped that Stowell would apply for leave, but it was solely for the other's sake. Command? What did command mean now? The leadership of a weak platoon labelled a Company, as war-weary as himself, needing to be nursed and inspired—and where would he find the strength to lend? Long since he had stopped envying the collectors of bars and stars; that had departed with the aging he had undergone since Cold Harbor. He was ready to pick up the responsibility if Stowell must drop it, but no more. Ambition was not the eternal motivation of striving; there were few indeed in '64 who would have accepted a promotion if it were to cost them a furlough.

The Captain finished reading and laid one paper on top of

the other. "Quite a budget of news. Tidings of our missing Hubbard. . . ."

"I hope from the Provost Marshal's pen."

"Thomas, you malign him. That wounded veteran who tried to keep up with his Company but failed because of sickness —I rather enjoy that double emphasis on disability—has been rewarded with a comfortable and quite safe position in the Conscript Office in Richmond."

"How the devil . . .?"

"When he gets away from those who know him, Hubbard has real ability as a malingerer. 'Wounded'—I can trace that to its source. He had a bullet graze on the shoulder at the First Manassas. Six months later it would have got him thrown out of any hospital, but his name was on the casualty list. He may have been sick, he usually said he was. I recall how frequent and how lingering his spells were until Dr. Snowden began prescribing a mixture of Epsom salts and axle grease as a quick and certain cure. Some innocent surgeon who doesn't know soldiers has been listening to Hubbard's version of the *Arabian Nights*. The averages work out that way. A good many really ill men get returned to duty, so there are bound to be a few who get excused. The wicked flourish like a green bay tree."

"I'd like to cut him down," said Brice contemptuously. He was thinking of Home Grown Smith.

The Captain had picked up the second paper, and his expression had changed. The grim cheerfulness had become only an ineffectual disguise for a deeper feeling.

"I mentioned a little earlier that I was going to apply for a furlough. I find that I am not."

He held the sheet close to his eyes as if he had trouble reading it, but Brice wondered if he were not using it to conceal his expression.

"I thought our usefulness here was over, and I asked the Corps Commander to transfer our Company back to the Battalion. That's true, Thomas, as far as it goes, but it's not all."

Stowell abandoned all attempt at pretense.

"I had the furlough in mind, of course, but more than that. Once we were back at Petersburg, I would have asked Dr. Snowden to certify me as unfit for duty and recommended you to relieve me. I owe it to the boys; I'm not what I was. I know it, and I'd rather not hear it from some superior. Perhaps I might have had an assignment to the Conscript Office on my own account and withered our green bay tree. Here is General Early's endorsement:

"'During its service with this Corps this command has benefited by improved discipline. It has been kept free of desertion, though its Captain, upon joining, admitted his inability to control his men. Individuals among them have rendered useful service as guides. In view of these facts it is recommended that it be retained in the Valley.'"

The stark injustice brought Brice off the porch rail, dropping his empty cup.

"Goddam him, the whole thing's a lie!"

"But it isn't," said Stowell with a shrug. "It's absolute truth on the face of it. Early just omits the full circumstances. We used an excuse to avoid being sent back. Now that we want to go, it is used against us. I'm afraid we must have done more than just annoy Jubal Early."

Brice was afire with rightous indignation, but a level glance cut off the words at his lips.

"The decision has been made for us. I never liked him, and now I reckon I'll have to admit that I hate him from the hide inwards, but I won't squabble with him. One side of him is a patriotic man and a good general, the other's what we've seen. He may lose his dignity, but I won't lose mine. When you come to my years, you'll value it as the last asset you've got left."

He occupied himself in folding the paper and putting it back in the envelope. When he had finished, only the dark flush on his cheeks betrayed his disappointment.

"That being settled, who do you recommend for Corporal?"

The naturalness of his manner called for a like response.

"Niedlander, sir." Brice had rallied his wits to meet the implied challenge.

The Old Gentleman gave a tug at his beard and dropped his lids. Had he another name in mind? His son? No, it couldn't be Murray. Nepotism was the last offense with which Brice could charge him.

Yet Murray had done well. The picket had lived up to their

pledge, but it was more than their constant vigilance which had made the change in the boy's personality. In a wry way, a reversal of Hubbard, the wicked had again flourished. Vigilance had meant companionship, advice doled out to an intelligent mind shocked into a willingness to listen. He had begun to understand his shortcomings and to remedy them. His messmates had closed ranks with him. Niedlander must have been firm with both Zollinger and German Smith. He did his share of the work eagerly and was beginning to be rewarded by grins or jokes at his expense. His father's still strictly routine questions were answered as they should be, not with that childish sullenness that had cut off all intercourse between them. Sometimes Brice gave Murray credit for at last appreciating the not too obvious benefits of his relationship. He must have overheard part of the persuasion which had been directed at Brice in the darkness of the ravine, the example of leniency which had been followed. Possibly too he recalled who had made him scrub that unspeakable uniform after the Monocacy and who had stood over him while it dried.

"I'm inclined to agree with you," the Captain's voice rumbled across the porch. "Tell Niedlander and have him negotiate some stripes with the Quartermaster. They ought to have that much of a uniform in store."

The westerly sun had moved until it shone between the pillars above the porch steps. The Old Gentleman lifted his chair so as not to scrape the planks and set it again in the shade.

"I wish there were more buttermilk," he remarked. "There's nothing that nourishes the springs of thought like a glass in your hand. You can try and convince yourself that it's a toddy."

Perhaps it was no more than a distraction from disappointment, but he began to talk, detaching himself from present misfortune and speculating on the future.

"I reckon women are the most interesting subject, but we've got none of them around, so I'll drop down to discussing men. I often wonder what these boys will do after the war, the more so when one of them gets crippled up like Kirk. I know it isn't the youngsters alone that have fought these campaigns, but it's them I'm thinking about most. You see . . ."

"This is a young Company," finished Brice with a grin.

"Seems to me I *have* mentioned that before. Well, maybe I've come to see it from their outlook, a localized viewpoint, you might say, but I still wonder. To go home, to meet parents who can remember only their own sacrifice in sending them, who expect no change, who can't visualize, no matter how honestly they may try, a man messily dead nor the dread of being the next, that's going to be a task beyond most. Better for a boy to strike out for himself, even if he has to dig ditches, if he keeps what he's gained. There is a gain, even though it's hard to see. When a whole generation has been dropped into the pit of hell, it's better to be along with them, not sitting on the brink by yourself. That's why, though it's come near to finishing me, I can't help being pleased that Murray came out."

Stowell was thinking aloud, and Brice was too interested to make any comment that might check the flow.

"If he's killed or maimed, a woman would cry that it's all a waste. I'd agree with her right heartily. All war's a waste, the worst there is, but I don't see any sense in merely bewailing it and not trying to salvage what we can. A boy can gain independence and self-reliance as well as bad habits. His family's been raised in peace; they know right well what made a man a success in their own generation, but they don't know what'll make him one in the next. And these boys are the next, what's left of them. They'll set their own standards, not have them imposed on them. I tell you this war will settle the West. The best blood and the best minds too will pick up stakes because they won't conform to what's already static. And if there's nowhere left to go, they'll still make a stir in the millpond. I don't know whether they'll be radical or conservative, depends on who looks at them, but they'll make a change."

Once again the lids were dropped, but this time their motive was to hide a strong emotion.

"You can say I've had some failures; Carney, for one. Well, I reckon Carney wouldn't have been much different even if he hadn't been in the Army. A man can fail young, just as he can fail old, and it doesn't make much difference where he is. I don't know but that he may come through still—that isn't in the hands of a Company Commander, it rests a lot higher. People can change mighty surprisingly."

His eyes opened, and he looked straight at Brice.

"I've seen that in a personal way. I'm mighty glad you made Niedlander a Corporal. I know you'll say I did it, but you sounded like a torchlight procession for him, and I'm following in the crowd with a mighty happy heart. I don't know what happened on that picket, but I've got a pretty good idea."

Brice made a noncommittal sound which came more from confusion than any other reaction. Stowell paid no attention.

"I think Murray probably made a fool of himself that night. I believe I know why, and I respect your judgment in handling it as you did. Oh, I missed him all right. When you'd taken out your picket there were only eight of them to think of—and I'd watched him, of course. McComas and Niedlander were doing a lot of scurrying and didn't tell me why. I didn't need to ask, and my heart was in my throat until we mustered the Company to march off and Murray answered to his name. There was a lot of thoughtfulness wandering around in the dark. They say that youth is cruel, but I haven't found it so. They've been mighty tender and so have you."

He put the cup to his lips, found that it was empty and set it carefully on the planks.

"I don't know just how Niedlander is mixed up in it, except that he is. I'll never ask him nor am I asking you. I don't want to know ever. McComas sent him instead of Beeler whom I'd told to go. I recollect I spoke right violently about it. After that I compromised with my conscience."

The bees were thinking about home; there was a smell of frying bacon.

"We'd best return the cups," said the Old Gentleman. "I want to oversee Watts's cooking. I never thought there could be a worse cook than Heenan until we found him."

Sergeant McComas coughed gently from the stone steps.

"Sir, Private Stowell requests permission to talk to the Captain."

"Very well."

Brice snatched up the china and made for the door. The farmer's wife was inside it, carrying a pitcher.

"There's a little more buttermilk," she said. "We can spare it."

Her presence left Brice in involuntary earshot of the porch. As he babbled inanities to the surprised woman, he could hear the boy's voice, diffident and respectful.

"Father, I've got some letters from home. I thought you might like to read them."

XXVII

"I KNEW it," said Zollinger cynically. "We never get to walk through Virginia, we've always got to footrace through it. You hear what they're shouting? Forced march an' all that goes with it—'close up the column,' 'step out, men,' an' young sprouts of Sergeants yelling abuse at their betters."

"He's got Niedlander now to sing bass to his tenor. Wish they'd find a different tune, though."

"We've sure been swirling around the Valley. Reckon Old Jube aims to fool the Yanks into thinking there's a lot more of us than there really are. Maybe Jubilee's the one who's lost count; *that* don't sound like Sheridan has."

The shuffle and clink, the sweat and the dust, were carrying them towards a steady pounding of guns eastward of Winchester.

"Ever notice how many big fights there are in June and September?" asked Watts, as if he were revealing the fruit of long meditation. "We're right in season for one. Generals just can't stand equinoxes peaceably, the weather does somethin' to 'em. The Seven Days were in June, and Sharpsburg in September."

"And the First Manassas was in July, and so was Gettysburg. . . ."

"Well, that's near enough, ain't it?"

"I tell you Generals don't need no equinox to have something wrong with them. Ever hear tell of the Surgeon what told an officer, 'I can't do anything for you, my poor fellow, your head's been shot off'? Didn't bother the officer a mite. 'That's all right,' he says, 'I'm a General, and I don't need one.'"

There was a little laughter, but not much. The guns were too insistent.

They halted to let a battery of artillery join the column from a side road. A light carriage followed and turned off towards Winchester.

"That's Mrs. Gordon! Well, if she's going to the rear, what we're hearing is more than a skirmish."

"More than a skirmish," agreed the rocking air.

Brice, tramping at the rear of the Company, heard too, but did not dwell. A good counter-irritant was operating against the crawling of his nerves. He had a problem and no one with whom to discuss it. McComas as First Sergeant must be at the Captain's elbow, so Niedlander had taken over the duty of shepherding the last files. Niedlander had possibilities, but a single month had not been enough to establish between them the sort of intimacy which Brice needed. Still, words were a help. . . .

"Corporal, do you believe in premonitions?"

The big man took his time in replying.

"I don't know," he answered honestly. "There's a lot of talk about them, but I can't say I take much stock in them."

He coughed gently. "If I was you, sir, I wouldn't pay no attention."

"Oh, it's not me," said Brice, with so much haste that he knew that the other was only the more convinced that he was speaking of himself.

The firing was nearer, but with so swift a contraction of distance that the speed of their advance could not entirely account for it. Ramseur must be falling back on Winchester. We'll be in action soon, and if I get hit, Niedlander will swear that I knew about it beforehand, whereas I've got no feeling one way or the other. It's the Captain I'm thinking about.

He remembered their breakfast, "coosh" done over a quick fire to the squawking of birds disturbed by the smoke and the voices. The Old Gentleman had looked at the greasy mess on his tin plate and laid it aside untasted.

"Thomas," he had said abruptly, "I think I am going to be killed today."

He had made the statement in so matter of fact a fashion

that Brice had not taken in the meaning of the words at first. When he had, he had said nothing.

"If I am," Stowell had continued calmly, "I'd be right grateful if you'd give Murray whatever I have on me. I reckon there'll be little more than my watch and some money. Keep William for yourself. He'll be a useful companion as long as he lasts. He's thinner; I decided on *King Henry the Sixth*."

"Of course."

"At least, I'll get my furlough." The tone carried a trace of forced humor, but was not mere bravado.

There had been no discussion, for the Captain's manner had invited none, but Brice had been mulling the matter over as they marched. Stowell might have decided that he had had a warning, but Brice remained unconvinced. Every combat soldier had at one time or another such an experience, possibly a recurrent one. The anticipation of danger wore away the will until the subconscious dread of death burst through, expressing itself in a certainty that had no actual foundation. If chance and a minnie made it a fact, it was remembered, quoted portentously, and the many times it had been proven false forgotten. He did not think that God was offended, not He who was their refuge in trouble.

Brice could do no more than add the incident to the increasing signs of the Old Gentleman's breakdown. There had been a release from stress, but it was only partial. Father and son had been completely reconciled. That was an advantage, but not a decisive one. The risk to the boy remained, and the necessity of its being taken directly under the Captain's eyes. There was no anonymity in the ranks any more, a single glance would reveal every one of the stalwarts who were still with the colors—or with the spade. Though there might be high happiness in those evenings when Murray would seek out his father for a chat, it could not be unalloyed with combat rubbing its bloody hands in the background. Brice had witnessed and both pitied and feared. On his own initiative he had gone to Kyd Douglas and begged for his good offices. Send the boy, at least, back to the Battalion, if Early's grudge was too persistent to rescue the Captain. The staff Major had been sympathetic, so had Sandie Pendleton—men of high character.

There had been a private note from Douglas. The General was yielding. He thought the Company's orders for Petersburg would be issued in a day or so. Brice had not mentioned it, even when Stowell had confided in him. An Army is a thick compendium of disappointments.

If good was to come, it must come quickly. During the rapid maneuvering the Old Gentleman had ridden a wagon twice; right now he was showing his fatigue, shoulders hunched, big head thrust forward, a lag in his stride. There had been an unusual irritability over minor difficulties. Brice and McComas were counting the days to the final breakdown as once they had counted the hours on the Charlottesville road.

"Halt!"

"Load!"

As they became a part of the battle, it became equally a part of them. They picked up its mood as they formed line and went into it behind Burke and the spade. They were old inhabitants of the smoke and the noise, on intimate terms with its emotions.

"Forward! Guide center!"

Sheridan had three corps and a plethora of cavalry, but they stopped him for a while—thin, screaming brigades who clutched at victory and forgot the odds against them. Late in the afternoon they were reminded.

I Company crouched behind a stone wall, shooting across it. Ordnance wagons rumbled and bounced, soldiers dropping boxes of ammunition over the tailgates, and the men ran back to them, stuffing pockets and haversacks with fresh charges. Their shoulders were sore with the recoil of their rifles, their faces stung from the spit of the priming as the exploding caps ignited it. Nobody had been hurt bad thus far, but they knew that things weren't going right.

Goddam it we had won one battle, and here was a second boiling up with fresh Yankees and repeating carbines. Those Spencers were real nasty! A Federal pulled trigger, worked a lever, and there was another cartridge in the chamber with five more behind it. We fired once and handled cartridge, bit cartridge, poured and rammed before we could shoot again.

The purple smoke rolled over them, and the bullets that

271

came out of it struck flying fragments from the uppermost stones. Their casualties began.

Matthews rolled on the grass, crying in agony. He had exposed his arm working the ramrod, and a bullet had smashed the bone. That kid! Hines—you'd think he might have been spared, wounded at Front Royal, wounded at Cold Harbor, just rejoined—was open-mouthed and staring, shot through the brain. I Company was deadly tired. They felt they were clinging by their fingertips above a bottomless drop, but the Old Gentleman was striding the line as he always did, calm, self-possessed, a word or so bracing the flinching men who did not relish exposing head and shoulders to the licking lead. Brice picked up Hines's rifle, one officer was enough when there were so few to command, and took shots at the enemy, deliberately dwelling on his aim for the set example, though he was cold with fear when the stones chipped beside him.

Part of his brain could hear Niedlander shouting at Murray Stowell, the rest was busy with the mechanics of reloading.

"It won't take the bullet? Your rifling's fouled. Grab Matthews' gun and use that."

Brice got a flashing impression, one boy scuttling over to the other, face averted from the crying, rocking huddle, to snatch up the Enfield.

"How many more of the bastards?" sobbed German Smith, who wasn't so old himself, and the Captain stood over him, booming in his battle roar:

"Just enough for us to whip!"

Cabell shouted a high warning.

"Look at that! That's cavalry off there! Christ Almighty, here they come!"

It was a mounted charge, sent forward by some fool of a *beau sabreur*, yelling and thundering out of the cloud. Gordon's infantry blew it apart. Yet there was no questioning the courage of the troopers who made it. One of them put his blocky chestnut at the wall and landed among the Marylanders. He wheeled his horse, aiming with a pistol, but Lucas, squat and terrible in his strength, seized the bridle and thrust the beast back upon its haunches while Beeler, grinning savagely, swung his rifle butt and smashed the rider to the ground.

There was a gasping cheer as the rest wheeled off and retreated.

The Spencers crackled again, and the Rebel infantry found their fire beaten down. There was a pervading uncertainty. The word was spreading, snatches of gasped, ugly rumor:

"Watch the left! Our cavalry's been swamped, and Breckinridge has formed square."

This was new, this was frightening. Forming square had been in the drill books since the time of Murat, but the Eastern cavalry had never been bold enough to force it, nor had superiority of numbers and equipment ever before rested so completely with one side. Nathan Bedford Forrest had wrecked the blue horsemen in the West using new methods, and his victims had learned them, were applying them. Leave your sabers at home, use your pistols and pray for fifteen minutes of bulge rather than three days of tactics.

Throats dried up, heads turned towards the rear. Brice threw down his rifle, snatched out his sword and stood close behind the men.

"Just a little longer, boys," he pleaded, "just a little longer, and they'll have enough of it."

The wall remained manned and defiant, but Brice knew that had the Company been larger, had the officers' influence been less, there would have been a drift backwards across the plowed field towards the roofs of Winchester. How had those houses gotten where they were? Good Lord, we've been bent back at right angles.

The Confederate batteries, magnificently handled, were firing rapidly, but the wavering in the exhausted infantry was becoming more pronounced. They had fought against odds of almost three to one like men struggling to move a heavy weight up a hill, but now the levers were snapping, the digging heels sliding under them. Rumor bellowed fiercely, and they had begun to listen.

"The left's caved in entirely. They're working round our flank."

The plowed field suddenly was sown with overtried soldiers, some in open flight, but the majority trotting with their rifles at the trail. They were veterans who knew only too well the tactical effects of being flanked, the enemy at right angles to their line, the bullets ripping through the files with no chance to answer, no room to wheel and face them.

The remainder still frantically used their rifles, black-faced, powder-ringed, wholly desperate, but the knowledge that their left was naked was a living wound. The next shouting rammed a fist into it and twisted the nerves into an agony of panic.

"They're behind us! God Almighty, they're behind us!"

What they had seen was their own reserves advancing, troops bled from one part of the line to prop another, but no one listened. They were the ones who had had enough. They could stand no more. The stone wall in one obliterating minute became the strand mark of their defense. They turned their backs on it and ran.

Another Federal attack was being mounted. There was nothing to stop it, and the wall heightened itself with dusty blue climbing over the gray stones and shooting down at the gray men.

"Rally, boys, rally! For God's sake, stay together!" roared a great voice. Brice obeyed it, returning to the source of his strength, the leadership of an old, broken man, but one in whom he trusted. He thrust himself into the little group that snarled and struggled as it retreated, firing and swinging butts until the attackers left them alone. In any disaster there are such nuclei, their sheer belligerence a guarantee of respect. Only the most determined would attack such a ring of scorpions. The rest of them were running, weren't they? Follow along and leave them be.

It was a rout, the first in the history of the Army of Northern Virginia. Yet there was enough of that stout infantry left to shake itself free and form the semblance of a rearguard. They fell back in clusters, very tough, still integrated. The houses of Winchester were close with their false promise of shelter, but Brice and the others listened to the shout that repulsed panic.

"Don't break up, don't run. We've never run. Shoot low and stick together."

There was a sound like a stone thrown hard against wood,

a wrenched-out cry of pain, and their bulky reliance fell at full length.

It was true then, it was true, thought Brice. Stowell had known what was going to happen. Burke dropped the spade, forgetting it, as the haggard men stared down at the real symbol of I Company. McComas was kneeling beside the prostrate body, cursing a steady stream.

"We've got to get him off!" shouted Niedlander, and Brice came out of his momentary paralysis.

"No, leave him!" he ordered through his tight throat—and faced a mutiny.

"Leave him, hell! Grab ahold of him, Lucas."

"Watch that ankle, you fool, the bone's smashed."

Brice spun McComas aside and stooped over. The Old Gentleman's face was gray with pain, shoe and ankle were a bloody mixture with a white splinter of bone showing, but he was alive.

"I thought he was dead," the Lieutenant muttered, then roused himself.

"You're damned right we won't leave him. Burke, lend a hand here, the rest of us will hold them off."

"The rest of us" seemed mighty few when the bearers had picked up their burden, but they were enough to cover the retreat into a street, packed with fleeing soldiers. The minnies rapped the buildings, the shells exploded with whizzing splinters, but a hand clutched at Brice, and woman's voice screamed pleadingly at him:

"Go back and fight, boys, please go back. I've never seen Confederates run before."

It was Mrs. Gordon, tears streaking her beauty. A minnie sent a soldier to his knees, then over onto his face, a shell bared a dining room as it burst, the chairs neatly ranged about the round mahogany table.

"Go into a house," Brice shouted to her. "Get into shelter."

She paid no attention, but Kyd Douglas split the crowd with his horse.

"Your carriage is ready. Come on quick. I've got Frank here."

275

His arm encircled a wiggling, excited six-year-old. Mrs. Gordon pointed to Captain Stowell.

"Put him in with me first."

The Old Gentleman was conscious, though in obvious agony. He groaned as they pushed him onto the cushions.

"For God's sake, boys, give us room here!" Douglas was shouting, as he dropped the little boy into his mother's arms.

Mrs. Gordon thrust another wounded man ahead of her and climbed after him. The carriage door slammed at her back, and the soldier on the box picked up his whip. Then Brice heard a grunting, pain-laden comment from a sweat-beaded face.

"It seems I was mistaken, Thomas. I've got my furlough without going to extremes. Well, they're yours now."

The wheels turned, the horses went into a gallop. Brice knew what the Captain had meant. He grabbed at McComas.

"Help me get them together and come on. The Yanks will be here before long."

Wagons of the train struggled down the Valley Pike three abreast, intermingled with the infantry. The Rebel artillery covered the rear, retiring by sections, swabbing the canister-heated barrels. The dusk was thickening to night, the prayed-for darkness that would block pursuit.

There were no organizations left, the hurry, the confusion, the obstacle of the vehicles with their teams, broke up every attempt at coordination. Yet Brice knew that some of his men were still with him, the final fragment of I Company paying its last tribute to the Old Gentleman, clinging to its remaining officer in stubborn survival.

Night at last, gunfire dying away, but no moon to lighten their way, only a glimmer of stars. The panic departed, but not the bitterness of defeat.

"Goddam those bluebellies. I hate those bastards. . . ."

Brice did not recognize the voice, but he knew the one which answered.

"I don't," said Lucas. "I believe in the Fatherhood of God and the Brotherhood of Man, and I don't hate nobody."

Beyond Strasburg was Tumbling Run and a bridge. They knew it by its sound, the echo of planks under the feet and

276

the wheels. Here there was an end to flight, control fighting
the rout with the names of regiments.

"Over here! Over here, Thirty-third Virginia!"

Brice crossed with his men and stood aside in the fields,
seeing the wagons and the troops dip down, come level on the
bridge, then climb again.

"What do we do now, sir?"

Plaintive and heartbroken, Murray Stowell had appealed for
help. There was no one now to whom Brice might turn. It was
his to answer in the starlight, beside the beaten Army.

"Sergeant McComas?"

No reply came, and he called again:

"Corporal Niedlander?"

"Here, sir."

"Get out to the road and rally the stragglers."

The catalogue of necessities opened its pages to the dog-
weary Lieutenant. Nearly four months ago he had heard for
the first time the Old Gentleman cope with them.

"All right, boys, let's see who's here and then we'll build a
fire. It'll make us feel better. There's water in the run there."

Rations? There might be some in the haversacks, though he
doubted it. If not, he'd stop a promising wagon by strategem
or force. His men had to be fed.

They had shuffled into a short line. Oh God, was that all
there was left? Brace up, you fool, there's bound to be more
of them, scattered and separated along the dark road of the
retreat. McComas was with us leaving Winchester. He'll be
along.

His memory arranged the roll, tiredly considering the omis-
sions. What was the first name? Abbott? Not any longer.

"Beeler!"

A silence, then a quiet volunteering of information.

"I saw him killed at the wall."

"Bufford!"

Zollinger answered for Bufford.

"Captured, sir, I'm pretty sure. He was running over to join
us when the line broke and a bunch of Yanks busted in between."

"That's true," said Lucas. "I saw him put up his hands."

"Burke!"

"Here!"

"Cabell!"

No answer, and no news of Cabell.

"Carney!"

"Here!"

Well I'm damned, thought Brice. I never expected he'd show up, believed he'd be the first to run. The Captain said he and Carney understood each other; maybe I'd better learn how.

No use calling Hines, he'd seen Hines dead.

"Lucas!"

"Here!"

Brice rubbed the sweat from his forehead with his sleeve. His voice went on, name and answer or name and silence. From the roadside came the sound of Niedlander calling into the night of the Confederacy:

"The Maryland Line, rally here! I Company, rally here!"